DIRE'S CLUB

A NOVEL

KIMBERLY PACKARD

abalos
publishing

Copyright © 2021 by Kimberly Packard

All rights reserved.

No part of this book may be reproduced in any form or by any electronic or mechanical means, including information storage and retrieval systems, without written permission from the author, except for the use of brief quotations in a book review.

Book cover designed by okay creations.
Edited by C.A. Szarek
The text in this book is set in Baskerville.
Library of Congress Cataloging-in-Publication Data
Available Upon Request

ISBN-13 Print: 978-0-9992015-8-9

ISBN-13 Ebook: 978-0-9992015-9-6

For Mason and Makenna
To a long life filled with adventure

ALSO BY KIMBERLY PACKARD

The Phoenix Series

Phoenix

Pardon Falls (Phoenix Book 2)

Prospera Pass (Phoenix Book 3)

Standalone Titles

Vortex

The Crazy Yates

1

A storm was coming.

The ocean staring back at Charlotte Claybrooke was frothy. Angry. The glass balcony doors pulsed beneath her fingertips with the gusting wind. It was months too early for a hurricane, but an occasional nor'easter would whip around and lick the barrier islands of South Carolina. This one seemed to have a long enough tongue to reach her house on the far northern edge of the Isle of Palms.

There was no reason for her to drag it out any longer.

She should batten down the hatches, close the shutters, and tie down anything that could catch the wind. It didn't matter.

The storm would still hit.

She was still going to die.

She just hadn't decided how…or when.

Charlotte watched the gulls ride the rising winds. Didn't they know what was coming? Shouldn't they be preparing their nests for impending doom? Instead, they were…playing.

Then again, that was exactly what she was doing. Instead of preparing for her death, she was packing for a globe-trotting vacation.

Charlotte turned from the gulls and faced her half-packed suitcase.

Her clothes lay neatly rolled—everything she'd need for a three-week trip. A sabbatical. That was what she'd told her staff at her life coach business.

She had to get away. Didn't want her colleagues, who'd come to see her as a guru to the grieving, hero to the hopeless, and lighthouse to the lost, to realize that she was, in reality, a liar. A fraud.

An imposter.

These moments always overwhelmed her. The two Charlottes battled for dominance. The broken, beaten Charlotte who still slept in her dead fiancé's sweatshirt—a piece of clothing she never washed, for fear of losing the last piece of Jason. Really, after nearly a decade she'd worn the sweatshirt longer than he ever did.

Then there was the healed, survivor Charlotte. The woman who penned self-help books. Headlined conferences. Had a social media account with one hundred thousand followers. Was often invited as a special guest on talk shows. She counseled celebrities who tried to relate to their fans by pretending to be broken.

It was all so superficial. If she'd actually counseled someone who was truly troubled, they'd see past the veneer, past the perfect hair and eye-grazing bangs. Past the forced smile and calm confidence.

They'd see Charlotte for who she was.

Someone flawed just like them.

That was the Charlotte who was in control when she'd signed up for Dire's Club. Her life-coach brain had taken over and booked the tour. She'd told herself; if she was dying, she needed to be among her tribe. She suspected her life-coach brain was also using reverse psychology.

Damn, she was starting to believe her own life-affirming, uplifting social media posts.

Her phone buzzed from her night table.

"Hi, Ms. Claybrooke."

Charlotte could hear the hum of road noise over her driver's voice.

"I'm coming over the bridge so I should be there in about fifteen, twenty minutes. Looks like your flight is on time. You all ready to go?"

"Sure, Chuck. Just need to throw a few more things in the bag."

"You're smart, getting away when you can. Storm's gonna be a nasty one."

The storm *was* going to be a nasty one.

Just not the one Chuck was talking about.

She thumbed through the stack of books on her nightstand for one to bring on the plane. It was a self-help smorgasbord. How to better yourself. How to accept yourself. How to not give a damn.

When was the last time she'd just lost herself in a novel? A romance even? A book so good that her heart would skip when the lovers finally kissed?

Instead of wrapping herself in fiction, Charlotte had plunged into the Arctic Ocean of information.

The picture she'd been avoiding all morning finally caught her attention. A decade-younger version of herself. Newly engaged, her cheeks flushed pink, her lips kiss swollen.

Jason was half-facing her, his eyes closed and a crazy-in-love smile on his face.

She recalled everything about that day perfectly.

Or maybe she'd told herself the narrative so many times, the story endured where the memory faded.

The perfect weather. A walk along the beach. A promise of forever.

She and Jason had only been dating a couple of months. They couldn't agree on how they met. Charlotte swore it was when he'd nearly blown his Achilles trying to keep up with her on a ten-mile training run. Jason said he had to save her from a riptide while they were on the swim of a triathlon.

Both were right.

She clearly remembered the cute bald guy who'd nipped at her heels during a run. He'd huffed and puffed right behind her while Charlotte had held tight to her eight-minute mile pace.

Afterward, when the training group met up for a beer, he'd joked she'd run like the beer keg was nearly tapped. Between his Australian accent and playful ice-blue eyes, she'd stammered over a suitably flirtatious comeback and lost sight of him among the group of people.

The next time she'd seen him was her first triathlon. A cold wind had whipped up the ocean and the sun burrowed behind thick clouds.

Charlotte hadn't been worried about the swim. She'd spent many days crossing the pool at her gym. However, the minute she'd hit the water, trouble lapped at her like an unexpected high tide.

Her muscles had seized at the shock of the cold sea. Her legs had dragged as she'd hopped over the waves, trying to get past the throng of eager athletes.

Charlotte hadn't been the only one feeling the effects of the cold. People had clustered together, seemingly unable to command their legs and arms to sync up and propel themselves forward.

All she had to do was swim a couple of kilometers perpendicular to the beach and it was over, but she was never going to get through the crush of people.

Unless she swam farther out. Deeper into the Atlantic, *farther* from the shore.

The kayakers keeping the racers from getting off track were focused on the barrage of swimmers.

She'd slipped right between two of them. If they called out to her, their voices were lost in the heaving and sighing ocean.

Once Charlotte had gotten her rhythm going, she felt good. Her body warmed up, her breathing regulated. It was just her and the water. Lifting her. Enveloping her.

After what felt like her usual time for the swim, she lifted her head, checking to see if it was time to cut back to shore.

Instead of being twenty feet from the coastline, she was a good forty feet.

Dammit. I'm going to have to make this up on the run.

Charlotte switched to the breaststroke, pairing the power of the ocean with her arms, but instead she got carried farther out.

Panic hit her like a rogue wave, capsizing her heart, leaving her breathless. Fear soured in her gut like she'd swallowed half an ocean.

She'd gotten caught in a riptide.

Her mind had churned on the instructions she'd learned as a child for surviving a riptide.

Stay calm. Conserve energy. Stay calm. Swim diagonally toward

the shore. Stay calm. Call for help.

Stay calm.

Charlotte took a deep breath and started a conservative swim. Winning the race be damned. She just needed to stay alive now.

The shore came into view.

Racers climbed out, stumbling over the waves as they pulled on helmets, readying themselves for the forty-kilometer cycle.

She kicked harder, wishing she could turn her legs into fins to propel her out of the water. After two hard strokes, her left quad seized so suddenly, she gasped just as a wave washed over her head. The riptide sucked at Charlotte, pulled her under, pissed her off.

The ocean wasn't going to take her.

She pushed with her arms, and burst through the surface, coughing and sputtering, waving the best she could to try to get someone's attention.

Stay calm. Call for help.

"Hey! I'm cramping up! Lifeguard!" Terror seized Charlotte's body, like a deep-sea monster come to life. She shouted, but the rising wind swallowed her words.

Another wave crashed into her from behind, tossing her forward.

She tried to push up again, but the waves were stronger. Instead of a deep breath of air, she choked on saltwater.

That was when that little voice first whispered to her.

Sleep. Let it go. Rest. It's okay. Let me take it away.

She kicked, trying to find anything that could propel her up. After a lifetime in the ocean, her old friend was betraying her.

Charlotte screamed into the water, releasing the last little bit of precious oxygen left in her body.

The voice of the deep called to her again. *No more trials. No more late-night toiling over legal briefs. No more mindless depositions. No more droning judges. Only peace. Only light. Let it go. Sleep.*

For the first time since she'd gotten into the freezing ocean, she relaxed.

She quit fighting and let her body sink.

Let the water consume her.

The first inhale of ocean water burned, but after that...

Nothing.

It was like waking up from the best dream ever, into the worst nightmare.

The air was frigid, but her lips felt warm.

People surrounded her.

Sand scratched at her back.

Her lungs were on fire, legs clenched tight.

The faces around Charlotte were distorted, like she was seeing them through a snow globe.

Except for one.

Jason.

"Sorry, I think I banged you in the head a bit." He grinned, even though concern touched the corners of his eyes. "I saw you go under. Didn't have time to pull off my helmet."

"You," she choked out.

"Yep, me." His Aussie accent was like a sip of chamomile tea

Jason stayed with her while she fought off the concerned race directors and paramedics on the empty beach. The race had moved on with the clouds, following the cyclists as they'd set off on their forty kilometers.

"Well, seems they left without us," Jason said good-naturedly, as if he hadn't spent months of training and hundreds of dollars for the triathlon he'd never finish. "Since I got a kiss from you, giving you mouth-to-mouth, seems only fair I should buy you a pint."

Charlotte never gave that race another thought.

It was less than two months after he'd saved her life that he'd taken her back to the beach, got down on one knee, and asked to spend the rest of their lives together. He hadn't proposed with a traditional ring. Instead, he'd given her a life preserver. "For when I can't be there to save you."

That life preserver now sat in a chair in her bedroom.

A place where Jason would've sat to put on his shoes before work or going for a run. Some nights she'd put it in bed with her, resting her cheek against it. Begging it to save her.

Charlotte glanced out the window at the ocean. The same body of water that'd brought her to the love of her life, in the same moment, threatened to take her away.

It was a beautiful monster.

She filled her lungs with a deep breath, and grabbed her phone, then launched the video app.

This was where her duality was the hardest. Pulling herself out of the past, and diving into a present that felt as real as the stock images that come in picture frames.

A type of happiness that could only be found by people playing a role.

She hit record. "Hey, y'all. Charlotte here." Her reflection looked calm, yet excited. "Just a quick video about knowing when to say it's time to replenish your soul. We all work so hard, give so much, pull from our well of what we offer others. But, that well can run dry, and when it does, it's time to fill it back up. That's what I'm going to be doing over these next few weeks. Taking time to do some traveling, to fill my well. I'll be checking in from time to time and posting videos, so stay tuned and take care of yourselves." She sent the video to her social media manager, letting Jules work her magic with filters and hashtags.

Truthfully, she would've deleted it if it wasn't for her obligation to her team. Obligation was like living on junk food. It kept her going but did nothing to offer nourishment.

Was that what'd gotten her to this point? A decade of living for other people and fulfilling obligations left behind the outer shell of Charlotte Claybrooke, and on the inside was nothing more than ash.

The doorbell chimed throughout her house.

Time to go.

She threw the last of her things into her suitcase. Her eyes lingered on their picture.

The girl in the frame smiled with her eyes, gazing up at the man she loved.

The man who'd saved her once.

The man she prayed could save her again.

2

There was something about meeting a new group of people facing death that made Jimmy Dire feel alive.

Not that he luxuriated in their demise. Quite the opposite. His job boosted their lives. Like a battery. He plugged into their world, charged them, powered them through the pain, turned their despair into delight. Like a business suit-clad genie, he wafted out of a bottle and granted them their final wish. Their final adventure.

Everybody dies.

Despite the potions and the notions, the crunches and the punches, and the all-absorbing nutritional demands, we all turn to dust. A nip here, an injection there won't stop the march of time. It beat a cadence with the jarring accuracy of an army of a thousand men.

Some fear it, some fight it, and others welcome it.

Some see it on the horizon like a meteor racing to shatter the earth.

For others, death is a sneaky bastard lurking around the corner, waiting until that final moment to snatch their life away.

Jimmy had seen the end of many, many journeys. He'd been around more death than life. Seen graceful exits and violent departures. Witnessed people on their dying breaths begging for forgiveness, or for more time, or even just for it to be over. Jimmy'd seen anger, denial, sadness, and finally, acceptance.

Everybody dies.

His job was to give the lucky ones something—a memory, a secret, a smile—to hold onto before the grand finale.

He pushed out of his chair and stared out over Biscayne Bay. His high-rise office offered the perfect view over Miami Beach to the ocean. The water was flat and calm, completely incongruent with the storm churning in his stomach. No matter how he did the math, the numbers came out the same.

His business wasn't just sinking; it was plummeting to the ocean floor with the speed of the Titanic.

If he could just hold Fiore off long enough to find more cash. To take care of this incoming group. Three weeks. That was all he needed. He did his best thinking in the company of the dying. Surely he'd come up with something.

Jimmy crossed his large office and fell into his chair. The 'Diers' as he called them, were scheduled to meet in just a couple of hours. He had just enough time to review their bios, double-check their medical records and releases, review the travel itineraries, confirm with the destination management companies.

Triple check everything for the fourth time.

"Darla, got a minute?" he asked into the phone's intercom.

She didn't answer, just opened the door and strode in. His assistant was decked out in her professional best. Buttoned-up black suit, with platform four-inch heels. She wore them less for the sexy factor and more for the height. Without them, she'd have to stretch to be five feet tall. Her blonde hair was teased up Texas big.

Some people merely were from places. For the native Texan, Darla wore her birth state like a Medal of Honor.

Was there something in the air in the Lone Star State that gave women gravity-defying hair?

Maybe they pumped aerosol hairspray into the atmosphere down there.

Darla handed him a stack of papers and perched on the side of his desk. "The jet is fueled and ready." She launched into the recap.

Years of working together had worn down the formality between them. Now their relationship was as comfortable as an old sweatshirt, each other's quirks were imprinted on the other, stretching them out. Sure, some parts got a bit threadbare, but it was softened to perfection.

"What about—"

"Management at Madison Square Garden has started building the stage, backup musicians confirmed, and we'll have shills to fill the audience if the fans don't come out." She kept her eyes on her checklist, not giving him an opening to question her bad-assness.

"And Peru?"

Darla flipped to the next page. "Weather's looking good. We should just be coming out of the rainy season when y'all get there."

Jimmy opened his mouth, but she continued.

"The one I'm worried about is Dylan's experiment in Switzerland at the research lab. We may need Enzo to call in a favor…"

He got it. Having Enzo call in a favor was one bad hand short of making a deal with the devil. "How much Texas charm have you turned on the Swiss?"

Darla's gaze flicked up from beneath her thick lashes, and she smirked. The former barrel racer wasn't afraid of much, especially after being rolled more than a few times by a horse that outweighed her ten-fold. Some poor Swiss scientists didn't stand a chance against her. "I dunno, maybe Austin, with a side of Lubbock."

"Can you crank it up to Dallas, with double Houston?"

She blew out a long breath. "You realize that's an atomic charm bomb. Not many people can withstand that."

"The scientists will appreciate it." Jimmy reclined in his chair. "Whatever it takes to keep from bothering Enzo."

His assistant's playful smile dropped and she pinched her brows together. "You haven't called him back, have you?" Her bright blue stare dared him to lie to her.

He swallowed and covered his mouth in a quick cough, hoping she wouldn't see his Adam's apple bob. Like an old married couple, she knew him better than he knew himself. "Oh yeah, thanks for the reminder." Jimmy jabbed the plunger on the end of his pen on the desk and scribbled something on his grocery list. "I'll do that before the guests arrive."

"Want me to get him on the phone for you?"

He grinned and leaned on his forearms, covering up the paper, in case Darla glanced down and noticed he'd written, *'pick up toilet paper,'* instead of a reminder to call Enzo. "Why don't you save that ass-kicking for the science guys. Oh, and we have one more to check on." He shuffled through real notes. "This last wish, dive with a pod of humpback whales. Drinks with that marine biologist get you the inside track?"

While their business was one hundred percent legit, now and then they had to resort to using tactics that fell just outside the lines of professionalism.

"Do you know how long I had to hear about how humanity is killing the oceans? I mean, I don't disagree, but I was about to slap him with a salmon to get him to shut up." Darla's Texas accent picked up annoyance, like a hitchhiker on a dark highway.

He covered his mouth. If she saw his smile, she might turn that salmon on him. "So, is that a no?"

"We're going out again tonight." She pushed up from the chair and straightened her jacket. "But you bet your sweet ass if he goes on about turtle extinction I'm going to shove one of those turtle eggs up your you-know-what." Darla spun around, her blonde hair whipping behind her.

"I love you, Darla," Jimmy shouted to her retreating figure.

"You'd better," she threw back to him.

He was still chuckling when he opened the final folder.

The Diers.

Five paper-clipped sets stared back at him. A photo attached to the upper left-hand corner, their formal applications, proof of insurance, completed legal documents, acknowledging they would not hold Dire Enterprises liable for any damages, dismemberment, or death.

That last one always made Jimmy chuckle. That was why people sought him out. They were dying. Terminal. Tangoing with the grim reaper. What did it matter if they died on their adventure? It just fast-forwarded them to the inevitable.

Past the legal documents were the official medical diagnoses. Most of his guests over the years had been cancer patients. Those handed the cursed words *'inoperable' 'metastasized'* and *'stage four.'* He'd also had several Alzheimer's diagnoses. Eager to experience what they could while they still knew who they were.

Occasionally, there were more exotic ailments; Parkinson's, Huntington's, and ALS. These people approached their adventures with an almost feral desperation. The need to cling to their bodies for as long as they could.

Jimmy thumbed past Levi Livingston; liver disease.

Scanned over Celeste Bennett; Alzheimer's.

Glanced at Dylan O'Keefe; poor kid had an inoperable brain tumor the size of a golf ball.

When he flipped to Lourdes Peña, he paused. The *telenovela* star's picture looked up at him. Dark, sultry eyes, luscious hair caressed one bare shoulder the faintest hint of a smile, as if the camera caught her either before it was fully formed or after it was spent.

Breast cancer was her initial diagnosis. After a battle, it'd changed tactics and turned into ovarian cancer. A brief respite later, the diagnosis was terminal.

These were the guests that pierced his heart the most. Sure, everybody dies, but it was the hardest to accept when seeing someone so full of *life*. As if they had further to fall than everyone else.

He cleared his throat and set Lourdes' file to the side.

The one that shocked him the most, because he'd turned to her books on grief and forgiveness time and time again, stared up at him next.

He had a rule, don't get close to the dying, don't become invested in their lives. But this one, he knew her from afar.

Charlotte Claybrooke; dying of…

Her application was meticulously completed. Legal indemnifications perfectly notarized. Payment completed with no problem. Insurance intact. However, her medical releases were missing.

That was strange. Everyone had to provide full disclosure from their doctors.

"Hey, Darla." Jimmy didn't bother using the intercom.

She appeared in his doorway, her cell phone to her ear. "Yes, my favorite pain in the patootic?"

"Charlotte Claybrooke, do you have her full packet? I'm missing her medical worksheet." He shuffled through his papers to prove it wasn't there.

"Probably. I'm on hold with the lab, can I check when I'm done?"

"Sure."

Jimmy didn't see his assistant leave his office. His gaze had fallen back to Lourdes' picture. What had she been thinking? Boredom at having her picture taken yet again?

A little bit of that. The sharpness of her eyes said there was more. Disdain, perhaps. Who wouldn't feel disdain at constantly having to battle delinquent cells?

No, there was more to her. A lot more. If he could just get inside the picture, ask her…

Jimmy swallowed and ran his hands through his hair. He bolted from his desk, staring at his reflection in the plate glass window.

Running kept him lean and in shape, but he did it more to wear out his nervous energy. His auburn hair ran from his forehead, but it was still pretty thick throughout. His long, thin nose took up very little real estate on his face, letting his wide, green eyes take center stage.

Jimmy never had trouble getting the ladies' attention, even as he crept closer to fifty. Suddenly he found himself studying the handful of wrinkles he'd earned after living in Miami for two decades.

When his eyes landed on the picture of Lourdes, air fled from his lungs, lungs that decided to take their lunch break, as if they'd unionized and forgot to tell him.

If a photo could do that to him, what would the actual woman do?

3

Darla's boisterous Texas greetings reverberated through the office. "Hey, y'all! Welcome! How y'all doin'?"

Jimmy shook his head and laughed. She was the only person in the world who could turn a one-syllable word into ten.

The previously quiet office was filled with excited chatter.

This was his favorite moment. A group of strangers on the cusp of becoming friends. Comrades. The hesitation, slight nervousness wondering if they would like each other, before realizing they would share an unbreakable bond.

Those who lived like there was no tomorrow.

He strained his ears, trying to discern the voices and attach them to faces he knew from a photo and lives he knew only through sheaths of paper.

A gravelly male voice met Darla's ebullience with his rock star rowdiness.

Another voice joined the mix. Strong, clear, matronly. It was a voice that could dress down the toughest hitman, and have him offering to carry her groceries.

His assistant's next greeting was met with a soft murmur. A young man's voice. Reluctant, not yet hardened by life.

Jimmy could almost hear the air escape the conference room next to him when the next person arrived.

Everyone quieted until Darla broke the silence.

"Well, hey girl, so glad you could make it." His assistant's voice kicked up an octave higher.

Lilting words wrapped around a Spanish accent answered her.

The movie star had arrived.

He couldn't make out what she said, but the sound of her voice entered his ears, shocked his heart, tugged his stomach like he'd just gone over the first hill of a roller coaster.

Jimmy glanced at his watch. Three o'clock on the dot.

He counted four voices. Four of his five Diers. Perhaps the last one had snuck in during Lourdes' wake, and he'd missed her.

Jimmy cleared his throat. He opened the door of a hutch and used the mirror hanging inside to smooth his hair, check his teeth and steady the racehorse galloping in his chest.

"Welcome, Diers!" He practiced in a low mutter to his reflection. "Welcome, *ahem*. Welcome." He tried on different tones and inflections, but none of them seemed to fit. Facing his professional idol, and a woman whose picture stole his breath like he was sprinting a marathon, rocked the foundation of his confidence.

"Jimmy," Darla whispered from the door. "It's time."

He took a final glance at his reflection, and closed his eyes. A slip of a memory raced across his mind. Travel magazines with the pictures cut out. Elaborate collages. The drip of an IV, the foul-smelling chemicals. It was his private meditation. A reminder that he could give these people a special gift.

Something no one else could.

"Showtime." Jimmy exhaled, then closed the cabinet door.

Like his office, the conference room looked out over the bay. Contemporary furniture, with white ergonomic chairs encircled the glass table with an array of trendy succulents nestled in a large planter.

The platter of finger food was untouched, but the guests were chatting, sipping wine, and enjoying Darla's tall tales and effortless charm.

He recognized Levi Livingston first. Head to toe black—including black sunglasses—made his thick head of white hair even more shocking.

Levi's face was thin, with deep lines creasing his forehead and down the sides of his mouth. The man sipped from a full glass of red wine, probably against his doctor's wishes since he was dying of liver disease.

Where Levi was a piece of grizzled meat, the boy standing next to him was like veal.

Dylan O'Keefe was tall, gangly. His dark hair was curly, and looked more like someone who didn't think to get a haircut, rather than someone growing it out. Oversized glasses framed his soft, pale face. If he shaved, he hadn't been doing it long enough to thicken his skin.

He winced as he sipped his white wine. The kid was a study in contrasts. He stood tall, not like other slouchy twenty-somethings who shuffled through life.

Jimmy found Celeste next. The woman's silver hair was pulled into a low bun and her black kaftan featured a smattering of white stars that matched a band encircling her head. A professional-looking camera hung around her neck and she clung to a thick journal like a secret.

She talked with her hands, her bright red nails miming the words coming out of similarly colored lips. The woman's life force was a warm lightbulb, glowing, illuminating, spotlighting everyone around her.

The glow she emitted fell on the woman to whom she spoke.

Lourdes.

She listened intently to Celeste. Her dark eyes narrowed, as if visualizing the words coming out of the older woman's mouth. Her long hair bounced with each nod. The star shifted her stance, the skirt of her dress swaying like a tree in a gentle breeze.

When Celeste got to the punchline of her story, laughter erupted from Lourdes, a lovely, throaty sound that was both joyful and sultry.

In the climax of her laugh, her gaze flitted in his direction. She tilted her head, studying him. Questioning him.

Challenging him.

Jimmy's mouth dried up like the Sahara. He opened it to say something, but the words fled like fearful prey, so he could only stare.

She pursed her lips, lifting one side in a smirk before turning her back to him.

He rubbed his chest. Not that it hurt, he was afraid a cartoonish heart was beating out of control.

Darla appeared at his side.

"We're missing one," Jimmy murmured to her, begging his eyes to leave Lourdes' backside.

"Charlotte should be arriving any minute. Flight got in late." His assistant turned her back to the room. "Are we sure Dylan's really over twenty-one?"

Jimmy glanced up at the young man. Sure, he looked young, but so did everyone under thirty these days.

That was one of the rules his attorneys enforced the most when drawing up the contracts. All participants must be over the age of twenty-one and of sound mind and body.

The sound body definition ranged but the mind was mostly to ensure that the Diers could deal with the cards they were dealt. He'd seen everything from impassive acknowledgment to utter despair.

While he didn't have a personal problem with age, the attorneys convinced him it was better for insurance and legal drinking age, adulthood ... yada, yada, yada.

The kid was a mathematical prodigy and game developer-millionaire. What did it matter if he had to get someone else to buy his beer?

"Twenty-three, to be exact," Jimmy said, hoping that would shoo his bulldog assistant away.

"Um, hello."

He turned at a soft voice behind him.

Charlotte Claybrooke stood before him.

The Charlotte Claybrooke.

Her brown hair hung straight past her shoulders, bangs covering her forehead and grazing her eyelashes. Steady green eyes, with just a touch of brown, held his gaze.

Charlotte wore a crisp, off-white sweater over matching pants. If meditation could be personified, it stood before him. Fitting for someone who'd quickly risen to become one of the nation's most sought-after life coaches.

The fact that Charlotte now faced death felt both poetic and grotesque. Heroes were mere mortals, no matter the pedestal he put them on.

Jimmy knew her words thoroughly. He'd often turned to her books and lectures early in his business. Her story of surviving her fiancé's sudden death had helped the early groups of Diers cope with their guilt of leaving loved ones behind. Charlotte's story of conquering her grief was like a warm fire on a chilly night.

For many years, he'd wanted to reach out to her. To share with her how he'd come to rely on her wisdom from a distance. Jimmy could never muster the courage to do it. Somehow, he felt like he cheapened her purpose in life.

She helped survivors survive.

He helped the dying die happy.

Two stars orbiting the same planet that was never meant to meet.

Until now…

"Charlotte," Jimmy stuck his hand out. "It is truly an honor to meet you."

She blushed and diverted her gaze to the carpet. "Well, the honor is all mine, Mr. Dire." Charlotte's Southern accent was all grace and lightning bugs and fried green tomatoes. "I apologize for my tardiness; my flight was a bit late taking off."

He stretched his face into his widest grin. "You're right on time, Charlotte. And please, call me Jimmy." He offered her an arm. "Shall we?"

She shyly locked her arms with his. "Let's."

He led her into the conference room, and the conversations quieted.

"Hello, Diers!" Jimmy stretched out his arms and lifted his chest.

The small group broke into applause.

"I'm Jimmy Dire." He'd make a connection with each person. He looked at Charlotte. "I'm your host, your concierge." Then Celeste. "Your travel companion." A nod to Dylan. "Your wingman." A toast to Levi. "Your drinking buddy." When his gaze slid to Lourdes, she lifted her chin. "Your...confidante."

She pursed her lips and looked away.

"For these next three weeks, I'm a genie, and your wish is my command." Jimmy paced the room, his hands clasped behind his back, before launching into his scripted spiel. "You're probably wondering why we share these adventures as a group. Well, dying is lonely. Your families feel such a range of emotions. Disbelief, anger, sadness. And, maybe you're feeling that, too. What we've left undone, unsaid. What we're leaving behind, and what we're taking with us." He paused to take a sip of his water. "There's survivor's guilt, but I believe there's also Dier's guilt. Dying is hard on the living, but I believe it's harder on the Diers. The remorse for not being there to walk daughters down the aisle, or see grandkids graduate, or even finish that masterpiece novel you've toiled over."

He clasped his hands and leaned forward. "Here is a guilt-free zone. You owe each of us nothing other than enjoying yourselves and each other's company. Here, no one is going to be upset with you if you go first. Because everybody dies. You are the lucky ones. You get to have fun doing it."

Exhales and self-conscious laughter rippled through the group, giving way to relieved applause.

Levi whistled and Celeste cheered.

Even Lourdes unleashed a wide grin.

"A few housekeeping items, per my attorneys." Jimmy rolled his eyes. "I must have a waiver indicating that Jimmy Dire, Dire Enterprises, its employees, and vendors are released from any liability. Please sign that before you leave this evening. As for other documents," he glanced down at the checklist in his hand, although he didn't need it. "I need proof of insurance and, of course, a release from your doctor. I believe I have almost everyone's." He leveled his gaze at Charlotte, but she was studying the glass of wine in her hands.

"So, we start tomorrow, with Levi Livingston who will get to live his dream of playing one last gig at Madison Square Garden. While this is Levi's adventure, you all get to participate. We've got a jet leaving first thing tomorrow, so we'll share more on the flight."

As rehearsed, Darla entered the room with an armful of packets.

"Darla Steele, who you've all met when you arrived, is my rock, my right hand, my left hand too, my keeper and best friend." His voice broke. She'd come such a long way from when he hired her on the spot at a nursing home. He cleared his throat. "She has your welcome packets with your hotel keys. Please spend some time getting to know your fellow Diers. And, welcome to Dire's Club."

4

Jimmy made a beeline for her as soon as he finished his welcome.

Charlotte darted her gaze to the *hors d'oeuvres*, studying the wine and broccoli to avoid answering his questions about her medical forms. She'd thought about faking the forms. Filling in some rare ailment that wouldn't spawn too many questions, like what was the treatment, or what were the symptoms, or how long she had to live.

She couldn't bring herself to do it. There'd been enough lies piled up in her life. One more might be the lie that broke the camel's back.

Omission was a better choice.

Jimmy reached for a plate and started piling on cheese.

She could feel it in him. The question. The accusation. It would be better if she just cut it out of him.

"Jimmy, do you have everything you need from me?" she asked, plucking a carrot stick from the tray.

"You know, I'm glad you brought that up. I'm sure it's our fault, but we can't seem to put our fingers on your medical files." His face was sincere, as if he truly thought they'd lost it. "I hate to bother you with this, but could you ask them to send another copy to Darla?"

Charlotte kept her eyes on the food. "Oh shoot, I'm so sorry about that. Of course. I'll call my assistant right away for you."

He laid a hand on her arm. "No rush, really. It's a formality is all. Just when you get to it."

She felt safe enough to look at him and nod.

Jimmy held her gaze for several seconds, as if he were going to say something else, but a husky, accented voice wafted in their direction. His head turned in the direction of the pretty Latina, and Charlotte couldn't help but let her gaze follow.

In her career as a life coach, she'd been around plenty of celebrities. They were easy to spot in a crowd. Their otherworldliness made them seem like they were too big for the space they inhabited. Even if they stood in the middle of a football stadium.

This woman had the same aura. However, it was different. She loomed large, but held herself taut. As if every muscle and every fiber was tightly clenched. Tightly controlled.

"Who is she?" Charlotte asked, unable to place the celebrity in her own memory bank.

"Lourdes Peña, *telenovela* star from Mexico City." Jimmy didn't so much as speak the words, rather he sighed them. "Excuse me," he added, before floating across the room to the woman.

Damn, he's got a crush. I hope he's in therapy.

"Ello, love," hoarse English-accented words pulled her from watching Jimmy swoon over the star. "Come here often?" Levi Livingston topped off his red wine, filling it nearly to the top of the glass. He tilted the bottle in her direction but she shook her head.

The former lead guitarist for Fistful of Devils swallowed half his glass before refilling it again.

"Had nothing better to do on a Thursday night," she quipped. "You?"

"Heard there was free booze so I thought, what the hell." He grinned, his temples crinkling behind his dark glasses. "So what you in for?"

"Beg your pardon?"

"You know, like prison, what're you doing hard time for?"

Charlotte buried her answer in a long sip of white wine. She'd expected this question, but like the medical form, she'd hoped she could skirt it. "Shanked some guy," she answered with a wink. "Cut him groin to neck. And you?"

He threw back his head and howled with laughter. "Brilliant. I'm Levi Livingston." He offered his hand.

She took his hand. It was clammy, but she tried not to recoil. "Charlotte Claybrooke." She leaned in. "I was a huge fan of Fistful of Devils when I was a kid."

"Really?" He seemed genuinely surprised. "Did you ever see us play?"

She shook her head. "No, my parents could never make the time to take me to a concert." Charlotte gasped at the slip. While there was no secret that Levi was old enough to be her dad, she didn't need to remind him. "Sorry, I didn't mean to make you sound old."

"No worries, love." He waved off the apology. "Age is but a number, right? Anyway," he dropped his voice to a conspiratorial whisper. "I can still lure the young lasses to bed. What's your favorite song?"

She chewed on her inside cheek. His band really was one of her favorites.

They'd been big in the eighties, known for upbeat, rebel rousing, dance-like-you-don't-give-a-damn anthems. She hadn't listened to anything by Fistful of Devils since before…

Charlotte swallowed a big sip of wine. "Oh gosh, I think 'She's My Girl.'"

Levi bowed his head. "Perfect song for a sweet southern girl. For you, tomorrow, I shall play it. If you'll excuse me, I'm going to see if that captivating little blonde has plans for the evening." He nodded toward Jimmy's assistant, Darla. "Cheers."

"Cheers, and good luck."

Charlotte moved to the back of the room, where she could watch the group.

Jimmy managed to capture Lourdes, but the woman didn't ease up no matter how animatedly he spoke.

Levi leaned against the wall; his charm cranked up to eleven as he spoke to the petite blonde.

Darla had an amused look plastered to her face. It was likely not the first time she'd been hit on by someone who had nothing to lose, and a gorgeous-girl-in-his-bed to gain.

The older woman and young man were huddled over a camera.

He was clicking through settings, his face pinched in concentration.

What am I doing?

They were all dying. And yes, there was the belief that everyone was dying from the moment they're born. These people were legitimately dying. They had the paperwork to prove it.

What did she have?

A heart that refused to glue itself back together. A brain that told her the world would better off without her.

A future that looked darker than the past.

She'd spent so much of the last decade being a fraud that she wasn't even sure who the real Charlotte Claybrooke was anymore.

The words she'd written; it was only to make herself believe them. That there was life after Jason. That she *could* go on. That the grayness would give way to color.

Fake it til you make it.

Right?

Except she'd never made it.

No matter how many stages she stood on, how many talk shows she visited, or how many celebrity endorsements she racked up, Charlotte never once started believing her own words. Even when everyone else did.

She could just slip away. Out the door, down the elevator, through the lobby. She could sneak off to the beach. Say she was going for a swim. Maybe the same current could capture her. Whisk her away, pull her under. Jason wouldn't save her, but that was okay. Because he'd be there waiting for her on the other side.

"Oh, you poor thing, standing here by yourself."

A warm, grandmotherly voice snapped Charlotte back to the conference room.

"Don't be shy, hon." The woman had the loveliest blue eyes. Not just the color, but the warmth that oozed from her. "I'm Celeste Bennett, early-onset Alzheimer's. Are you Charlotte?"

"Yes, Charlotte Claybrooke. It's nice to meet you, Celeste. And, um, sorry about the Alzheimer's. How're you doing?"

"That's kind, but don't you worry about me. I finally get to embrace that crazy, absent-minded old lady I've always wanted to grow up to be."

She smiled. Judging by her dress and matching headband, she was embracing it, whole hog. "What's your adventure, Celeste?"

Like a three-way lightbulb, the woman lit up to the next level. "Oh, I'm so excited, we're going to hike to Machu Picchu." She clapped her hands like a child. "Have you ever done that?"

That was actually on her and Jason's list of possible honeymoon destinations. He'd wanted an adventure, she'd wanted romance. Charlotte had won, but promised him their next vacation would be Peru.

"No, never made it there. That'll be fun. Why did you choose that?" She had to keep the woman talking. The more Celeste talked, the longer she had to fight the urge to walk into the ocean.

The older woman's eyes misted. "I always wanted to be a photographer for *National Geographic*. But I met my husband when I was young, married, kids, grandkids. You know how that goes. He's been gone for a few years, and when I got the diagnosis, I thought well, what am I waiting for?"

"That's why you've got the camera," Charlotte nodded to the camera still in the young man's hands.

"Oh, Dylan is so sweet. He's optimizing it for me." She turned to the boy. "Dylan, honey, come meet Charlotte."

The young man pushed his glasses up on his nose and joined them. "I think I've got it all set for you." His voice was deep, yet youthful.

The faintest stubble dotted his chin. His complexion was perfect, as if the awkward teenage years had missed him. There was a seriousness in his eyes, like he'd lived many lifetimes before the one in this body.

"How do you do?" Charlotte asked.

"Poor Dylan has a brain tumor. Doctors can't do anything for him. Bless his heart."

He winced. There was something in Celeste's words that bothered him. Instinct told Charlotte it had more with the pity being laid on him, thank his prognosis. "Sorry to hear that," she whispered. There was something especially bothersome about Dylan being among them. She could understand Levi and Celeste, and even Lourdes, in some way. The woman appeared to be about her own age. They all had a good chunk of life behind them. But Dylan. He was barely into his early twenties. "Excuse me." She sat her glass down and escaped the conference room, in search of a ladies' room in the hall.

Charlotte braced herself on the counter and breathed deeply. "This was a mistake," she muttered.

Why did I think this would work?

The door flung open, and Lourdes stopped just inside, her hands frozen on her half-lifted wig. Fear flitted across her face, like a rabbit caught in a predator's stare.

"It's okay," Charlotte said. "My bark is much worse than my bite."

The TV star pushed past her. "If you lose your hair, just embrace bald." The woman set the wig on the countertop and dabbed her head with a paper towel. Her light brown skin glistened under the overhead lights. The diamond earrings dangling from her lobes sparkled, tossing even more light against her skin. Standing there bald, she seemed even larger than life. As if her charisma was tucked away under the cap of fake hair. Without it, her true power was freed.

"For what it's worth, you do bald beautifully," Charlotte said.

Lourdes blanched. "Says the lady with the full head of hair." She then took a deep breath and closed her eyes. "Sorry, it's funny the things you become envious of." With her wig back in place, her light dimmed just a bit. Her back stiffened and her body tightened. "Well, I'm sure we'll talk again soon."

She followed the woman's escape with her eyes.

Is that what would happen to her? If she shed the baggage of grief? Would her light warm like a rising sun?

Or, would it snuff out like the darkest of nights?

5

The jet was airborne before the sun finished its climb into the eastern horizon. Charlotte slipped her off shoes, tucked her feet under her legs, and rocked her seat back.

Levi sat in front of her. He hummed songs from her youth, mumbling the lyrics, only to get one wrong, curse and start over. When he wasn't fumbling over the words, he'd hammer out a beat on the window.

"Are you getting excited?" She leaned forward.

"What? Oh, yeah, tonight. Yeah, love." He turned in his seat. The faint smell of alcohol wafted in her direction. He was clad in much the same uniform as the night before, except today he wore skintight black jeans with an oversized black sweatshirt. "Just been a bit since I've sung some of these."

"So, why this instead of something you've never done before? Like summiting Mount Kilimanjaro or hang-gliding off the Grand Canyon?"

The rocker lifted his sunglasses. "How do you know I haven't?" Levi winked before lowering them. "This was my best performance ever. October 1987. I was in my prime, as was the band. The fans fed off us, we fed off the fans. It was a beautiful feast."

Charlotte laughed. "Sounds more like a feeding frenzy. Did you ever get nervous? Up on stage?"

He shrugged and took a sip of his orange juice. "Maybe, but I stayed pretty well blitzed through the eighties." Levi pointed his glass in her direction. "But what about you? You can't hide behind instruments, hairspray, and screaming fans."

She withheld the tremor that rumbled at her core.

Charlotte the charlatan.

That was what she called herself when she gazed out to an audience of people staring up at her with desperation in their eyes. Begging her to say the right thing to give them the lift they needed to get out of bed each morning. To stumble past the life's-so-unfair. To step over the why-me's.

The verbal shot of adrenalin to their souls.

They looked to her to cling to life.

She didn't launch into her career of being a life coach to defraud others. It had been for herself. Like an actress, if she recited her lines enough, she'd eventually step out of her real life and into the story she'd written.

That Charlotte could overcome the worst life could give her. Not just overcome, but find a new purpose. A new mission.

New life.

Except, she never fully believed her own lines.

Lately, she'd felt her delivery had grown flat. That she'd need to look off stage and ask the director to give her the next line.

"You've obviously never been to a personal improvement conference, Levi," she quipped. "There's lights, dancing, speaking in tongues." Charlotte hid her smile behind a sip of coffee.

"But are there girls lifting their shirts?"

She pursed her lips and darted her gaze up to the ceiling of the plane. "Not at mine, but the other guy's…When was the last time you played a show?"

"Ah, it's been a good many years." He held his hands up.

She hadn't noticed the trembling the day before.

"The worst part about being a drunk is you're damned if you do and damned if you don't." Levi took a long sip of his vodka and orange juice. "I've learned to stay in this in-between place. If I don't let myself dry out, or get too sloshed then I'm pretty good."

"But playing guitar…" During the height of the band's popularity, he'd been a well-regarded guitar virtuoso. His riffs were studied and imitated, applauded and snubbed. The band always hovered just outside the orbit of acclaim.

"I can still do some chords, but I aim to focus on singing this go." He unscrewed the top from a flask and filled his cup to the top, diluting the orange juice to a light peach color. "I've always been better than that wanker of a lead singer anyway."

"You're really lucky. Do you know how many kids want to be rock stars and grow up to be doctors or lawyers?" Charlotte thought about her own childhood fantasies. Standing in the middle of her bed, her hair teased up, her face painted in her mom's makeup, singing into her hairbrush to a crowd of stuffed animals.

"Or life coaches?" Levi's voice lifted with a smile.

"That obvious?"

"When you stand on stage, when you look out over people all staring back at you…" His eyes grew wistful. "Do you know why they say so many musicians are larger than life?"

Charlotte shook her head.

"Because they have to be. Thousands of people, who all want something from you. Your talent. Your music. And, if you're any artist who's worth a damn, your art is your soul. So they want a piece of your soul." Levi drained the rest of his juice and filled it with straight vodka. "You have to be willing to give your soul to be up there. And while it's thrilling to hear shouts of your name, when you come off the stage, after the crowds have bought their shirts and albums, after the groupies have passed out, and after the adrenaline and booze wears off, you find yourself spent. Depleted. Empty. It's a hell of a feeling. Knowing that you gave so much that if someone touched you, you'd crumble like one of those hollow chocolate Easter bunnies." He held her gaze for several long seconds.

Could he see it? That every time she'd speak at a conference, or appear on TV or even just work with a client she'd come home a shell of who she was when she woke up that day.

"How're ya feeling, Charlotte?" he asked, his British accent becoming more pronounced as he drank. "We need to watch out for each other. Us, Diers as Jimmy calls us."

Her eyes burned and she blinked quickly, shooing the tears away, like naughty children. "I'm good, just a little tired. Overwhelmed, maybe."

He nodded and pursed his lips. "You've never told us what's killing you."

"I haven't," she agreed.

Levi looked out over the cabin, studying their travel companions. "That's okay, death is something we all have to do alone. This just helps us feel a little less lonely." He pulled his phone and a set of earbuds out of his pocket and passed them to her. "You remember the words to 'She's the Girl'?"

"Mostly. Why?" Charlotte reached for the phone.

"It's a duet. I need someone to sing with me."

The previously cool interior of the plane cabin suddenly sparked with heat, and she recoiled from his outstretched hand. "Wait, what? No, how do you know I can even sing, I couldn't. This is your adventure Levi; you should have professionals." She tossed out every excuse she could summon to decline his request.

"You've got a lovely voice; I imagine it's only more beautiful when you sing."

"What if I'm tone deaf?"

"Who the hell cares?"

"What if your fans complain?" She shook her head so hard that her bangs stuck in her eyelashes.

"I'll tell 'em to fuck off. I'm dying, I can be a bastard." Levi softened. "It'll be toward the end of the set. I won't force you, Charlotte, but if I look off to the side of the stage and call your name, I hope you'll be there to answer me." He swiveled back around.

Charlotte put the earbuds in and found the song in his playlist. When she pressed 'play,' the song washed over her. Her heart found the heavy guitar riff and danced with it. The lyrics played, her lips forming silent words that just needed the lift of her lungs to give them life. Her body rocked, swaying side to side with the bass.

She closed her eyes and found herself back in a time of braces, first periods, awkward growth spurts, and trying to find her place in life.

A threshold between childhood and adolescence. A time when she read teenage magazines, but wasn't quite ready to give up her dolls.

The summer the song was popular had been when her parents fought the most. Her dad's business wasn't doing so well, but he didn't want to let her mom go back to work. What would the neighbors think?

It was the summer they'd dropped the country club membership, so she missed the days spent poolside with her friends. It was the summer they couldn't afford to send her to cheerleader camp, so instead of trying out, she said she'd play school sports instead.

It was the summer she'd learned adults cried much more than kids.

6

Hell hath no fury like a pissed-off liver.

Or was it cranky knees? Those were pretty ill-natured. Then again, these days everything in Levi's body was angry.

Ears?

Irritated.

Heart?

Vexed.

Hips?

Outraged.

Then, there was his liver. It burned with every sip of vodka, yet screamed when he let it dry out for too long.

Maybe he'd drank to the point when it was no longer an organ, but instead one of those spiny sea urchins, stabbing him from the inside whenever it got its fill, and then again when it was thirsty.

Levi wiped the steam from the bathroom mirror and leaned in. His eyes were damn useless. His whole life, twenty-twenty vision, then suddenly he had to squint to see if the young lady he flirted with at the bar was young.

Or, even a lady.

Water dripped off his shoulder-length white hair. At least he still had hair.

It'd gone white almost overnight when he was in his early thirties. The band manager had wanted him to dye it back to jet black, but he rather liked it. That shock of a white, lustrous mane in a sea of hair-sprayed, teased, permed eighties hair bands.

He was a white tiger.

The rest of them were nothing more than rowdy kittens.

He pulled the lid off the travel-sized vodka bottle and took a healthy swig.

Levi turned to study his profile, gripping that little bit of fat that tended to settle on the waists of men, as they aged.

Thank goodness that ladies' corset company started making products for men. Slipping into leather pants was harder on the blokes. A lot more to have to cram into tight places.

He downed the rest of the bottle and tossed it in the hotel trashcan. The alcohol bounced around his stomach, jostled by nerves like a crowd-surfing groupie.

The pre-show jitters were also new.

Back in the day, he and his bandmates barely gave it a second thought before they'd hop on stage and give it everything they had. Instead of coming off at the end of the set feeling exhausted, they'd felt pumped. They were just getting started. The night was young. Booze and babes were waiting.

Now, his hand would ache for days after just strumming a few basic chords. He'd find himself unable to talk after belting out half-assed words sung on puny notes.

Levi used to think of his music as a love letter to his fans. Now, it felt like he texted them in that blasted shorthand and smiley face shit his daughter always used.

Leave it to today's youth to send us back to using hieroglyphics.

He peered at his reflection.

When did I get so fuckin' old?

The answer stabbed at his gut.

When he was diagnosed with liver disease.

There was nothing in the world to make a man feel both dead and alive than to hear his pending expiration.

Suddenly, he became more aware of the feel of the sun on his face. Of the smell of the crisp winter air of the English countryside. Hell, even London smelled beautiful to him. His daughter's voice; he marveled at how her American accent would ease into its English roots during their conversation.

Would he ease back into being Levi Livingston, frontman of Fistful of Devils, in the same way that Olivia had slipped on her father's accent? Or, would he trip over himself like a clumsy stripper?

His phone buzzed. Group text from Jimmy, reminding everyone that they were leaving for the Garden in thirty minutes.

Thirty minutes to get himself together.

Thirty minutes to convince himself he wouldn't make an arse of himself on stage.

Thirty minutes to get enough of a buzz going to walk out that door.

"Eh, fuck'em," he growled at his reflection. "I'll be dead soon. What does it matter?"

Levi sat on the edge of the bed, getting the tight leather pants to his knees before he popped his bum out to get it over his hips, only to then have to thrust his pelvis forward to get them zipped.

Thankfully, the white ruffled shirt went on with nary a protest.

He tossed his signature red sequin blazer in its garment bag on his bed. It was going to be bloody hot on stage, but he couldn't let them see the sweat stains under his armpits.

The compact on the counter taunted him. Sure, he'd donned his fair share of eyeliner back in the day. Might even throw it on from time to time now.

That didn't bother him. What bothered him was the foundation he'd picked up to cover the sickly gray that made him look like a character out of a Bela Lugosi film. If he were one of those drab goth singers, he'd welcome the pallor, but for his final gig, he wanted to project prowess and health.

For his final gig, Levi wanted everyone to know he was alive.

Even if it killed him.

He secreted a couple more travel-sized vodka bottles into his blazer pocket and headed downstairs for an energy drink chaser.

Levi was handing over cash for his purchase when a soft Southern voice caught his attention.

Charlotte stood with her back to him, her phone held high, the camera flipped around to selfie mode. "Hi, y'all, Charlotte here and—" She stopped and pulled her phone down, head bent over the screen before holding it back up again, shaking her curtain of chestnut hair and clearing her throat. "Hey y'all, it's me. Just a quick hello from the Big Apple. Tonight is going to be a special night, where I get to see one of my childhood favorites, Fistful of Devils. Stay tuned, I might even sing a surprise—" She brought the phone down again. "Dammit."

He watched her fumble with her phone and start and stop the recording several times. She didn't act like a self-help guru. All the ones he'd come across while married to Naomi, his yoga teaching, New Age-y ex, were either over-sexed, long-haired men who thought they could screw their clients happy, or barefoot prophets who hopped on couches and expounded the benefits of primal screams.

Charlotte was neither of these. She was as subdued as an early summer day. All soft sunshine and gentle breezes. There wasn't the blast of heat that usually accompanied people full of you're-in-charge-of-your-own-destiny bullshit.

Especially someone as young as her, as alive as her.

She was unlike the other Diers, people eager to burn out the rest of their energy in one final burst. Although, there were all types of dying stars. Not everyone went supernova. Some just faded away.

When she lifted her phone again, his gaze collided with hers in the camera.

Guess being a creepy old bloke is par for the course.

"Nothing makes you feel your age like technology." His face burned as he pulled his mouth up to a grin.

"That, and social media." Charlotte shoved the phone into her back pocket. "You ready for tonight?"

Levi held up his mini-bottles of booze and wagged the energy drink. "Working on it." He winked and let his official Fistful of Devils smirk cross his face. "How about you? Getting your vocal cords warmed up?"

She laughed. A delightful sound, that reminded him of a tropical beach.

"I have to admit, I might need some of your liquid courage." Pink touched her cheeks. Cheeks that already had the perfect glow of health.

What *was* killing her?

She didn't have the gaunt, hairlessness of a cancer patient, like Lourdes.

She wasn't past the prime of her life, like Celeste, succumbing to her brain's short circuit.

Nor did she have the pissed-off pinched face of someone dying too young, like Dylan.

No, Charlotte's toned body and porcelain complexion sung health and vibrancy. Yet her demeanor hummed acceptance. Readiness.

Levi offered an arm, leading them to the front of the hotel lobby. "You still haven't told me what's killing you."

One of her shoulders lifted. "Does it matter? Will you think any less of me if my death was uncool?" Charlotte pressed her lips tight, as if tucking away any other words that threatened to slip from her full lips.

What did it matter? They were all dying. One person's death wasn't necessarily sexier than another's. Messier, maybe.

But dead is dead is dead.

It didn't matter how they got there; they were all on the Good Ship Dead-You-Drop.

He waved away his question. "Fuck it. How you die doesn't matter, it's how you live, right?"

Her face relaxed. "That's true. So, what do you think? Did you live as good as you're dying?"

"Tabloids sure as hell think so." Levi stopped at an oversized couch and invited her to sit. He plopped down next to her. "My exes seemed pretty happy with what they got in the divorces." He took a pull from the bottle. "My daughter." His eyes misted and he rubbed his nose. "Olivia's proof I did something right in this world. Her mum and I always made it about her. I cut back on touring when she was young." A tightness cinched Levi's chest.

Olivia was a young woman now, with a successful career, never riding her father's famous coattails. That made him most proud. He'd raised her to be her own person.

That was also his greatest regret. He wouldn't get to see more of how that strong woman would change the world.

"She's brilliant, but I'm sure all papas say that about their kids."

Charlotte smiled at him, full of light and life.

Whatever was killing her hadn't snuffed the glow inside of her.

"It really is about those we touch, isn't it?" She looked away, her gaze sweeping the lobby, but somehow, he knew she didn't see Terrazzo tile and bellhops hurrying by, or oversized floral arrangements with birds of paradise standing sentry.

She saw something that perhaps only someone with the sixth sense of their impending death could see.

The song winding down to the final notes. The last few pages of a beloved book. There was a strange calm with knowing the calendar held more days in the past than the future.

No, it's not that, it's about those who change us. Sometimes the people we know for the shortest time have the greatest impact," she said quietly.

That was when he saw it. Beneath the surface of a beautiful woman in the prime of her life, there was the weight she carried.

Like a ship heaving its anchor across the ocean. While it was pulled up, it glided effortlessly. Once it loosened, the anchor had the potential to bring the whole ship down.

Levi downed half his vodka in one drink.

She was right.

They'd only just met, but he found himself wanting nothing more than to keep her on the surface.

7

They arrived at Madison Square Garden early but got snarled in the pre-concert traffic. While they waited, the car crept past throngs of fans lined up outside, taking selfies in their vintage Fistful of Devils T-shirts.

Charlotte sat at the back of the SUV, studying the group of total strangers. Strangers, yet in some way, they felt comfortable. Like coming together with long-lost family at a reunion.

People who had nothing but shared genetics, or in this case, destiny, who found each other. It felt a lot like when she'd first met Jason. The locking together of puzzle pieces that made a beautiful portrait of her life.

A portrait shattered by a sleep-deprived driver on a rain-slicked road.

She swatted away the memories, mumbling under her breath about a mosquito following them from Miami, but the young man seated next to her didn't seem to notice.

His eyes were focused on the filled notebook in his lap.

She peered at the markings. A formula of some kind for some math that was light years beyond her nascent ability to balance her checkbook.

"What's that?" she asked.

Dylan made a few more marks before he jumped; obviously startled that she was speaking to him. "Oh, I was just running through my theory one more time."

Charlotte didn't think it was a final 'one more' time. More like one more time for that day. "What's your experiment?"

"In layman's terms, I'm trying to prove that time isn't linear," Dylan spoke to his notebook.

"So you're building a time machine?"

If that's the case, can I be first in line to go back ten years?

"I wish, but when you break time down to its smallest unit, I believe we can manipulate it. Tweak it, just for a moment, before it skips ahead."

"What could we use that for?" How many split seconds could be reversed before hearts are broken? A hairpin U-turn of time to right a listless life.

The young man looked out the window on his side.

She watched the passing buildings through his glasses. Magnified. Distorted.

"Everything starts small, right," he said. "Imagine if we could start changing time at the smallest units, but then could build up to something bigger."

Charlotte chewed on the inside of her cheek. "You *are* building a time machine."

"Think of me as laying the rebar."

The van pulled into an underground garage, thrusting them all into darkness, shadowing her thoughts.

"Aren't you worried that this could be used for harm?"

An orange garage light illuminated Dylan's sheepish grin. "What do I care? I won't be here." His expression morphed into a joker's smile. "Just kidding; not like this is going to work. Lately, my numbers seem to be different each time I run the equations. I can't tell if this tumor is making me smarter, or making me miss something."

The SUV lurched to a stop and Jimmy popped out. "All right folks, you're all welcome to hang out backstage or you can be down in the pit, but we'll meet back in the green room when the concert's over." He handed out all-access credentials. "Enjoy the show."

They followed him through the bowels of the arena. Concrete buttresses held up one of the most iconic venues in the world. A place where athletes and rock stars alike dreamed to hear the roar of a crowd.

"Char," Levi called.

The nickname, riding on a lilting accent chilled her, as if carried by a ghost.

Only one other person had ever called her that.

"I'll be looking for you." He lifted his sunglasses. Sincerity poured out of his dark brown eyes. Sincerity with a side of understanding.

He didn't really *need* someone to sing with him. His request was for her; for Charlotte to laugh and play and throw her carefully constructed persona into the winds of spontaneity.

Charlotte could only nod.

The ghost had stolen her voice.

Fans were already filling the seats when she peeked out from the side.

The floor was standing room only, but plenty of people climbed into the seats in the upper levels. Who knew that an aging rock star without his full band could still draw a crowd?

Celeste positioned herself in the photographer's pit, just below the stage. Her camera clung to her face, as she captured photos of the incoming crowd and sound check.

Dylan sat on a speaker, hunched over his notebook, and chewing on the end of his pen.

Jimmy stood across the stage from Charlotte, phone to his ear and his eyes glued to the ground in front of him. His gaze flitted up in her direction, and his face softened.

She glanced over her shoulder and found Lourdes standing just behind her. "Have you ever heard of his band?" she asked the *telenovela* star.

"No, we didn't have a radio when I was young, so the only music we heard was what we played." She crossed her arms over her chest. "Actually, this is my first rock concert."

Charlotte dropped her gaze to study the woman's outfit. Skintight leather pants ended at stiletto heels. A matching tight leather jacket covered a snug lace top.

She looked at her own clothes. Dark jeans tucked into riding boots with a tan sweater. Charlotte looked more likely to go to a farmer's market than a concert. "Well, you've certainly got the outfit down."

Lourdes smiled tightly at the compliment.

"I was reading," Charlotte continued. "Your adventure, to sleep under the stars in Namibia, why did you choose that?" She'd expected Lourdes to want a shopping weekend in Paris or Milan.

"Mexico City is one of the most populated cities on the planet," Lourdes said on a sigh. "You can't see any stars, except for the brightest ones. I want to know what it feels like to be alone. To bask in the light of the weaker stars."

The undertow of the woman's words hit Charlotte's chest. She'd intentionally bought her house on the far end of a barrier island. Hiding away from humanity. What was it like to be an ant in a crowded colony?

Everyone trudging one way or another, always in a line, always flanked by another ant.

She searched for the right response, but luckily, the swell of the crowd filled the awkward silence.

Levi came out on stage from the opposite side. Clad in his usual black pants and boots, but this time he donned a bright red sequined jacket over a ruffled white shirt. His guitar was slung around his back. Hands up; greeting his adoring fans. "Hello Madison Square Garden," he rasped into the microphone. "How the hell are ya?"

Like a surging wave, the crowd screamed and cheered.

He launched into his set. The first song was one of his band's biggest hits, and the fans shouted and sang along.

As he played and sang, Charlotte could almost see it. What he meant about needing to be larger than life.

Levi seemed to grow several inches, and an orb of light flowed out of him, shooting out across the crowd, feeding them with his energy. He danced, ran from side to side. Threw up his hands and encouraged the fans to sing along with him.

Before she knew it, she was singing along with every word. Her hips swayed, her hands over her head, as she danced and tossed her hair side to side.

Even Lourdes sashayed, clapping along and singing along with the chorus with one of the more repetitive songs.

The master showman, Levi gave the crowd a break with a quiet ballad.

She glanced at Lourdes, about to whisper something, but the woman's gaze was focused across the stage, past the star, settled directly on their host.

Jimmy stared down, scowling at something on his phone.

Charlotte tried to read the star's expression, but it was tucked away, hidden behind a wall so thick it could only be reached with a jackhammer. Or, friendship.

Levi finished that song to a tidal wave of applause. "Thank you, thank you," he said, taking a swig from a cup.

Charlotte hoped it was water. Or, at least had water in it.

He whispered something to his lead guitarist, who nodded and moved back from his mic stand.

"For this next song, I'd like to invite someone very special out to help me with it. Char, my dear girl," he glanced at her side of the stage.

Lourdes giggled next to her. "Get it, *chica*."

Charlotte demurred, but her companion gave her a gentle shove. Before she knew it, she was out of the safety of the curtain and a spotlight found her.

The crowd roared. Some of them likely recognized her as America's Self-Help Sweetheart.

Behind the bright lights, the audience haunted like an apparition.

She could hear their shouts and screams and whoops and whistles. Could even almost see them. The first few rows a specter before fading into the ether of the arena.

"They're not really there," Levi breathed in her ear, his voice slicing across the din of the crowd. "You've got this." His lined face warm, sincere.

Charlotte had spoken in front of numerous audiences. Some probably the same size as the one that turned out for Levi's adventure. But that was *speaking*, not singing.

That was Charlotte Claybrooke, the guru, the savior of lost souls. The woman who pretended she had her life together.

That woman wasn't going to save her. Not standing in front of a microphone with a band behind her. That woman turned to dust three inches in. If she was going to keep from making a mockery of Levi's dying adventure, she'd have to dig deeper. Deeper than she'd dared to look in a very long time.

The music and words started simultaneously.

Levi launched into a raucous song. An anthem of hope and love and who-the-hell-cares-we're-young-and-gonna-live-forever.

Charlotte found herself harmonizing with the frontman. Singing backup until they finished the first chorus.

When the music bridged to the second verse, Levi stepped back from his microphone, holding his arms out to indicate it was her turn.

Like discordant gears that finally sync, the song clicked deep inside her.

The crowd turned into her audience of stuffed animals.

The darkness became her bedroom.

When Charlotte grabbed the microphone, her hand felt the soft handle of her hairbrush.

With each lyric flowing from her mouth, she flew back in time from forty to fourteen. As if she'd found the winning formula to Dylan's time machine.

Levi joined her for the final chorus.

Back-to-back, they shared the microphone. Feeding off each other's energy. Egging each other on. Laughing as much as they sang.

When the song ended, they collapsed into a tight hug. How long had it been since someone had hugged her like that?

"Thank you," Charlotte said. "I haven't had that much fun in...well, ever."

"Me either, love," he said. Levi took another swig from the cup. He wheezed, audibly enough that she could hear it over the cacophony of the crowd.

"You okay?"

The musician pulled a handkerchief from his back pocket and wiped the perspiration from his forehead. "Oh yeah, just a bit winded." He turned from her and gripped his mic stand. "Give it up once more for Charlotte Claybrooke."

The crowd whipped into another frenzy, but she barely noticed.

Instead, her attention was drawn to the white fabric tucked into Levi's back pocket.

A smear of tan makeup marred the otherwise pristine fabric, matching the same smear of ghastly gray marring the otherwise healthy rock star.

8

The adrenalin flowing through Levi's veins was better than any drug he'd ever tried. Maybe that was why he did it. Why he sang and danced and played until the audience spun around him like he was back on the old merry-go-round in the neighborhood park.

Why he'd called Charlotte up to sing with him.

For him.

That was going to be his last song. He'd planned to call it a night and follow it with a half-assed encore, but the roar of the audience was a siren's song to the stage. The chants of his name were the electricity driving his heartbeat.

The power that flowed from his fingers, that lifted his voice was nothing more than magical.

Levi ran from one side of the stage to the other, ignoring the pain radiating from his knees. He hopped up on the drummer's platform, reveling in the view of the crowd. Camera flashes flickered like the lightning of an approaching storm.

He wished he could've died right then, glowing like a star and then fading away, like a meteorite burning out high above the earth.

That would have been poetic.

Hell, he almost willed his heart to stop working. To seize up right at the dying chords of the final song of his third encore.

It mocked him, pounded against his chest.

Kept him alive.

The band rushed off the stage.

Levi took one more bow. One more wave. The moment soaked into him like the first rays of the summer sun after a long, dark winter.

He had to pull himself off stage. A few more seconds of standing there, and he'd run the risk of going from being adored to abhorred.

The hallway leading to his dressing room was mobbed with people. His management team. Record label execs. A few ladies he could only guess were groupies back when everything was perky and tight without the assistance of underwire and shapewear.

Hugs. Slaps on the back. Well-wishes and fuck-yeahs. Hands grabbing at him. Lights, shouts, whistles.

Overwhelming was an understatement.

Everyone wanted a piece of Levi.

It was cliché as hell, but he could feel them absorbing his being, his essence, like sponges soaking up spilled wine.

He'd never been one of those stars who scorned the limelight, who threw punches at photographers, who tossed insults to fans who spent their money and time worshipping him.

Quite the opposite. The more of himself he gave away, the more there was out there in the world.

Levi was the fluffy white seeds of a dandelion. On the breeze of his stardom, he floated to far reaches of the world, embedding himself in someone else's soul, keeping him alive, bad liver be damned.

A shout of his name rose over the rest.

He glanced over his shoulder.

Jimmy stood with the rest of the Diers.

He should be with them, after all, it was Jimmy who'd made this happen. Who gave him one last chance to be Levi Livingston, frontman of Fistful of Devils, instead of some bloke dying of liver disease.

He took a step toward them, toward a group of strangers who, at this moment in his life, had more in common with him than people he'd known for years.

Another wave of fans crashed into him, drawing him into their wake, pulling him out to sea.

When the froth cleared, a young blonde woman stood before him. Her clothes weren't just painted on, they were borne on, like the dolls his daughter had played with as a toddler.

"I've been a fan my entire life," she said, her voice was equally sweet and smoky like she was trying to channel a starlet who'd been alive in her great-grandmother's time.

"Oh yeah? All of what eighteen, nineteen years?"

My God, I have leather pants older than her.

"My mom had all your albums, so I grew up listening to Fistful of Devils," she said.

Shite, way to make a wanker feel old.

Levi shuffled his feet, eager to get away from the insulting ingenue. "Well, that's, er, nice. Always glad to hear my music is a family affair."

The young woman took a step closer to him, threatening to stick against him like her flimsy clothes. "I've heard you liked to party." She pressed against him, despite her repeated use of 'kid' and 'my mom' she felt very much like a grown woman.

Levi cleared his throat and scooted back. Not enough to completely disengage, just enough for his traitorous male anatomy to not encourage her more. "I've been known to have some fun back in my day…"

"What about now?" She closed that little blessed space he'd made. "Do you still party?"

It wasn't a question of if he still liked to party. He loved to party. It was just that partying didn't always love him back. By the time the club really started hopping, it was time for Levi to climb into bed.

Or, that sometimes the hangover would kick in while he was still drunk. Never mind the fact that most days his penis acted like an ornery old dog; waking him up in the middle of the night to take a piss, sleeping when he wanted to take it out for some exercise, humping someone's leg at inappropriate moments.

He craned his neck to the side, looking for anyone who might be able to save him from the fledgling vixen. His bandmates were busy hitting up their own groupies.

It was only the Diers that watched him, with expectant intensity, waiting for him to finish a polite conversation with a nice young fan before turning back to join them for an evening of hot tea and crumpets.

To slip into cozy footwear and compression socks. To talk about their aches and pains, good days and bad days. About how this was all temporary, that soon enough they'd be in a better place. Nothing will hurt. Soon enough, it would all be over.

Fuck that.

Levi wasn't ready to slip into a comfy cardigan and put his feet up. That was the purpose of this little encore performance, of joining Dire's Club, wasn't it? To give himself one more go, one more song. To lap up the cheers of the audience like a thirsty man rescued from the desert. It even meant giving into the darker side of his rock and roll lifestyle.

He took a step closer to the woman. Her scent washed over him, vanilla with an undercurrent of pheromones. "Listen, sweetheart, if you promise not to make any references to listening to me as a kid, or that your mom was a fan, I promise not to ask you if you've planned for your financial future, or when you're going to meet a nice guy and settle down. Deal?"

She pulled her pretty mouth into a salacious smile. "Deal."

Levi hooked his arm around her shoulder, and lead her down the hall, but not before catching a glimpse of Jimmy and Charlotte.

Their disappointment didn't take long to register. It was a look he'd seen in Olivia time and again as he set off to tour. It clouded the eyes of his ex-wives, as they sat across mahogany tables to dissolve marriages that shouldn't have happened in the first place.

It stared back at him in the mirror when he'd wake up and promise himself he'd get clean, that *that* was the absolute last time he'd get so fucked up he couldn't remember whose hotel room he was in.

Disappointment, like the torment of making an album, had a way of being forgotten.

He tightened the grip on the young woman, not bothering to ask her name. What did it matter? If he had his way, he'd get so blitzed, whatever it was would fly out of his mind like a freshly forgotten promise.

"I hope you've got some good party tricks," Levi said, tapping the side of his nose.

"That and some you've never seen before," she pinched his bum with enough force to leave a bruise.

That was one thing he loved about today's young people; they were completely unafraid of making an ass of themselves.

They hurried out of the backdoor of the arena.

There were far fewer camera flashes here, but enough people shouting his name to remind him he was Levi Fucking Livingston.

He was a rock god, and gods don't die.

At least, not in his mythology.

9

The late February morning was temperate enough that Jimmy decided to jog Central Park, instead of the hamster wheel treadmill at the hotel's gym.

Some days he didn't mind being on a treadmill. There was something freeing about not having to watch for traffic or pedestrians or cracks in the pavement. Other days, he just needed to move. To put as much distance between where he was and where he wanted to be.

He picked the longest path he could find.

This was one of those days where Jimmy needed to be far, far away.

Not from the Diers. They seemed to have gelled together with the adhesive power of Super Glue.

He'd only been half-watching Levi's set. The other half of his attention was focused on Lourdes, standing across the stage, and the barrage of text messages coming in from Darla.

His assistant had been on her date with the marine biologist. Between threats of stringing Jimmy up with a fishing net, and feeding him to Great Whites, he was able to glean that a pod of humpback whales was known to frequent an area near Baja, California this time of year.

An off-the-radar location that would be the perfect opportunity for Charlotte to dive with these rare giants.

He'd never judged anyone for their dying adventures. From jumping out of airplanes to scaling mountains. Diving to the depths of the ocean to feeling the weightlessness of sub-orbital flight. Jimmy had seen it all.

It had even become a sort of a game. An application would come in to join Dire's Club. He'd read the person's bio, their diagnosis, and try to guess what they wanted as their final adventure. Over the years, he'd become a sort of an expert at picking the antidote to the person's death.

Afflictions of the nervous system, those that robbed the person of their ability to move until it finally stole their breath, usually went with something to test the limits of their bodies. To prove they were still in control.

Diseases of the mind. Those people wanted to show they still had all their mental faculties or wanted to sear memories into their brain.

Cancer. Well, those with a terminal cancer diagnosis were always a mixed bag. Some of their dying wishes had nothing to do with the disease. Others wanted to shove a middle finger at death and hop out of a helicopter and go flying down a ski slope.

However; Charlotte's wish. Jimmy couldn't quite figure out what it meant.

It didn't help that her paperwork was incomplete.

He should've been more forceful. Should've told her she couldn't join the crew until everything was turned in. She was *Charlotte Claybrooke*. Her name alone would drive business. Well, assuming he could find a way to skirt the confidentiality clause after her death. Maybe he could get a new contract drawn up for her. Levi, too. That upon their deaths, Dire Enterprises could use their likenesses and endorsements in marketing.

Jimmy pulled off the trail and typed a reminder into his phone. As soon as they were on the plane to Peru, he'd get Darla to call the attorneys.

Assuming she'd answer his messages. She'd seemed pretty serious about feeding him to the sharks.

Heart attacks were child's play to his Texas firecracker assistant.

He waited for a running club to pass before jumping back on the trail.

Just as the lake came into view, he felt the presence of another runner behind him.

Seconds later, the runner overtook him.

Her back straight, long dark brown hair pulled through the back of a baseball cap. With a strong stride, she didn't so much look like she was running, but flying.

The pride Jimmy had in his solid nine-minute mile hit rock bottom. This other runner was probably clocking a seven-minute mile, and she seemed to be hardly breathing.

She moved on, folding into the gaggle of joggers.

His music paused, and a trilling sound blasted in his ear, instead of guitar licks and drum solos. Jimmy accepted the call without even looking at the screen. "Hey Darla," he said, slowing his pace only slightly.

The pause at the other end was so pronounced; Jimmy glanced down at the screen to make sure he hadn't dropped it.

He cursed.

Not Darla.

Enzo Fiore. His investor.

The man who held his entire world in his well-manicured, non-callused hand.

Also, the sharpest pain in his butt.

"Dire," the man said. If his voice were canine, it'd be a Doberman.

Drooling. With a spiked collar.

"Why do I get the feeling you're avoiding me?"

Jimmy slowed his pace to a walk. "Enzo, you should never feel that way." He tried to match his investor's tone, but the best he could muster was an eager-to-please Lab. "I've got a new group of travelers that kicked off. I have to give them my full attention during this critical bonding time." He looked down, just to make sure he didn't step in his own bullshit.

"I fund this little...endeavor," Enzo said. "I'd say, any time I summon you, you'd stop in the middle of whatever you're doing to talk to me."

A group of speed-walkers sashayed past him.

"I do!" Jimmy's voice spiked so suddenly the walkers jumped and gave him the side-eye before pumping their arms and legs faster. "That's what I just did. It's what I'm doing. So, talk to me. What can I do for you, Enzo?" He winced as the question left his mouth.

The man cleared his throat. "You could start by returning my calls as soon as you can."

"Yes, sir. Absolutely. I would've called this morning but I didn't want to wake you."

The water station came into view.

Runners stretched; twisting, tugging, pulling, pushing, squatting. The runner who'd passed him with the perfect stride bent over a fountain.

When she looked up, Jimmy caught the first sight of her face.

Charlotte?

He'd seen many of his Diers in great physical shape, but he'd never seen one who could run like her.

"I also need to see projections for this year. Two months in, and I've seen nothing. No projected budget. No anticipated revenue, profit. We're not running a non-profit, Dire."

Dread climbed up his spine with the cold, clammy hands of a zombie clawing out of the grave. Frankly, he was surprised he'd made it this far into the fiscal year before Enzo asked for it.

It wasn't that Jimmy avoided budgets and finances, along with fiscal projections. It was just that he'd rather be strung up by his toes over an open flame with cannibals sharpening their knives.

"Yes, Enzo, I've got it nearly done."

Charlotte pulled her heel up to her glute. The woman only had the slightest flush to her cheeks, which was more likely from the cool winter breeze than exertion. A small circle of sweat darkened the top of her top, and by her effortless stretches, her long, lean body seemed lithe.

"Look, I'm leaving for Peru this afternoon. I'll work on it on the flight and get it to you ASAP."

"I'm not fucking around, Dire."

"Me either. All right, gotta go. Bye." Not only did Jimmy want to get his investor off the phone, but he wanted to catch Charlotte before she jogged off in the other direction. He quickly hung up and sprinted to the water station.

It was less than thirty feet to where she was, but Jimmy huffed. Was that from exertion or talking to Enzo?

"Charlotte?"

She tugged her ball cap further down her forehead and ducked her head. It seemed like an impulsive move. Something she'd done a thousand times when someone said her name before she'd had a chance to steady herself and put on her outward appearance. "Oh, Jimmy, hey." She straightened, hiding it in a side stretch. "Fun time last night."

"Yeah, Levi had a blast, so that's all that matters," he said.

Another running club approached. This one even bigger than the last, threatening to swarm the water station.

Threatening to swoop Charlotte up and take her away before they talked.

"Wanna get a coffee and start heading back?" Jimmy asked.

She checked a fitness tracker on her wrist. "Um, sure, I got a few miles in."

They walked in silence to a street vendor. Gray-white steam rose off their black coffees, floating between them.

He studied her as they sipped.

Her bangs clung to her forehead, and even though a sheen of sweat trickled down her face, she didn't have the tell-tale yellow-gray complexion of someone with an expiration date.

"I learned a lot about you in just the last twelve hours," he said.

Charlotte froze. That healthy runner's glow fled from her cheeks. "Oh?" her voice was tight, constrained.

"Yeah, I learned you could've easily been a rock star instead of a life coach." He paused for a sip. "And, I learned you can outrun the devil."

Her body relaxed, starting with her jaw loosening and her shoulders dropping. Maybe Charlotte had something neurological afflicting her. Something that tensed her muscles and relaxed them like a slow leak of air from a balloon.

"Maybe he's chasing me." The twinkle in her eye was part jest, part dare.

They turned up the street toward their hotel. "Well, I'd put my money on you," Jimmy said. His phone buzzed in his hand. His gaze darted down long enough to see a text message from Darla.

He sighed. Even though Charlotte had paid in full, and they had her credit card on file for any incidentals, he needed to follow protocol. Especially with Enzo on his ass.

"By the way." He glanced behind them before dropping his voice. "We have intel that there's a pod of humpback whales with relatively no watchers. The timing should work. We can head straight out to the Pacific after Dylan's experiment."

The color that had drained from her face resurfaced, and her mouth pulled up into a wide smile. She was genuinely excited by the possibility that her dream adventure would become a reality. "Thank you," Charlotte said.

The flags outside their hotel beckoned them from a block away.

Something told Jimmy that once they crossed that threshold, once the doorman pulled open the glass doors to their luxury hotel, the little bit of her wall he'd managed to chip away would instantly repair itself. "I'm curious," he said. "Why did you pick that as your final adventure?"

Charlotte slowed to a stop. Tendrils of her chestnut hair pulled free from her ball cap and whipped around her face. She chewed on her lower lip, bringing her coffee cup up to her chin before dropping it again. She opened her mouth to answer, but a heavy hand crashed down on Jimmy's shoulder.

"Mark Mercer, how the hell are you doing, buddy?" A big man stood in front of them. His cheeks were ruddy, and chunks of his straw-colored hair lifted in the cold wind. A plump woman with equally ruddy cheeks and dark hair streaked in gray stood next to him. "It's me, Ralph, Ralph Owen, from back in Cleveland."

His heart plunged like a skydiver with a failed chute. "What? I'm sorry, you must've confused me with someone else." He tried to push by the man, but he was as big of an ox now as he had been in high school.

"Nah, man, I'd know you anywhere. Remember that night we got stoned and stole your dad's police cruiser?"

He searched for his voice, but it was nowhere to be found.

Ralph continued rattling off high school escapades in non-sequential order.

Maybe Jimmy could turn around and run. It was obvious, judging from Ralph's girth that he hadn't exercised since his high school football days. There'd be no way he could catch him, smother him in a name that belonged to another man.

"I'm sorry, sir," Charlotte stepped between them. "Some people have familiar faces. For example, I'm confused for that lifestyle coach, Charlotte Claybrooke, all the time." She rolled her eyes as if the burden of someone calling her out was too much to bear.

Ralph's wife came alive. "Oh my gosh, you do look like her!" She eyed Jimmy.

She'd been a couple of years behind them in school, and her face was as forgettable as her name.

"Ralph, she's right, he looks a lot like him, but Mark had a lot more hair."

The man scratched his head and furrowed his brow. "Yeah, guess you're right, sorry to bother you." The man offered his thick hand in apology.

Jimmy stared at it, almost afraid to touch it, afraid the man would feel the truth like a palm reader tracing the lines of someone's future. "Think nothing of it."

The ghost of his past trudged on, carrying with it secrets that had no business in his present.

"Jimmy?"

He jumped. His name the shot of adrenalin needed to kickstart his heart.

"You okay?" Charlotte asked. Her gaze as intense as a laser cutting through metal.

He laughed. "Yeah, that poor guy was pretty convinced he knew me. Thanks for the help there."

She pursed her lips. "Yeah, anytime. Well, I need to get cleaned up and packed before the flight."

The doorman pulled open the heavy, ornate door for her, but Charlotte didn't turn to enter right away.

She studied him for several seconds.

Was she seeing if the name Mark Mercer fit him? Was she looking for a quickened pulse, shallow breathing?

He held her stare, refusing to look away and breathe life into her suspicions. Jimmy swallowed, clearing away the cobwebs of his forgotten history. "Charlotte, we still need your paperwork."

Her body shifted slightly, like a door clicking into place, shutting him out. "Oh, yes, sorry. I'll have my assistant follow up with the doctor."

The busy hotel lobby swallowed Charlotte.

He hovered outside. Sipping the cold dregs of his coffee. His hand shook as it brought the cup to his lips.

Some people talk about the fright of facing a brush with death.

That never scared Jimmy.

A brush with his past…was the most terrifying thing in the world.

10

Darla had held on to her old convertible for days like this. The Florida winter sun smiled down. The tangy smell of saltwater wafted off the ocean. Not overpowering, just enough, if she squinted and cocked her head just right, she could pretend she was pulling into some exclusive beach-side resort instead of a nursing home.

Then again, in Florida, same difference.

That was the other reason she held on to her seen-better-days Celica. She could hardly afford her mother's care, never mind a car payment, or insurance beyond basic liability.

Darla parked and grabbed the boxes of donuts from her backseat. That was something she'd learned early on from her momma. Bad news was best delivered with a side of sugar.

Moving. Chocolate donuts.

Couldn't afford cheerleading camp. *Tres leches* cake.

Gotta sell her horse. Four dozen chocolate chip cookies fresh out of the oven.

Her no-good father didn't pay child support again, so no new clothes for her freshman year of high school. A gallon of butter pecan Blue Bell ice cream.

It'd worked with Darla while she was growing up; maybe it'd work with the administrator at the nursing home.

"Hiya, Janice," she sang out in her most pronounced Texas drawl like a soprano at the Grand Ole Opry. "How's that grandbaby?"

The woman working the front desk lit up and pulled out her phone, updating Darla on everything her new grandson had done since she'd seen her last.

Every. Thing.

"Hey, is Sam around?" Darla asked, cutting the woman off when the conversation turned toward the color of his poops.

"Yeah, I'll buzz you right back," the woman said.

The heavy automatic lock clicked over and the door sighed with relief, like a satiated man loosening his belt after Thanksgiving.

She handed the woman one of the boxes. "This is for all y'all do for Momma."

The woman feigned surprise, with a few well-placed you-shouldn't-haves, but Darla's mom had been there long enough and through several bill hikes that the woman had to know when the staff was being buttered up.

Literally.

Darla walked down the administrative wing of the nursing home. The heel of her boots thudded against the Linoleum floor. She paused at a glass case housing awards and checked her hair. The ocean-breeze blow-out gave the perfect oomph to her Texas locks. She knocked at an ajar door and peeked in.

Thinning gray hair stared back at her.

Sam looked up; his glasses dangled off the tip of his nose. "Ms. Steele, I wish I could say this is a surprise..." Sarcasm dripped with every word.

She might not have enough donuts for this.

Darla cleared her throat and pushed through the door. "I was coming to see Momma, and thought your team might like some sweets." She held the box between them like a shield.

The man sighed and put his pen down, leaning on his forearms. "And, this has nothing to do with the letter you received."

She set the box on his desk, and took a seat in a guest chair, perched on the edge, the same posture she'd taken many times in the high school principal's office. Back straight, knees together, head bowed. If it got her out of trouble for getting caught with Cody Roy in the janitor's closet, then maybe it'd help her talk Sam out of raising the cost of her mother's care. "Well, now that you mentioned it," she said, lacing her fingers around her kneecaps just enough to let her push-up bra do what she'd paid a pretty penny for it to do. "I do want to talk to you about that."

"Of course you do, Ms. Steele." An old spring groaned when he reclined in his chair.

Maybe she should've brought him a fruit basket instead.

"You can call me Darla," she said.

"No, I think Ms. Steele will do just fine." He crossed his arms over his wide belly. "Look, I did the best I could last time, and I wish I could do something this time, but costs are rising."

"But fifteen percent more, Sam, that's insane. I can't afford that."

He sprang forward, the chair coughing as it catapulted him. "That barely covers the increase in salaries."

Tears stabbed at the back of her eyes like ice picks. If Sam would respond to a crier, Darla would let them go, but something told her to buck up and hold them back. "She just sits there." She could feel her voice rising, getting nasally. "Doesn't cause no trouble, isn't hitting any buttons. If I move her, you might get someone who needs more help. Wouldn't it be better to have a low-maintenance patient than the unknown?"

The man's face softened, compassion creeping in the small crevices of wrinkles. "Darla, someone new in her room would pay twenty-five percent more than you do. Everyone here has a soft spot for Nell, for you. We don't want to see you go, but we're running a business. If you need me to, I can make some calls, and see if someone else can take her." He dropped his gaze. "Someone more in your price range."

She glanced out the window. Palm trees hid the view of the highway but the glare of windshields flickered in and out with the rhythm of a ticking clock. "How much time do I have?" Darla pushed the words past the lump in her throat.

"I can give you thirty days, but by the end of March, you'll either need to pay more or find her a new home."

She sat there for several seconds before nodding and pushing out of the chair.

Her boots shuffled down to her mom's wing.

Staff would pass her by, opening their mouths to greet her, but either the redness in her eyes or the scowl smeared across her face scared them off.

Darla paused outside her momma's room. Took a deep breath and shoved her shoulders back.

The doctors weren't sure how much Nell was aware of her surroundings after her stroke. But her momma always said fake it 'til ya make it, and by God, if Darla had to become a plastic doll, she'd do it.

"Hey, Momma," she said, as she burst into the room.

The woman kept her gaze out her window. Dark blue eyes staring, where, into the past? Her own mind?

She walked around to the other side of the bed to get into her mom's line of sight. Her mother hadn't made eye contact with her in years. Not intentionally. Darla grabbed a hairbrush and smoothed it down the side of her mom's head. Blonde locks pulled through the bristles.

Her face looked even more youthful, softer, unlined, unburdened. Even in a catatonic state, her mom remained beautiful.

Maybe that was why she didn't try harder to wake up. Lying there locked in a bed, locked in her mind, she didn't have the worries of paying bills, of no-good men, of a troublemaker daughter, of having to sacrifice her morals to make sure there was enough food on the table.

After a lifetime of losing, Nell had finally won after Darla graduated high school. She'd caught the eye of a good, albeit older, man. When he whisked her away to Florida to retire with him, Darla had assumed her mom would live out the rest of her days in retirement luxury.

Little did she know, after he'd died suddenly on the golf course, his other wife, the one he neglected to divorce and didn't think to tell Nell about, would lay claim to what little fortune he had.

That was what had done it for her mom. It wouldn't have been so bad if Nell had been down at the bottom where she spent most of her life. It was because she'd climbed higher than ever before. Waterfront condo. Nice clothes. Car with working A/C.

She didn't trip on the sidewalk. Her mom had come crashing down from the penthouse.

Lucky for Darla, to protect their father's reputation, the man's other family had settled with enough money that she used it to put her mom in a good nursing home, thinking that it would cover however many days she had left. When it became obvious that, 'Give 'em Hell Nell' was still in there somewhere, she'd taken up the only job she knew she was good at.

Dancing.

Not in the ballerina sense.

Dancing in Miami had been different than dancing in Houston. The girls were taller, more exotic, more alluring. In Houston, she was the main event. In Miami, she was demoted to dancing for the kiddie tables.

Crossing paths with Jimmy Dire at the nursing home had seemed like a godsend. He'd been there to check on a client in the room next to her mom.

When Darla went toe-to-toe with the call nurse for him because the patient was being neglected, Jimmy had hired her on the spot.

Her phone buzzed in her purse. Enzo Fiore's name stared up at her.

"Hi, Enzo," she put on her most chipper voice. "Are you still looking for Jimmy? I told him you'd called."

"No, I got him on the phone." The investor's voice was set against a backdrop of *boing* sounds and grunts. Either he was in the middle of a tennis match, or was into some really freaky stuff. "He's putting the final touches on the budget and projections for this year, but I wanted to see if you could go ahead and send me what you've got as a draft."

She moved away from the bed. Darla was pretty sure her mom could still smell her BS, even when catatonic.

"Oh yeah, I'm not in the office yet, but let me see what I can find when I get in," she lied. There was no budget for the new year.

She'd been harassing Jimmy for it, for months. Every time she sat down to balance the books, it was like trying to scoop water out of a submarine with a child's plastic bucket.

Money flowed out of the bank account way faster than it came back in.

Boing. Grunt. Screech. "You're not covering for him, are you?"

She glanced behind her.

Nell continued to stare into the unknown.

"I'm more likely to string him up with barbwire, don't you think?" Darla had learned a long time ago that a truthful non-answer was much better than a lie.

Grunt. Shout. *Boing*. Shout. "You're probably right. Get it to me as soon as you can." The phone cut off mid *boing*.

Was Jimmy lifting her too high?

11

"One cup sugar, one cup butter, one cup peanut butter," Celeste rattled off her favorite peanut butter cookie recipe from memory. She closed her eyes, but the tropical sun still blazed behind her lids. "One cup brown sugar, three eggs. No, two eggs. No, three. Two, definitely two." She finished reciting the recipe and glanced at the notes in her journal.

It was all there.

The eggs nearly threw her. Was that because once, she'd messed up and doubled the eggs? That had been when the kids were young and her husband, Ed, was away on a business trip overseas. That slip-up had been from being a busy mom, not an Alzheimer's-addled grandmother.

Celeste jotted down how long it'd taken her to recall the recipe. A few seconds slower today. She'd lost precious time on the eggs.

Next up, the pictures.

She launched her photo app and flipped through the grandkids. Those were the ones the doctor had said she might forget initially. Last in, first out. "Charlie, Paige, Sam, Skye, and Jeffrey." They were easy today, and she marked her time.

Now her kids. A brown-haired woman stared up at her. She had the haircut most women did these days. Long, something she could style for a night out with her husband, but with enough length to stay in a messy ponytail for busy days carting kids from school to whatever over-scheduled children did these days.

"Katherine, my sweet first baby."

Would Celeste become Katherine's fourth child? As the disease ate away at her brain, would her only daughter feel compelled to mother her mother?

She couldn't, *wouldn't* become a burden.

Once she was home from the trip with Dire's Club, she planned to march into her attorney's office and have him draw up her plans. She'd rather waste away in the corner of a nursing home than ruin her children's lives.

Celeste took a deep breath and swiped to the next photo. "Kevin."

So much like his father, clean cut with glimpses of gray just beginning to show in his brown hair. His bright blue eyes always got him into trouble, and also got him out of trouble.

Like her late husband, Kevin had launched himself into the oil business, hopping up the corporate ladder with seemingly one hand tied behind his back. Where was he now? Dubai? Central America? Was that the Alzheimer's, or the fact that her middle child was much more his father's child than hers?

She swiped again. The mischievous grin of her youngest smiled up at her. "Michael," her voice was soft, as if she cooed at him while in his crib rather than staring up at her from a glass phone screen.

Where Katherine had been born as a little adult, and Kevin was a clone of Ed, Michael was all hers. Unlike his brother and sister, he had reddish-brown hair he always kept a bit on the shaggy side.

His siblings had taken school seriously, but Michael focused more on the social side, easily rising to most popular, most likely to be president or a beach bum. The yearbook prediction fit him perfectly, and while she wished her youngest was with her every day, knowing he was an ocean away in Hawaii made her feel better. He wouldn't see her brain turn to Swiss cheese.

Celeste glanced at the clock. It was time to load up and prepare for her hike to Machu Picchu.

Her camera was fully charged. Three new ink pens in her bag, plenty of pages in her journal. This was the trip she'd waited her whole life to take, and she'd be damned if she'd forget it before she got back home.

The open-air lobby was buzzing when she got downstairs. With the energy of people eager to make this iconic trek, and mosquitos the size of her youngest grandchild. She shook the can of her all-natural, organic bug spray, chuckling to herself. She was already sick, poisoned by living in a modern world. What good would it do to keep avoiding chemicals?

The beautiful Mexican movie star sat by herself in the lobby's corner. Over-sized sunglasses and steam rising off a cup hid her face, but the woman glowed despite the veil of sunglasses and steam and sickness.

"Hi, Lourdes, how are you this morning?"

The woman's lips formed a thin line. "Hot, sticky." She slapped a slender hand against the side of her neck. "Eaten alive by bugs. Couldn't you have picked a less humid adventure?"

Celeste hid her grimace behind a long drink of water. Was this woman nasty to everyone or just her? Was it an attitude accompanying being beautiful and famous, or was she famous because she found everyone disdainful?

"Well, if you're too delicate for Peru, I'm sure we can just meet up with you somewhere else. Maybe after you've done some shopping or something." These were the moments she loved being an absent-minded old woman. The award for living a long life is the ability to say whatever the hell she wants to whoever the hell she wants to.

Lourdes frowned and opened her mouth as if a snide retort was ready to leap out, but the woman drowned it in a long pull of her coffee. "No, I'll be fine. I was just thinking all of us with our suppressed immune systems, we could pick up Dengue fever or something."

"And then what, we die faster?" Celeste shrugged. "I wouldn't mind going while I still know how to wipe my own butt."

Charlotte entered the lobby. The woman's athletic frame was draped in hiking gear. Her shiny chestnut hair pulled back into a perfect ponytail.

I'll have whatever's killing her.

"Excuse me," Lourdes croaked before pushing herself off the sofa and abandoning Celeste.

She chuckled. "I could get used to this senile thing."

Dylan flopped into the seat Lourdes had vacated. "You got your camera ready, Celeste?"

She held it up. "Fully charged and ready to go." She studied the young man.

His skin was pale, a clammy sheen covered his forehead like dew on the morning lawn. "What about you, are you fully charged and ready to go? Aren't you kids made up of batteries these days?"

"Almost, but—" he wrung the back of his neck. "My head hurts, and my neck's sore."

"Is that the—" For some reason, calling this young man's brain tumor out felt like cursing in church. Sure, everyone said it or thought it, but to say it in his presence was blasphemous.

"Nah, probably more like dehydration." As if it to punctuate his point, Dylan took a long swig of water.

The boy's apprehension about the hike enveloped her like a swarm of gnats. Maybe Lourdes was right. Maybe she should've picked something less daunting.

Celeste was old, but more physically fit than women twenty years her junior. She'd prepared for this hike, trained for it. And the humidity, well, that was the one benefit to living in Houston for all those years.

Celeste gnawed on her lower lip.

Levi had looked pretty ragged after performing a few nights earlier. Exhaustion deepened the lines on his face and dulled the mischievous twinkle in his eye.

What if her adventure did it in for the rock star? What if it made them all fall flat? There'd be no way they could be put back together in time for everyone else's adventure.

This is a marathon, not a sprint.

Jimmy entered the lobby, his phone glued to his ear. "Yes, yes, I understand, but if you'll just listen… Okay, but there's real value here. Think of it as a service industry. Hello? Hello? Are you there?" He pulled the cell back from his ear and looked at the screen. "Dammit Peru, and your shitty cell service."

She approached their tour guide before he could stick his phone back to his ear. "Good morning, Jimmy, do you have a few minutes?"

The man looked up. His eyes were wild, harried, like a trapped animal. "Celeste, hey, yeah, sure." He pecked at his screen a couple more times before putting it in his shirt pocket. "What can I do for you?"

"Well, I, uh…" It was so much easier when she'd just thought about this. What if he said no? What if everyone was looking forward to it? What if they were insulted by her thinking they weren't healthy enough?

Jimmy cocked his head and leaned down. "Celeste, you feeling okay? Do you want me to call a doctor?"

She straightened her back. The last thing she intended to do was bother a busy doctor with her insecurities. "Oh no, I'm fine, well, except for the Alzheimer's, or old-timers, as I call it." *Good lord, I'm rambling.* "I was just thinking, if it's not too much trouble, but you can say no, and that won't hurt my feelings one bit, and I know all the hard work that goes into planning things." *Please make it stop.* This wasn't so much a symptom of her deteriorating brain, as her deteriorating will. She took a deep breath and lowered her voice. "I worry that hiking to Machu Picchu might be too strenuous for some of the others."

He narrowed his eyes and stared hard at her.

It was a stare that dove in deep, swam around, searched for the truth.

"Too strenuous for the others or you?" His words were soft and understanding.

"Oh no, I'm ready for this. The others—"

"Will be fine."

Celeste nodded, searching for the rest of her argument. "I don't want anyone to be—"

"What about you?" Jimmy lightly gripped her elbow and pulled her into a secluded corner. "Celeste, when was the last time you did something for yourself?"

She frowned. She did things for herself all the time. A couple of months ago, she'd bought a week's worth of frozen dinners that Ed would've complained about being too salty, just because she planned to drink wine and dig into her favorite author's newest book. That was for herself. Wasn't it?

"I got a pedicure…"

His mouth quirked into a gentle bless-your-heart smile. "When was the last time you were selfish?"

The word hit her like a cocktail to the face. "I'd never."

"I know, and there's nothing wrong with that. There are far too many selfish people in the world. You're here because you want to have your final adventure, that thing you've waited your whole life for. You're dying. If you're not going to be selfish now, when are you going to be?"

Hot tears sprung to her eyes. Why did tears always burn? Was it the emotion fighting to stay tucked inside, deep down where it belonged? Or was it like a splinter, hurting as much coming out as it did going in?

"What does it matter? I won't remember it anyway."

"True, there will come a point when you don't remember this trip, but *we* will. We will remember the joy of seeing you climb to the top of ancient runes, the sense of accomplishment that will radiate from your body. Most importantly, we will remember you, as you are *today*, at that moment of doing something you've waited your whole life for."

The tears had broken free of their captors and streamed down Celeste's face, taking with them guilt, apprehension, and regret.

12

The bus lumbered like a lazy elephant. Charlotte had traveled to some far-off destinations for triathlons, but she was starting to question just how difficult it would be to hike to Machu Picchu.

Especially for Levi.

She never once doubted the physical demands of being a performer, but after the concert, the man seemed even more spent. Like a beach after the tide had gone out. Still, flat. Traces of where the water whipped the sand into a lively frenzy scarred the otherwise pristine surface. Life had teemed just moments earlier, but the receding tide was like death.

Charlotte glanced behind her. A good day and a half after his adventure, Levi seemed refreshed, rejuvenated, recharged, and any other 're' word she could think of.

Or, maybe he'd just reapplied the makeup that hid his gray pallor.

The rock star made eye contact with her and saluted with his bottle of water.

Well, his bottle of clear liquid. Doubts about if it really being just water flowed in and out.

The man hovered over the line of sober and drunk, never really seeming to put his foot down in one exact state.

She met his raised toast with her bottle of electrolytes.

The air in the jungles of South America sucked the moisture from inside her and coated it on her skin.

Charlotte turned to her seat-mate. She'd made a point of beating everyone on the bus to sit next to Celeste.

The woman had deviated from her usual attire of matching kaftan and headband to cargo pants, a button-down shirt—held down by a vest with more pockets than a human could use—and brand new, unmarred hiking boots. Her journal lay open on her lap, the front and back of the pages filled with her tight handwriting.

"Are you writing a book?" she asked.

Celeste startled, as if forgetting that someone sat next to her. "What? Oh, this. No, this is for when it starts."

Charlotte cocked her head. *That's right, early-onset Alzheimer's.* "Is it starting? The forgetting?"

Celeste narrowed her eyes and her bright red lips pulled up into a devilish grin. "If it were, I wouldn't notice it, right?" Then she winked. "But no, I think I forgot more when my kids were little than I do now."

"When was your diagnosis?"

"Six months ago." She sighed and looked out the window. "The first thing I did was book this trip."

Charlotte thought about her parents. They were roughly the same age as Levi and Celeste. Would she have let either of them run off on these adventures with a clock ticking down their mortality?

After Jason, they hovered around her more than they had in her youth. As if he could reach up from the grave and bring her with him.

How many times had she wished *that* could happen?

"I'm impressed your family supports you coming." She had to get away from her brain.

"Oh, I haven't told them yet." The older woman spoke to the passing landscape.

Her words hung in the air. How could she risk her life, her health, on a far-flung adventure without her children knowing?

The core of Charlotte's self-help empire was honesty. Honesty with oneself. Honesty with those around them.

Then again, Charlotte was the biggest liar she knew.

"You can stop right there, missy."

Her companion's sharp reprimand jolted Charlotte. "I'm— What?"

"You're analyzing me. Judging. You tried to hide it, but it was there before you could catch it."

She opened her mouth to argue, but Celeste was right. It was an impulse sometimes. Like an actor reciting his lines but realizing later he was among friends. There was no reason to dissect the woman sitting next to her. She didn't need a life coach.

Quite frankly, Charlotte could barely navigate *her* life much less someone else's.

"I was just thinking about my parents," she said, apologetically.

Celeste nodded. "You haven't told them, either." She pursed her painted lips tight and looked out the window. Her skin was soft and supple. Rather than lined with age, it hung loosely like a gentle curtain around her jowls. Without her long white hair, she would've looked decades younger.

"I don't talk to my parents as much as I used to," Charlotte said, looking past her fellow dier, and watching the hazy countryside roll past them. The last time she'd seen her parents was like sitting in a doctor's waiting room with strangers. Everyone in their own world, pretending to not notice the other.

The woman patted her knee.

Where Celeste's face lied about her age, the woman's hands told the truth. Knobby and lined, her knuckles swollen with arthritis and liver spots dotting her otherwise flawless skin.

"It's hard telling the people you love you're dying." Her seat-mate didn't look at her as she spoke. Instead, she pulled the camera up to her eye and snapped several pictures before jotting down indecipherable words in the notebook.

Charlotte's throat froze shut, as if she'd just swallowed an ice cube

Chapter 12 | 73

instead of lukewarm water. It felt wrong to sit there with a stranger on the way to climb Machu Picchu, rather than visit with her parents. However, there was truth to the adage that one would tell a stranger on a plane more than they'd tell their spouse.

Could she do it? Could she tell a woman she'd known less than a week something she couldn't tell the people who'd raised her?

There was a peace about Celeste.

An otherworldliness that either prompted her parents to bestow that name on her. Or, maybe she lived up to the name. Whatever it was, it defined the woman perfectly.

"What made you choose this adventure?" Charlotte asked. The question leaped forward, over the admission poised on her lips, knocking it out of the way, as if she were about to drink a glass of poison.

Her new friend closed her journal, the pen marking her place in the middle of the book. She looked at Charlotte, her pale blue eyes shining. Would that light go out as her disease progressed?

She couldn't imagine Celeste as anything other than bright, lively.

"As a little girl, I never imagined myself getting married, raising children. I always thought I was made for grand expeditions and adventures," Celeste said. "But, here I am. Sixty-something years, three kids, five grandchildren, and a dead husband later."

"I'm sure there was adventure in raising a family." Her voice was weak, submerged in sorrow.

"Oh, I wouldn't trade it for anything." She touched Charlotte's arm, her face serious with love. "My children were everything to me, and my husband was the most amazing man I'd ever met." Her expression didn't so much as fall, as it stumbled a few steps. "I raised them to be the free spirits I longed to be."

"And they're scattered around the world," Charlotte finished the sentence.

She nodded, her eyes dewy with tears. "As a parent, your greatest accomplishment and curse is raising strong, independent people."

Is that who *she* was?

Her parents didn't so much as raise her to be strong but raised her to have no other choice.

Charlotte had lived two lives for so long she couldn't remember which one was the truth.

Was it the popular high school brainy athlete, or the girl who'd gone home to care for her mom during one of her bad spells? Or, was it the college co-ed who'd eschewed sorority life to keep her grades and her track time in place to retain her scholarship, because her father had thrown away her college fund after a string of bad investments? Or, the law school student who'd worked two jobs?

Whoever Charlotte was, she didn't feel like the woman who still mourned her dead fiancé, nor did she feel like the self-help guru who made a career out of surviving.

Survival was for the strong.

After a lifetime of being strong, she'd earned the right to be weak.

Charlotte scanned the bus.

Jimmy sat next to Lourdes. His head bent close to hers.

The *telenovela* star smiled at whatever he said.

Levi leaned against the window, his arm resting on one leg perched on the seat, swigging more from his whatever-was-inside bottle.

Dylan sat behind him, his head bent over his notebook, likely checking and re-checking his mathematical equations. If he was successful in his time machine, could she beg him to take her back?

If she couldn't go back to the day of the accident, could she at least go back and 'forget' to take her birth control pills? Then maybe she'd have a piece of Jason.

Maybe she wouldn't be so alone.

"How would your life have been different?" Charlotte asked, her voice so quiet she could barely hear herself over the choke of the bus engine. "If you hadn't met your husband, what would you have done?"

Celeste's red lips pulled up into a wide smile that brightened her face like the sun emerging after a rainstorm. "Why, this, honey." She gestured out the window like a game show vixen presenting the grand prize. "I was working at a magazine, aiming to be the travel writer when I met Ed. Planes made him nervous. Ironic, huh? An aspiring travel writer marries someone afraid of flying." There was a kind of wistfulness in her voice.

Not like Celeste regretted her life. More, someone who wished she could've lived both lives.

Maybe there was a duality about her as well. Perhaps it wasn't uncommon to feel as if someone had two, or more, distinct paths laid out in life, and every one of them would have been the right choice.

Charlotte smiled and grasped her friend's hand, marveling in the softness that reminded her so much of her own grandmother's hands. "So, here you are."

"Here I am." She squeezed Charlotte's hand. "And, here you are. What's your adventure?"

"Well, we're going to be much more grounded for mine, than walking through a cloud forest for yours. I want to dive with humpback whales. You guys get to hang out on the boat if you want." Saying it as they approached the trailhead for their hike to Machu Picchu sounded so simple. As if she was told she could have any dessert in the world, and she'd opted for plain vanilla ice cream. She laughed. "That sounds so lame sitting next to the lady leading us up to Inca ruins."

"Not at all, Charlotte. It sounds beautiful." Celeste dropped her hand and gazed back out the window. "I'm choosing a culture that's been gone for centuries, a place where we cross a peak known as Dead Woman's Pass. A place that is essentially a graveyard." When she met Charlotte's eyes, tears streamed down her face, cutting pale lines through her blush. "You chose a species that fought extinction. You still have hope. That's what makes you different."

That's the biggest lie.

The one Charlotte slipped into every day like a comfy cardigan. Despite everything, she still had hope.

The lie was starting to tatter, show wear.

It was only a matter of time before she ripped a hole in it.

13

The rainforest threatened to consume them. Not just as they entered the heavily-canopied trail, but in every other sensory detail.

The screech of birds and monkeys pierced Charlotte's eardrum so sharply it squeezed her head. The smells were a cacophony of animal musk, rotting vegetation, and the sweet notes of fruit and flowers.

Because of the sensitive nature of the ecosystem, they passed no other hikers.

It was just this randomly thrown together group of Diers, local trail guides, and their leader, Jimmy.

Most of the trail was narrow, forcing them to walk in a straight line. Their labored breath served as the only conversation.

The guides led the way. Their backs were weighted down with the group's gear, but the men still managed to walk with light, nimble steps.

Levi was behind Charlotte, mumbling under his breath. "Bloody humidity," he cursed. His hand slapped against his neck. "And these mosquitos. For fuck's sake."

She glanced over her shoulder. "Do you want some bug spray?"

"And cover me in poison?" he shook his head. "No thank you."

She bit her tongue. What would it do to argue that maybe a little bit of poison was worth not getting any number of mosquito-borne jungle illnesses?

Then again, his liver disease might kill him way before Dengue fever did.

Jimmy walked with ease, sweat barely dotting his forehead, even though he carried a full pack.

Unlike the others who kept their gazes on the trail or peering around at the rainforest around them, he stared at his phone, fingers feverishly pecking at the screen.

"You can't be getting service up here?" Charlotte asked against her better judgment. She'd mastered the art of avoidance, but curiosity brushed it aside. Sure, it was hot and sticky, and could cause someone to keel over from exertion, but how often does one go for a hike in a rainforest?

Not just any rainforest, but in a few thousand feet they'd climb into a cloud forest, and then a little further, and they'd emerge on the ruins of an ancient civilization.

People who loved and hurt and laughed and died just like them.

"What?" His head jerked up, his eyes wide and jaw slack. Jimmy looked like a kid who got caught with his pockets full of candy. "Oh, yeah, no, just typing up a few emails. Guess you could say this fresh air and native beauty inspired me." He slipped his phone into his shirt pocket.

It would probably come back out as soon as they turned around.

The trail widened, and she used it as an opportunity to walk next to Lourdes.

Despite the hike and humidity, the *telenovela* star wore her wig and a face full of makeup, but the jungle seemed to be a step ahead in the battle for beauty. Sweat cut lines down the woman's face, washing away her carefully constructed cheekbones and leaving dark trenches of mascara in its place.

The fake brunette curls that made up Lourdes' wig hung past her elbow on one side, while the other side was hiked up to her shoulder.

Charlotte's scalp tickled with each drip of sweat and her bangs clung to her forehead. How unbearable was it for Lourdes to make this climb in what was essentially a fur coat for her head?

This would be a perfect time to record a video for her followers. To examine why women felt such a need to keep up appearances so much so, in the face of the ultimate discomfort they'd go out of their way to make up their faces and don fake hair.

For what? For some equally sweaty, disheveled men to find them attractive?

But who was she to judge? Charlotte rarely scrutinized her reflection in the mirror. She was always comfortable in her own skin. It was what hid beneath the surface she couldn't stomach seeing. Her rich, brown hair, hazel eyes, and porcelain skin were simply a disguise to the ugliness that lurked deep inside her heart, constantly reminding her that she was a fraud.

As much as she wanted to close up her business and walk away from it all, there were her employees. People who relied on her for paychecks and livelihood, who believed in the narrative she wrote. *Narrative. Lies.*

The ground leveled out and the guides paused for a water break.

Lourdes shrugged her pack off her shoulders and it hit the ground with a soft *thump*.

"That climb was hell," Charlotte said, hoping to find some words to defrost the woman's shell.

The star held her wig in place as she threw her head back to gulp water. "I grew up in the mountains of Mexico, so luckily elevation doesn't bother me." Her words had a slight breathiness to them, making her already throaty voice throatier. "But cancer… The cancer isn't so much a mountain, but a pit with incredibly steep walls." She took another drink. "Steep walls with nothing to grab onto."

Charlotte nodded through her swig of water. "I know what you mean."

Grief was much the same. That feeling of being at the bottom of an icy crevasse. The desire to climb out, but forces holding her in place. As if a step up on either side would result in her falling so much further down.

Right after Jason died, she'd spent so much time in the bottom of that pit, she'd grown numb.

Numb to sadness. There was only so much sadness one could feel before it ceased to even be.

Numb to basic human needs. Why eat, why breathe, why sleep? Jason would never do any of those again.

Numb to the people around her. They all went home after the casseroles were eaten, and after the last of the funeral flowers had died.

The crevasse slowly melted. Waking in her the need to eat, to bathe, to write about her grief at losing her fiancé just weeks before their wedding.

Charlotte didn't climb out of her icy pit. Instead, it'd melted around her, leaving her standing in boggy mud that threatened to trap her there forever.

"Well, whatever cancer you have, you've barely broken a sweat," Lourdes said. "I'm jealous. I got the bitch cancer."

She opened her mouth to argue, but what could she say?

If she countered that she didn't have cancer, then the next question would be what *did* she have?

What was killing her?

No, it was better to let Lourdes believe they were sisters in delinquent cells.

"May I help?" Charlotte asked, not waiting for an answer before straightening her fellow dier's wig. Once it was back in place, she pulled the sleeve of her shirt over the palm of her hand and used it to wipe away the errant makeup.

"Thanks," Lourdes said.

Maybe the makeup wasn't for them. Maybe the makeup was for her. Much like how Charlotte would prepare herself for a race with ample water and energy gels, compression tights, and sturdy shoes, did Lourdes prepare herself for this hike, her life, with as much normalcy as beauty products could allow?

"Which chemo drug are you on?" she asked.

"Oh, um," Charlotte stumbled, not wanting to outright lie. "I'm not."

One side of Lourdes' mouth quirked up into a smile. "Ignoring the doctors. I'll admit, I wouldn't have thought you the type."

The self-help guru in her scoffed that she didn't need the star's approval. The only person whose opinion mattered was her own.

Not clarifying was the same as lying, but her inner pre-teen always eager for winning over the popular girl shushed her. Told her, sometimes fitting in was more important than standing out.

"I bet you didn't think I was the type to rock out at the Garden, either?"

Lourdes' smile drooped slightly. She looked over her shoulder, her gaze tracking their host. "This seems to be quite the trip of self-discovery."

"Let me guess." Charlotte ventured deeper, into the just-two-girl-friends-gabbing territory. "He's not your type but yet there's something about him."

Her chest heaved. "When you start to lose everything that defined you, it makes you ask who you really are." She winced, as she lifted her pack. "Because when all of that is gone, what's left can be beautiful, or it can be horrible."

The words slammed into Charlotte with the force of a tsunami. "I can't imagine you being anything but beautiful."

This time, the woman's smile was tight, but her eyes were coated in sadness. "Don't be so sure."

The group resumed the hike, and while her feet followed those in front of her, her mind played with Lourdes' words.

She and Jason had been together for just a little over a year, but it'd taken no time for them to become known as *Charlotte and Jason*.

Char and Jay, as they'd called each other.

After the accident, her grief had filled the hole he'd left. While she'd built a career on letting that go, she hadn't in reality.

Charlotte hadn't forgiven herself for choosing work over a bike ride with Jason. She hadn't forgiven the new mom, who was sleep-deprived with a colicky baby, and had nodded off on her way to work.

She hadn't forgiven a child who was so uncomfortable that he cried all night.

She hadn't forgiven Jason, for making her fall in love with him, and then leaving her all alone.

14

One thing the dying did better than the living was looking around.

They studied every sunset as if it were their last. Welcomed every sunrise as if it were a salute to their final day. Embraced every inhale. Mourned every exhale.

Jimmy saw it time and time again. The living never truly appreciated life until they were told it was coming to an end. That was when they finally looked up.

This was especially true as this group trudged up the trail toward Machu Picchu. Celeste led the way, since it was her adventure, chatting with the guides, and furiously clicking away at pictures.

Lourdes paused at a tropical flower. Her long, graceful fingers gently caressing the petals, kissing them with her touch before moving on to another plant.

He'd swear the flower looked brighter, healthier after her touch. What would happen to him if she was to trace her finger along his jawline? Would he stand up taller? Look stronger?

Be able to stand up to Enzo?

Of all the adventures Jimmy had done around the world; this was his first hike up to Machu Picchu. If he couldn't figure out how to make the balance sheet show a few more zeroes, he'd never have the chance to climb it again. He'd be lucky to pull himself out of the street. Especially tinkering with his budget from his cellphone while trekking through the jungle. God knew what kind of mess he'd made for Darla to decipher.

He had to make the numbers work.

For Darla.

His heart stumbled. He called his assistant his *work wife*. She did everything for him. Dry-cleaning, grocery-delivery, car inspections, memorials for clients who'd passed away.

They were a married couple without shared residences. Jimmy and Darla hadn't bonded over hobbies or mutual attraction.

They'd bonded over death.

Over people's final days. Tears of happiness and wails of heartbreak. They'd bonded over goals achieved and lives not fulfilled. Over regrets, denials, and desperate pleas for forgiveness.

They might not have had a physically intimate relationship, but Jimmy and Darla had shared more intimate moments than most couples would in a lifetime. They've cried together and comforted each other. It never mattered that they hadn't slept together.

Until now.

Until Jimmy had found someone who sparked something within him he didn't think he had. Not anymore.

The desire to love.

The desire to be loved.

The way Lourdes' gaze found his, across the stage in the middle of a concert, in a busy room, or on the jet, it wasn't out of the realm of possibilities.

But it *was*.

Don't fall in love with the Diers.

That was the first thing he'd told Darla when he hired her. It was his guiding principle as well. For professional purposes obviously, but also because he *knew*. He knew the pain of seeing someone he loved fading before his eyes. Of seeing their bodies wither away, almost decomposing before they were truly gone. The smell of death.

It was something that got into his clothes, his heart. It never left, either.

Death stole his mother. Piece by piece. Breath by breath. In some ways, death had stolen his life, too. The life he'd had, could've had.

However, it could also give. It'd given him this new life.

Jimmy put his phone in his pack, refusing to let an unbalanced budget ruin the moment.

He went back to watching his clients; all marveling the serene cloud forest.

All except Charlotte. She trudged ahead, not slowing down to study flowers, admire fauna, or inhale a deep breath of rainforest air.

She simply walked. As if she'd done it before.

As if she'd do it again.

Had Darla received her completed paperwork?

Jimmy's hand itched to pull out his phone and type in a reminder, but he fought the urge to scratch it. It would only lead to another itch to look back at his budget, and another itch to tweak some numbers, and another itch to plan some marketing programs to attract more clients.

Then he'd be covered in hives all because he needed to type in a reminder about paperwork.

Not worth it.

The trail ahead of them climbed sharply. The summit for Dead Woman's Pass neared.

Dead Woman's Pass. Had it been named because of the paper-thin air? Because no matter how deeply Jimmy inhaled, it was like he was breathing through a plastic stir-straw for coffee. Or, was it the altitude? At more than four thousand meters they were closer to Heaven than Earth.

Or, maybe an ancient civilization built this challenging, beautiful trail in hopes that one day, a dying woman who'd lived her life for everyone but herself would finally fulfill a lifelong dream.

Levi stumbled.

Jimmy lunged forward and grabbed the aging rock star around the chest, heaving him back upright.

"Thanks, mate." His words came out thick and heavy, as if they too were weighed down by the humidity of the jungle. He took a weaving step to the right. "Would it have killed her to have picked something more…sedentary?"

Jimmy chuckled, but held on tight to the man. Was Levi was drunk or oxygen deprived? Maybe both. "Says the man who played his heart out on stage a few days ago."

The rocker took a deep, wheezing breath and gripped Jimmy's shoulder. "Yes, that must be my problem."

He peered closer. Levi's skin had an eerie gray putty color to it.

Jimmy had seen this color before. The same final color his mom's skin had taken. As if the oxygen in her body was being drawn away from the surface. Away from the living. From him.

"Why do you do it?" Levi asked. "Why do you surround yourself with our sorry lot?"

He chewed on the question for several steps, partially to get his thoughts in order, but mostly to get enough air for an answer. "It's a service. Like a priest giving last rites."

The man coughed into his sleeve. "Your therapist must make a killing off you."

"Would you believe I haven't been in therapy since I've been doing this?"

The rocker stumbled to a stop and whipped his head in Jimmy's direction, leaning in close. "You…?" He lifted his pinched fingers to his mouth and inhaled. "Because if you do, help a bloke out. It'll ease my pain."

His heart cartwheeled. Was this hike too much? Sure, all his clients were dying, but he'd never had one expire on a trip. "Are you hurting?" His voice was an octave too high.

The man smirked and rattled a nearly empty water bottle. "Nah, I'm not feeling much right now. Except some chafing."

Jimmy couldn't help but laugh. Liability-wise, he shouldn't know that someone under his charge was drinking while on a treacherous, strenuous hike. However, he had a feeling that sobriety would hurt worse. "Running," he said after several steps in silence. "I go for long runs. It helps clear my head." He stared at the back of Charlotte's head.

The image of her dark brown ponytail waving in the wind, as she flew past him in Central Park flashed in his mind.

Everyone else around them showed signs of physical strain.

Not her.

"Hey, so you and Charlotte have gotten close, right?" Jimmy asked.

Levi side-eyed him. "We've bonded. You got your eye on her?" The man leaned over and dropped his voice. "I saw how you were looking at her."

His jaw dropped, but he caught it quickly and shook his head. "No, no, that's not it. I'm just asking if you guys talked about your, um, situations. You know, your afflictions."

"You mean what's killing us?"

"I was trying to avoid being so blunt, but yeah."

The rock star grabbed his arm. "What, you don't know? I thought we had to fill out paperwork, and releases and diagnoses, and promises to never sue and the like. Didn't she do all that?"

Jimmy kept his face still, not letting it betray his mistake. "Oh yes, of course, I've got it all back at the office. I just, uh, I forgot." He hated lying, but he also hated casting any doubt into a man who'd trusted him with his life. At least what was left of it.

A soft smile of pity slid across the man's face. "You do have a lot to keep up with. But no, I asked, but whatever it is must be tough for her to talk about."

He nodded. Denial wafted off her whenever he'd spoken to her, and she always tensed, like an animal preparing to escape prey.

It must be new. Her diagnosis. The death sentence still fresh in her head. Her brain still processing it. Aware it was happening, but refusing to speak the words, to breathe life into the fact she was dying.

She wasn't his first denier. These were the ones he had to treat as if they were fine. Jimmy couldn't coddle her, couldn't ask how she was feeling. If he did, if he forced her to confront her diagnosis before she was ready, she'd be crushed.

Charlotte wasn't quite a Dier, but she wasn't fully alive.

15

Charlotte expected the wound over her heart to have been ripped open at the first sight of Machu Picchu.

Instead, she felt…nothing.

Sure, she was in awe over the Inca ruins of a long-gone civilization, but throughout the climb her brain assaulted her with memories of Jason.

Planning their wedding had been the easy part. A small ceremony with family and close friends on the beach where he'd proposed.

Where he'd saved her life.

The reception was to be at their favorite restaurant.

The only disagreement had been over where to honeymoon.

"What if I promise to rub your feet when we get to the top?" Jason kneaded her sore arches with his knuckles. She'd had a long day in court and collapsed on the couch before changing out of her suit.

She would've married the man for his foot rubs alone.

"Mmmm?" Charlotte drifted off from a combination of exhaustion and his magic hands.

"If we hike Machu Picchu for the honeymoon," he said. "When we get to the top, or anywhere along the way. C'mon, Char. For me?"

"Or, I could promise to bring you any drink you want if we go to the beach, instead," she countered.

He flashed his crooked smile. The one that always made her heart stumble like a runner tripping at the starting line. Before she'd lost him, her heart would recover and take off sprinting like interval training. Now, thinking of that smile made it crash to the ground.

"Throw in sunscreen on my back and you've got yourself a deal." Jason sealed the compromise with a kiss to the inside of her ankle.

What if she'd given in? Granted him his wish to hike this same trail. Would he have spent more time hiking to train rather than his usual bike ride?

There was a lesson there. A video post to her followers about not playing the *woulda-coulda-shoulda* game. There were no winners in that game.

Life was linear. Even if Dylan was somehow able to build a time machine, it still moved forward.

The past was simply for viewing. A movie she could watch a million times in her mind, but there'd be no changing the script.

The only part she could change was the blank pages ahead of her. What was yet to be written. Each day forward was a day closer to the end.

A day closer to Jason.

The sound of someone gagging dragged her away from the past.

She followed the noise around one of the stone edifices, tucked out of sight of the rest of the group, as they milled about the tiered ruins.

Levi leaned against the other side. His cheeks flushed, but the rest of his color was a muted gray. A large puddle of bloody vomit lay at his feet.

"Are you okay?" Charlotte shoved her shoulder under his armpit to help him stand.

"Yeah, yeah." His words were low and raspy. "I guess I should've done more for exercise than walk down to the bodega for cigarettes." He winced and gripped his ribcage.

"Wait here, I'll get Jimmy."

A cold, clammy hand gripped her wrist. "Char, dear, please don't."

"But you're vomiting blood." She pressed the back of her free hand against his forehead. Even though a sheen of sweat dotted his forehead, his skin was too cold for someone who'd just completed a hike. "Levi, this is serious." She glanced over her shoulder and lowered her voice to a terse whisper. "You need a doctor, a hospital."

His breath came out in shallow wheezes. Levi hugged one arm across his body, the other clung tightly to her. "He'll send me home."

Charlotte put on her best scowl. The one she'd used with opposing counsel. The one she'd used during the part of her presentations where she talked about pulling herself up and out of a dark place and putting her life back together.

The one she'd give herself every time she looked in the mirror, and the lie stared back at her.

"Maybe that's where you need to be," she said.

The old rock star took off his signature dark sunglasses. Faint, light blue cataracts spread across his dark brown irises, but it did nothing to snuff the pleading look emanating from within. "It'll kill me."

"We're all dying." She flipped her scowl off and softened her face, leaning in close. "Remember?" Charlotte hoped humor would get through to him where begging had simply bounced off his denial.

He shook his head in a slow, mournful back-and-forth. "I can't do this alone, Char. I'm afraid to die." Levi's voice trembled on unshed tears.

Charlotte eased him to the ground and sat next to him. "This is where I say we all die alone and we're all afraid." She exhaled and rested her head against the cool stone.

The self-help guru part of her wanted to cheer him up with a meme-worthy witticism. The suicidal, heartbroken bride wanted to collect his despair, as if it were a trophy for losers proving that life treated some more harshly than others. "But it's all bullshit."

A sharp laugh escaped the man's throat. "You sing one song on stage and suddenly everything's bullshit. Imagine if I'd let you have an encore. You'd've trashed your bloody hotel room."

It was Charlotte's turn to laugh. Something she'd found it easy to do around her new friend. Something she'd found herself doing more and more since joining Dire's Club.

Signing up for Dire's Club had been a long-form impulse. She'd heard of the travel company. Applauded it for its mission to grant a final adventure to the terminally ill.

She'd completed the paperwork a dozen times before she worked up the nerve to click 'submit.'

The diagnosis part would be tricky.

She wasn't ill.

But, she was terminal.

"What's your secret?" Levi asked.

"To managing my rock and roll lifestyle?" She quirked an eyebrow in his direction.

"To not being afraid."

What would he say if she admitted she welcomed death?

That she'd give anything to see Jason's crooked grin.

Including her life.

"Is that why you left with the groupie? After the concert?" she asked.

Levi owed her nothing, but Charlotte couldn't shake the bitter taste of disappointment. Like an empty spot in the bleachers where her parents should've been, the rocker choosing to leave with the young fan instead of the Diers had taken her back to her teenage years.

He exhaled, dropping his head. "When I signed on for that adventure, I wanted everything. The lights, the screams, shouts of my name." A sly smile crossed his lined face. "Girls lifting their shirts." His face fell like a cloud darkening the sun. "And, Char, that includes groupies. What can I say? I wanted my last hit of a drug only a few get to experience. It's a weakness. I'm a junkie for stardom."

She swallowed and looked out over the ruins.

A place where a whole civilization of people had lived and loved. Thrived and died. Had they been afraid to die? What about the last one of their kind? He or she truly had died alone.

Even though Charlotte had made up her mind, it was the logistics of it she'd struggled with. Non-violent for sure. Drugs were a possibility, but they felt too unstable.

But drowning…It felt like the perfect ending to her story. To her and Jason's story.

Everyone was going to die. How they died was a reflection of how they lived.

Celeste was going to die from a disease that robbed her of who she was. Fitting for a woman who wished she could've lived another life.

Dylan's brilliant mind was going to kill him.

Lourdes' womanhood, something that defined her, rebelled against her.

Levi, the man she'd only known for a week—but felt like she'd known him her whole life—his fast and furious lifestyle would be his undoing.

As for Charlotte, it was appropriate for her to infiltrate this cadre of dying with a lie. After all, she'd lived one for the past decade.

She'd die the way she lived.

A liar.

All alone.

16

Celeste absorbed everything about the hike to Machu Picchu like a dry sponge. The air, crisp and clean, burned her lungs with each inhale. The silence of the jungle roared in her ears, only broken by the occasional shriek of a monkey or call of a bird. The humid air dancing on her skin.

Could her body remember what her mind wouldn't?

The mountaintop ruins hovered in the mist like a ghost. Rocks lined what were once homes. Broken walls no longer sheltered families. Steps led to nowhere. It was the remnant of a long-gone society.

Would she become the same way as her disease advanced?

A remnant of a long-gone person.

"Magnificent," Jimmy whispered beside her. "What do you think, Celeste? Is it all you thought it'd be?"

All she could manage was a nod. Not because she was speechless by the beauty, but because she couldn't quite understand her swirling emotions.

How much of her life had she spent waiting for *this* moment?

All the books she'd read. The photographs she'd scoured. Celeste should feel accomplished. She should feel fulfilled, instead she felt…nothing.

It wasn't that it wasn't beautiful, or mystical. It was just, somewhere deep inside, where she'd tucked away her diagnosis and the warnings from the doctors, was the knowledge that the images from the books would outlive what her mind could remember.

Last in, first out.

She moved away from the group, shuffling to the edge of the cliff. It wasn't a sheer drop into oblivion. If she fell, the worst that would happen would be a turned ankle.

If she looked out, straight ahead, she could almost convince herself that she stood on the edge.

On the edge of the world. On the edge of her sanity.

Celeste pulled her camera up to her eyes. She could've used the screen, but seeing the world through the small window lens comforted her. The limited view forced her to focus on committing small glimpses to memory.

That was all she wanted. To die with at least some small view of her life goal in her mind. Even if it was a swath of the bright blue sky. Or a petal of a tropical flower. Maybe even just a shadow of the crumbled rock wall.

Her memories would start dropping out of her mind like autumn leaves falling from a tree. At first, it would be just a few random thoughts. Like where Celeste had put her keys or the name of the nice kids next door. Then there'd be a storm that would shove the others out, until finally, the only thing left would be a few stubborn remembrances holding on.

That storm was coming.

It might be next week or next year, but there'd be a point where all she had left would be the thoughts in her journal and a photo album full of pictures and people she didn't know.

What would it feel like to look at something, at someone, and not know them?

Would she feel remorse for not recognizing them, or would it be as disassociated as walking by a stranger on the street?

Would she even know herself?

Celeste crossed the ruins, climbing to the highest point, standing at the edge. Wind whipped her clothes, slapped her face.

Her mind wandered back to the last church sermon she'd heard. The preacher had talked about the soul, how it lived on, how who they were would continue long after the vessel decayed.

She perched on the precipice between science and religion, finding herself teetering to one side before the other side dragged her back to it.

After that sermon, she'd hung back, wanting to ask the minister where the soul lived. Celeste always assumed the brain, because that was where her hopes and dreams, thoughts and impulses came from.

With her brain deteriorating, what did that mean for her soul? Would she find herself in the afterlife with little recollection of who she was?

She could end it.

She could jump, quit her life before she lost who she was. While that would end her story, it would set the journey her children took on a very different path.

Her grief would simply transfer to them. What signs had they missed? Who'd seen Mom last? What could they have done to stop it?

Jimmy had given her permission to be selfish, but not *that* selfish.

Celeste straightened her back, inhaled deeply, and screamed off the side of the mountain.

Her angst reverberated back to her. Wings flapped in the distance; birds distraught by the shouts of an old woman losing her mind.

Literally.

"Celeste?" Lourdes appeared next to her. "Are you okay?"

She looked at the scared starlet. The shout dislodged something inside of her. Celeste was more than okay.

She was free.

"Come here," Celeste motioned for Lourdes to join her on the ledge. "Try it."

The woman looked at her, a perfect eyebrow arched. Skepticism marred her pretty face.

"Go ahead," she nudged.

Lourdes squared her shoulders and inhaled, like a big bad wolf readying to blow down a house. Her demur scream flowed from her lips.

Celeste pursed her lips and nodded. "Not a bad first try. How about this," she took a deep breath. "Fuck you, Alzheimer's!"

The name of her disease echoed back at her. If the curse hadn't come from her it would've been mocking. Instead, with each repeat, the word's potency lessened.

"Oh, that felt good," Celeste said. "Lourdes, your turn."

Another inhale, and her mouth opened. "Fuck you, cancer!" The star's eyes widened and her hand slapped over her mouth. "Oh my God, you're right! That felt so good." She glanced back to the misty canopy of the rainforest. "Fuck you, chemo. Fuck you, hair loss. Oh, and fuck you, radiation." Her chest heaved. "Why are we doing this?"

"I want to make sure I remember it." The whisper felt unnaturally quiet after the shouting.

A throat cleared behind them.

Jimmy and Dylan were standing there.

Their leader's expression somewhere between mortified and proud.

Dylan looked like a kid eager to take a turn with the coolest toy.

"Dylan, come here, honey." Celeste reached for the boy who wasn't much younger than her baby. "Come try it. Like this. Fuck you, HMOs!" The O reverberated back at her.

He hesitated before joining them on the edge.

As if the crazy women shouting obscenities off the side of the mountain might throw him off.

Dylan cleared his throat. "Screw you, brain tumor." A laugh bubbled up at the end of the shout. "Screw you, headaches. Go to hell, nausea."

Lourdes smirked. "Oh, that's a good one. Yes, fuck you, puking!"

They took turns shouting at their ailments.

With each scream, Celeste felt lighter. The burden of her disease expelled with each faded note of her shouts.

"How do we get in on this?" Levi's gruff English accent sliced through an interlude. He stood with Charlotte at his side, his arm over the woman's shoulder, but in a way that the woman propped him up.

Celeste stepped back, making room for the rocker on the edge of their world. "Come on in, Mr. Livingston."

Charlotte and Levi walked to the edge.

He puffed up, like a rooster ready to crow. A cough wracked his body, forcing him to double over.

Charlotte bent over him, whispering in his ear.

He nodded and straightened. "Fuck you, you cock-sucking liver."

The group dissolved into laughter.

Charlotte stood silent, looking out over the valley below them. She gnawed on her lower lip and took a step closer, her toes hanging over the edge.

Celeste felt the urge to reach out to her, to grab her and pull her back to the safety of solid ground. What if she slipped?

What if she did exactly what Celeste wanted to do? Keep walking until she stepped into oblivion.

The anticipation hung in the air like the mist over Machu Picchu. The moment when she'd shout what was killing her.

"Fuck you, death!" The self-help guru turned back to look at the group; the need for approval, as evident as a child taking her first steps.

Celeste reached and pulled her closer, lacing her fingers in the woman's cold hand.

The chant changed then, from shouts at their diseases, they cursed death.

Because in the end, that was what was killing them.

They were all on the same journey.

Different paths, but the same ugly destination.

17

The numbers on the computer screen mocked Darla. No matter how she shifted expenses, the revenue always had a big fat negative sign in front of it.

"Crap on a cracker." She laid her head on the desk. Her coffee had long gone cold, and her smoothie had gone warm. She didn't just need to get that number into a huge profit, she needed to find enough money in the budget to ask Jimmy for a raise.

The big fat negative sign had a companion in her personal budget. If she couldn't find the money in Dire's Enterprises' budget, then she couldn't keep Momma in the same care facility.

Maybe there was something she could sell. Minimalist living was all the rage these days.

Plasma. She probably had plenty of it. Couldn't think of anything she needed it for. She could sell it. To someone else who does need plasma. For plasma-y things. Whatever those were. Did they use human plasma for plasma TVs? Living a plasma-less life would be pretty minimalistic.

Her computer chimed, with a meeting reminder at the same time an email from Enzo came into her inbox.

She didn't need to open it to know what it said. The budget was for last year, he needed this year's budget. Could she get it to him ASAP?

Darla was no ditz, but she also wasn't above playing one to get what she needed. In this case, it was to get Enzo off her butt about the budget, while she figured out how to keep her momma in her nursing home.

Five more minutes of playing with the numbers. Five more minutes to figure out where to cut, what to skimp on, where to find money tucked away in a couch-cushion of a line item. No matter what she cut, it wasn't adding up.

Jimmy couldn't keep the business running without some major overhaul.

She locked up the office and rode the elevator down to the garage. The mirrored walls were a funhouse of her reflection. So many Darlas, each one fighting for her place in the world.

Fighting to keep her momma safe. Fighting to keep Jimmy's business going. Was there a Darla in that amplified reflection that fought for *her*?

Fought for the woman who was too smart to dance, but also knew life favored those born into a certain social class. The one that didn't assume that because a girl was blonde and pretty, she couldn't think. The one that didn't force those in hard times to twirl their naked bodies around a pole so sweaty, smelly predators could fantasize about them later.

She wasn't going back there. Back to the clear high heels, the dead eyes, the body glitter, the fear of seeing someone she knew while on stage, the embarrassment of meeting a nice guy and eventually having to tell him what she did for a living.

Darla leaned in close and studied her face. If the harsh fluorescent lights were telling the truth, at thirty-five, she'd be stuck dancing at an interstate club that advertised eighteen-wheeler parking.

Even Momma had never sunk *that* low.

Her mind played with numbers as her GPS guided her to the nursing home. It was a good way inland. *That's good, for hurricanes.*

Darla pulled into a small parking lot, way under-sized for the building it served.

The nursing home itself looked like a series of portable buildings, hitched together like a child's train set. The beige siding was dirty, and weeds grew through massive cracks in the uneven sidewalk.

"Okay, maybe they spend more time cleaning up the inside," she mumbled before opening the glass door.

The smell hit her immediately. Darla was used to the typical smell of nursing homes. The bleach covering the tang of urine was just par for the course of caring for invalids.

This smell was different. Harsher. It didn't ride up on a current of air conditioning, it enveloped her like a hot Houston summer, seeping into her clothes, her hair, her brain.

She paused inside the doorway, waiting for her eyes to adjust from the sunlit parking lot to the dimly lit hallway. Only every other overhead light was working.

A man wheeled toward her. One of his socked feet sat crooked in the footplate, the other pulled him forward in small, slow strides. Dried, white spittle clung to two-day-old whiskers on his chin. His mouth moved like a fish out of water, but no words came out. A gnarled hand reached out of her, threatening to drag her into whatever Hell he was in.

"Mr. Watts, what're you doing out of your room?"

Darla jumped at a voice behind her. An older woman stood in a doorway; her hands hitched on her ample hips. Even though they were the same height, the woman seemed to tower over her.

"You must be Darla. I'm Merrie, like Merry Christmas but with an 'ie'." Her thick, stubby fingers gripped her hand. "Let me get Mr. Watts settled, and I'll be right with you."

The woman pushed past her and spun the old man's wheelchair around.

A guttural cry escaped his floundering lips, and he leaned out of his chair, reaching for Darla, his eyes pleading with her.

"Um, Merrie, is he okay?"

She glanced over her shoulder. "Well, why wouldn't he be?" Her voice was full of who-do-you-think-you-are. She glanced down at the agitated man and shifted her features back into neutral. "Oh, this? Mr. Watts is our resident flirt. Any pretty young thing that walks through the door, and he instantly turns into Casanova."

The man's grunts grew louder as he was pushed further down the hallway.

Merrie rolled him into a room and slammed the door behind her.

Darla's feet finally thawed, and she moved farther inside the nursing home. She peeked into the first open door.

A woman lay on the bed. Rotting food sat on a bed tray, and the woman stared at a repeat of a game show. When the audience laugh track played, she chuckled along in a high-pitched, child-like giggle.

She moved to the next room.

A man lay flat on the bed, eyes closed as if sleeping, but his face was waxy, pale.

She counted several of her own breaths, waiting to see if the man's chest moved with an inhale, but nothing happened.

Was he recently departed?

Should she mention something to Merrie, offer to reschedule sometime in the future?

Like never.

She tiptoed backward, easing out of the room, hoping to slip back out of the nursing home, but she hit a wall. Not an actual wall, but a woman as stout and unmoving as one.

"Is he…" Darla couldn't finish the sentence. Tears rushed forward. She'd sell a kidney, her right arm, and then strip as part of a fetish freak show to keep her momma from ending up in this place.

Merrie pushed past her. "Mr. Tomlinson is a real light breather." She picked up his frail wrist, squeezing it so hard Darla feared she was going to break the man's bird-like bones. "You wouldn't believe how many times…Well, huh, I guess the old coot finally did it." She dropped his wrist and pulled the sheet over his face.

"Are you kidding me?"

The woman narrowed her eyes and huffed. If she'd been a bull, steam would have puffed out of her nose.

It wasn't the first time she'd stared down an angry beast, and it wouldn't be the last.

"These people deserve your respect. They're humans, for goodness sake, not just old rugs you can toss into a room and forget about."

Merrie's body heaved and she ducked her head down. If she'd had horns, she would've charged.

Just in the short time she'd been there, Darla was convinced the woman *did* have horns.

"You think *I* tossed them in a room?" She stalked forward. "You think *I* forgot them? Look around you. What's missing? Go ahead, look."

Darla was afraid to let go of the woman's gaze, afraid she'd charge her as soon as she looked away, but she backed into the hallway and glanced to her right.

Several elderly people sat idle in wheelchairs, even a few younger people. People who for one reason or another had been shorted the gift of time.

Back to Darla's left, the doorway to freedom. The hallway stood empty. No one else entered the building. No one else came to visit an aging loved one, or inquire about a caring place to tend to a parent's final days.

That was why the parking lot was so small.

This place was a graveyard for the living.

"You're just like them." Merrie's voice was low and seething. "You want the Ritz but you're only willing to pay for a Motel 8. So, forgive me if I don't cater to their every whim or wipe their asses with golden toilet paper, because I'm doing a helluva lot more for these people than their families are."

The woman's words were a sucker punch to Darla's gut. That was the last thing she wanted to do. She'd give her own life for her mom to wake up, to complain about her choice in men, to chastise what she was wearing, and to tell her she needed to puff up her hair and straighten her back.

She opened her mouth to argue, willing some snappy comeback to leap up her throat and slap the woman's smirk off her face.

All she could do was walk back down the hallway, back out into the Florida sun, far away from neglected people, and the bitter woman who cared for them.

It didn't matter that Jimmy was on a trip. As soon as he called to check in, she'd tell him she needed a raise. She was worth it. Her mother was worth it.

And if he couldn't...

Plasma. Kidney. Her body.

Her soul.

It didn't matter what she had to sell.

Darla wouldn't let her mother end up in a place like that.

18

The convoy of Jeeps flew down the highway. A herd of giraffes raced them. Their long, graceful necks reached and bobbed as they sprinted.

Lourdes twisted in her seat in front of Charlotte, her dark eyes following as the herd veered toward a copse of trees. "Do you think it ever gets old?"

She followed the *telenovela* star's gaze. Two young giraffes played a game of chase, while the adults pulled leaves off trees.

People would ask her the same question when they learned she lived in a beachfront home surrounded by water on two sides. Did she ever get tired of staring at the ocean? Did her ears ever become numb to the sound of waves rolling in? Did her skin stop feeling the spray of saltwater?

The relationship with her home was complicated. She'd bought it after her business had taken off. It wasn't the grand gesture of someone who'd grown up clinging to the middle class, suddenly coming into money. Her home was a way for her to be close to Jason, while as far away from people as possible.

Living by the ocean was anything but static. Some days it was languid, like a lazy teen disinclined to barely lap at the shore. Other days it was a hyperactive child, crashing like thunder on the erosion barriers.

"Why such a remote adventure?" she asked.

Lourdes' chest heaved with a deep breath. "Have you ever been to Mexico City?"

She shook her head.

The Jeep slowed to allow a herd of elephants to cross the road. Beautiful creatures that seemed far too docile for the harsh African terrain.

"Americans think New York City is the epitome of a big city, but they're wrong. Mexico City is vibrant and complex, with ancient and modern culture. Sometimes in the same block." Her eyes misted, as if she spoke about a lost love instead of a city. "It's the fifth most populated city in the world, and incredibly suffocating."

"This is less about the adventure and more about being able to breathe," Charlotte ventured.

Lourdes held herself so still, when she nodded, it seemed like a big movement. "It's about sleeping under the stars. Real stars."

A radio buzzed in the SUV. Rapid words were spoken to their driver and he quickly pulled off the road.

The other vehicle pulled up.

Jimmy leaned out the window. "We just heard rumors of bandits hitting some campsites a few days ago." His forehead was as wrinkled as a pair of slept-in pants and dark bags stained the skin beneath his eyes.

"By hitting you mean…" The chill of fear doused the afternoon heat clinging to Charlotte.

"Robbing only so far, but someone could get jumpy."

Concern coated his every word; rightfully so. Despite the waivers and forms and indemnification clauses, they were still his responsibility.

She glanced to the back row of Jimmy's vehicle.

Levi was slumped in his seat, his head rested on the back, chest moving in slow, gentle breaths.

Charlotte exhaled. She'd held her breath until she was reassured Levi still possessed his.

"The guides, they have guns, no?" Lourdes asked, her voice terse.

"Well, yes, but—"

"But nothing. If I wanted to be scared into submission by robbers, I could've stayed home," the star declared then mumbled Spanish under her breath.

"Lourdes, are you sure?"

She looked away. Back over the vast African landscape with gentle hills, dangerous creatures, and deadly men. "The cartel tried to control me; cancer tried to control me. These *pendejos* can *vete a la chingada*."

Jimmy's gaze darted toward Charlotte, obviously pleading with her to talk some sense into the woman.

She shrugged. "I think I'm more afraid of Lourdes than any bandits right now."

Their leader heaved a heavy sigh and told the driver to continue.

They rode in silence.

The driver gripped the steering wheel so tightly his dark skin paled to a milk chocolate color.

Dylan had been napping next to her, but now he sat up straighter, his head swiveling to try to take in their arid surroundings.

Lourdes stared straight ahead. Whatever thoughts raced through her mind were on display to the road ahead of them.

"Call me Lulu," Lourdes' voice was so quiet it was almost lost in the road hum. She made eye contact with Charlotte. "Thank you for backing me up. My closest friends call me Lulu. I would like for you to do that, too."

"Thank you, I appreciate that. But you're right, we can't live in fear."

"What's the worst that can happen? Death? We're all headed there now." The starlet chuckled, but it wasn't the soft, warm sound of a sincere laugh, but it had the hard edge of irony.

"Or we could live," Charlotte said. "Today, tomorrow, and the tomorrow after that, until we're out of tomorrows."

Lourdes' eyes filled with tears. She reached over the seat and clasped Charlotte's hand. Despite the heat surrounding them, her hand was ice cold. "I'm glad you're here."

She smiled and squeezed her new friend's hand. Was it wrong to wish she truly had some terminal disease? To wish that a rare and untreatable illness battled her body, killing healthy cells, turning her organs to dust from the inside out.

Was it possible to equally feel as though she belonged with this group of Diers and apart from them?

What would happen if Levi found out she'd lied? Would he feel ashamed for letting her see him at his weakest in Peru?

Or, Lourdes.

Dying was dying. Right?

The Jeep pulled off the main highway and trundled down a one-lane dirt road. The more treacherous the road became; the more Lourdes' obvious excitement grew.

The road pitched up.

The Jeep climbed at a decent incline.

Everything seemed exaggerated.

Prairie grass grew out of bright red dirt. The blue sky was so vibrant Charlotte reached out her open window. Everything looked like a backdrop for a movie set.

Zebras munched on grass, glancing up only briefly to eye the passing cars and then returning to their meal.

Tears sprang to her eyes from a place inside her she didn't know existed. A place that celebrated the breathtaking beauty of life. A place that wanted to see and smell and taste everything that life had to offer. That wanted to wrap its arms around the world and everyone who inhabited it.

At the end of the climb, the road leveled out to a plateau. Several large tents were erect, a wooden table sat close to a fire pit, and lanterns encircled the campsite. Hammocks hung from frames, one for each of their group.

When Jimmy said they'd be camping out under the stars in Africa, she'd assumed it would be in the type of tents that youth groups across America used for summer outings to earn badges.

Now she understood why the man was nervous about their plan. If thieves were indeed roaming the area, their "glamp-ground" would be a beacon in the night.

Lourdes ran out of the Jeep as soon as it came to a stop. She halted short of their home for the night, her small hands clenched into tight fists.

Jimmy climbed out of his Jeep slowly, his gaze on the woman and his face taut. "Did I get it right?"

The pretty Latina twirled on her heel; a wide smile filled her face. She took three fast steps and threw herself in his arms. "It's perfect! Thank you!"

The relief on Jimmy's face reminded her of the look on Jason's face when she'd accepted his marriage proposal. A lazy smile crossed her lips just thinking about that moment.

Everything was amplified in the African desert. The sky, the colors in the landscape, the crisp earthy smell.

The two people falling in love.

19

Lourdes stared into the mirror of her compact. Her eyebrows were a bit too close together, making her look like she was scowling. After seeing what Jimmy delivered, she had nothing to scowl at.

Jimmy.

Her breath caught on the thought of their tour guide. *Nothing* about him was her type. The man was nearly fifty. She hadn't dated anyone that old since she was in her twenties.

Thinning auburn hair, receding hairline. Granted, it was more hair than *she* had, but still, she didn't want to run the risk of pulling some out every time she ran her hands through it.

Tall, wiry frame. If there was a six-pack under his shirt it was more because he was thin, but not because he spent hours in the gym.

Yet, her cheeks warmed every time his eyes studied her. Every time he said her name, her heart stumbled like a clumsy schoolgirl. She could feel him nearby, even if he never spoke.

Lourdes slammed the compact shut. "Stop it."

These feelings had no place in her life. Nor in her heart.

She was dying.

If that wasn't the worst time to start a relationship, what was?

A bell rang outside.

"Cocktail hour," Jimmy shouted.

The tone of his voice caressed her, sending her blood thrumming through her veins at a quicker pace. *"Basta!"* she hissed. Lourdes took a deep breath and let it out slowly. If she walked out flushed, if her voice wobbled or if she stared too long, the others would worry.

She'd learned to deal with a lot since her diagnosis, but pity was not one of them. Lourdes Peña was someone others looked up to, never with downcast, sad eyes. It was amazing how pride could drive the pain away.

If only her pride could rid her body of cancer.

The chatter outside grew louder.

She hadn't asked for a night on the African planes to spend it all inside her tent, but it was the only place she could hide from Jimmy. From the feelings he stirred. He was oxygen to the hope she couldn't afford to have bubble up.

The early evening air was warm, with a cool undercurrent. The sun drifted toward the horizon. Large, orange, unencumbered.

Lanterns dotted the area around their campground. The guides worked in tandem at the campfire; one stirred a large black pot while the other flipped food on a grill.

"Welcome to the most beautiful adventure in Dire's Club history." Jimmy appeared beside her; a glass of wine offered in his outstretched hand.

"Is that so?" Lourdes took the wine. "Out of the whole world and all the adventures, this is the most beautiful one?" Her mind told her to walk away, not flirt with the mildly handsome man standing before her, but her body wanted to spend more time in his warmth.

Red tinged his cheeks and his mouth parted, as if about to speak, but one of the guides called him over. "Excuse me."

The minute Jimmy fled, she chilled. She glanced around the campground, studying the random group of strangers.

The older woman stood off to the side, camera to her face, furiously clicking away.

"Celeste," she said, hooking an arm around the woman. "How're you doing?"

The woman's mountaintop shouts at Machu Picchu had stirred something within Lourdes. While her body died, her mind remained fully intact. Would it have been easier if it were the other way around? To let her body remain strong and beautiful while her mind wasted away? After all, everyone knew Lourdes was renowned for her beauty, not her brains.

Celeste patted her forearm. "Thank you, dear. I'm better. How are you?"

She pulled her mouth into a smile. "Still dying."

The older woman laughed and leaned in closer. "Fuck dying," she whispered.

Lourdes giggled. "Yeah, fuck dying." Arms wrapped around each other; they watched the sun dip lower.

Death was a strange bedfellow.

So was life.

Footsteps approached from behind them. "Dinner's ready, ladies," Jimmy said. He held his arms out. "May I?"

Lourdes hooked her arm through his. Electricity zipped through her body. They hadn't touched each other since they'd shook hands the first day they'd met.

His eyes sparkled as they studied her, his cheeks reddened. He deposited her at the head of the table, and took a seat at the opposite end.

She kept her gaze down, avoiding the eyes of the man staring a hole in her from the other end of the table.

Why was this happening now? All she'd wanted was to die happy. To die alone. To finish her journey with no cliffhanger.

She was *dying*. A sequel was not in her future.

The conversation at the table flowed as easily as the wine. Lourdes found herself in a conversation with Celeste, then called over to join in a story with Levi, but in the space between the words, she'd always find Jimmy watching her from the far end; his expression content.

"What's it like, being a movie star?" Dylan asked. "Being famous?" He directed the second half of his question to Levi and Charlotte.

Like the night sky, stars came in all sizes and intensities. Some burned bright, fast, flaring into nothing. Others warmed slowly, their glow turning up, saving their energy for the long game. More seemed to be in it for the duration, but a sudden super-nova-like explosion darkened their sky too soon.

Lourdes opened her mouth. Words crouched on her tongue, ready to tell the young man all the opportunity it afforded her. Instead, the truth leaped forward, pushing the lie aside. "It's lonely."

Charlotte nodded. "I'm not even a real celebrity, and I could tell you that."

"Yeah, everyone acts like they're your best mate, but they just want to say they know you. They won't be there when you need them." Levi stared at his nearly empty wine glass.

"Like when you're sick," Lourdes said. "People act like cancer's contagious."

"But, making movies and TV shows." Dylan shifted the conversation back to his question. "That must've been cool."

Lourdes straightened, shaking the long hair of the wig off her shoulders. "Of course, who wouldn't want to be someone else? To have the glamor of playing dress-up and make-believe every day. To jet off to exotic locales." She picked up her wine. "But it's so easy to forget who you are, to lose yourself in each role you play." She tipped her glass, watching the legs of the wine run down the inside curves. The sounds of the African sunset filled in the gap of the conversation.

Birds chirped. A chorus of frogs. Somewhere in the distance, an animal snorted.

"Sometimes." The word came out in a watery whisper. "Sometimes, I can't remember if I'm me, or if I'm still playing a role. That I'm playing the part of a cancer patient, and this is one of those roles where I'm fully immersed, so far as to lose weight and shave my head. As if I'm doing it for award season."

The mood shifted.

That happened a lot when she told the truth.

They weren't expecting her to be so acerbic, so serious, so dour. People expected light-hearted tales from her. They expected someone who vowed to use her disease as a platform for raising awareness, but screw that.

Being terminal gave her permission to be brutally honest. Cancer was an asshole. Life was never long enough.

She threw back the rest of her wine and refilled the glass. "But, since I'm dying, I can tell you all sorts of gossip," Lourdes leaned on her elbows. "What do you want to know?"

Celeste perked up, her blue eyes sparkling. She sucked in her lower lip, coating her teeth with bright red lipstick. "Brock Gardner," she said the name of the latest action hero, one Lourdes had shared the screen with just a few years ago. "He's so handsome, what's he like in real life?"

She leaned back, cupping her glass against her chest. "Truthfully, he has the worst breath, but no one is brave enough to tell him."

A laugh erupted from Charlotte's throat. "What about Arturo Altayo? You guys dated for a while, right?"

Lourdes hadn't thought about the famous *futbol* player in years. They had made a beautiful couple. The Brazilian soccer player, with his dark blond hair and tattooed skin. "He's a horrible kisser."

"What?" Dylan shouted. "A dude like that?"

"Yep, kissed like a snake." She put her glass on the table and darted her tongue in and out in demonstration. "I think he was going for quantity over quality."

It felt good to share all these secrets. To shed the past.

The table erupted into laughter. Except for Jimmy.

Lourdes cocked her head and narrowed her eyes. Something told her he'd be a good kisser. Long, deep, a kiss that would stop time, making them forget where they were.

Who they were.

20

There'd been only once, in the twelve years that he'd owned his business, that Jimmy had to cancel someone's adventure. To have to look in a client's eyes, to say the words that would snuff out the last flicker of light.

You can't have your dying wish.

Poof. Gone.

They wouldn't die happy. They'd die disappointed. They'd die like his mother. Marrying a man incapable of love. Bearing a son cursed to carry the mark of his father's anger. Living a life that only accomplished dying.

The news of possible bandits hadn't dimmed Lourdes' fire. It ignited it. Doused it in gasoline.

With dinner over and drinks in hand, his group of Diers gathered around a nascent campfire to watch the sun sink below the horizon. Giant trees loomed in the distance, backlit giants watching over the desert.

A pair of binoculars made its way around the group. When he brought them to his face, Jimmy observed the shadowed figures of giraffe moving in a straight line against a brilliant fiery orange sunset.

It was the second most beautiful thing that evening on the African plains.

The most beautiful sat three chairs away from him.

Radiant. Serene. Full of life.

And, dying.

Stories filled the evening air. Levi entertained with raucous tales of life on the road. Celeste cackled with her infectious laugh. Even Dylan had put away his journal full of numbers and mathematic formulas to join in the conversation.

Lourdes faced the dying light of the day, her glass of wine held close to her chest. The orange fire had diffused to a warm glow. Her golden skin was luminous, as if the waning sun escaped the sky only to be soaked into her body.

Jimmy remembered his mom the same way. The sun didn't shine from the sky, it shone from within her. Basking in it warmed him on a cold day. It'd dried his tears. It'd brightened the days darkened by his father's mercurial tendencies.

Her light hadn't turned off like a switch when she'd gotten sick. It waned, like an ending day, saving its beauty until the very end.

Then, it was gone.

The darkness set in.

A darkness he could only escape with a new day.

A new life.

A new name.

Jimmy pushed off the chair and checked on the guides, who were now serving as security guards. "How's it going?" he asked Thomas, the lead guide.

The man kept his gaze on the darkening landscape. "Quiet, but not too quiet." As if on cue, an animal grunted in the distance against the symphony of insects and night sounds. Thomas twirled his finger in the air. "When all that goes silent, get everyone in the tents."

It didn't take long for the cacophony to settle into a white noise hum.

Jimmy strained his ears to pay close attention to every grunt, every chirp, every hoofbeat in the darkness around them. "Need a refill?" He held up a bottle of wine.

Every hand thrust a wineglass into the air.

Lourdes giggled, covering her mouth with her delicate hand.

"Lourdes," he said, pouring her wine nearly to the top. "Are the stars bright enough for you?"

"Lulu," she said through a gulp of wine. "You all can call me Lulu. The group that dies together…" She lifted the glass again, this time for an air toast.

After the celebratory gesture, a tempered, yet pensive mood settled over the group like the cooling night air.

"I grew up very poor, but also very happy. We didn't have a lot, but we also didn't need much." She stared into the fire, with the faraway stare of someone looking into the past. "It was my parents, my brothers and sister, and my *abuelita*." Lourdes smiled. "I was my *abuelita's* favorite."

The crunch of footsteps echoed to Jimmy's left. His heart choked his throat, only climbing back into place when one of the guides came into view, making a pass by the group.

"She used to tell me stories of movie stars. Glamorous women and handsome men." The starlet looked up at the canopy of the Milky Way stretched overhead. "I thought they lived in the Heavens. I wanted nothing more than to be one of those women, to be the story another *abuelita* tells her little granddaughter. To have another little girl think I lived in the sky." Lourdes took a long drink. "What she didn't know was that once you soar that high, you can never come back down. Not without a crash. A falling star."

The tone of the group grew somber.

Jimmy watched their faces in the flickering firelight. Each seemed to be pondering Lourdes' story. He stoked the fire, sending embers flying into the night.

"You'd burn up before you hit the ground," Dylan quipped.

It started with Celeste's gasp.

Charlotte covered her mouth, but then her eyes crinkled with a giggle.

Levi snickered, mumbling something rendered inaudible by the alcohol.

Lourdes' jaw dropped for a second before her laugh rose above the sounds of the desert night. It was a hearty laugh, robust, full of life.

"What?" Dylan asked, his eyes wide. "It's true, something like ninety-nine percent of all meteors burn up before they hit the earth."

His explanation launched another round of guffaws. The laughter died down with the slowness of a sunset.

The fire burned down to a soft glow. The wine bottles ran dry. Yawns filled the void of the conversation.

"The cartel invaded my town," Lourdes spoke in the darkness. "Most of my family got out, but I could never go back. I could never look up at a sky full of stars and wonder where mine will be when I'm gone. You can never go home again, but you can find home in the most unlikely place, with the most unlikely people."

Jimmy's group of Diers toasted their nearly empty glasses and called it a night.

Except for Lourdes. She seemed in no hurry to crawl into her tent and bid the night goodbye.

"This must be depressing work," she said. "I'm sure you could've found a niche that didn't involve dead people."

"You seem pretty damn alive to me." His words were coated in wine.

Her smile was lit by the star shine. "What does Mrs. Dire think about you taking all these grand vacations?"

Jimmy grinned. If his mother were looking down, she'd giggle at the use of her fantasy name. "I think my mother would've been quite proud of me."

"And Darla…"

"Is my wonderful office manager."

Lourdes crossed the small seating area to stand in front of him.

The shadows of the night accentuated her beauty. Dark hair a black hole that drew him in. Her strong cheekbones sliced through the softness of her face. Brown eyes glittered in the last embers of the fire.

She put her hand out. "Walk me home."

He took her hand but didn't stand. "It's a short walk."

"Guess you better walk slowly."

Jimmy stood, but she didn't back up. His heart slammed against his ribcage, pumping blood like he was sprinting, making his brain fuzzy, drunk from her nearness.

"Is there a rule?" Her accent was thicker, her voice hoarse.

"About walking you home?"

She leaned up on her toes. Wine-stained lips parted, just inches from his mouth. "About kissing a client."

When her mouth crashed into his, every nerve-ending in his body ignited. The softness of her full lips caressed his. Her warm fingers wrapped around his neck, pulling him into her body.

Jimmy reached around her waist, but her free hand found his and laced her fingers into his. His ears rang with his rushing blood, filling the silence of the night...

The silence.

He broke their kiss and held his breath.

"What's wrong?" she asked.

"Shhh."

When his pulse slowed, the quiet of the night was all-encompassing. "Thomas?" Jimmy shouted.

Approaching footsteps echoed in the night. First two, then another two sets, finally more footfalls than he had men working for him.

"Money, jewelry, passports." The man stepped out of the darkness and into the circle of the campsite.

Jimmy had always heard people held up at gunpoint were unreliable witnesses. Their attention wasn't on the person robbing them, but the weapon staring at them.

They were right.

That was the first thought flashing through his mind. There'd be no way he could tell someone what these men looked like.

He tucked Lourdes behind him, shielding her from the bandits. "Okay, no need to hurt anyone, we pose no threat."

"No talk." The man glanced behind him and spoke in a hurried foreign language.

Two other men broke from the group and entered the tents.

Screams and shouts of his clients filled the air.

Charlotte pulled Celeste close, holding the older woman.

Dylan slunk his shoulders forward, as if trying to make himself small.

Levi, in true British rocker fashion, cursed. "Get yer hands off me, you bloody wanker."

"Hey guys, just do what they say." Jimmy let his gaze drift up from the gun to the man holding it.

"Money, jewelry, passports," the man repeated.

Passports. Money and jewelry could be replaced, but passports were a different story.

Especially Jimmy's. There'd be far more questions than he was prepared to answer.

"Money and jewelry," Jimmy countered. "No passports."

The bandit lifted the gun higher, its nozzle now eye level with him. "You don't negotiate."

"Would you rather us stay, and report this to the police, or leave the country and get on with our lives?"

The other bandits murmured, distracting the gunman.

Lourdes growled behind him.

He could feel the feisty Latina tighten.

A lioness ready to pounce.

She lunged for the poker.

A chorus of clicks filled the silent night as the gang of bandits pulled out their weapons.

"Lulu, put it down." His even tone betrayed the fear sprinting through his veins.

"I don't want to hurt your woman."

"You think I'm scared of you?" Lourdes hissed. "You're children compared to the cartels."

The head bandit took two steps in her direction, holding the barrel of the gun just inches from her forehead.

Her jaw tightened and her eyes narrowed. "I'm not afraid to die."

Jimmy reached behind and gripped the poker. She resisted, tugging it back before he stroked her fingers. With a sigh, she handed it to him.

He held the poker up, loose in his hand in a gesture of surrender. "Money and jewelry, no passports, so we can leave the country. And, don't hurt anyone."

The man dropped his weapon and glanced at his gang. He twirled the gun in his hand, and, as quick as a jaguar striking, crashed the butt of it against Jimmy's temple.

21

Jimmy collapsed with the speed of an in-demand director's career after a sex scandal.

Lourdes allowed her gaze to follow him long enough to reassure herself he'd have a killer headache, but would otherwise be okay. Anger and fear twisted and turned in her gut, churning the wine, threatening to send it back up.

She wanted to fight back; wanted to pick up the poker she'd dropped and jam in through the eye of the man standing in front of her.

In the end, all she could do was cross her arms over her chest. Acceptance of their situation, with a side of defiance.

It was no different than when she'd discovered the studio she'd spent her career with was laundering cartel money.

Deep inside she wanted to object, to call attention to the atrocities, the criminality. Of that fact that somewhere a family was being pulled apart with the savagery of a medieval torture device.

Rather than fight back, Lourdes learned her lines, turned on her otherworldly charisma, charmed critics, wowed the *telenovela* fans. All to stay out of the crosshairs of powerful men who ruled with toxic machismo.

Because who was she, but an actress? A beautiful woman who made people laugh when they were sad, who drew them out of their poverty and into the fantasy world she inhabited on screen; who gave little girls sweet dreams of finding their own happily ever after.

Behind her, the rest of the group was huddled together behind Levi. The rock star stood shirtless; his barrel chest thrust out like a protective shield.

"Everyone on the ground, face down." The bandit indicated with his weapon.

"Let's all just do what they say," Lourdes murmured, squatting slowly to kneeling. "Listen, like he said, leave our passports. Without them, we can't leave the country."

The man regarded her. Annoyance flared in his dark eyes in the reflection of the dying fire. In a quick move, he raised the gun and jammed the muzzle into her forehead.

The metal was cold against her hot forehead.

"Everyone down or she dies."

She kept her gaze tight on the man. She wanted to see every breath, every blink, every flinch of the man who could take away her pain.

If this was how she'd end up dying, she wouldn't look away.

Like how she'd refused to look away when the needles carrying drugs to kill the cancer cells pierced her skin. Like how she'd refused to look away when the doctor held up scans to show the milky white splotches of disease invading her body.

Like how she'd stood naked in front of the mirror after her surgeries, studying the swollen, puckered incisions reminding her what she'd sacrificed in hopes of living just a little bit longer.

Lourdes had refused to look away then, and she'd be damned if she looked away at the moment her life was going to end.

The other Diers lay face down.

Levi growled behind her, a mix of prayer and curses.

Someone's teeth chattered so loudly the sound competed with the crackling of the firewood.

Charlotte whispered reassurances at someone. Celeste? Dylan? Maybe herself?

The leader stood there, pressing his gun into her forehead while his minions checked their tents. He spoke in a quick, foreign language. It felt like a shout in the quiet of the night. "No passports," he said to Lourdes. "You should be afraid."

"If you'd lived my life, you'd realize that this isn't the scariest thing I've experienced. Losing my home to the drug cartel, being alone with a director who was known for taking what he wanted. When the doctors stopped fighting and used words like 'managing pain,' and focused on making me comfortable." Lourdes swallowed hard. "*That's* scary. A gun at my head. That's a relief."

The man's head pulled back as if she'd slapped him with words. His lips parted, but nothing emerged.

Several seconds ticked by while they regarded each other. A thief with a victim who refused to *be* a victim.

She'd learned a long time ago that people only had power if it was given to them. He might take her money and her jewelry, but he'd never have power over her.

Finally, a long whistle cut through the night. "Let's go," he called. He pulled the gun from her head. "On the ground. Don't move until you count to one hundred."

She could fight him, beg him to shoot her. Fighting bandits would be a more theatrical end to Lourdes Peña than wasting away with cancer.

Her gaze fluttered back to the curled, prone figure of Jimmy.

His kiss was still fresh on her lips. The tingling wasn't dulled with fear, instead, it enhanced the sensation. Like champagne bringing out the brine of caviar.

Staring at her death had only made their kiss sweeter. Made her want it more.

She slowly lowered herself to her stomach. The ground was still warm from the heat of the day, but the air above her was cold.

Four sets of footsteps drifted off into the darkness.

The only sound was Dylan counting under his breath.

Lourdes strained her ears, waiting for the sound of an engine starting, but there was nothing but unmarred silence.

Then she heard it, the click of an insect. A snort of an animal followed.

The bandits must be far enough away that the night sounds felt safe enough to exhale.

"I think they're gone." She leaned up to look around.

The fire was now just a hulking mass of black with a glow of orange deep in the middle.

"Levi, will you check on the guards? Charlotte and Dylan, check our tents, see what they got." Lourdes pushed herself to her knees and crawled to Jimmy.

He moaned when she turned him over. Blood ran down one side of his face, pooling around his eye.

She pulled his head into her lap to get a better look at the cut.

"Lulu?" His voice was strained. Jimmy tried to open his eyes, but he winced. "Shit, what happened?"

Her mouth tried to pull up into a smile, but it faltered and froze into a grimace. They'd been warned. *She'd* been warned. Bandits were hitting tourists. Her pride could've gotten them all killed. "I'm sorry, this is all my fault." The tears rushed forth like a river bursting its banks. A few splattered on Jimmy's cheeks.

He reached up, thumbed a few. "Hey, no crying. They could've just as easily not hit us."

Levi emerged from behind the tents.

The two guards staggered beside him, both sporting similar red dribbles of blood, their hands zip-tied behind their backs.

"They're fine, we just need to cut them free," the rocker said.

Charlotte knelt beside her. "You guys okay?"

Lourdes could only nod.

The woman studied the gash on Jimmy's forehead. "It could be a concussion, so we should take turns sitting with you until daylight," the self-help guru said. "Seems they mostly took cash and credit cards. Levi might be missing a watch. Unfortunately…" she looked over her shoulder. "Unfortunately, they took Celeste's camera."

Shame punched Lourdes' heart, battering it, berating it, belittling her. Because she had to have her adventure a woman with a failing mind was going to lose any remnants of hers.

The scene already playing in her head was not the one in front of her.

Instead of Dylan comforting a distraught Celeste, the woman was dabbing a tissue to a cut on the forehead of one of the guards.

Jimmy sat up, freeing Lourdes to run to the older woman and wrap her in a tight hug.

"Lulu, is everything okay? Did they hurt you, honey?" her voice was muffled in her embrace.

"I'm so sorry, please forgive me. Charlotte said they took your camera, and I know that your trip meant everything to you, and your pictures…" A sob rode up on a hiccup. Lourdes hadn't cried this hard in a long time.

Not when the drugs stole her hair. Or, when she'd had to step away from the show she'd been part of for so long. Not even when the grim-faced doctor told her the cancer wasn't responding. The last time she'd cried this hard, she'd been standing in the shower, her fingers prodding a diamond-hard lump in her left breast. That was the only time she'd let herself cry, that moment before it'd all started.

Somewhere in her tears, the embrace turned, Celeste held her tight while Lourdes cried.

"You're going to forget and then you won't have anything," Lourdes whispered into Celeste's hair. "You're going to forget it all because of me."

"You're right, Lulu. I am going to forget." Celeste let go and held her at arm's length, her bright eyes smiling as they studied her. "I might forget what something looks like, but what will never leave me is how you made me feel. How all of you made me feel. The brain forgets, but the heart will always remember."

22

Her trilling cell phone invaded her restless sleep. Darla's clock flipped over to four-eleven. There were only two logical calls this early in the morning.

Both made her heart plunge.

Jimmy's name flashed on her screen.

She sighed a prayer of relief. "You'd better be bleeding." Her early morning voice sounded roughly like someone with a two-pack-a-day habit.

He laughed nervously. "Thanks to twelve stitches, not anymore."

Darla sat up in bed, his words a combination of an ice bath and espresso shot. "Wait, what? Jimmy, are you okay? Are the clients okay? What happened?"

The phone line shuffled. "Had a little run-in with some bandits."

"Bandits!" Her voice lost the smoker's husk and gained a pre-teen squeak. She swung her legs off the bed and switched on her bedside lamp. "Give it to me from the start."

He cleared his throat. "We were just turning in when they struck. Knocked out our guards. Stole our money, some jewelry."

"But you got hurt." Her chest heaved. Did they have something in the paperwork that protected them from this? What if the clients sued? What if someone else had gotten hurt? Died? There'd be no reason to ask for a raise if there was no company to give it.

"Butt of the gun to the temple."

"They had guns!"

A dog barked in the unit next door. Darla's squeak was now only audible to canines.

"I doubt they were loaded." Jimmy's words wobbled on a lie. It was his tell.

As if he spoke on an unsteady foundation, one she could blow off with a breath.

She took a deep steadying inhale. If she could feel his panic thousands of miles away, it must be deafening to the clients. "Where are you?"

He shuffled the phone again.

She could almost see him transferring it from his bad ear to his good ear, the one he used when he was about to say something he didn't like.

Something she'd seen him do for years. Something she doubted he even realized he did.

"We're back at the hotel. Everyone's fine." Jimmy cleared his throat again. "Darla, they knocked me out. I was hired to give these people their dying adventures, and to keep them safe. I couldn't do anything for them because they knocked me out."

She could hear it now.

The tears in his voice were as thick as the Florida humidity.

It was also as suffocating.

"Shhh…" she said, swaying on her bed as if she were comforting a baby. "You're okay, you're safe now."

"You're right. I'm just a little freaked out. I need your help though. They took all my cards, my cash. Got a little from the clients too, so we'll need to reimburse them. I might even need you to file an insurance claim."

Darla's mind sped up with the whine of a jet engine. "Ohhh-kaay."

The last time she'd looked at the bank account, it had just enough to pay the office rent, the insurance premium, and her salary for the next two months. If she had to wire money to Jimmy to replace what he lost, that'd clean them out faster than vultures on a corpse.

Then the insurance. Insurance companies were in the business of deferring, not paying. Dealing with them for her momma taught her that.

"Here's the rub. I don't think we have enough." He voiced what was in her heart. "I was doing the numbers in my head while we were driving back to the city. To replace what we lost, that'll clean out our account, right?"

Darla nodded into the phone before answering. "What else can I do?"

He sat there so long she worried they'd lost the connection.

Only when she called his name did he let an exasperated exhale cross the ocean.

"Can you talk to Enzo?"

"Jimmy." His name said all she needed it to.

Are you sure you want me to do that? Do you realize what door this opens? He's going to ask about the budget. It'll be safer to sell one of our kidneys. Maybe even both of our kidneys.

"I know, I know. Trust me, the last person I want to ask for money is Enzo, but I don't know what else to do."

It was Darla's turn to be silent. Would it be easier to just walk away? To let Jimmy figure this out so she could focus on her momma?

Or, could she use this in her favor? Tell Jimmy she walked into the lion's den for him, now it's time for her reward.

"It's not even five yet." She sighed. "I'll go see him first thing and call you back."

"Thank you," he said, his voice finally sounding stronger, steadier. "Darla, you know I couldn't live without you, right?"

His words caught her breath. Like a puzzle piece clicking into place. Sure, she wanted to wring his neck and feed him to wild hogs some days, but they were so enmeshed in each other's lives, if he were suddenly gone, it'd be like losing a limb.

"Yes, I know, why do you think I stick around and answer the phone at four-eleven a.m.?" She disguised the catch in a throat-clearing. "Take care of yourself. I'll call you in a bit." Darla ended the call and stared at the dark phone.

Had they been dancing around their relationship for so long neither of them noticed they were orbiting closer and closer together?

She could almost feel it. The gravitational pull of two stars, heating up, swirling around each other, faster and faster until…boom. Maybe it was time for the boom.

Time for Jimmy and Darla to become *Jimmy and Darla*.

She wouldn't need a raise then. If they were a couple, Jimmy could help out with her momma. After all, that was how they'd met.

She pushed off the bed and padded into her bathroom. Darla studied her reflection. Her blonde hair stood up in the back and dark circles smeared under her bright blue eyes. This was going to be one of those days of extra concealer and extra hairspray.

Out of the shower, she put a large glob of mousse in her hair and dried it straight, putting thick rollers in the crown to give it extra oomph. Today would be a day for sleek and professional, not for a brassy big-haired, big-mouth Texan. She needed to be CEO Darla, not assistant Darla.

The suit she picked was her favorite splurge. Fitted, it hugged her butt perfectly but was loose enough down her legs that she could walk with a long, confident stride. The bright blue color accented her eyes. The low-cut lace shell underneath would draw Enzo's attention right where it always landed.

Most days she'd tell him that her mouth was nowhere near her boobs, but this was one of those days she'd let him talk to whatever body part he wanted to, as long as she could get Jimmy some money without much of a fight.

The sun was straining through a low haze when she pulled up at his racquet club. A young valet tilted his head at her, seemingly torn between wondering who had a crazy CEO-dominatrix fetish, and why their hooker was showing up at seven a.m. in an older-than-he-was Celica.

"You can leave it nearby," she said. "This shouldn't take long."

She followed the *boings* and grunts until she found Enzo deep in a game of racquetball. Darla leaned against the wall outside their glassed court, watching the venture capitalist sprint and slam his racquet into a ball.

There was no doubt the man was as good-looking as his money. Tall, Italian, with a youthful face dotted by a graying beard. His wide shoulders heaved, the muscles rippling beneath his tight workout shirt.

If she hadn't had enough of his type in the past, she might've been attracted to him, but men who were as in love with themselves as Enzo rarely had enough room in their hearts for someone else.

"Darla," he said, wiping sweat off his face with a fluffy white towel.

"Enzo."

"You hand delivering my budget?" His dark eyes peered at her over the edge of one of those expensive water bottles that promised to keep water colder, wetter, waterier for eternity, or as long as a fifty-dollar water bottle could provide.

"There's been an…incident." Darla had practiced a half-dozen ways to start the conversation in the car, but there was no easy way to say it.

He paused stuffing his racquet in its case. "What kind of…incident?"

"Bandits robbed them in Namibia. No one was hurt, but they took all of the cash. I'll file an insurance claim, as soon as I get into the office, but in the meantime—"

"Jimmy needs money." Enzo folded his arms across his broad chest, the corded muscles in his forearms flexed. "Want some breakfast?"

Her mouth dropped open. Food was the furthest thing from her mind. "Thank you but I need to get into the office and start working on replacement cards, filing the insurance claim, and whatever else Jimmy needs me to do."

The investor pinned her to her spot under that dark gaze. As if probing her, checking for any cracks in her foundation.

Darla straightened her spine and pulled her shoulders back, tilting her chin up just enough to say 'I might be blonde, I might be petite, but I can still stab you in the heart with my stiletto.'

"You're too good for him," Enzo dropped his voice. "How about a cup of coffee, then?"

Now he was talking. Three hours into what already looked like a never-ending day and she was having inappropriate fantasies about coffee.

She followed him to the want-to-be-hip-but-still-in-a-country-club coffee bar, where he ordered a concoction that sounded like a lot of words to just say coffee with some milk and vanilla flavor.

When it was her turn, she ordered it black. Not because she didn't know what his too-many-words coffee drink was, but because she wanted to prove she had bigger balls than he did.

Coffees in hand, they sat at a small table in a lush outdoor garden.

Enzo leaned back, his left arm draped over the back of the chair, the face of his expensive watch winking at her in the sun. "No clients hurt?"

"Nope, a bit scared I'm sure, but they are all safe."

He nodded. "Good; lowers the chance of a lawsuit." Enzo took a long drink of his coffee. "You probably think I'm an asshole."

Darla's jaw dropped. Blatant honesty wasn't a play she'd expected the man to make. "I, uh…"

"You have to be a bit of one in my line of work." He dropped his gaze and brushed some dried flower petals off the table. "Just the same as you having to tuck your heart away in your former line of work."

The sips of coffee in her stomach threatened to travel back up. Darla swallowed again, pushing the acid back in its place, but all she succeeded in doing was choke on it, a cough exploding from her throat. She looked away, studying the tropical plants in this little bit of paradise she had no business being in.

"I'm not judging you," Enzo said. "The opposite, I admire you. That desire to be so much more than what life had given you." He straightened. "We're not that different. You and me."

Tears crowded her eyes like an angry mob. Trying to push their way through, but she clenched her jaw and forced her ducts to hold tight. Once they breached the barrier there'd be no stopping them. "What do you want?"

"I want to help you. And, believe it or not, I want to help Jimmy. I believe in his business. I wouldn't have invested if I didn't. But I'm worried about him, Darla. I'm concerned about his mental health, being around so much death."

Darla forced her gaze off the plants, back to the man sitting across from her.

His face loosened. Gone was the pinched brow, the tight jaw, the aloft nose.

"And, you're worried about him, too. I can see it," Enzo said. "I'd be a terrible businessman if I didn't admit to wanting to protect my investment. I think he needs a break. A reset. I'll loan Jimmy whatever he needs to bring the group home. Refund the people who didn't get their trips, offer to reschedule them if, well, if their health allows."

"Wait, you want to do what?"

"Bring him home, Darla. Convince him to take time off. Not to close the business, but a sabbatical. He'll listen to you. He trusts you."

His words slammed into her with the force of a bucking bronc.

How was she going to explain this to Jimmy? To Dylan and Charlotte, and the rest of the Diers?

It was their lives and she wasn't going to take away what little time they had left.

Enzo cocked his head to the side and studied her. "I'll even give you a little bonus. How about I pay for your mother's care for the next three months?"

Her jaw dropped. "How?"

He shrugged. "I've got to know everything about my investment. The money will be wired to the corporate account this morning. You'll want to run home and pack. I'll have the jet waiting for you. You'll do this for me, right?"

She stood, her chair screeching on the concrete.

"You're doing the right thing, Darla. Your mom needs you." He gripped her wrist, his hand searing her numb skin. "I need you."

Darla's feet carried her away from Enzo. The man who'd vacillated between friend and foe. The man who'd both saved her and asked her to sin.

The man who pretended to be just like her, but in all reality was nothing more than a hollow shell who only pretended to be human; only pretended to know who she was.

Only pretended it would be easy to choose between two people she loved.

23

A good strong cocktail worked wonders on the soul.

There was no denying, by the time Jimmy lifted his third drink, his hands shook less and his heart didn't sprint away at the sound of the waiter approaching from behind.

Renting a cabana at the hotel's rooftop pool was worth the small fortune he'd have to charge to help everyone relax. This, on top of the other small fortune he'd promised his guides, as soon as Darla wired him cash. Added to the first small fortune he'd spent already on Levi's night headlining Madison Square Garden, and the albeit, smaller fortune for Celeste to hike Machu Picchu.

It was funny how all these small fortunes were draining his account, like a submarine with a screen door.

Jimmy frowned at his drink; pink and frothy with a cheerful umbrella. Completely opposite of his mood. He attempted to drink himself happy with a carefree cocktail, but happiness wasn't at the end of a straw.

Maybe he should switch to something that matched his temper better. A dark and stormy. Or a shot of I'm-flat-ass-broke served out of a paper bag.

Luckily, he was used to being at the bottom of the barrel. It wasn't his first time to be down. However, he was not out.

Instead, this was where he thrived. Where he had to get creative to climb up. Had to do whatever it took, become whoever it took, to crawl out the other side and thrust his arms up in the air and shout, "fuck you!" to whoever doubted him. Jimmy relished being so low he had nothing to lose.

He rubbed his lips, remembering the feel of Lourdes' kiss. His mouth tingled, chiding him that he *did* have something to lose. Some*one* to lose.

A hand slapped his shoulder.

Jimmy jumped, spilling the sweet cocktail down his arm. A curse slipped from his mouth.

"Mate, I wish I had a few more years left in me." Levi sat on the lounge chair across from him, with Dylan following. "I could write a helluva song about bandits in the night." He held his drink up, and the young man clinked glasses.

"I know, man," Dylan slurred. "That was insane. The guns, the way the men just came out of nowhere. And, Lourdes—Lulu—standing up to them like a badass. It was just so…badass!" The boy tossed back a good bit of his drink, his face blanching before he managed to get it all down.

Jimmy leaned into Levi. "How many of those has he had?"

"Second one, mate." The rocker dropped his voice. "I told the bartender to go easy on the liquor. He's mostly drinking flavored soda."

"Good man."

The young man prattled on, rehashing the robbery Jimmy had been knocked out during for the billionth time. Suddenly, Dylan's excitement skidded to a stop and his brow pinched, his facing pivoting to remorse. "I hope my real death is as exciting as my near death." He sniffed and rubbed his nose on his sleeve. "My whole life, and that's the most exciting thing that's ever happened to me." The boy stared into space, his light brown eyes filling with tears.

Jimmy didn't have a lot of young adults go through Dire's Club. It wasn't that they didn't die, they just did it surrounded by family.

Dylan's presence on this trip was an anomaly, not just for the young man, but for everyone with them.

What was it like to be part of a group of people dying, like him, but who'd lived two or three times his short lifetime? Did he feel cheated?

"How old are you, Dylan?" Levi asked, his jovial spirit dampened by the younger man's tears.

"Twenty-three."

A curse fled Levi's lips on an exhale.

Dylan wiped his face with the heel of his palm. "I've been thinking." His voice broke, and he cleared his throat before another long drink. "I've been thinking about what I'll miss most from not living, and I think… I think it'll be not having a family."

The aging rock star snorted. "You ask me that question at your age, and I would've said the girls."

The boy shrugged. "Maybe I would've been a terrible dad. Mine wasn't awful, he just didn't know how to relate to a son who went to college at twelve."

Jimmy lifted his glass to his mouth. "Sometimes fathers get the sons they need, not the ones they want. At least I told myself that every time my dad and I fought."

Those fights were tattooed into his memory. They were like cooking frogs, gradually turning up the heat so they wouldn't jump out of the pot. Especially after his mom died.

The tension in the house warmed, bubbles of an argument roiling beneath the surface. As he aged, the temperature had soared, until the night it'd all come to a head. Raging and angry, their fight had spilled out of the house and into the street like a pot of pissed-off water boiling over.

It didn't help that when the cops had shown up, the men his dad called brothers because of a shared uniform rather than shared DNA, his father had turned his back on his son, his own blood, and told them to take him to holding.

When he'd been released five days later, Jimmy didn't go back home, didn't go back to the world of drunken fights and lashes with a belt so severe that it'd broken the skin. He didn't go back to the man who'd given him a name, but little else.

He couldn't go back to the home where the memory of his mom had faded like wallpaper in the sun.

He'd walked away. New life. New name.

"Me, I loved my Da," Levi said. "You always hear of rockers and their torrid relationships with their parents, but mine were great. My dad taught me how to play the fiddle, my mum taught me the piano." The older man cupped Dylan's shoulder and gave it a gentle shake. "I think the fact that you worry you'd be a bad father would've made you a decent one."

Dylan gave him a weak smile and nodded.

"Here, let me buy you another drink." Levi stood and threw back the rest of his drink. "And, when I say me buy, I mean Jimmy will buy us another drink."

He opened his mouth to say something about keeping Dylan from overdoing it, but Levi winked, silencing his warning.

Alone in the cabana, Jimmy pulled his phone out and tried Darla again. She'd said she got cash from Enzo, but she was cagey about how the money would be transferred to him. Several hours of calls only went to her voicemail.

Darla has never been out of touch before. And, she wouldn't while I'm on a trip. Unless something happened to her mom...

That was the other thing that'd bonded him to Darla. Granted, he was his mother's caregiver when he was much younger, but somehow, he didn't think it would matter if he was eight or forty-eight. No one was ready to face caring for a sick parent. Parents were for comforting children, scaring away monsters, and kissing boo-boos. There was no manual for shooing away a mother's monster.

Like the eleventy-billion times he'd called Darla before, it went straight to voicemail. He didn't bother leaving a message; he'd left her several already and at this point, he was torn between anger and concern.

Maybe both. It was so unlike her to not even send him a message to let him know something happened.

Even if the unthinkable, she always thought about him.

Unless...

A siren wailed in the distance. Its banshee screech bouncing off the buildings. Bouncing off his heart. Settling in the pit of his stomach. The siren grew louder, amplifying the dread pumping through his veins.

What if something had happened to Darla?

Visions of her demise flashed through Jimmy's brain, like a movie on fast-forward. Darla lying dead in the middle of a busy street. Darla raped and murdered in a dark alley. Darla mangled under her old convertible, flipped upside down in the Everglades. Darla shoved in the marine biologist's freezer, waiting to be fed to the fishes.

He hit her name again on his phone. This time the message wouldn't be for her. This time it would be for whoever found her body. To let them know he'd take care of everything, her funeral, her mom, all of it, because she always took care of him.

Jimmy plugged his free ear, since the wailing siren was louder than the blood rushing through his ears.

The phone rang once.

Twice.

Maybe they'd found her. Had she listed him as her 'in case of emergency'? If not, they might not answer. Why haven't they had this conversation before?

She was his 'in case of emergency,' it seemed only natural he'd be hers. A more responsible, adult version of the 'best friends forever' broken heart necklaces.

A third time. Then...the wailing of the siren filled his ear, putting his fear into overdrive.

"Hey, Jimmy," Darla answered over the cacophony.

"Darla, you're alive. Right? I mean, you're okay."

The *bee-doo* rang out in stereo, the siren on the phone in perfect sync with the siren outside his hotel.

"Where are you?"

Where her voice didn't answer, the sounds around her did.

A car horn blaring filled both of his ears.

The siren faded now, moving off into the distance. Street sounds, cars, chatter, the chaos of humanity.

All of it assaulted him.

He pushed off the lounge chair and crossed the rooftop in a few long strides. Jimmy leaned over the edge, his gaze skimming the street just six stories below.

It didn't take long to spot her.

Her thick blonde hair was a beacon on the busy street. She stared at the door of the hotel; her suitcase clutched tightly in her hands.

As if sensing being watched, Darla looked up. There was something different about her bright blue eyes. Whether it was the distance of seventy-odd feet or the fact she'd just finished an eighteen-hour flight, but something was…off.

A harshness in her eyes. Tension on her face.

"I brought your money." Even her voice had a sharp edge, the soft Texas corners gone. "And, I'm here to help."

24

Numbers and letters danced on the page. Formulas, that to the non-mathematician, would appear as gibberish. While Dylan was fluent in math, even a master at it, the equations now jumbled around his mind with no rational coherence. Like someone suffering from the type of head injury where they wake up suddenly speaking a language other than their native tongue.

He was now no longer confident in his hypothesis. No longer confident it was even grounded in anything that wasn't crackpot science.

Dylan stood from the particleboard desk in the hotel and paced the room. The soles of his sneakers smacked on the tile floor. The only sound competing was the wind through the open French doors.

The few pieces of furniture were scattered in the room like distant stars. He avoided them, afraid to get pulled into the orbit of his bed or a chair and risk falling into it. There was no guarantee he'd get up, get back to work.

After looking down the black hole of a gun, he didn't even want to travel to Switzerland for his adventure. Like an actual black hole, the shot from that gun could've been his undoing. It would've pierced his head, ripped through his brain, shattered his skull. But it hadn't. He'd fought that event horizon, so maybe it was possible to stand up to another.

Assuming he wanted to.

He glanced at the clock on the bedside table. The group had agreed to meet up for dinner in just a few minutes. A final meal before the next day's flight to Zurich.

The last supper.

Plop him in the middle of the table, because the next day he was going to be marched to the cross.

Adventures were for coloring outside the lines. For facing danger and living through it. For being so scared dying didn't seem so terrifying.

While the thought of presenting to a team of the world's best scientists scared the crap out of him, no one was going to die if Dylan made a miscalculation.

The death would be his legacy.

The only casualty would be proving his father right.

He was always punching above his weight. He had no business finishing high school at age eleven. A pre-teen had no business going to college.

Instead of getting his driver's license, Dylan had walked across the stage with his master's degree. Instead of going to senior prom, he'd started his own software company.

And, instead of spending some of the final days doing something truly memorable before his brain tumor robbed him of his conviction, robbed him of his life, he was trying to prove an impossible theory was just that, impossible.

Why would anyone want to go back in time?

The past was there for a reason. Like a fossil captured in amber, if cracked open it would disintegrate, but left encased it could be studied, fretted over, forgotten about.

Was his hypothesis the misfiring of a dying brain?

A thin line separated genius from madness. It wasn't a matter of *if* Dylan crossed that line, but how long ago had he done so?

A searing pain clawed through his head. He pushed himself from the desk and stumbled into the bathroom. The pill bottles were stacked up like soldiers ready for battle.

He didn't bother looking to see which one he popped open. At this point, it didn't matter if it masked the pressure at the base of his skull or alleviated it.

Migraines plagued him, just thinking about his presentation.

Maybe this pain wasn't a result of stress or his tumor. Maybe it was from the drinks he'd had on the rooftop with Levi. Dylan had never had a hangover before. Was it supposed to feel like his head was going to explode?

A buzzing filled the air like an annoying fly. With one hand over his eyes, he stumbled back into the bedroom and found his phone dancing across the bed. "Hello?" His voice was rough, like he'd lived three lifetimes within his twenty-three years.

"Hey, Dylan, got a second?" Iain Johnston, his company's COO, sounded like he was more than half a world away. A galaxy away.

He dropped on the edge of the bed. Work conversations never took *just a second*. "Yeah, Iain, what's going on?"

The man hesitated, the background noise filling the space of their connection. "It's your dad. He flipped out today."

He fell back against the bed. "Shit, guess he got the papers from the attorneys."

"And, then he set them on fire in the lobby."

Great, nothing like being overly dramatic to get your point across, Dad.

"Was anyone hurt?" That was the other part of the reason he'd wanted to go on the Dire's Club trip.

To be far away from his father when his lawyers drew up the legal documents for how his company and his fortune would be handled after his death.

It wasn't that his dad wouldn't receive anything. After all, Dylan owed it to his father for raising and supporting him.

It was just that his dad assumed he'd get everything.

"No, luckily, security was looking for him," Iain said, pausing a beat before continuing. "How's the trip going? You sound...tired. Are you resting? Eating enough? What about the pain? You're not overdoing it, are you?" The man peppered him with questions.

Where his father saw Dylan as a source of income, Iain stepped in as the worrisome father figure.

"I'm fine." He'd save the robbed-by-bandits story for after he was back in Boston. "But hey, I gotta go, they're waiting on me for dinner."

"The presentation is up next, right? This could be huge, if you pull it off. Break a leg."

He ended the call and dropped the phone next to him. The headache numbed to manageable.

With each second that ticked by, his resolve decayed like an atomic half-life. Why would he want to go back in time? His father's incessant ridicule filled his past.

No son of his would spend more time with his nose in a book than out perfecting a spiral pass. O'Keefes were athletes; lacrosse, tennis, even rugby. Not nerds. Not brainiacs. They were supposed to wear letter jackets, not skip high school.

Dylan didn't want to go back to that. He didn't want to spend another minute reliving the past. If anything, he wanted to fast forward to his fate. To finally be free of his father's control.

Somehow, getting on that plane tomorrow felt like he was still just a scared little boy under his father's control. If he was correct, he'd be just rewinding himself to that same boy who'd wanted nothing more than to be loved for who he was.

Cherished, no matter what.

25

Group dynamics were just that. Dynamic. Charlotte marveled at how the addition of one person could change everything. It was something she'd always been able to pick up as a trial lawyer. Which juror was in charge? Who was the one person she needed to connect with? Who could be swayed with fact, and who needed to be touched with emotion?

When Jimmy's assistant had shown up, unannounced from the way his mood shifted, the dynamics became…explosive.

Especially as the group gathered for dinner their last night in Africa. Tomorrow, they'd be on a plane heading to Switzerland so Dylan could have his dying adventure—conducting an experiment at a world-renowned lab.

Lourdes—or Lulu as she constantly reminded everyone when they slipped—furrowed her brow. Gone was the adrenalin of being held up. The light that burned from within her had waned.

For a little bit, Charlotte saw the *telenovela* star for who she was before cancer had stolen her hair, stole her health, stole her beauty. Now, dark cushions cradled her tired eyes, and her color resembled the pale hue of adobe.

Celeste chewed on her lower lip, gnawing off her brightly colored lipstick. The ice in her forgotten cocktail was nearly gone.

Charlotte sat next to her at the dinner table. "Hey, you doing okay?" Deep down she had the urge to hug the woman. Maybe it was the far-off look in her eyes, as if she looked into a place that couldn't be seen, only remembered. "Celeste?"

The older woman stirred as if awoken from a memory. "Oh, Charlotte, dear. I've been trying to recall where I know that pretty young lady from. Has she been with us this whole time?" She leaned in close, whispering behind her hand.

She inclined her head toward Celeste, lowering her voice. "That's Darla, Jimmy's assistant. We met her in Miami. She got here earlier today."

Her friend exhaled, slouching against the back of her chair. Relief washed down her face, but it didn't manage to clear away the concern knitting her brow. "I'm afraid it's beginning." Her voice quivered.

What would it feel like to constantly worry that every misplaced object or forgotten face was the beginning of the end?

Charlotte had a good memory, but it was far from perfect. Too often she'd find herself forgetting what she wanted to remember; the feel of Jason's hand in hers, the sound of his snore, what she said to him that final morning. Somehow those memories were gone, but she could recall a closing argument from a long-ago trial.

There was nothing fair about Celeste's disease, but memories weren't fair.

Forgotten or remembered.

She pulled the woman in for a side hug.

Dylan skulked into the dining room, falling into the chair opposite her. He tossed his journal on the table and his shoulders hunched forward.

"You're up next," Charlotte said. "Are you ready?"

"No, the numbers aren't adding up." He scratched the back of his head with his pen. "I've got to present to a team there before they'll run the experiment, defend my thesis in a way, but this is all shit." He threw the pen down and sunk even farther in his seat. "I don't want to be the kid who got to play with million-dollar equipment because he's dying. I want to be the man with a breakthrough."

This was the other thing Charlotte was good at. Seeing someone's self-doubt and teaching them how to conquer it.

"It'll only be scary until you're there. Once you start your presentation, your fear and self-doubt will be pushed aside by your instinct and your flawless knowledge."

A cynical laugh erupted. "No offense, but you get paid to say that."

She shrugged. "No one's paying me now."

"Yeah, have you had to stand in front of a room full of people to plead a case for something you believe, and they are there to rip it apart? The people you speak to are there because they *want* to believe you."

"To answer your first question, the entire time I was an attorney. I argued cases in front of judges and juries who waited for me to mess up." She perched her elbows on the table. "Anyway, I'd rather talk to a room full of critics instead of a room full of fans any day."

Dylan tilted his head. "Why?"

She took a deep breath and brushed her bangs from her eyes. It'd been a long time since Charlotte had faced a roomful of critics.

People with pinched faces, arms folded across their chests, and narrowed eyes. Her first—her hardest—had been a room half-filled with people who thought they were attending a Lion's Club meeting.

"They expect you to fail, and if you do, you meet their expectations. But if you succeed, you gain their respect."

He nodded as he sipped his water, obviously taking in her words.

The day that'd launched her career, as *the* Charlotte Claybrooke, peeked out from the corner of her memory.

The blog she'd started as a way to work through her grief had grown in followers to the point they'd started meeting in back rooms of restaurants.

The Charlotte Club was what they'd called themselves. People who'd come together to embrace their loss. Embrace it, give it a name, and crush it.

Embrace it. Name it. Crush it.

A mantra she'd told herself daily, but the words never melted into her heart.

It'd taken a while to work up the courage to attend one in person. She'd picked Tulsa, Oklahoma. A place where she knew no one. Where no one knew her.

Not the *real* Charlotte.

She almost didn't go. When she finally went, the meeting almost didn't happen, because of a scheduling mix-up between two groups. Finally, they had agreed to share the hour.

It'd been weird. Sitting there, half the faces beaming at her, the other half scowling. Half the room vibrating with excitement, the other half checking their watches. She'd decided to speak to the scowlers.

Her presentation had been rough. Read from handwritten notes, hastily scribbled on the plane. The cadence of her words hadn't quite worked verbally, as much as they did on paper.

She'd made it through.

The scowlers had leaned forward, some even wiped tears away. Her fans, well, they had turned into this weird combination of excited, elated, and heartbroken.

"Find the grumpiest person in the room. That's what I did," she told Dylan.

The man was probably long gone by now, but his image was still seared into her mind.

He was someone who wore his decades like a suit of armor. The deep lines in his face, the tanned-leather skin on his arms, the corded muscles of someone who'd gotten them from hard work, not time in the gym.

"There was a man, I think he would've rather been getting a root canal. Without the drugs. At first, I didn't want to look at him, but I knew if I could win him over, I could win anyone over."

As Charlotte talked that day all those years ago in Tulsa, the man's arms had loosened, his face had softened to the point that his jaw had gone slack.

"How did you do it?" Dylan asked.

She smiled. "I spoke my truth. It was rough at first, especially when I tried to talk to everyone, but something told me to talk to *him*."

He'd come up to her afterward, his ball cap proclaiming him a veteran of a foreign war in hand, and the wrinkles of his face carrying water like a river.

"His wife had died two years earlier, and that was the first time he'd let himself cry for her."

That man, Dennis, had hugged her with the ferocity of someone holding on for dear life. They'd stayed at the restaurant through the afternoon and well into dinner service.

Talking about grief, losing the loves of their lives, and how hard it was to continue.

How he could go days without knowing what day of the week it was.

She shared how, in the weeks following Jason's death, she'd spend her entire day sitting next to his freshly dug grave.

That night Charlotte had learned everyone grieved, everyone hurt, but it was the process of their grieving that was intensely private.

She couldn't walk them through it, but she could be a lighthouse, guiding them through the fog. To keep them from crashing into rocks.

However, not even lighthouses were permanent. Their gears ground to a halt. They ran out of fuel. The light waned.

She blinked away the tears brought on by the memory of the man who was the foundation of her lighthouse.

A man she'd met only once, but who'd changed her life.

"Talk to that one person. You might find someone who's been struggling and something you say might be the inspiration they need to continue to their own breakthrough. Don't embellish, don't try to overcompensate. Just be the charismatic, brilliant Dylan O'Keefe we've come to adore." Charlotte offered him a sly smile. "Knock 'em dead."

26

Jimmy needed to sprint. It was his first thought when he awoke. Never mind that they needed to be checked out of the hotel in just a few hours, and be on their way to Switzerland for Dylan's excursion. Never mind that a hangover squeezed his brain with the grip of a bodybuilder.

Never mind that he wanted to knock on Lourdes' door to remind himself what her lips felt like.

No, he needed to run.

Run away from the concern over why Darla had shown up unannounced, leaving her mother behind without anyone to care for her in case of an emergency, and leaving his business unattended.

Luckily, their hotel had a small gym with an ancient treadmill that no one else wanted to use. He powered up the machine to an easy warm-up jog, letting his legs work through what his mind couldn't figure out.

She could've wired the money, but maybe she wanted to finally be included on a trip.

He'd always wanted to invite her. To make it a perk for all of her hard work. Jimmy had always assumed Darla wouldn't leave the country with her mom in a nursing home.

She smiled. "I spoke my truth. It was rough at first, especially when I tried to talk to everyone, but something told me to talk to *him*."

He'd come up to her afterward, his ball cap proclaiming him a veteran of a foreign war in hand, and the wrinkles of his face carrying water like a river.

"His wife had died two years earlier, and that was the first time he'd let himself cry for her."

That man, Dennis, had hugged her with the ferocity of someone holding on for dear life. They'd stayed at the restaurant through the afternoon and well into dinner service.

Talking about grief, losing the loves of their lives, and how hard it was to continue.

How he could go days without knowing what day of the week it was.

She shared how, in the weeks following Jason's death, she'd spend her entire day sitting next to his freshly dug grave.

That night Charlotte had learned everyone grieved, everyone hurt, but it was the process of their grieving that was intensely private.

She couldn't walk them through it, but she could be a lighthouse, guiding them through the fog. To keep them from crashing into rocks.

However, not even lighthouses were permanent. Their gears ground to a halt. They ran out of fuel. The light waned.

She blinked away the tears brought on by the memory of the man who was the foundation of her lighthouse.

A man she'd met only once, but who'd changed her life.

"Talk to that one person. You might find someone who's been struggling and something you say might be the inspiration they need to continue to their own breakthrough. Don't embellish, don't try to overcompensate. Just be the charismatic, brilliant Dylan O'Keefe we've come to adore." Charlotte offered him a sly smile. "Knock 'em dead."

26

Jimmy needed to sprint. It was his first thought when he awoke. Never mind that they needed to be checked out of the hotel in just a few hours, and be on their way to Switzerland for Dylan's excursion. Never mind that a hangover squeezed his brain with the grip of a bodybuilder.

Never mind that he wanted to knock on Lourdes' door to remind himself what her lips felt like.

No, he needed to run.

Run away from the concern over why Darla had shown up unannounced, leaving her mother behind without anyone to care for her in case of an emergency, and leaving his business unattended.

Luckily, their hotel had a small gym with an ancient treadmill that no one else wanted to use. He powered up the machine to an easy warm-up jog, letting his legs work through what his mind couldn't figure out.

She could've wired the money, but maybe she wanted to finally be included on a trip.

He'd always wanted to invite her. To make it a perk for all of her hard work. Jimmy had always assumed Darla wouldn't leave the country with her mom in a nursing home.

All through dinner she'd avoided him. Avoided his questions. Avoided his gaze.

Was Darla mad?

He cranked it up to a light sprint.

Maybe...

Maybe she was pissed about having to get close to the marine biologist to get an inside scoop on Charlotte's wish. He hadn't asked her to do anything immoral. Just make friends with the guy.

Unless...

Jimmy upped the speed.

Unless something had happened. Maybe the guy wasn't as nerdy as Darla made him out to be. Maybe he'd assaulted her. Harmed her, and she was running to him for help.

That had to explain why she'd seemed so afraid. In the years he'd known her, his tiny Texan wasn't afraid of anything. The bigger the adversary, the tougher Darla got.

This had to be bad. Really, *really* bad.

He hit stop and let the treadmill wind down. The gym was the last place he needed to be. His best friend needed him.

Jimmy jogged through the lobby, skidding to a stop when he saw a blonde ponytail pacing behind a potted tree.

"I've been thinking about what you asked me to do. Can we negotiate? There's only two left." Darla held herself tight, her free arm clutching her waist. "These are dying wishes we're talking about, not some weekend in the Hamptons." Another pause. "I know what you promised." She rubbed her temple. "I can't do that. I won't do that." She whirled, and her gaze collided with Jimmy's. "I've got to go."

The tree stood between them for several seconds.

Darla's face was a Salvador Dali painting of emotion. Defeat smeared across her brow. Strokes of anger flushed red across her cheekbones. Her blue eyes lit up with remorse. Her mouth twisted in fear, paling the hue to a dying pink.

"Are you okay?" Jimmy said through the plant. "Who hurt you?"

She shook her head. "I'm fine." A frond danced with her words.

He moved two steps around the tree, but she scooted away.

Was she afraid of *him*? Had he done something to hurt her?

"Darla, you're starting to scare me."

She broke their stare, and glanced in the direction of the restaurant. "I'm craving pancakes. Want pancakes? Let's get breakfast." The words tumbled over each other, shoving aside punctuation.

"I need to shower."

"Have pancakes with me, Jimmy," she pleaded.

He nodded. This was less about Darla's sugar craving and more about something she had to say.

They settled into a table near the front of the restaurant.

Darla ordered the biggest, sweetest breakfast on the menu, and Jimmy asked for toast with black coffee.

The wall his assistant put up was like bulletproof glass. He could see her there, on the other side, but every time he tried to shatter it with a word, it ricocheted back to him.

Finally, after their food was delivered and she shoved a few mouthfuls down, he spotted a chip in her wall.

"Are you going to talk now?" Jimmy asked.

She shoved another bite of whipped cream with pancake in her mouth. A dollop of the cream clung to the corner of her lips. Darla licked at it, but still missed the whipped cream.

He leaned across the table and scooped it up on his fingertip, offering it to her before putting it in his mouth, when only a blank stare answered him. "You never really explained why you're here. Not that I'm not happy to see you, but your mom, and filing the claims from the robbery, and just all the other stuff that goes on back in the office." He'd never had to pull the boss card with her, but maybe it was time to reach for it, just to remind her who he was. "You didn't ask me if you can come, you just showed up. That's…unusual."

"Enzo sent me."

Jimmy flinched. He hadn't expected her to have a boss card of her own. "What for?"

Darla frowned and looked away. "Guess he wanted to make sure the credit cards made it."

"Over-nighting would've cost a helluva lot less, and wouldn't have left your mother an ocean away."

It was her turn to flinch. The leaving-your-momma-behind play was a low blow, but he needed it to knock the last of her wall down.

"Is that who you were on the phone with?" Jimmy asked.

She shoved more whipped cream into her mouth. "Switzerland's off," Darla mumbled once she swallowed.

His coffee shot up his throat at her words. "What do you mean *off?*"

"I mean that running Dylan's experiment is off."

"Why? I thought Enzo knew people." His legs twitched, wanting to go, needing to run. Far from Darla, far from a young man who'd not only been denied living a full life, but was now being denied the one thing he wanted to do before he died.

Jimmy wanted to run far from this life.

Maybe he could even start a new one again.

"It doesn't matter how many people he knows. We can't do it."

"You haven't answered why," he barked. The rage inside him flexed its claws. The one that lived deep inside him. Besides a name, it was the only other thing he'd inherited from his father. "Call Enzo and tell him it's unacceptable. We're going to get on that plane, fly to Switzerland and—"

Darla slammed her hands on the table and pushed herself up. "No, Jimmy, we're going to get on that plane and fly back to Miami."

He shot out of his seat, the chair clattering on the floor. "What's going on, Darla?"

She narrowed her eyes to steely blue slits, the color of the bay right before a storm. "Enzo's pulling the plug."

"On the lab?"

"On all of this. The lab, Charlotte's adventure. Us. He's bringing us home, Jimmy. It's over. Dire's Club is over."

Her words echoed and turned, twisted, and floated. Taking up residence in the air all around him, and in his heart.

That was why she'd avoided him. Why she was sent.

To bring him home. To bring his Diers home.

How was he going to tell Dylan? Charlotte?

Lourdes.

He wasn't ready to give up his time with her. Her magnetic pull was too strong. Sending her back to Mexico City would rip him in two.

"Why?" His voice was softer now. "Why is he bringing us home now?"

Darla glanced down. Her face red, and her chest heaved, like she'd just sprinted a marathon. "We're broke, Jimmy. We've got no money in the account and Enzo gave us just enough to get home. There's nothing we can do."

The force of her words crashed into him like a tsunami, tearing the ground out from under him, tossing him about, the debris of his life, of his mistakes, plowing into him.

What if's floated around him.

What if he'd finished high school and gone to college? What if he'd gone to business school, had a better network of investors?

What if he'd charged more?

His assistant, his best friend, looked at him with thick tears running down her face.

What if he'd never put Darla in this impossible position?

"No," Jimmy whispered. "I've got emails out to people. I can get a loan, second mortgage on my condo."

"Stop." Sobs shook her small body. "Just stop. It's too late."

Too late was the diagnosis of a disease. Too late were the words his father had said when Jimmy rushed home from school to find his mom had passed without him there.

Too late was how he'd felt when he'd found his father's obituary online.

He'd always vowed his clients, his Diers, would never know the power of those two words. Until now…

"But, I'll—we've got credit cards—there has to be a way." He ran his hand through his hair, pacing a few short steps.

"We could always win the money you need, mate."

Jimmy twirled at Levi's voice.

There stood his Diers. Shoulder to shoulder.

Connected by their collective dying.

"How long have you been there?" he asked, swallowing down another wave of nausea.

"Long enough to know you're out of money," Charlotte said, her mouth pulled into her signature soft smile.

"And, that my experiment's off," Dylan added.

His gaze drifted to Lourdes. Her face was unreadable, the theater mask back in place, covering whatever she was thinking. Feeling.

"But I think it's safe to say none of us want this to end," Celeste said.

They nodded in agreement.

Levi's lined face pulled up into a wide grin. "Like I said, we can always win what you need. My band once found itself flat broke. A few lucky bets at the casino was all it took."

Jimmy pinched the bridge of his nose. His headache, his heartache, worsened looking at the people he'd disappointed but stood ready to help him. His father had relished in reminding him he was a loser.

Although the bastard was long dead, he expected him to lurk around every corner, ready to jump out and shout 'loser!' at every mistake.

"Guys, they call it gambling for a reason," he said. "We could just as easily lose it all. Don't worry, I'm going to figure this out. We're going to be on our way soon, and we won't miss a beat."

The group stayed silent for a moment, as if ruminating on adventures not taken. A raucous party interrupted by the money police.

"I've changed my mind." Dylan's soft voice crept across the restaurant.

Jimmy gripped the young man's upper arms and looked him square in the eye, calling forth everything ounce of truth he'd ever told. "Don't worry, this won't stop us from granting your wish."

He smirked and threw his journal to the side. "Good, I have a new wish. I've always wanted to cheat a casino."

"Wait, whoa, no, no." He backed away from his group. "It's in the rules that we don't break any laws, everything is on the up and up."

"I don't mean really cheating, just *sort of* cheating. Cheating with my mind, not with cards up my sleeves."

"Counting cards is still illegal."

"Only if they prove we can do it."

There was a gleam in the boy's eye. The same one from the rooftop when he'd proclaimed that nearly dying at the hands of bandits was the most exciting thing he'd done.

Was his wish to test a ground-breaking hypothesis a young genius trying to leave his mark before being ripped off the planet too soon?

Was it the sign of a man who'd missed adolescence because he'd worked it away in school?

Was this his last chance to play?

Jimmy opened his mouth, the promise of possibility looming on the horizon like the rising sun, but reality clouded over and he shook his head. "I appreciate the gesture, but the plane is going back to Miami."

Lourdes tilted her head and held her phone up. A smile crept across her beautiful face. The smile of a mischievous goddess, eager to bestow her gifts on her followers.

Jimmy would follow her *anywhere* with that smile.

"You think you're the only one with access to a private jet? We'll leave for Monaco this afternoon."

27

Charlotte blinked at her reflection, dazzled by the sequins of the gown twinkling back at her. The spaghetti straps rested against her shoulders, dipping to a sweetheart neckline that managed to look both sexy and classy.

The dress brushed the ground and a perfectly placed slit gave a peek-a-boo view of one of her thighs as she walked.

The beige gown covered in both silver and gold sequins emanated light. It was as though the glow came from her, not the megawatt dress.

In addition to paying for the group to fly to Monaco, Lourdes had insisted that everyone was going to have the full Monaco casino experience, black tie and all.

Charlotte had instinctively reached for a simple black dress. Something that would allow her to fade into the background. Forgotten, overlooked. For some reason, she'd kept circling back to this dress, like a hungry vulture.

"Aren't you glad I ripped that hideous black thing out of your hands?" Lourdes appeared in her bathroom doorway.

The *telenovela* star had also offered to do her hair and makeup. All those years at the receiving end of makeup artists' skillful hands, Lourdes had claimed to have picked up a few tricks.

"You're luminous. Sit."

Charlotte obeyed, hitting the velvet ottoman with an exhale.

"Heavy, huh," she said, gently brushing Charlotte's long brown hair. "You'll get used to it, and when you take it off tonight, you'll feel weightless." The woman smiled, and a soft laugh tumbled from her throat. "I wonder if that's what it'll feel like when our souls leave our body. As if we'd just taken off the heaviest dress."

Charlotte tried to leave her smile in place for her friend, but it faltered. Somehow she didn't think it'd feel like taking off a luxurious ball gown instead, it would feel like shucking shackles. Chains that'd held her to her body, to the world, keeping her from Jason.

A hostage to life.

Lourdes separated the top and bottom half of her hair. "I'll say it again. I'm insanely jealous of your hair," she murmured. "What do you think about an updo, to show off this gorgeous neck and skin."

She could only manage a weak nod and a weaker smile.

"Is there someone special in your life?" the starlet asked, through a mouthful of bobby pins. "Boyfriend, husband, girlfriend?"

"I had a fiancé."

"Ahh...past tense. We've got a lot more of those than future tense." Lourdes winked. "At least we have the present tense."

The first year after Jason had died, she'd catch herself referring to him in the present tense. It was a glitch. Momentarily forgetting he was no longer with her, no longer alive. Like a computer that refused to save, Charlotte's brain couldn't write the new memories.

Now it felt as though Jason had never been in the present, and any glimpses of a future felt more dream-like than real.

Now, all she had *was* the past tense.

Her eyes burned and she blinked, shooing away the tears. It was as unfamiliar as thinking of Jason alive.

There'd come a point when crying was no longer a relief. When it no longer eased the ache in her heart. When the tears spent had only made her eyes puffy and dehydrated her.

It was as meaningless as bingeing on a bag of jellybeans. Might help her immediate hunger, but an hour later, she'd feel empty again.

Charlotte cleared her throat; cleared the phantom emotion that threatened to strangle her. "What about you? You've never talked about if someone waited for you at home."

One corner of Lourdes' cupid's bow mouth pulled up into a mischievous grin.

It was the kind of smile that preceded suggestions like breaking into a liquor cabinet, stealing dad's car, or toilet papering a rival's house.

"I've dated enough men who spend more time in front of a mirror than me. Do you know what's good about dying? No more fear. No more worrying about what someone thinks, because I'm dying and soon, I'll only be a memory. No more worrying about rejection, because it's not as bad as death. No more worrying about what other people think, because what do I care when I'm dead and gone? Death is quite liberating." Lulu pinned Charlotte's dark brown hair into place. "Can you keep a secret?" she whispered at their reflection.

"Of course."

Lourdes sat next to her. "The night the bandits struck…Jimmy and I were…I, um, I kissed him. I don't know what came over me. Maybe it was the wine, but…" She took a deep breath. "I've been with some of the most handsome men in the world, and they didn't make me feel a tenth of what *he* did in that kiss."

She clasped her friend's hand. "Lulu, I can't say it's a surprise. I've seen how he looks at you, and how you look at him." For the first time in ten years, Charlotte missed that. She missed someone looking at her like she was the only person in the room. That feeling in the pit of her stomach like she'd taken the first plunge on a rollercoaster.

Lourdes closed her eyes. Her false lashes rested against her cheeks. "Which is why it was a terrible mistake."

"What do you mean? You just said he made you feel something."

Lourdes pushed herself up and leaned into the mirror, her ring finger rubbing some non-existent smudge under her eye. "There's a reason we're all here together. The dying. We can be as selfish as we want with each other. We're vampires, trying to suck as much from life as we can while we still have time. It's not fair to do that to the living."

She watched her friend staring at her reflection.

Lourdes wasn't looking at her expensive wig and perfectly made-up face. She didn't see the skin-tight red dress that accentuated her curves. Lourdes was looking into something much deeper. Something that only *she* could see in the mirror.

"Marcos and I had been together for a while. A power couple they called us. I broke things off when the doctor told me I needed a double mastectomy."

"Lulu…"

She shook her head and smiled. "He was nearly ten years younger than me, and while I was healthy and beautiful no one would whisper, but the minute I got sick, I knew my beauty would fade. I set him free." Lourdes turned from the mirror. "*Pues*, let's put some makeup on you so we can help Jimmy."

While she creamed, powdered, and highlighted Charlotte's face, Lourdes pinched her brow in concentration. When she moved out of the way for the reveal, Charlotte barely recognized herself.

Light shone from her cheekbones, and her eyes stood out like dark emeralds, the smoky, seductive eyeshadow cushioned her irises like velvet. Her full lips were tinted with the softest pink, enough to draw attention to her pout but not so much as to upstage her eyes.

"Wow," she breathed.

Lourdes smirked. "What would your ex say now?"

Charlotte let that designation float past her. It wasn't worth ruining the magic to correct her. "I think he'd be as speechless as I am. You're a magician."

"You're proof that there *is* beauty in death."

She breathed as deeply as the dress would allow. The way Lourdes was dying was ugly. Stealing the woman's beauty, taking from her what defined her womanhood. The way Levi was dying was brutal, albeit some might say appropriate. The way Celeste was dying was atrocious, slowly robbing her of everything that made her *her*. And

Dylan's was barbaric. A brilliant young man whose mind was killing him.

Since the days of Romeo and Juliet, suicide has been romanticized. The burden of living was simply too much for a fragile soul.

It was far uglier than what was killing her friends. It was a monster, inside her head and her heart. A monster that whispered she was a fraud. She didn't know the first thing about pushing past grief. The monster took every moment she smiled and turned it into guilt. For being alive.

For living.

There was no beauty in how Charlotte was dying.

It was the most hideous death of all.

28

Dylan looked more like a nervous young groom than a genius about to cheat a casino. He paced the elevator lobby. His tuxedo fit his tall, thin frame like a second skin and his normally longish, curly dark hair had been recently trimmed. Dark framed glasses perched confidently on his nose.

If Charlotte were two decades younger, she'd have a crush on him. "Are you ready?"

His Adam's apple bobbed and a high-pitched laugh escaped his throat. "I was less nervous when I was thinking about presenting to a bunch of stony-faced physicists." He raked his hand through his hair, mussing what'd previously been controlled. "What if I mess up? What if I miscalculate the odds?" He lowered his voice and leaned in, his gaze darting up to the corners of the ceiling. "What if they know I'm cheating?"

"And what if you win big and save the day? Just think of it as an adventure."

Dylan grimaced, as if her encouragement was a bitter pill.

"Plus, it's not all on you," Charlotte said. "I've been known to roll some dice here and there."

The younger man nodded, but his tight jaw betrayed any ease he might've been trying to display.

Levi and Celeste joined them in the lobby.

The rocker wore a sleek tuxedo, with the bow tie hanging untied around his neck and his signature dark sunglasses perched on his nose. The devil might not care, but he cared enough to try to look like he didn't care.

The older woman was resplendent in a bright blue taffeta gown. Her white hair was pulled back into a tight bun and a sequined headband clung to her forehead.

"Celeste, you're magnificent." Charlotte pressed her cheek to the woman's. "And Levi, you're dashing."

He took her hand and brought it to his lips. "Char, my dear, just when I thought you couldn't get more beautiful…"

It was silly. Like playing dress-up. These tuxedos and gowns were a glitzy disguise to who they truly were. Unlike being a little girl trying to fit into too-big shoes, the gown, the hair, and the makeup, the glamor felt appropriate. Like supernovas flaring out before they went dark and died.

Lourdes joined them next. Her fitted red dress clung to her body. The hair in her wig tumbled down her bare shoulders in dark, luxurious waves, and her brown eyes shone under a canopy of glittery eye makeup.

To the un-knowing, Lourdes looked like a beautiful, healthy woman in the prime of her life. The woman standing there was her true self.

The cancer was a disguise.

Darla and Jimmy were the last to join them. They walked together, but a foot separated them. Like a long-married couple in a bitter argument, but still had to act normal to make it through the evening.

Their leader looked dapper in a classic tuxedo; his auburn hair slicked back. His gaze bounced around the group before it anchored to Lourdes. His pale cheeks reddened, and his mouth quirked into a smile before it tugged back to neutral.

His assistant was an absolute bombshell in her short, black dress and platform heels. Her blonde hair was folded into a French twist, and her makeup was only slightly heavier than usual.

"Well, I'd say we all clean up well." Levi's gravelly voice cut through the quiet classical music playing in the lobby. "Shall we go raise some hell?"

The elevator opened onto the casino floor. Charlotte's eyes burned against the gold light. Not just the light overhead, but the reflection bouncing off the gilt gold covering every inch of the ceiling, the walls, the tables. It was like stepping out of the shadow of the moon and directly onto the surface of the sun.

A cocktail waitress who could moonlight as a supermodel approached; her megawatt smile drowned out by the competition of the casino floor. "Welcome," she said, her accent undefinable in its origin, but definable in its sex appeal. She offered her tray of champagne. "Can I direct you to a table?"

Dylan's jaw dropped and red crept up from his collar.

Charlotte grabbed a flute and thrust it into his hand.

The liquid quivered like ripples in a pond before he threw back the glass and guzzled it all in one sip. Dylan handed the empty glass to the now aghast model. "Craps."

She quickly recovered herself. "Right. Follow me."

He glanced over his shoulder, with a crooked smile and disappeared into the casino with Jimmy and Levi in tow.

Celeste and Darla took off in the direction of the slot machines.

Lourdes opted to try her luck with the roulette wheel.

The group dispersed, heading to their corners and leaving Charlotte alone in a sea of flashing lights, gleaming gold, and a tasteful, muted cacophony of raucous cheers and classical music.

She didn't mind being left behind. It felt good to shed the skin of Charlotte Claybrooke, America's Self-Help Sweetheart, to peel off the sweater of Charlotte the Charlatan.

For the few minutes, until she took her spot at a casino game to help save Jimmy's business, she was simply the heartbroken woman who couldn't move past the grief of her dead fiancé.

Ten years later.

Ten *years*. She'd only known Jason for a little over a year when she'd lost him. How could it have taken her ten times as long to get over him? What was she mourning, him or the promise of the life they'd have together?

Maybe both.

By now she'd expected to have a couple of kids. Spirited children with her dark hair and his dancing blue eyes. They'd live in a comfortable Colonial-style home in the suburbs, somewhere near great running and biking trails.

Maybe she'd made partner in her old law firm by now, or maybe she would've taken a job at a non-profit, so she could spend more time with their kids.

A whoop and cascade of music from the slot machines sliced into her fantasy. The could-have-been life drifted away like flotsam on the ocean, leaving in its wake the depths of her depression.

Charlotte turned away and found the closest bar. "Bourbon, neat," she said to the bartender.

"Beautiful on the outside, tough on the inside," a male voice spoke next to her.

The man sported a thick head of black, wavy hair which capped a chiseled, freshly-shaved square jaw. His dark eyes scanned the casino floor, but she could feel him study her from his periphery.

"Maybe I just like things in their true form." She matched his posture; one elbow propped on the bar, studying the people gambling.

How many were there simply to pass the time? It didn't matter if they won or lost, it was the game that was important. The journey. The highs of victory and lows of defeat.

How many were there because it was their last chance? However they woke up tomorrow was solely dependent on what happened this evening. They could wake up high on hope, or in the deep abyss of despair.

"You're thinking too hard," he said, still not looking in her direction. "I can feel it. Your thoughts make the air quiver around you."

A short laugh escaped her throat. "I bet you say that to all the girls."

One corner of his mouth quirked up. "I doubt any of my usual lines would work on you." He pivoted, offering his free hand. "Javier."

"Charlotte."

His hand closed around hers, warming it while sending a chill down her spine. How long had it been since she flirted with someone? Since she felt the tug of attraction?

Too long.

Not long enough.

"So, Charlotte." The *r* and the *l* rolled around on his tongue like lovers. "Who left you all alone?"

Such an innocent, flirtatious question meant to determine if she were fair game or not.

Maybe she should answer it truthfully.

Would it send this bar fly Casanova into someone else's kitchen?

A cheer erupted from a crowded craps table. All of the Diers had congregated around the game.

Levi's "Fuck yeah!" rose above the laughter and clapping.

Celeste's bright blue gown stood out among the sea of black dresses and tuxedos, and Lourdes' cascade of curls tumbled as she clapped. Jimmy side-hugged Dylan, jostling the young man like storm debris on the ocean.

Just as being with the group suffocated her, their absence, even just for a few minutes, left her light-headed, as if going from labored breath to an infusion of oxygen.

Was she her truest self with the other Diers?

In some ways yes, except in the biggest way.

If she didn't belong with them, where *did* she belong?

Watching them across the casino, an ache grew in her chest. If they were successful tonight, they'd only have a week left with each other. After that, they'd go back to their homes. Back to their lives.

Back to their deaths.

"You have it wrong," Charlotte leaned in close, her nose filling with the spicy, woodsy scent of the man's cologne. "*I* left my friends all alone. If you'll excuse me."

Javier grabbed her hand, as she took two steps from the bar, stroking the inside of her wrist, making her more light-headed than the bourbon. "I'm not ready to say goodbye."

Her lips stretched into a lazy smile. "If you bring me a drink, you can come say hello." She nodded to the craps table, where an even larger crowd grew.

She pushed through the people, sliding into a spot next to Lourdes. "You fled tall, dark, and sexy like he carried the plague."

She cut a glance to her friend, unsurprised that Lulu would have watched her flirting with the handsome man. "I didn't want to miss all the action," Charlotte said.

Chips dotted the various plays on the table, and both Levi and Jimmy had large piles in front of them.

The game of craps reminded her of trying to plug a leaky ship with her fingers. New holes would pop up and eventually she'd run out of fingers. Looking at the bets that could be placed on the *Come*, *Field* or *Pass*, or any of the variation made Charlotte dizzy with possibility. Or, maybe that was the hastily consumed liquor while chatting up a sexy Spaniard.

Lourdes twirled on her heel and narrowed her eyes. "What about the action *you* could have gotten?"

"I just met him."

Fire flashed in the Latina's eyes but the rest of her paled. Paled, then flushed green. "I saw how he looked at you. How he held on to you." Her friend's voice was strained.

Charlotte bit back her concern. There was one thing she'd learned with her time among the dying; they don't want to be asked if they were okay. Because the answer was almost always unequivocally, 'no.' She forced her focus back to the table.

Levi cupped the dice, holding it in front of a buxom brunette so she could blow on them.

"Anyway," Charlotte whispered to Lourdes. "I think he's an escort."

"So?"

She rolled her eyes. "I'm not paying for sex."

No matter how good it might be.

The starlet swayed and gripped the edge of the table. "We all pay for sex. There's always something transactional about it." She sipped her drink. "In some ways, there's something cleaner about money."

She opened her mouth to argue, but a glass of amber liquid appeared in front of her, attached to a bronzed hand. Her eyes traveled up to the sexy smirk.

"Hello," he said.

Lourdes whispered something. Her lyrical words in fast Spanish.

Javier furrowed his brow.

Her friend ignored him and leaned her cheek against Charlotte's. "Sleep with him or flirt with him all night and leave him wanting," she breathed in her ear. "All that matters is you enjoy yourself. I'm feeling a bit worn out, so I'm going to call it a night." She glanced at Jimmy, but their host's attention was on the full table. "Let me know how it ends."

Charlotte squeezed her hand. "I'll text you all the details."

Javier took over Lourdes' spot at the table.

"What did she say to you?" Charlotte asked.

"She, um, she asked if I take credit cards."

She whipped her head in his direction, her jaw dropping before a laugh bubbled up from a place so deep down inside, she thought it was out of air. Charlotte laughed so hard that her drink splashed over the side of her glass, dousing her hand, and for just a few minutes, she forgot she was dying.

"I take it the answer's *no*."

"Why would I take—" His face stilled and he shook his head. "Oh, did she think I was an escort? *Dios mio*, I don't know if I should be embarrassed or flattered."

"Well, you have to admit, handsome guy, by himself at a casino bar." She checked the status of the latest game.

Darla had joined the table, leaning close to Jimmy.

Whatever iciness hovered between them earlier had melted away.

The brunette with Levi snuggled so close, Charlotte could only see one of her hands.

"I'm here on business."

Charlotte's skin erupted in goosebumps with his breath in her ear. "An escort could also say that," she teased.

Celeste rolled the dice.

Shouts and arms filled the air.

Javier leaned in, his chest warming Charlotte's bare shoulders. "Which are your friends?"

"You met Lourdes. That's Celeste." She nodded to the older woman getting ready for another roll. "Down at the far end, the man in the dark glasses with white hair is Levi. The handsome young man is Dylan. The man next to him is Jimmy and Darla is the blonde."

Javier's gaze roved over their motley group. As he said earlier, he could feel her thinking, she could now feel him trying to piece them together.

"How do you know each other?"

She twirled in her spot, her back to the table.

The man, the stranger she'd just met who made her insides churn like an angry sea, stood over her. Not in a menacing way. Warm. Enveloping. Like someone who would hold her well into the night.

Charlotte downed the last of her bourbon. "Shared interests."

Javier tilted his head. "Shared interests? Like music or art?"

Or, dying.

"You could say that."

She held his gaze, searching inside herself for a grain of guilt. Just enough to grow like a pearl. Instead, she felt nothing but the tide of desire pulling her to him.

Was that what she wanted? To be held by another man? Loved by another man?

Reason bobbed in the distance, but the alcohol pushed it away.

Maybe Lourdes was right. It was simply a transaction. It wouldn't be anything like with Jason; where every time they'd touched, kissed, made love, he'd taken a piece of her soul.

"I think I'm going to call it a night." Charlotte pushed past him.

Javier followed her away from the crowded table. "Charlotte, I'm still not ready to say goodbye."

She reached, tugging on his wrist, pulling him to her. "Then don't."

29

The craps table spread out in front of Dylan like a treasure map.

The croupier stood with only three other players, people who looked as if they'd stepped off a cruise ship on the French Rivera to waste a few hours before pushing back off.

They were vacationers. Amateurs. People who had nothing to lose except a few hours of boredom.

He watched a couple of rounds of play. It was like jumping on a moving merry-go-round. Dylan had to pick the perfect moment to jump on.

"What're you thinking?" Levi asked into a glass of whiskey.

He sipped on yet another glass of champagne. He didn't have the heart to tell Levi and Jimmy he'd spent the entire flight to Monte Carlo Googling how to gamble.

It'd been an impulse. An urgent need deep inside, of him to feel the same flush of fear the bandits had drawn. To be standing in front of death. In front of loss. In front of failure.

That was what frightened him more than a drawn gun.

Failing.

In his brief life, the only thing Dylan had failed at was making his father love him. A son wasn't supposed to be responsible for a father's love. That was solely on the parent. Logic told him that, but it didn't stop him from feeling like he'd flubbed an easy math question.

The numbers on the table danced in front of his eyes. What was the bet he was supposed to make? Put chips on the *Pass Line*? Then what was the winning roll?

He'd never had a problem remembering in the past. Was this a new symptom or was it just exhaustion from being awake for nearly twenty hours?

Dylan pulled some chips from his pile. He'd nearly maxed out his credit card, and in hindsight, it would've been much more of a sure bet, if he'd just given Jimmy the money instead of playing this game. "I'm in," he said to the croupier, dropping his chips on the *Pass Line*. He'd start small, ease his way into the game; decide if this was where he could win.

See if it scared him.

The croupier nudged the dice down in his direction. "You're up, sir."

Dylan palmed the dice, closing his eyes to will any combination of numbers that formed a seven or eleven to show when they landed.

The dice flew from his hands, tumbling over the table until they landed on the opposite side.

"Four and three, well done, sir," the croupier said, good-naturedly enough to keep him engaged, but not too cheery to confuse the players, as to whose team he was on.

Chips were handed out.

More people joined the table.

The lights in the casino brightened. Or, maybe it was the pills wearing off.

Dylan glanced up; the Beaux Arts architecture shone down on him. Pale yellows and golds, ornate carvings that were too perfect to have been constructed by hand.

"Bets down," the croupier said, his French accent both refined and gentle. "Sir, when you're ready."

He cupped the dice again.

There are six ways to roll a seven. A one in six chance. To roll an eleven is a one in thirty-six chance.

Numbers danced in his mind, as he calculated the possibility of a winning roll.

The dice sprang from his hand.

"An eleven sir, well done."

Cheers went up around the table.

What'd started as three or four passing vacationers had turned into a gaggle of gamblers.

Jimmy pulled him into a tight side hug. "Dylan, my man, I don't know how you're doing it, but you have the golden touch." He handed over a glass from a passing cocktail waitress, just a bit of amber liquid stared up at him.

He threw it back, the liquor burning the whole way down. It was like all the times he'd gotten sick. The same acidic fire, only in reverse.

"Slow down," Jimmy said. "That's a fifty-year-old Scotch. Meant to be sipped, buddy."

Dylan's hand acted on its own. Placing bets on every corner of the table. Bets against himself. Bets against his friends. Bets that made no sense.

His hold on reality loosened, like a child letting go of a balloon. Was he supposed to have alcohol on his pain pills?

He tried to recall the warning from the doctor. He'd mostly ignored that discussion. He never drank. Why store useless information, it just took up precious memory.

Lights. Drinks. Dice.

Girls. Women he'd never seen before appeared out of nowhere.

Shouts. People touching him, slapping him on the back.

Pressure.

Pressure in his head.

Pressure to *win*.

Pressure to be the person his father wanted him to be.

Pressure to leave behind something; something to make the world a better place, to allow people to correct their mistakes.

The crowd clawed at him. Threatened to consume him.

"Bets down." The words were spoken in slow motion.

Or, maybe that was just how Dylan heard them. Then, like watching a video with a flaw, everything around him sped up, people moved faster, the words came out in a high-pitched squeak.

He abandoned his experiment, but perhaps his experiment didn't abandon him?

Was this how it would've worked?

Time would slow down, speed up. Reverse, pause.

Jimmy and Levi were huddled together, their heads much bigger than usual.

Darla had joined the table.

Dylan didn't remember her joining them. It was like she'd materialized out of thin air.

"Dylan, you okay?" Her voice floated into his ears, but he didn't see her mouth move.

"Sir, any bets?"

"Dylan?"

"Bets down."

"Dylan."

More acid burned at his throat. "I gotta—" he didn't finish the thought; he pushed through the throng of people, escaping the claustrophobia.

He was free of the craps table, but all he did was move from one festoon of people to another.

Unmoored from the table, Dylan was lost, floating in a sea of bodies.

A ticker of formulas passed behind his eyes. Pythagorean Theorem. The Denumerability of the Rational Numbers. Prime numbers. Impossibility. ABCs.

He jogged toward the exit. Where he was going?

Out. In. Up. Over.

Shouts of his name assaulted him from behind like bullets, "Dylan, Dylan, wait up, stop."

He burst through the front door of the casino hotel.

The cool night air wrapped its arms around him, pushed air into his lungs.

The evening was instantly quiet. The sounds of the casino died away, replaced by the whooshing of cars and the low mewling of cruise ship horns.

"Dylan," Jimmy jogged up next to him. "You okay?"

He bent over, his hands resting above his knees. Deep inhales steadied his racing heart, calmed his erratic mind, pushed back down the alcohol that threatened to spill all over his tuxedo. "Too much," he gasped.

Jimmy rubbed his back, gentle circles with enough pressure. The touch of a parent when a child was sick. "I'm sorry, I shouldn't have given you the liquor. And that table heated up pretty fast. You were on fire."

Dylan stood up and shook his head. "Everything. Too much. Dying. Living. All of it."

The man's face softened. He'd probably had this conversation many times over. "I know, son, there's no easy way—and especially someone as young as you. I couldn't imagine how your family must be feeling."

He scoffed. "I only have my dad left, and he can't wait for it to be over."

"It must be hard on him. Seeing his only child, his son, going through what you're going through. Not being able to help you."

Tears burned behind his eyes. Dylan shook his head, dislodging them. "That's not it." It would've been so much easier to let the lie Jimmy believed float between them. Some lies warmed the heart where the truth was a stinging barb.

"Dying is hard on everyone. It's especially hard on the living, the family members, and those who'll be left behind. While everyone grieves differently, I can guarantee you—" The man continued. Either ignoring him or because he'd given this speech so many times it practically gave itself.

The pointless rambling pierced his heart. Not because of the pain his father might one day feel, but because there would be no pain. No grieving. No mourning a life cut short. "Jimmy, stop. Because you have no clue." His voice rose on the sea breeze.

Jimmy stopped speaking. His face went slack, as if he'd never had his pep talk not work on a Dier. "I-I-well, we all experience death differently…"

Dylan ran his hands through his hair. The gelled strands stuck to his hands. "My dad wants me dead," he shouted, the words so acerbic, a couple getting out of a Maybach cut side glances at them.

Jimmy winced. "You can't mean that," he whispered.

Dylan fell to the curb, his elbows resting on his knees. "He's doing everything he can to fight my will. Says my COO is manipulating him to keep him out of the company." He lifted his eyes from the insanely pristine concrete to study the courtyard in front of them. "I could almost see the dollar signs in his eyes when the doctors said it was terminal."

"Are you sure? People process these diagnoses in different ways."

"We were walking out of the hospital and he asked how much I'm worth."

Jimmy crouched on the curb next to him. "Ouch. That's—wow." The muscle in his jaw flexed and he rubbed his chin. "Even my old man wasn't that cold." He kept his gaze on the scene in front of them. "My father saw me as just the hired help. When my mom was sick, I was her caregiver, but I also took care of the house, the cooking, bills. After she died, I grieved and expected to be a normal ten-year-old. Pop had another plan for me."

"It wouldn't be so bad if…" The words hitched in Dylan's throat. Suddenly, he felt less like a twenty-three-year-old man, and more like an eight-year-old boy. It didn't matter how high his IQ was, a child was still a child. "How hard would it have been for him to just say he was proud of me?"

A heavy hand crashed down on his shoulder and squeezed.

"Not being able to say that is more about him than you. It's because of his own shortcomings. Admitting pride of someone else, especially your son, is impossible to do when you're damaged. They've got to save all that sentiment for themselves. Their bank is empty. You can't fault a bank account when it has nothing to withdraw from."

They sat in silence for several minutes.

Zero, times any number always equaled zero. It was a basic math lesson, but one that stretched beyond the realm of numbers.

No matter how much Dylan poured into his relationship with his dad, it was always met with a zero.

30

It wasn't going to work.

Those words weighed on Darla like a two-ton bull stepping on her gut.

Jimmy had lit up like a poor kid waking up to a tree full of gifts on Christmas morning, and there was no way she was going to crush him with the truth that they were only just wrapped empty boxes.

They couldn't gamble their way back into a flush banking account. The fantasy had given him what he needed, and what would be his undoing.

Hope.

Hell, it'd even given Darla a little hope. Like the time that her momma's gaze brushed against hers and held, like a mother grasping her child's hand. Then she'd looked away, her gaze sweeping out the window, tossing Darla's hope out to the parking lot.

The cheering at a craps table pulled her away from the mindless slot machines. It wasn't that she wanted to play the slots; she was just trying to avoid Jimmy.

Avoid his hope; afraid it would rub off on her.

It was going to hurt when they lost, but there was nothing she could do.

He was riding high. Flying too close to the sun. Sooner or later, his wings would melt. Darla just had to be there to catch him when he came crashing down.

Jimmy's face was flushed. A lock of his slicked-back hair had fallen across his high forehead. He huffed into his closed fist, then released the dice on the table. His tongue poked through his parted lips before a cheer and high fives erupted around the table.

The crowd was already two people deep when she pushed through to his side. "What's happening?" she muttered to her boss. "Where's Dylan and Lourdes?" They were missing a couple of Diers.

He leaned in close to her ear. "Levi's up ten grand, I'm up four. Dylan and Lourdes both went to their rooms."

"You mean…we're winning?"

Jimmy flashed his million-dollar grin and turned back to the table.

The croupier passed around chips with the dexterity of a musician, and announced the table was open for bets.

Her friend rolled again. A five and a two stared up from the other end of the table. The shouts and whistles rivaled that of a sporting event.

More chips handed out. Strangers high fiving each other. Cocktail waitresses started circling the table like sharks. A busty woman, siliconed, botoxed, and collagen-injected to the point she was more plastic than human, sidled up to Levi.

The excitement rolled off the gamblers like pheromones.

A glass of champagne ended up in Darla's hand.

Jimmy chugged his own in a long gulp before rolling once more. This time, half the table cheered, the other half *ahhed*. A few of his chips went to the dealer, the rest of his bets stayed on the table.

"This game makes me dizzy," she said, taking another long sip. "Or, maybe it's the champagne."

"Wanna play?" Her boss held up four five-hundred-dollar chips.

Darla resisted the urge to shove those chips into her purse. It was more than she'd had in her bank account since…ever.

"I don't know how."

"I'll teach you." His eyes sparkled, then narrowed. As if seeing her for the first time.

Was he feeling it too?

She'd been here all along.

Jimmy put the chips in her hand and closed her fingers around them. "Next bet, I'll help you."

Darla tried to swallow, but the lump in her throat wouldn't budge. She emptied her champagne flute, and handed it off to a passing cocktail waitress in exchange for a full one. Was she drinking to calm the nerves of the game, or the butterflies in her stomach from Jimmy's stare?

Both were a serious gamble.

Her phone buzzed in her purse. A text from Enzo.

Why did my jet return to Miami empty?

She nibbled on her lower lip and hastily tapped a reply. *Maybe because we weren't on it?*

Shit. What was she doing? It wasn't good to fuck with a bull before stepping into the ring. Was it the champagne? The gambling?

Bumping into Jimmy every time the crowd jostled them?

Darla erased the message and left the question unanswered.

Enzo's name flashed with an incoming call. It rang twice, and she declined the call.

YOU don't decline my calls, was the quick follow-up text. It was amazing how the man could lob an accusation through a message.

Then again, he held her mother's well-being in the palm of his hands, or wherever he kept his no-limit credit card.

She retreated from the table and found a spot outside of earshot. Darla hit redial.

"Where are you?" Enzo barked, his voice echoing, as if he were in a glass-enclosed racquetball court.

Was that all he did?

"Sorry, I hit the wrong button." Her lie was as flimsy as the walls of their old trailer.

"Are you in a *casino*?"

She looked up and around. Which of the cameras did Enzo have access to? "Yep."

"Was I not clear, Darla?" The barking settled to a growl. A ball bounced in the background. "You were to bring them all home."

She drained the last of her third glass of champagne and hiccupped. The way she was downing the booze, Darla was at the risk of waking up hungover. Or, fired. Both? "Yes, you were clear, but Lourdes Peña paid—"

"Don't blame this on the clients. You work for *me*, not them."

She plucked drink number four off a passing tray. The alcohol would fuel her words or numb the burn. Either way, she needed as much liquid courage as her liver could handle.

"I do work for them. I don't work for you. We're on our dime, not yours, so don't worry your pretty little head."

Cheers rose at the craps table like the soaring voices of a church choir. Levi and Jimmy embraced like brothers in arms.

"We'll be home when we're done. Oh and Enzo, all that racquetball isn't helping your stress. Maybe you should try getting laid instead." She ended the call and turned her phone off.

She'd just tied a rope good and tight around the bull's balls. Next time she saw Enzo, it was sure to be one hell of a ride.

Darla pushed back through the growing crowd to the table.

Now people stood four deep, and casino floor managers stood with their hands clasped behind their backs, watching the players like hawks, ready to swoop in at any signal of cheating. Judging the stacks of chips at each of the gamblers, this table was hotter than Houston in August.

"Was that Enzo?" Jimmy asked.

"Yep."

He leaned down and placed chips on the table. "Was he wondering where we are?"

Darla held her glass like a shield against her chest. "Yep."

"Did you tell him to go fuck himself?"

She cocked her head to one side.

Her boss thumbed through his chips, his mouth moving as he counted his winnings.

"Thought I'd save that honor for you."

He stopped counting and shook his head, laughing. "Just when I think I can't love you anymore."

Her heart stumbled like a drunk college girl walking home from the bar. He'd said he loved her before. She always tossed those declarations in the platonic pile.

"Are you ready?" he asked.

Darla stared. Her champagne-numbed mind struggled to understand what he was ready for.

"To play?" Jimmy asked. He grabbed the flute from her fingers and set it on the ledge in front of him. "Maybe you should slow down. I've never seen you speechless. Darla Steele without words is like an empty museum."

Thoughts whizzed through her mind like they were on a Tilt-a-Whirl, but only three small words staggered from her lips. "Right, yeah, sure."

"Okay, so here's how it works." His words slurred together.

Or maybe that was just how she heard them.

Darla didn't so much as listen to Jimmy, as watch his lips move. It didn't matter what he said, it made little sense to her. Even if she were completely sober, it would still be too much to hold in her brain.

"Here, why don't you place a bet at the *Come*, and then on the eights." He pointed at the table, indicating where she should put her chips.

The croupier pushed the dice toward her with his stick. "Bets down. Madam, the roll is yours."

Darla cupped the dice. Was she supposed to shake them? Blow on them? She opted to close her eyes and make a wish. Recalled one childhood birthday where her mom had had enough money to get her a cake. The promise of a wish. With a simple exhale, she could have anything she desired.

Jimmy. Please dear God or whoever grants wishes, nothing has ever felt more right. Let me have one good thing in life.

She opened her eyes and released the dice. They flew through the air, just a few inches off the table before they collided with the green felt, tumbling end over end.

One stopped.

A single black dot stared up.

The other teetered on its edge, almost falling over before it settled down and landed.

The one faced up, winking at her like a genie granting wishes.

Cheers flew up around her.

Champagne rained down on her as the woman next to her thrust her full glass into the air.

Jimmy shouted and punched the air. "Yeah! We did it!" He grabbed her by the waist and pulled her close, his lips colliding against hers before she was able to inhale.

Darla's body went slack, as if forgetting how to kiss.

Maybe she had. It'd been a good while.

She reached for the table to steady herself, but then she remembered it was Jimmy. She should hold on to him rather.

He could steady her.

Just as she'd commanded her arm to wrap around his neck, he was gone.

"You won, Darla." He smiled down at her, his eyes glistening, and a bit unfocused. "We won. We saved Dire's Club." Jimmy focused on the table. "Woo! I can't wait to tell Enzo where he can shove his money."

Chips were dispersed, and the croupier asked if she wanted to bet again, but Darla shook her head.

The lights. The gold. People crushed into her.

Her stomach twisted like a wet rag, and champagne shot up her throat. She swallowed it down. "I need to go lie down," she said through her fingers.

"You okay?" Jimmy asked, but kept his eyes on the table.

"Too much champagne and excitement. You staying?"

He glanced in her direction. "What? Oh yeah, not leaving while the table's hot. I'll check in with you when I leave here, see if you need anything."

He looked up at the ornate ceiling. "Fuck you, old man. I won." Frankly, if he really wanted to talk to his dad, he should look down.

Side effect of being around the dying. They were always positive that their elevator would be heading to the top floor instead of the basement.

"I'm a winner."

His winning feet took him left and his winning hand rapped on Lulu's door.

She didn't seem surprised to find him there. "Well don't you look like the cat who just ate the canary," she purred, clutching the doorframe.

That red dress, the one that Jimmy was certain had been made just for her, still covered her body. Dark circles cushioned her eyes, and her face was pale under her makeup, but her dark hair had a slept-in messiness.

He opened his mouth to speak, but instead, he pulled her toward him and crushed his lips against hers.

She parted for him, and Jimmy deepened the kiss, pushing forward until they were in her room.

Lourdes broke the kiss but didn't pull away. "I take it we won."

He nodded; his breathing too shallow to form words. "I wish you could've been there. Beside me."

She dropped her arms and moved across her room, picking up a glass of red wine. The rim was covered in her bright lipstick. "You didn't need me." Her voice was a watery whisper.

In the shadows of her room, he saw it.

The dark cushions under her eyes weren't from exhaustion, but from crying. Her hair wasn't just mussed from sleep, but it was…crooked.

Jimmy picked up the bottle of wine. Only a splash left.

"Okay, I'm a drunk, so what." Lourdes took a defiant sip.

"I didn't say anything."

"But you thought it," she snapped back, her gaze glued to the carpet. Lourdes took a long breath and met his eyes. "I'm sorry. I wasn't feeling well, so I came back here, where I proceeded to feel sorry for myself. Long story short, I drank a bottle of wine."

He crossed the room and cupped her cheek.

Lourdes leaned into his hand, her skin cool and waxy.

"I wish I could make it go away," he said, thumbing at the smeared mascara.

"Sometimes I feel like that's all that's left of me, cancer cells."

Jimmy smiled and leaned down, inhaling her scent. Jasmine laced with Bordeaux.

He'd smelled plenty of death in his life. The sour stench of decay creeping into a person's body. Organs shutting down. Skin graying, hair falling out. It was a smell that grabbed him by the throat and squeezed.

Sometimes it was accompanied by the chemical tang of medicine. Morphine leeching out of someone's pores. Or maybe a last-ditch chemo treatment. A medical Hail Mary that was destined to fall short of the end zone.

The smell was as familiar as the freckles on his arms, and it had yet to invade Lourdes' essence.

When his lips found hers again, the kiss was less urgent. It was slower, methodical. Like savoring a fine wine.

Her hands found his hair, nails caressing his scalp before traveling down to his jacket, shoving it off his shoulders.

His own fingers traced the skin along her arms. Jimmy's mouth left hers only to taste the delicate flesh of her collarbones.

He could feel the groan deep in her throat when he kissed the hollow of her neck.

"I shouldn't be here," he whispered in her ear. "This is so unprofessional. You're a client. I'm overstepping every rule in my book, but dammit Lourdes, I want you." Jimmy nipped at her ear. "I want you like I've never wanted anyone else."

Her body went stiff and her arms dropped to her side. She stepped away, rubbing her forehead with one hand, while the other arm clutched her stomach.

"What is it? Did I do something?"

She nodded. Her heart slid into her gut.

Her wishes still plummeted to earth like lead balloons.

The only difference between her childhood wish, and the one she'd just made with Jimmy was the size of the hole it left.

"Darla," her boss called, as she walked away. "You saved me. Thank you."

A half-hearted smile tugged at her cheeks.

They were two lost souls, adrift in the world, holding on to each other like their lives depended on it.

What would happen if one of them let go?

31

It had to be the dumbest thing Jimmy had ever done.

Maybe not *the* dumbest. There was a long line of contenders for the top spot. However, kissing Darla when he got a little too carried away…

That shot to the top of the list after she'd run away; toppling that time in high school he'd gotten stoned and stole his dad's police cruiser. Yeah, he'd screwed up more than breaking the law.

He wrapped his untied bowtie around his knuckles, wishing he could slam his fist into the mirrored walls of the elevator lobby. To punch out the guy who might've ruined things with his best friend.

If he went right, he'd walk into his room.

If he walked left, he'd be at Lulu's door.

A little further past the *telenovela* star's door, he'd be at Darla's. He'd said he would check in on her, but after that look she'd given him, if he knocked on her door she'd slap him.

Tomorrow she'd be better. Sober.

Maybe she wouldn't even remember the kiss.

Jimmy reached into his pocket, running his fingers over the chips. He was a winner. The ridged edges told him that. The dice told him that. The good juju from the table told him that.

She nodded. Her heart slid into her gut.

Her wishes still plummeted to earth like lead balloons.

The only difference between her childhood wish, and the one she'd just made with Jimmy was the size of the hole it left.

"Darla," her boss called, as she walked away. "You saved me. Thank you."

A half-hearted smile tugged at her cheeks.

They were two lost souls, adrift in the world, holding on to each other like their lives depended on it.

What would happen if one of them let go?

31

It had to be the dumbest thing Jimmy had ever done.

Maybe not *the* dumbest. There was a long line of contenders for the top spot. However, kissing Darla when he got a little too carried away…

That shot to the top of the list after she'd run away; toppling that time in high school he'd gotten stoned and stole his dad's police cruiser. Yeah, he'd screwed up more than breaking the law.

He wrapped his untied bowtie around his knuckles, wishing he could slam his fist into the mirrored walls of the elevator lobby. To punch out the guy who might've ruined things with his best friend.

If he went right, he'd walk into his room.

If he walked left, he'd be at Lulu's door.

A little further past the *telenovela* star's door, he'd be at Darla's. He'd said he would check in on her, but after that look she'd given him, if he knocked on her door she'd slap him.

Tomorrow she'd be better. Sober.

Maybe she wouldn't even remember the kiss.

Jimmy reached into his pocket, running his fingers over the chips. He was a winner. The ridged edges told him that. The dice told him that. The good juju from the table told him that.

She hid her face from him.

"Lourdes, talk to me. What is it?"

She grabbed her glass of wine and sat on the edge of her bed; her face still hidden away. "You don't want *me*."

He sat next to her, grabbing her free hand. "Every time I see you, I can't breathe. When those gorgeous eyes look at me, I want to cry. When that beautiful mouth smiles, I feel like I'm in a free fall." He tilted her chin toward him with a finger. "I don't want you for just one night. I want you for every night. Every day."

Fat tears clung to Lourdes' eyelashes. "You want the ghost of me. The me who *used* to be here. I'm sorry, but she's gone, Jimmy. I'm all that's left."

"You're wrong. You're all I want."

She stood. A sad smile lifted the corners of her mouth. "At first, the cancer didn't take much." She backed away two steps, and reached for a dinner napkin, dipping it in a glass of water. "For the first several months I thought the doctors were wrong, because I didn't feel sick." Lourdes wiped the napkin across her forehead. Only a blank slate of skin stared back where her eyebrows had been. "That treatment wasn't successful, so they tried a stronger chemo." She pinched her eyelashes, pulling them off and setting them next to the empty wine bottle. "That was a bitch. My hair started falling out in clumps. Some people told me to shave my head. To shove a middle finger in cancer's face, but I couldn't." Lourdes pulled the wig off, stroking the long dark hair before gently laying it on a chair.

Jimmy swallowed. Of course, it wasn't a shock her treatment had robbed her of her hair, he'd just never seen it.

Her bald head was luminous, the brown skin reflecting the low light of the room. Without eyelashes and eyebrows, her dark eyes glittered like uncut diamonds.

She held his gaze, a dare in her eyes.

When Lourdes seemed satisfied he'd passed whatever silent test she'd put him through, she reached behind her back and unzipped her red dress. "The chemo and radiation seemed to feed the cancer." She held the dress in its place for a moment before dropping it, then stepped out of the dress, still just out of his reach. She wore a skin-toned strapless bodysuit. "The next course was surgery. That's when my doctors got aggressive." Lourdes pulled down the top of the suit.

Where her breasts should have been, two white lines stared back at him.

She glanced down. "I've been meaning to have reconstructive surgery, but my white blood cell count was never high enough." She wiggled the suit farther down her body. A long white scar bisected her lower abdomen.

Lourdes shimmied out of it, padding at the hips and buttocks puffing out as she scrunched it down, stealing her curvy figure, leaving bony hips in its wake.

"It took everything, Jimmy." Her voice was soft. "So, I don't know why you want me, because there's nothing left."

He stood, closing the distance between them in one long step. "There's so much there. Your fire, your fight. Your passion. It took some things, but it didn't take who you are."

A sob tumbled from her mouth, but she tried to hide it in a laugh. "You're a sadist. Hanging around people like me."

"You're beautiful."

"You're insufferable."

Jimmy quirked his mouth up. "I'm suffering all right."

She laughed. Not the snappy, haughty laugh of someone trying to keep him away, but the warm, honey-coated laugh of a woman drawing him in. "I'm afraid," she said.

He leaned in, touching his forehead to hers. "Everyone's afraid of dying."

Lourdes shook her head. "No, I've accepted that. I'm afraid of living." She looked up, her lips just brushing his. "I'm afraid once I acquire that taste for life again, it'll be harder to give it up. Like a junkie out of rehab tasting her drug again."

Jimmy picked her up, trying not to show his shock for how light she was. He gently laid her on her bed and hovered over her, wanting to cover her with his body, but too afraid to crush her. "You should never have to give it up, not until your last breath."

Once they were both undressed, stripped from their clothes, their shields, their pretenses, she felt more real, more womanly than he could've ever imagined.

Making love to Lourdes was like making love to an angel. Her cool touch, her fiery passion felt otherworldly.

Once it was obvious he wasn't going to break her, she felt stronger, reinforced by something tougher than steel. As if the physical manifestation of love and desire had fortified her, enlivened her to embrace everything life held for her.

32

The sun could take all the time in the world. Jimmy was in no hurry to have his night with Lourdes end. It wouldn't be just one night. He wouldn't accept it.

There was something so beautiful about that first night. Like hearing a favorite song for the first time. The excitement of its chords, the thrill of a falling crescendo.

The thrill of falling in love.

He studied her face. The golden sun filtered through the curtains, softly kissing her tanned face. Unencumbered by hair, her high cheekbones took center stage. Her soft, full lips were like fluffy clouds against a brilliant blue sky.

Lourdes took a deep breath, her small nose scrunching before exhaling, releasing all tension.

What did she see when she slept? Did she dream she was healthy? Did the cancer cells invade her sleep, giving her bad dreams, or mocking her broken body? Was she dreaming about him? Reliving their passion?

Or, would she wake up filled with regret?

She rolled toward him, her eyes fluttering open. For a moment, she was still, her gaze studying him. A warm smile stretched across her face. "You're still here," she sighed.

"Where would I go?"

Lourdes opened her mouth, as if to answer him, but instead leaned in for a long, soft kiss.

"You don't regret it?" Jimmy asked.

She answered him with another deep kiss, this time covering his body with hers.

Her mouth pulled away from his and traveled to his neck, her searing cold kiss warming his body.

His heart sprinted, banging against his ribs like a runner in the final leg of a race. Blood rushed in his ears, a shushing sound, with a shrill undertone.

Lourdes moved further down his body, and the ringing grew louder, deafening.

Jimmy barely heard it, his body was paralyzed under her touch, his brain addled with anticipation.

"Do you need to get that?" Her voice was husky with desire.

"Get what?"

"Your phone, it's ringing."

He reached for his phone.

Two missed calls from Darla. A voicemail waiting to be heard.

He swallowed, but his mouth was still a desert.

Darla.

Jimmy had never checked on, despite his promise. Had she made it back to her room okay? She'd been pretty drunk. What if someone had intercepted her?

A text message popped up on his screen.

Where are you? I need you.

His body turned to ice. The phone burned in his fingers.

She'd never needed him before. That was always *his* role in their relationship. Jimmy needed Darla. Couldn't run his business without her. Couldn't run his life without her.

She was more than his rock.

Darla was his foundation.

She framed his life. Held up his walls.

His assistant covered him, kept the monsters of his past away with her feisty take-no-shit-from-anyone demeanor.

Now that she needed him, could he do the same for her? Hold her up when he couldn't exist without her?

"Everything okay?" Lourdes pulled herself up the bed.

"I don't know." Jimmy stared at the message, at the red voicemail notification. Dread snaked into his blood, coiling in his heart. "Let me check this."

He pressed 'play' on the voicemail. "Jimmy, answer your door." Her voice was quiet, tight, as if holding something back. There was a banging noise. Like she was pounding on his door. "Dammit."

Jimmy pushed off the bed and crossed Lourdes' room, staring out the window at the waking city.

Shopkeepers hosed down the sidewalks outside their businesses. An old woman waddled down the street, tugging a cart behind him. Everything outside the hotel looked fine.

The world continued spinning.

His thumb pressed on her name. The phone didn't even ring on his end.

"Where are you?" Darla demanding, her breathing shallow.

"What's going on? You sound—"

"Levi's dead." The words came out on a sob. "Levi's dead, and I can't find you."

Her panic strangled him. "What do you mean *dead?*"

Sure, everyone was dying, but in all the years of running his business, no one had ever died on a trip.

"I mean dead-dead. The police are here, and the hotel manager. A woman was with him. I think she's a hooker, and she woke up and he was—"

That was when he heard the low murmur of voices in the hallway. A mechanical buzz of radios. Words in French.

Hushed, as if trying to not make a fuss over something as inconvenient as a guest dying.

His heart tumbled, crashing into his stomach, forcing tears to his eyes.

Darla needed Jimmy.

Jimmy needed Darla.

"Where are you?" The words scratched their way out of his throat.

"I was checking to see if you were in the gym. I'm coming back up to Levi's room," she said.

He dropped to all fours, crawling on the plush carpet, gathering his strewn clothes. "I'll meet you there." Jimmy ended the call without waiting for her response. He couldn't let Darla see him leaving Lourdes' room. It wasn't that he felt the need to sneak around behind her back, but he couldn't answer those questions.

Who was he kidding?

Those *accusations*.

He'd kissed his assistant, and then spent the night in the arms of a client. The combination of both would send the needle flying skyward on the scale of inappropriate behavior.

"Jimmy, you're scaring me." Lourdes wrapped a robe around her shoulders, her face paling.

They would all find out eventually.

He didn't have a playbook for this. All of his Diers were healthy enough to travel. Their illnesses not advanced enough to cause death on an adventure. He'd had doctors' assurances.

Goddammit, we have signed forms.

"I've got to go," his throat closed. "Levi..." He couldn't breathe life into the announcement. Not yet.

He pulled his undershirt on and stepped into his tuxedo pants, not bothering to tuck in his shirt. Jimmy shoved his feet in his dress shoes, skipping the socks. Well, sock. He could only find one. He shrugged his dress shirt over his shoulders but left it unbuttoned, then grabbed his jacket and bowtie. "I'll get you in a bit." Jimmy made it halfway to the door but jogged back to the bed, pressing his lips against Lourdes' with the urgency of a dying man.

The closer he got to the door, the louder the sounds in the hallway grew.

He stepped into the hallway.

Four uniformed officers stood in a circle, scribbling in notebooks.

A woman in a lab coat with latex gloves covering her hands took pictures of the outside of Levi's room.

"What're you doing?"

Jimmy jumped at Darla's voice.

His assistant stood halfway between her room and the door he'd just come out of, clutching a thick file folder against her chest like a security blanket. Her hair was pulled back in a messy ponytail. A winter coat covered her short pajamas, and her feet were shoved in her black platform heels.

"I, uh…"

She blinked at him, her shoulders rounding slightly before she straightened her back. Her gaze hardened, pinning him against the wall with the deadly sharpness of a sword. "Here." She thrust the folder at him. "This is your business; you deal with it. I'm going to get dressed." Darla whirled on her heel and slammed her door.

Jimmy wanted to follow her, to ask if she were okay, but the barbed fence of her rage held him back. There was no talking himself out of this one. He was as caught as a fish on a hook.

"*Monsieur* Dire?" An officer approached him. "May we speak?"

He stared at Darla's door for another long second before glancing at the man. "Yes, of course, whatever you need."

He followed the officer to Levi's open door.

The rock star, his friend, lay on the bed, naked except for a sheet wrapped around his waist. His signature dark sunglasses rested on the night table. Levi's face looked empty without them.

Or, maybe that was just the emptiness of death.

"What happened?" Jimmy whispered, trying to keep his voice steady, but failing miserably.

Yellow tape crossed his door, keeping him out. Keeping Levi's corpse in.

He scanned the room. An empty bottle of champagne sat on the floor. Two half-full flutes were on one side of a desk, one glass coated in lipstick.

At the other end of the desk a baggie with white powder coating the inside, the powder tumbling out in white lines on the desktop like soldiers lining up for battle, their general a rolled piece of paper.

Jimmy's gaze darted back to the dead man. White foam flaked from his mouth, his nose.

He didn't need the medical examiner to answer him.

"Were you aware that *Monsieur* Livingston had drugs in his possession?" an officer asked.

He shook his head. Sure, the older man was a dying alcoholic who faked sobriety, but in the two weeks he'd known him, Levi had never slipped away. Never sniffed uncontrollably. Seemed jittery. Unfocused. High.

"There was a woman." Jimmy cleared his throat. "Last night at the table, there was a woman hanging on to him. Brunette, wearing a green dress." He closed his eyes, trying to recall more about her, but all he could see was Lourdes in the dim light of her room. Darla in the glare of the hall.

"Yes, we believe she's the person who alerted the hotel staff, but she wasn't here when we arrived." The officer spoke while reading his notes. "We'll keep looking for her, but it's not uncommon for prostitutes to frequent casinos."

Jimmy surrounded himself with the dying, but it was always hard to see it manifest.

Death loomed like a shadow, stretching a space beyond its boundaries. Not just touching its victim, but slicing into the people closest.

When it was gone; when it followed the body, it left behind a deflated shell that would never snap back into place, no matter how the survivors tried to fit back into their lives.

It was always too big.

The weight of losing a loved one shrank a person's heart.

The elevator dinged and a stretcher rolled out pushed by another medical examiner.

"What now?" Jimmy asked.

"We'll take him to the morgue. An autopsy will be performed to determine the cause of death so we may close our case. Do you know of a next of kin?"

He stood aside to let the examiner through. Jimmy scanned Levi's paperwork in his mind. Emergency contact. A young woman in L.A. "He has a daughter."

"Very good. We'll need that, and anything else you have." The officer nodded once and followed the stretcher into Levi's room.

Levi was dying. Probably faster than any of the other Diers. But… he was also living.

Harder than the others.

What would he say to them?

To Charlotte. She and Levi were close.

Dylan. He looked up to the man.

Lourdes. Would she be so scared with the reflection of her own mortality that she'd slam the door between them?

The medical examiners rolled Levi into a body bag and zipped it up to his chin.

Jimmy stared, waiting for the British rocker to break a smile, to unleash his cackling laugh, curse at them with his gravelly voice.

The final zip covering Levi's face echoed around the room. Ripped into Jimmy's heart.

33

Light snoring next to her roused Charlotte from her dreams. Dreams of lounging on a catamaran on a calm sea. The boat rocked gently, like a mother sending a child to sleep. The sun caressed her shoulders, warm, comforting.

She shook the body next to her, hoping to silence him so she could lull herself back to that place. "Jay, roll over you're snoring."

He rolled to her, nuzzling her neck. "Mmm, pet names already, *mi amor?*"

Charlotte froze at the accent.

Spanish.

Not Australian.

Javier.

Not Jason.

Her nudity clung to her like the stench of decaying seaweed. The evening before crashed into her with the force of a tsunami.

Javier's touch, his lips on her body, her climax, sweaty, spent bodies gasping for air. Debris from a night of passion that should've never happened.

His lips traveled to her mouth, but she turned her head.

"I think you should go," she said.

He hovered over her for a second before leaning back on his elbow. She could feel him studying her. His gaze as warm as his touch.

"We don't have to make this awkward," he muttered.

She kept her eyes on the curtains. Heavy burgundy drapes with a gold *fleur de lis*. Sunlight peeked in from the edges, threatening to shine a light on her mistake.

Her regret.

"I'm glad you agree." Charlotte's skin hummed with the nearness of him. As if it had a mind of its own, and wanted to touch him.

Javier sat up in bed. Red lines dragged down his muscular back.

Did I do that?

He looked over his shoulder, capturing her stare. Stubble dotted his jawline; his dark hair stood up in the back.

Javier was even more handsome mussed than well-coifed.

"I know how this started, but...I'm not ready to say goodbye. Let's have break—"

"Goodbye." Charlotte had to push the word out of her mouth. It threatened to climb back down her throat, to hide from the handsome man in her bed. Other words were eager to bubble up.

Stay with me. Never let me go. Make me feel something other than hurt.

She couldn't let those words out. Like leaves scattering in the wind, she'd never get them back. Never get herself back.

He studied her for another long second before muttering in Spanish. Javier pushed out of bed.

Charlotte curled into the fetal position; trying to make herself as small as possible.

Invisible.

He dressed behind her. Clothes snapping back into place. The reverse of the evening before, when she couldn't get him out of his jacket fast enough.

Her fingers tingled with the feel of his chiseled stomach as she heard the snap of his shirt buttons. The zip of his pants...

The bed heaved under his weight when he sat to put his shoes on.

He stood, and the bed felt barren. His footsteps shuffled across the room, pausing before he reached the door. "Charlotte, for what it's worth, I don't do this either. One-night stands. It doesn't make you bad." He paused. "I left my card on the dresser. You know, in case you ever want to say hello."

She waited until the door clicked shut behind him before she let go of the tears. Charlotte buried her face in her pillow. Why was she even crying?

Jason's been gone for nearly ten years.

Hell, he'd *want* her to move on. To find happiness with someone, Javier, whoever. To have a life, a good one. The life they couldn't have together.

For the first few years, the thought of dating had made her stomach turn. Then she'd started her business, speaking and writing about grief, helping others find their way out of the storm. She couldn't focus on helping others while falling in love. Then, when the whispers in the back of her mind had turned into shouts, she couldn't allow anyone into her life.

Into her death.

Charlotte pulled herself out of bed and padded into the bathroom. Her hair was tangled. The dark eyeshadow that'd made her eyes look sexy and mysterious had migrated south and was now streaked with her tears.

She leaned into the mirror, trying to see whatever Javier had seen. Whatever had made him want to have breakfast with her.

Charlotte was in a committed relationship with her grief.

She didn't see it ending any time soon.

She ran the shower as hot as she could stand it, hoping to scrub away Javier's touch. To burn her skin to the point that it couldn't feel the remnants of pleasure, only the piercing sting of pain.

With her pale skin now a puckered angry red, she shut off the shower.

A pounding at the door filled the silence left in the wake of the running water.

Charlotte quickly threw the bathrobe on, tying the belt as jogged to the door. Her heart galloped. Who did she expect to see on the other side? Javier?

Yes. No?

Maybe.

Lourdes stood there instead. Her wig was in place, but she wore no makeup, not even eyebrows. Her eyes were red, and she wrapped her arms across her stomach, holding herself. She opened her mouth, but then pressed her lips in a tight line and looked down.

"What's wrong?" Charlotte asked. There was no disguising the fact something terrible had happened.

Lourdes wore it like a shroud.

"It's Levi, he's..." The *telenovela* star threw her arms around Charlotte, her body shaking with her sobs.

She looked over her friend's head.

Police meandered through the hallway.

Jimmy stood to the side, talking with one. His face pale, taut.

Celeste clung to Dylan's arm; her free hand covering her mouth.

The young man sniffed and rubbed his eyes.

Darla stood to the side, arms crossed in front of her body, her eyes puffy and nose red.

She'd seen these postures before. When the police had come to tell her about Jason. When she'd had to tell her friends.

Charlotte's knees buckled, but her friend held her up.

This was what death did. It destroyed the living. It took their plans; for tomorrow, for next month, for a lifetime, and it crushed it in its fist.

"I'm so sorry, I'm so sorry," Lourdes whispered. "Put some clothes on, then we'll all talk."

She dressed, but everything was numb. The movements mechanical, as Charlotte pulled a pair of running tights up her legs and topped it with a long-sleeved shirt and her running shoes. Maybe her mind told her she'd need to run from this.

Their group was gathered outside Levi's room.

A black body bag lay on a stretcher, the prone figure of her friend disguised by the thick plastic.

Less than twelve hours ago, he was alive.

Laughing and cheering.

Less than twelve hours ago, blood flowed through his veins, breath filled his lungs.

Less than twelve hours ago, they were on top of the world. At least their little corner of it.

"What happened?" Charlotte whispered.

"Appears to have been an overdose," Jimmy's voice was flat, lifeless.

She snapped her head in his direction. Sure, her friend embraced the rock and roll lifestyle, but she'd never seen him with drugs.

"The police think it was the woman he was with last night at the table." He cleared his throat. "She was probably a prostitute. Likely supplied him with the drugs."

Charlotte blinked back tears. Her friend didn't have to die. He wasn't going to live much longer, but he would've been there with them, if it wasn't for that woman.

Her ears ached to hear his graveled accent calling her *Char*. Her eyes strained to see him walk through the door, in his signature all-black outfit and dark sunglasses. But, those sunglasses remained perched on his night table, never again to rest on his lined face.

Levi didn't have to die. It was senseless. Merciless. He was supposed to be there until the end of their trip. He was going to be there on the boat, standing beside her as they floated over a pod of whales, just the same as she'd stood beside him on stage, singing together, their voices twining and lifting each other.

Charlotte squeezed her fists, her fingernails digging into the palms of her hands. He wasn't supposed to leave her. He'd promised.

Jason had promised a lifetime together.

The investigators wrapped up their work, flipping notebooks closed, putting away cameras. They pushed past the group of Diers, two leading Levi's body out the room.

She wanted to reach out and unzip it, to see for herself that her friend lay inside, but she didn't want to erase her last memory of Levi. Instead, Charlotte gripped the doorframe, needing to hold onto something solid.

Death was a bastard.

She was tired of letting it rule her life. It was time to take control. It was time to fight back.

"Suicide," she whispered, her eyes glued to the black bag wheeling her friend away. Charlotte could feel the stares of the other Diers, their gazes stinging her like the spray of a cold, angry ocean. "That's how I'm dying. I'm going to kill myself."

34

"You mean that in a euthanasia sense, right?" Dylan was the first to speak. "Like before you get too sick?"

Charlotte lifted her gaze from the floor.

The investigators had left with Levi several minutes earlier. It was just their group, minus one, standing in the hallway.

Her admission hung in the air like a mist, warping the faces of the people with whom she'd bonded.

Lourdes' face pinched, her brow darkened. "Do you think this is a joke?" She took a step back.

Charlotte shook her head, her wet bangs clinging to her forehead. "Not at all. And, no, Dylan, not euthanasia."

Jimmy shuffled and ran his hands through his hair, blowing air out his puffed cheeks. "Maybe we should talk about this, as a group."

"What is there to talk about?" The star snapped. "She's a liar."

"Lulu," he spoke with the tenderness of lovers. "Let's hear her out. Come on, we'll go into my room."

Charlotte waited until they all filed in before she entered. She had to tell them, she owed it to Levi, to all of them, but seeing their betrayal-distorted faces, she wished she could go back in time. Back to when she sent her paperwork into Dire's Enterprises, with the plan that this would either save her or give her one final adventure.

They gathered in the sitting room of Jimmy's suite. Like hers, it followed the same rich burgundy and gold *fleur de lis* decor, but the window on this side looked out to the bright cloudless sky.

Lourdes and Celeste took the love seat.

Dylan fell into an armchair.

Darla pulled out the desk chair, and Jimmy perched on the arm of the love seat beside Lourdes.

There were no more chairs.

No one made room for her.

"Charlotte, why don't you start at the beginning?" Jimmy asked.

She'd heard this tone before; her colleagues at the law firm used it when asking a guilty client to come clean. They already knew it would be bad, they were just bracing themselves for the worst.

Her method of dying was her crime. The faces staring back were her jury. This was her trial. One she'd hoped would never happen but was likely to be the most important trial of her life.

She took a deep breath. "Lulu's right. I'm a liar. A fraud."

"Lourdes." The *telenovela* star spat her name.

"What?"

She scoffed. "You can call me Lourdes. Or better yet, Ms. Peña."

Charlotte swallowed. She understood why her friend was hurt. Everything their friendship had been built on was a lie. Her legs twitched, wanting to take her away. It was a finish line they'd all cross. What did it matter?

She could stand up there and beg forgiveness, but in the end, they were all strangers.

Except...

It *did* matter. It mattered more than anything else in her life. Because until she'd walked into Jimmy's office and met this random group of people, she'd been unmoored, floating in a tumultuous sea, hoping for anything, anyone, to grab on to. To save her.

These past two weeks have given her more to live for than her last ten years.

"When I lost Jason, I didn't just lose a piece of me. I lost *all* of me."

"Who was Jason?" Darla asked, her voice soft and quivering.

"My fiancé. He was hit by a car just a few weeks before our wedding. We were triathletes, so he was on a training ride by himself." The only thing Charlotte could remember from that day was the police officer who'd come to her door.

He'd missed a spot on his chin while shaving. That was all she could recall. Nearly ten years later, the last thing she remembered wasn't what she and Jason had said to each other, or if she'd told him she loved him, or exactly what the officer said.

It was that damn patch of dark hair the person who'd told her that her world was destroyed had failed to shave that morning.

"I know I'm the last person you'd think—" She looked off, her gaze finding the blue sky outside the window. "I don't know what to say. I'm weak. Weaker than I thought, and I couldn't pull myself out of this grief. And, suicide—depression—*is* a disease, it kills twenty-five percent of Americans." Charlotte added the fact sheepishly, as if data could excuse her betrayal.

"Spare us the statistical bullshit." Lourdes stood so quickly Jimmy nearly tipped over. "You have a choice. We don't. We're dying, and there isn't a damn thing we can do about it." The woman pushed past her.

Lourdes' anger trailed her like perfume.

"Lourdes," she said.

Her friend stopped, her hand on the doorknob, but she didn't turn.

Charlotte continued, "I don't have a choice. Some days it's all I think about. It's poisoning my mind, just like cancer is poisoning your body."

The starlet sprung on her, shoving a finger in Charlotte's face. "Do *not* compare us. We are nothing alike. I want nothing more than to grow old and die in my sleep. *You're* poisoning your mind. I didn't ask for this."

She flinched, the sharp words laced with the poison of truth. It would've hurt far less if Lourdes had just hit her.

The room rattled with the slamming door.

Celeste stood next. Big tears pooled in her eyes. "You should be ashamed of yourself." Her voice was soft, soaked in sadness. "You'd seemed like such a nice young lady. I'm sure you're hurting, but you're not one of us."

The door closed gently behind the older woman, a low click that pierced Charlotte's heart more than the crack of Lourdes' anger.

Dylan stood; his hands shoved in his pockets. He stopped in front of her, his dark blue eyes magnified behind his glasses.

More than anyone else, he deserved to live. Cutting his life short was cruel. It was an egregious crime, and if there was someone who should pay for it, Charlotte would've been happy to argue that case.

There was no villain, other than his delinquent cells. No criminal, no perpetrator, no one to pay.

He opened his mouth, but then closed it and shook his head, before just walking away.

The room should've felt empty, but the heaviness of her betrayal settled in, taking the space left by her friends.

Former friends.

Fellow Diers.

Darla stood next and wrapped her arms around Charlotte.

At first, she kept her arms at her side, her body flinching at her touch. Retreating in on itself, unwilling to be comforted. Undeserving.

Charlotte should be hit, kicked, screamed at. Not hugged.

"This must be so hard for you," she whispered. She released her and looked in Jimmy's direction. "We've got a paperwork nightmare with Levi; I'm going to get started on it."

Their leader slid from the arm of the loveseat to a cushion and patted the empty spot next to him. "Let's talk."

She eyed him; not that Charlotte didn't trust Jimmy. She didn't trust herself to not beg forgiveness, to ask to still be part of the group.

She didn't deserve that. Didn't deserve pity or mercy, understanding or sympathy.

Charlotte deserved exactly what she was getting.

"I won't bite," he added, at her hesitation.

She sat, hugging the opposite end. There were so many things she wanted to say to Jimmy. Guilt clouded her mind, stealing her words.

In the dark corners of her brain, her heart, she heard that mantra, *end it, end it, end it,* whooshing through her body with the rhythm of her pulse.

How long would it take her to fling the balcony door open and leap to her death? Would Jimmy stop her, or let her go?

"So, this is why your doctor never sent anything in." He spoke to his hands.

"If I'd seen a shrink, I'm sure the last thing she'd do is send me on a trip with dying people."

Silence settled between them like a ghost.

"Jimmy, I'm sorry. I wasn't here to make a mockery of death."

He turned, pulling one leg up on the sofa. "Why *are* you here, Charlotte?"

She took a deep breath. Why was she there?

Not there in the hotel room, but there on earth.

Was it because there were two Charlottes? One trapped inside, begging to get out, to leave her body, to join Jason wherever he was. The other, the one who wrote books on pushing through grief, the one who got up on stage and shared her story, who threw life preservers to the drowning.

Desperately hoping the words she wrote and spoke would eventually sink into her psyche.

They never did.

"The easy answer; I really am going to die. The harder answer, I want to fight like hell..." A sob strangled her words.

A muscle flexed in Jimmy's jaw, and his Adam's apple bobbed. "Phantom limb syndrome."

"What?"

"I've had a few amputees come through and they talk about losing a limb, but still feeling it. It's an itch, or a tickle, or even its pain sometimes. Losing someone is like losing a limb. She's gone, but you still feel her there."

Charlotte turned, matching his posture on the loveseat. "Who was she?"

"My mom, and even though it's been nearly forty years, some people leave such an imprint that when they're gone, the void they leave is inescapable."

Jason's death was an imploding star. The black hole of her grief devoured everything. Light. Hope. Happiness. Her future. The gravity of it was all-consuming.

"I'm trying to escape the void. But he's everywhere. Even places we've never been together; I feel Jason next to me. And, when I don't think about him, I feel guilt. Guilt of letting myself forget about him," she said. "That's why I'm here, I think."

Jimmy nodded and looked toward the door, where all of their friends had escaped. "It makes sense now."

"Care to explain it to me? Because nothing makes sense."

"Your dying wish, to swim with humpbacks." He whipped his head back in her direction, his gaze warm, understanding. "They fought to survive. Just like you. You're fighting, Charlotte. Even if you think you're done, you're not."

Was she fighting to stay alive?

She certainly didn't feel like it.

Maybe it was still there. Her will to live. Hidden deep inside the vault of her heart. Protected, only to be accessed when it was time to cash it out.

Was that why she wrote down her wish?

She didn't want to see more death.

Charlotte wanted to be confronted with life.

35

Charlotte wasn't shocked by the text message from Jimmy.
You might be more comfortable if you fly back on your own. We can reimburse.

After all, it was Lourdes' jet that had gotten them there. The woman was angry enough she would've tossed Charlotte out mid-fight. Without a parachute.

I understand. And, no need to reimburse. She responded. It was better this way. To not have to face their anger. Their judgment.

She was packed and ready to go. Javier's business card sat on the desk. A square that reminded her she was still capable of being loved. Of loving.

Charlotte shoved it in her purse. She probably wouldn't actually reach out to him, but at this point, decision paralysis was ravaging her body. The roadmap she'd laid out for herself wasn't just ripped in half. It was incinerated.

She tried to sleep on the flight home, but the movie behind her closed eyes was a highlight reel of the last two weeks. Sharing the stage with Levi, their voices dancing, playing off each other. Hiking Machu Picchu with Celeste, seeing the world through the older woman's camera lens. Drinking wine fireside with Lourdes, watching the African sunset. Boosting Dylan's confidence, sharing in his heartache of a life cut short.

It didn't help that she punished herself with a playlist full of Levi's former band on repeat. She might as well flog herself with his memory. Let his searing guitar licks slash across her body.

Her driver met her at baggage claim. "Miss Claybrooke, we didn't expect you back until next week." Chuck reached for her luggage. "I'm sorry to hear your vacation was cut short, but I hope it was fun while it lasted."

She kept her dark glasses on. If he saw her eyes, he'd realize that this was no vacation.

Spring had come to Charleston while Charlotte was away. The sky was a brilliant blue and the ocean sparkled like it was topped with diamonds.

When they drove across the bridge to her island, she looked out over the sailboats dotting Charleston Harbor. White beacons waving at her in the gentle breeze. White flags. Telling her to surrender. Surrender what?

Her fear. Her life.

Her grief.

Could she give it up?

Quit grieving cold turkey. Grieving Jason was all Charlotte had left of him. If she gave that up, what would she have left?

No past. No future.

Nothing but a hollow shell of a life.

Her home looked exactly as she remembered it, but it somehow felt different. As if she'd outgrown it.

"Are you going into the office Monday, Miss Claybrooke?" Chuck asked, lifting her suitcase from the trunk.

"Yes, I'll see you Monday morning." She reached for her suitcase. "Charlotte. We've known each other long enough, please call me Charlotte."

The older man looked down; his white eyebrows furrowed. "Are you sure, Miss Claybrooke—Charlotte?"

"Yes, thank you, have a great weekend." She took three steps toward her house and whirled. "I think I'm going to drive myself Monday. Why don't you take the day off?"

"Miss Claybrooke...Charlotte, is everything okay?"

Charlotte glanced at the point of the island, the breeze rolling off the ocean, and whipping her hair off her back. "Yeah, it will be. Thank you, Chuck, for everything."

She dropped her bag at the front door and jogged up the stairs to her bedroom. The life preserver waited for her where she'd left it.

Charlotte dropped to her knees and clutched it, holding it against her chest. What would Jason think if he saw her?

"Char," he'd say. *"What are you doing? Get back out there."*

This wasn't the girl he'd proposed to. The one he'd followed on a run. The one he'd saved from drowning.

Would he even recognize her?

Did she even recognize herself?

Charlotte wiped her eyes and stood, digging her wetsuit out of the closet. The water would still be cold, but she needed to swim. To dive deep.

The beach was empty. It usually was this time of year. Only in the height of summer would the vacationers spill over from the public beach into her private one. She didn't mind. The big house at the end of the island felt less lonely with kids playing in the tide, building sandcastles, doing cartwheels. It was as if the house breathed easier with children near it. A friendly, gentle giant.

The cool sand squished between Charlotte's toes, welcoming her home. She walked out toward the water, her footsteps alongside the triangle prints of the gulls.

The first wave nearly knocked her over, but by the time she'd waded into waist-deep water, she felt at home.

With a deep inhale, she dove in, kicking until she'd made it past the breaking waves.

Charlotte swam. She swam until she could no longer see the sandy floor beneath her. She swam until the water no longer tried to spit her out at the shore. She swam until she felt weightless. As if she'd shed her body to become one with the water.

After several minutes, she surfaced, treading water, pulling her goggles to the top of her swim cap. Her house was a dot on the horizon. The barrier island was a line of grayish beige. She paddled in a circle. As far as she could see, she was alone.

As far as she could feel, she was alone.

The others had likely landed back in Miami. Was Lourdes going to spend a few days with Jimmy before heading back to Mexico City? Dylan, was he on a connecting flight back to Boston? What about Celeste? Was she sitting next to some nice young man on her flight to Houston?

Levi.

Was her friend lying on a cold metal table in Monaco, his chest cut open, organs lying on scales, being examined for what killed him while the truth stared the coroner in the face?

Death.

Death had killed him.

Charlotte floated on her back, staring up at the cloudless sky. The sun was sliding down to the west. Jet lag and exhaustion tugged at her, threatening to pull her under.

She could do it.

Let it happen.

It would be poetic, in a way. That ten years later, she finally died the way she was supposed to. As if death had been waiting patiently for her to come back to its lair.

She took a deep breath of salty air. Her lungs still wanted to breathe.

The water under her rippled, a swirling jet tickling her calf.

Charlotte sat up, looking around her. Her heart froze at the first dark gray fin. It undulated in and out of the water, instead of gliding across the top. Tension flowed out of her body. It wasn't a shark.

The second fin was smaller, surfacing just to her left.

Two more appeared to her right, a mother and a calf, their bodies so close together they appeared as one. Big fin, baby fin.

She pulled her goggles over her eyes and took a quick breath, let herself sink.

A pod of a dozen or so dolphins swirled around her, circling her, twirling, making barrel rolls underwater.

Charlotte watched until her lungs burned.

She floated back to the top, afraid to move, to make any sudden movements to break the magic.

The dolphin spiraled closer and closer, their slick bodies gliding past her legs. Like dogs, they were curious, cautious, eager to play, but would also run off at any sudden movement.

Suddenly, one of the larger ones shot out of the water, landing on the water on its side, cold ocean water splashing in Charlotte's face.

Another splashed behind her. Then two, side by side, launched out of the water.

Could they feel it? Her depression. Did it carry across the water like flotsam, drawing this pod of caring creatures toward her?

There was always old sea tales of dolphin saving lost sailors.

Did they also save lost souls?

Her face burned from the cold water and the wide smile. She'd grown up in the ocean, and had seen the occasional dolphin from a distance, but never anything like this.

A young dolphin arched out of the water next to her, leaning up in the water, mimicking her treading. His mouth opened, tiny teeth smiling at her as he clicked and nodded. He bobbed and crashed his chin on the surface, splashing water on Charlotte.

She couldn't help but laugh. "You want to play, buddy?" She gently splashed water in his direction. He let out a long stream of high-pitched squeaks. If she didn't know any better, she'd swear he was laughing.

The sun kissed the western horizon and the air cooled.

She needed to get back to shore, but the last thing she wanted to do was leave the dolphin. Leave the moment.

The circle of porpoises widened, their arching dives moving away from her until they were further out at sea.

Except for one.

The young dolphin stayed by her.

He surfaced once more, his body floating next to her, shooting water out of his blowhole.

She reached out and ran her fingers over his back.

His skin was cool and rubbery, soft and solid under her cold fingers.

Charlotte looked into his eyes, silently thanking him for being there, for reminding her that no matter how deep the ocean might seem, she'd never be alone.

No matter how strong the undertow of death pulled at her, she had the strength to fight back to the surface and swim to shore.

36

There was nothing more sickening than two people who slept together and tried to pretend it never happened. The forced casual politeness. The avoidance of gazes. Fighting a smile.

Darla was literally nauseous by Jimmy and Lourdes' act.

The *telenovela* star struggled to put her bag over her seat on the private jet.

Jimmy casually assisted, but his hand lingered over the woman's.

Their gazes stayed locked for a breath too long.

That wasn't the only sign they'd slept together.

Jimmy slipping out of Lourdes' room with rumpled clothes the morning they'd found Levi, tousled hair and the sheepish just-got-laid grin was indisputable.

It'd been stupid for Darla to think there was more to them than employee and boss. It was stupid to think that he could love someone like her. Her momma had been right.

Like married like. Trailer trash didn't leap out of the garbage can and suddenly find itself in a Bel Air mansion.

Nope.

When it was finally time to take out the trash it went straight to the landfill. No matter how it tried to dress itself up and no matter how nice the private jet it flew in on.

"I'm going to check on Momma," Darla said, as soon as she retrieved her luggage. She didn't want to wait to see the long goodbye between Jimmy and Lourdes.

The late afternoon temperature was warm and muggy, a bit early for Miami. It could've also been her temper gradually turning up.

Everything about this last trip was a cluster. From suicidal Charlotte slipping by them, to the bandits, ignoring Enzo's commands to come home and the casino trip.

Levi's overdose was the whipped cream on this cluster sundae.

Jimmy and Lourdes, well, they'd put the *fuck* into cluster fuck.

Her mom was in her usual place, eyes staring out the window watching the sun set over the Everglades.

"Hey, Lupe," Darla greeted the nurse checking her mother's vitals. "How's she doing? Anything new?"

"Hi, Darla, welcome back." The nurse changed out the bag of nutrients that kept her mother alive. "Same old, same old. Did you have a good trip?"

Was she spinning her wheels with her mother, just as she was with Jimmy? Putting too much faith into something that would never happen.

Her mother snapping out of her catatonic state.

Jimmy falling in love with her.

Would it kill the universe to give her a win for a change?

Lupe finished her work and left them alone.

Darla grabbed the hairbrush and sat next to her mother. "Hey, Momma, so I just got back from Africa and Monaco." She ran the brush through her mom's long blonde hair. "I didn't see much of either place, but Monaco was…interesting. We visited one of those fancy casinos, got all dressed up. I won a bunch of money playing craps. You'd've been proud."

She put the brush down and grabbed the jar of moisturizer. Its tangy scent brought tears to her eyes. Or maybe it was the thought of

Levi alive. She put a dollop of the lotion on her palm and gently rubbed it across her mother's face.

This ritual had initially started as a way to keep her momma looking youthful. Darla cringed at the thought of Nell waking up and finding herself decades older. Now it was as much for her own well-being as her mother's.

"Then something really sad happened. A man, one of Jimmy's clients, died. That's the first time that happened."

Something even sadder had happened. Jimmy broke her heart. Darla wasn't ready to admit that to her mother.

Her phone buzzed in her purse. She set the moisturizer down and retrieved it.

Jimmy.

She stared at his face flashing on her screen. Auburn hair, receding hairline. Green eyes and a long straight nose. Truthfully, Darla could do better. Also, truthfully, no she could not.

"Hey, Jimmy. What's up?"

"How's Nell?" He huffed between the two words, like he was running. The sound of traffic filled the space between his question and her answer.

"Um, same old Nell. Where are you?"

"Good, I mean, not good, because you want her to get better, but I guess same is better than worse." He was rambling, and Jimmy only rambled when he was nervous.

"What's wrong?"

A car horn blew behind him. "Sorry, walking down on Ocean Front for a bit. Hey, so I wanted to talk to you about something."

Darla's heart plunged into an ice bath. Why did he want to talk about it? She'd been planning to sweep it under the rug, let it gather dust with all the other dashed hopes and failed wishes. Then again, there were so many of them, she was likely to trip over the rug and break an ankle. Maybe it was better to keep this one out in the open.

"Yeah?"

"Yeah, so yesterday morning, when you saw me, in the um, hall, with the stuff with uh, Levi." Huff, huff. "So, I know how that looked."

She crossed her arms. "It looked like you were coming out of Lourdes' room."

"Well, yeah, that's what happened." Jimmy's voice went up an octave. "But let me tell you why."

Oh God, no, no, please, we're not buddies who tell each other about the latest conquest.

"Jimmy, I'm with my mother."

"I know, I'm sorry, but let me finish."

Darla could hear the ocean behind him now. Could almost see him standing there, staring out at the Atlantic, the descending sun setting the waves on fire.

"She wasn't feeling well, so I went by to check on her."

Like you said you'd check on me.

She chewed on the inside of her cheek to prevent the words from slipping out of her mouth.

"And I guess from the booze and the excitement of the casino, I fell asleep in her chair."

Darla rewound to that moment. Not that she had to rewind too far. It'd been on a loop in her mind. Jimmy stepping out of Lourdes' room. Undershirt untucked. His tuxedo shirt unbuttoned, jacket and tie in hand. He wasn't even wearing socks, for God's sake.

Why would anyone sleep sockless in a client's chair?

"Uh-huh."

"Yeah, so I realize that it probably looked like something, um, inappropriate happened."

"Did it?" Her voice was barbed wire.

The pause had the ominous tension of a cowboy getting strapped on the back of a bronc. That moment before all hell broke loose. Either it would be a smooth eight seconds or one of them was going to get trampled.

"What? No." Her boss now sounded like a pre-pubescent boy. "No, Darla, come on, you'd known me for how long, what, no, no, nothing... You know me better than that."

He was now a stage five rambler. If he wasn't careful, he was going to step in his own bullshit.

"Do I?"

Jimmy sighed into the phone. "Darla, are you okay?"

No, she wasn't okay. She'd told their investor he needed to get laid. She'd kissed her boss and liked it, wanted more to happen. Instead of him coming to her room, she woke up alone, then found him coming out of an exotic movie star's room when she couldn't find him to tell him one of their clients overdosed. After all that, another client had admitted she was suicidal.

So no, Darla was about as okay as snow in Houston.

She took a deep breath and looked up to the tiled ceiling. What good would it do? He knew she knew. This would fester between them, like a splinter stuck in her foot. It would work its way out, or it'd get infected. Only time would tell.

"I'm fine. I'm just jet-lagged and mentally drained, with Levi and Charlotte…"

"So that's the other thing I wanted to talk to you about. Can we maybe, if Enzo asks, or I guess if anyone, future clients and what-not, but if anyone asks about Levi, can we just say natural causes?"

"You mean, lie."

"Or maybe we could say liver disease, since that's what he was dying of."

"But he overdosed."

"It would be for the best, for all of us, Levi included, because who wants that hanging over them?"

Darla crossed the small room. The last of the Florida sun winked goodnight.

Goodnight and good luck.

"Only if asked." Jimmy's voice was pleading, desperate.

God, she'd do anything for this man. Was she that loyal of a dog? Kicked, fed scraps, and then left to sleep outside in the cold.

Tears shot to her eyes and her throat closed up. "Fine," she whispered. "Yes, whatever you want. You're the boss."

"Darla, don't be that way. We're a team. You and me."

She squeezed her eyes shut, closing the levee before the tears broke through. "I've got to go. I'll see you Monday."

It'd been a long time since she'd given herself over to tears.

Steele women don't cry.

Her momma had told her that for as long as she could remember. Fall off her bicycle. *Steele women don't cry.* Had to sell her horse to pay the rent. *Steele women don't cry.* Had to move her senior year, away from her friends, because her momma's new boyfriend lived two counties over. *Steele women don't cry.*

Even when her momma had a stroke.

Darla had managed to keep it together.

It was high time for her to shed some tears, to lance the boil of hurt and disappointment.

She curled up on the bed, the medical-grade blanket rough on her cheek.

She cried for her momma, stuck in an earth-bound purgatory. Her brain too scrambled to be fully present, her body too strong to give up.

She cried for Levi, a man she barely knew who was headed toward death, but a night of bad decisions hastened his arrival.

Darla cried for Charlotte. How lonely of a place it must be to want to end her life.

Most of all, she cried for herself, for the person she could've been, the person she wanted to be. "Oh Momma, I would give anything for you to tell me what to do."

A weight landed on her head, not heavy, but with enough heft that she startled.

"Momma?"

Nell's cupped hand rested on her crown. A hand that she'd last seen at her momma's side had now moved five inches to stroke her hair.

Darla sat up slowly, hesitant to remove her mother's touch, but needing to confirm.

Her mother's gaze was still stuck to the spot outside, where she stared daily. Her expression impassive, not moving, but her left hand jerked again, grazing Darla's arm.

Her momma was right.

Steele women didn't cry.

Steele women fought back.

Darla grabbed her phone and tapped open the text app. *Can we talk?*

Three words. No bull.

There'd be a lot more to say when they met up, but for now, that was all she could muster.

She was officially in that moment. Getting strapped in, ready for the ride.

Because when she sat down with Enzo and told him everything she planned on telling him, there'd be no getting the bull back into the chute.

37

Charlotte took her time getting ready for work. Usually, she was up before the sun to get her run in, then she'd be at the door waiting for Chuck to drive her to the office. She didn't need a driver, except it gave her an extra precious half-hour in the car to get work done both to and from the office.

She sat on her balcony; her steaming coffee cup held close to her heart. Charlotte's gaze scoured the ocean, looking for her pod of dolphin. The magic of the experience hadn't waned in the days since she'd crawled out of the ocean, exhausted and exhilarated. It wouldn't happen again, but she couldn't help but hope.

She'd done that a lot in the past couple of days.

Hope.

Hope that her friends had made it home safely. Hope that their dying adventures weren't ruined because of her. Hope they'd forgive her.

It was okay if they didn't. She wouldn't blame them. But, she still had hope. Which was a hell of a lot more than she'd had when she'd gotten into the water.

Even though the morning was cool, Charlotte drove with the top down. Music loud. Fistful of Devils. Her go-to playlist for the past several days. Her hair whipped her eyes, but the stinging felt good. Made her feel alive.

Her office was a hive of activity.

Meredith, her booking manager, was pacing the open floor plan office, her earbuds hanging from her ears like electronic jewelry and her head bent over her phone. "I know you promised your employees a book signing, but Miss Claybrooke can't possibly sign that many copies."

"Sure, I can."

The young woman jumped and twirled, her brown eyes widening. "Hold on, let me call you back. Charlotte, I thought you weren't back until next week."

She shrugged and dropped her bag into a chair. "Missed you guys and came home early. Wanna catch me up?"

Charlotte's small team gathered around her, but her focus drifted out the window, watching the trees in the breeze.

Two branches moved together, like lovers, rubbing against each other. Like her and Javier, their bodies swaying together, hearing only the music of their passion.

The voices of her office stopped, the void of their words as screeching as a needle across the record.

She snapped her attention back to the table and four pairs of eyes blinked at her. "I'm sorry, I missed that last part."

Meredith glanced at her colleagues. "I was just saying the company has a thousand employees coming to their corporate conference, and even if just half of them wanted books signed, it'd make you late to catch your flight, which would make you late to the radio interview back in New York."

"Okay, move the interview."

Her director of communication, Veronica, sat up straight. "What, no, do you know how long I've been trying to get you on Sam Ellison's show?"

While Veronica and Meredith bickered over schedules, Charlotte's attention drifted back outside. She rubbed her thumb across her lower lip, remembering the electricity pulsing through her when she'd stood on stage, her and Levi, belting out one of her most beloved songs.

"Is that the song you were singing that night?" Jules, her social media manager, asked. "That was brilliant by the way." The young woman typed into her phone. "Lots of engagement, shares, and it introduced you to a whole new audience. By the way, you're a really good singer."

She stiffened. When she'd been up there, she was Charlotte Claybrooke, Fistful of Devils fan, a teenager trapped in a forty-year-old's body, a woman who'd momentarily forgotten she was going to kill herself.

When she was up there, Levi was still alive.

"I just read that guy died," Meredith said. "In a Paris hotel."

"Monaco," Charlotte muttered. The table grew quiet, the mood of the room shifting with her emotional tide. "Meredith, when is that keynote?"

"Two weeks, in Vegas, then you've got the Sam Ellison interview in New York the following morning."

Charlotte nodded. Had to stick around at least that long. Then maybe she'd quit, close her company, quietly shut down her public persona. There was no reason to disappoint anyone with her suicide.

The thought slipped from her brain like water through a sieve.

Ugh. I thought I was past this.

"Okay, let's not schedule anything before that." She pushed herself to standing. "I'll be in my office catching up."

She had to escape their naïveté. If she stayed there much longer, she might infect them with her depression.

They might infect her with their innocence.

She closed the door of her office and opened her laptop. With a browser open, she typed in *Lourdes Peña*. The star stared back at her, links to her biography, various news stories, images of her friend —*former* friend—because the woman would stab her in the heart with a stiletto rather than speak to her again.

Charlotte clicked through the image bank, going back in time. Lourdes on the red carpet, her hair, her real hair, pulled up into a tight bun. Strong eyebrows and long lashes framed her dark eyes. She was still thin, but not gaunt, her cheekbones prominent but not protruding.

There were never any stories about the starlet's illness; she'd somehow managed to keep it out of the media.

Charlotte could almost find the moment when Lourdes had gotten sick. The red carpet appearances had tapered off, the candid photos of her canoodling with the sexy guy of the week became fewer, then a year later, a different Lourdes emerged.

The light within her had dimmed, exhaustion moved into her eyes, and her hair lost the natural luster; instead had the cartoonish abundance of a wig.

Why couldn't she trade places with her?

Charlotte should be the one eaten alive by cancer. If she could, she'd gladly trade her life-force with this woman. *She* deserved cancer. Lourdes deserved life.

She opened another tab on her browser. This time typing, *Dylan O'Keefe*.

There wasn't as much about him. A few links to his social media accounts, and stories of his tech company.

Charlotte clicked on one story and quickly read the feature of the boy genius who went to college when he should've been going to middle school. Was well on his way to his Ph.D., instead of preparing for high school graduation, when his illness struck. Treatments failed; it was only a matter of time.

A matter of time before what made him Dylan, his brilliant mind, killed him.

Why couldn't she trade places with him?

To give Dylan the long, healthy life she didn't want.

Finding Celeste Bennett online was even more difficult. The only reference to her was in her husband's obituary. A man Celeste had loved, but because of him, she didn't live the life she set out to live. Now, she was on the cusp of forgetting it all. Forgetting her family, her joy, her loves, her achievements, her failures.

Why couldn't Charlotte trade places with Celeste?

She would be freed of grief that'd anchored her in the past, refusing to give up and let her move forward with her life.

Her cursor hovered over the search bar of the next window. She was afraid of typing in his name. Not that she was afraid of what she'd read. Charlotte had been there, seen it all. But…because of how she'd feel. How she wanted to trade places with Levi most of all, despite how buoyed with hope and life she'd felt after the dolphins.

When his face finally filled the screen, accusatory headlines glared back at her. *"Levi Livingston, Fistful of Devils Frontman, Dead at 72." "Drinking and Drugs Suspected in Rock Star's Death." "Rumors of Suicide Swirl Around Dead Rocker."*

The image of her friend smiled back at her. His dark sunglasses covered his face, a bright smile, even brighter white hair. Levi aged through the pictures, but the girls next to him didn't.

Charlotte went back to her search results, and a new story popped up. This one was less accusatory, more memorializing.

Levi grew up in Southampton, the only son of hard-working people. He'd been married a few times, but only his first marriage, the one that'd started before he'd become a star, produced a child.

The girl, a young woman now, remembered her father as being kind and caring, always there for her, despite a busy touring schedule and her parents' divorce.

Charlotte scrolled to the end of the story, eager to find something that would tell her it was all a lie, her friend was still alive, he hadn't overdosed after spending the night with a prostitute. Instead, she found a simple line. *"A private memorial service will be held on Friday, at Forest Lawn Cemetery in Hollywood Hills."*

She clicked open one more tab and pulled up the airline reservation system. Once her flight was booked, she sent an email to her team. *Cancel my meetings for next week, I have to fly to L.A.*

38

Stormy days were made for self-loathing. The clouds darkened the skies, casting an ominous cover over Miami, wrapping Jimmy in a dour mood.

His reflection stared back from his office window. The ocean frothed angry waves. If he didn't know better, he'd think the ocean was acting on Darla's anger, rather than atmospheric forces.

Then again, her temper was known to rile up a tornado or two.

It was a stupid act of a desperate man. Asking her to lie about Levi's death. Thinking she wasn't smart enough to catch on that Jimmy had done more than just fall asleep in a chair in Lourdes' room.

It'd been a while since desperation had squeezed at his throat with enough force to suffocate him. He'd climbed out of those moments before. Back when he was younger and had the strength and swagger of youth.

But, now?

Now he was a weak middle-aged man with a receding hairline who seemed unusually adept at making monstrous fuck-ups.

Jimmy pulled a bottle of bourbon from his desk drawer. No sign of Darla. No text from her that she wouldn't be coming in. Nothing to indicate anything was wrong.

He should reach out to her. Make sure everything was okay.

He already knew the answer to that.

Everything was *not* okay.

The amber liquid filled his glass. It was barely ten o'clock in the morning. A Monday morning. Jimmy was one low son of a bitch to be drinking in his dark, empty office on a Monday.

He pulled up the budget Darla had been working on. Bless her beautiful heart. She'd tried her best to make the numbers work.

A negative budget is a negative budget.

No amount of massaging was going to make it anything but that. Darla wasn't working with clay. She was working with a heaping pile of manure.

Jimmy blanched at the thought. His assistant shouldn't be cleaning up his shitty bookkeeping. She was working way above her pay grade. Way above what he should've asked of her.

There was also the dummy budget. The one that said Dire Enterprises was doing modestly well. He could send it to Enzo like he had last year. To show he *did* know how to manage his business. It wasn't *all* about taking lavish trips around the world. Maybe that would buy him time to pull it together and climb out of the hole he'd dug.

After all, this was Jimmy's calling. His mission. His ministry. He couldn't put a price on something as precious as that. Had Jesus charged people when he'd healed the sick? No, he did it out of the kindness of his heart. It was who he was.

He threw down the rest of his bourbon and refilled the glass.

Then again, look at what happened to Jesus.

Jimmy Dire was nowhere close to being the Son of God.

"Son of the Devil is more like it," he muttered into his drink.

He deleted the blank budget. There was no hiding anymore. He'd messed up big time.

Jimmy had two choices; face the music or run like hell from it.

Did he have it in him?

To walk away and start over again. He'd done it before, but he'd been much younger. It was easier to convince government workers. Kind women who'd seen in Jimmy the American dream. A kid from nowhere who was destined to go somewhere. Their belief in him had fueled his transformation.

If he tried it today, they'd just see a man who'd failed at his second chance and wouldn't be worthy of a third. Jimmy was no longer that kid desperately trying to shed his father's name and abuse.

This time he'd be shucking his own mistakes.

His gaze fell to the haphazard stack of file folders. The latest group of Diers. There was something different about this group from any other; overdoses and sexual liaisons aside.

They were a team.

All for one, one for all.

Jimmy shuffled through the stack until he found her file.

How had Charlotte made it through the application process?

Was it because she was Charlotte Claybrooke? Because he'd been distracted with his failing business? Entranced with Lourdes?

He thumbed through the paperwork. She was a clever one, without a doubt. Claiming her forms were lost in cyberspace, or her assistant was falling down on the job.

The woman stared up at him from her headshot. Chocolate brown hair with bangs grazing her eyebrows, as if she could hide under the curtain of hair. Golden green eyes smiled at him; warmer, more genuine than the sentiment on her lips.

Truth be told, there was nothing in the forms preventing anyone who was suicidal from participating. It was an unwritten rule. Everyone who came through Jimmy's door was dying of an honest-to-God illness.

Then again, depression was an illness of the mind. Charlotte's will to live was irreparably broken.

If that wasn't a sickness, then what was?

His mind flashed back through the slideshow of the past ten days. A woman who wanted to die wouldn't have jumped on stage with Levi. She wouldn't have befriended Celeste, someone sure to forget her in the coming months. If Charlotte truly wanted to kill herself, she wouldn't have admitted the truth to her friends.

No, she would've kept it to herself, to sneak away and do the deed leaving them all to wonder what warning signs they'd missed.

Maybe Charlotte needed the group, not to live out her dying wish, but to live out her living wish.

Jimmy took another long sip of his bourbon. Her adventure was the only one they didn't get to. Could he get the group back together, those still walking the earth, to be there for her? Would they put aside their anger to stand beside her as she stood with them?

Kintsukuroi. The Japanese word that meant something was more beautiful after being broken struck him like an unexpected slap.

Is that what they all were?

Beautifully broken.

Was that what drew him to Lourdes?

Had light seeped through the cracks, making her more luminous than before? Like a dying sun, was she shining her brightest before her light went out for good?

Jimmy rubbed his chest. Just two days without her, and he felt chilled outside the glow of her sun.

How would he feel when her final breath escaped those beautiful lips?

He grabbed his phone and hit *call* on her number. The phone paused before commencing the double ring of an international call. It was only an hour earlier in Mexico City, but Lourdes was probably already awake. Gently stretching. Her dark eyes fluttering open. Soft lips pursing into a gentle smile.

After the third ring, the unmistakable void of an answer.

He cleared his throat, pushing away the bourbon-coated cobwebs of despair.

"*Diga,*" a man said. His voice was throaty, thick with sleep.

Jimmy pulled back the phone and looked at the screen. It was Lourdes' number. The same one he'd texted with the evening before.

Did something happen to her? Was this man a doctor?

Would Jimmy feel the shift in the atmosphere with her death, or would the world keep spinning as it has for millennia through countless deaths?

"*Hola?*" The man spoke again.

Jimmy opened his mouth, trying to remember the words to ask if the man spoke English, but in that space of silence, he heard it.

Lourdes' sultry voice tossed a question in Spanish.

The man answered her, and the line went dead.

He stared at the dark phone in his hands.

The storm intensified outside. Lightning lit up his office, tossing shadows on his life. Shadows he'd tried to keep hidden in the bright Florida sun.

The brighter the light, the darker the shadows.

It was only a matter of time before the shadows of Jimmy's past overtook his life.

39

Even though it'd been a couple of years since her last visit, Charlotte navigated her car through the labyrinthian single-lane dirt road to the back corner of the cemetery with the ease of someone who made a daily trek.

The tombstones shrunk the farther she drove into the heart of the graveyard. The historic monoliths with the names of the dearly departed worn or covered by lichen gave way to newer, more conservative markers standing straight, gleaming like a teenager's smile after an orthodontist's handiwork.

It was back in this corner, hidden among the matching tombstones, tucked away under a grand oak tree, with Spanish moss draped like a bride's veil, where the love of her life had been lain to rest.

Charlotte hadn't started her day by planning for a visit to a cemetery. She'd been in a marketing meeting, strategizing the branding of her next book, when she'd gotten up and walked out of the meeting, ignoring the dropped jaws and uncomfortable side glances of her team. They didn't need her for this meeting. It wasn't her brand on that book.

Not anymore.

Her mind kept wandering to her upcoming flight to Los Angeles and Levi's funeral. It was both impulsive and, quite frankly, pretty desperate.

There were no guarantees the other Diers would be there. If they were, they'd most likely shun her. Or worse, cause a major scene that would upstage her friend's tribute.

She didn't *have* to get on that plane. She didn't have to put herself in the middle of the mourning. She didn't have to let people see her.

Charlotte escaped the cold air of her car. The heat and humidity enveloped her; her skin broke out into a flush of sweat.

Jason's grave sat under the dappled shade of a tree.

The plot next to him was empty.

It was hers. Bought with his, because she was unwilling to let a stranger be buried next to him.

Eager to rejoin him as soon as she could.

For the first few years after his death, Charlotte had visited regularly. Caring for it as one would nurture a garden. She planted flowers around the headstone, hoping something beautiful would grow out of something horrible.

Despite that, the grounds crew always cut them down. Always cut *her* down. As if reminding her life didn't grow from death.

Life grew from life.

Jason's granite gravestone was still pristine. No moss grew on it, nothing discolored it. It stood there, staring at the tree, watching life move on without him.

Charlotte sat on the ground, ignoring that her beige pants would likely be ruined when she stood. The grass was cool, a few drops of leftover dew clung to the edges of the blades, not yet burned off with the early afternoon sun. She plucked a long blade from the ground, twisting it around her finger as the wind whispered in the trees.

She avoided staring at the final date on the tombstone. The tenth anniversary was just over a month away. They should be making plans for a wedding anniversary getaway.

Maybe back to where they'd planned to honeymoon. Just them,

without the kids they'd hoped to have. Charlotte shouldn't be sitting in a beautifully somber cemetery.

Jason shouldn't be underground.

Life was full of "shouldn'ts." It was full of "could'ves" and "might-have-beens." Even a few "never wases."

Life was full of surprises. Of laughter and a baby's squeal of delight. It was full of tears of happiness and tears of sorrow. It was full of warm sunshine and cold rain. It was full of heartache and full of heart-warming happiness.

Life was full of death.

It was also full of life.

"Hey, Jason." As natural as it felt to talk to him, Charlotte couldn't help but look around to make sure she was alone.

Not like anyone would fault her for talking to a grave. It happened a lot out there.

"Sorry, it's been a while." She shredded the grass and tossed it to the side. "I miss you. With everything I have. It's funny, I think I'm more accustomed to the void you left than you. I guess grief can take shape."

She crawled forward and laid down, her head nestled against the base of the headstone. "I messed up, Jay. Not just on the trip, but before that. I've been messing up since you died."

Charlotte closed her eyes and imagined they were back in bed on a lazy Sunday morning. Jason listened to her intently, with no judgment. These were the moments she loved the most. The quiet hours where they told each other all their secrets. It was where she could admit she was scared. That maybe she missed something while preparing for an important trial. She could whisper her insecurities and he'd take them from her. He would lift the burden of worry and carry it for her.

"If you were here, you'd tell me I'm not as bad as I think I am. You'd say sure, they might be angry with me, but, given time, they'd understand." Charlotte sighed and rolled over to her back, staring up at the sunlight filtering through the newborn leaves. "It should've been me that morning." The words hurt as she pushed them through

her throat. "You are so much better equipped at life alone than I am."

The words had barely floated away when she could feel Jason's chastisement. Why did she have to be the weak one? Why couldn't she be the one who grew stronger from this? Dying was easy. Living was harder. She'd never backed down from a fight before him. Even after he died, she didn't back down. She fought.

What was she fighting against now?

Her grief? It'd been there since the beginning, but these days it hummed, like the white noise of a fan.

Charlotte covered her eyes with her forearms. The image of Sunday mornings with Jason faded to the night of passion with Javier.

Her cheeks warmed with the remembered feeling of his lips on her neck, how they'd left a trail of burning desire as they moved down her body. When it was over, when the rush of endorphins and lust left her body, guilt settled in like an incoming tide.

Her eyes popped open. Somewhere along the way grief had left her body and guilt had taken over.

She'd been honest about her grief, but she'd never told anyone about her guilt.

Charlotte leaned up on her elbows. What if she wasn't the only one? What if there were others out there, living with unbearable guilt?

Guilt so ominous it would crush them.

Her honesty could be the searchlights for others whose grief festered and turned to guilt. She could let them know that it was okay to feel like an imposter. Everyone was just trying to do the best they could.

She pulled her phone out of her pocket and launched the video recorder. Her image stared back at her. Her cheeks were red from the heat. Dark circles were smeared beneath her eyes.

Charlotte brushed her bangs back.

The world needed to see her sincerity.

Her thumb hit the red *record* button, and her lips pulled back into a soft smile. "Hi guys, it's Charlotte." She paused, noticing the gravestones in the background of the video selfie.

She hit the *stop* button.

What was she doing?

She shouldn't be making this confession in a cemetery. What if people thought she was making light of suicide?

Or, worse, what if she set off a suicide contagion.

No, Char, be authentic. No more of this bullshit.

Charlotte held the phone up and started the recording over. "Hi guys, it's Charlotte. You're probably thinking it looks like I'm sitting in a cemetery, and well, you're right. I'm sitting here with Jason." She paused and looked away. "It's been a while since I've come to see him. I've always thought of him as my compass, but I've realized I was wrong. It's you. Every single one of you who has found solace in my story and my words. So, with that, I have a confession."

She cleared her throat. "I'm an imposter. Yes, I'm really Charlotte Claybrooke and yes, my fiancé really died just a few weeks before our wedding. I was fighting through my grief, but somehow my company took off to a place where my heart failed to go. I haven't succeeded in any way, other than earning money and building a company on something that's an important part of the human experience. Grief." Charlotte stood, suddenly feeling the need to move. "I never moved on. I haven't found that kind of love again. Not yet, at least. Some hopes died with Jason, and the death of those dreams is worse than losing him.

"You all look to me to guide you through this, but here's the deal. I'm not through it myself. Ten years later, and I'm no better. I'm worse." Tears burned behind her eyes. "Recently I took a trip with a group of people with terminal illnesses. There, we bonded over the fact we were all dying. Myself included. But my death was different than theirs. Their death would be the result of something out of their control; cancer, liver failure, Alzheimer's. I joined this trip with the intention to take my own life, because dying sounded better than living with myself feeling like I failed each and every one of you." She walked to the far edge of the property, staring out through the copse of trees. The spring growth was already thick, blocking her view into what lay beyond.

"This isn't a goodbye post. It's the opposite. This is a post about shedding the shroud of guilt. And, if it means I lose every single one of you, and my business goes bankrupt, that's fine. I'd rather be poor and honest with myself and others than make myself rich on a lie." Charlotte sucked in a deep breath, like it would be her last. "I'm going to get help, for this depression that's eating away at me. If you're like me, hurting, unable to let go of grief and anger and guilt, get help. There is still a life for us to live." She stopped recording and quickly posted the video to her social media channels before she changed her mind.

The team would freak out when they saw it, and if it meant they all quit, she could accept that.

Charlotte went back to staring at the green abyss. The future was just as much of a tangled mess as the vines and undergrowth of the forest. Something terrifying probably lurked just out of her view, but that was okay.

Because now she was ready to give it everything she had to stay alive.

40

Darla hadn't snuck around this much since she'd climbed out of her bedroom window as a teenager to go parking with Ranger Bonner. Except this time, she didn't creep down the dirt road to meet Ranger at the turn off from the highway.

This time, she just didn't go into the office. Rather than sneak out of the trailer park, she turned off her phone so Jimmy couldn't reach her. Instead of Ranger and his tight Wranglers, Darla was getting in the car with Enzo Fiore and his cost-more-than-all-of-her-possessions-combined wristwatch.

Their investor waited in his slate gray Maserati; his eyes hidden behind a pair of flawless aviators.

Gawd, I hope he forgot about that getting laid comment.

The black seats hugged her butt better than her favorite jeans. She ran her hands over the supple leather. It was possibly the softest thing she'd ever touched. Like veal for a rich person's ass.

"Darla," Enzo said, his mouth barely moving. He glanced out his window. "I took your advice. You're right. It loosened me up."

She froze her fondling of the leather seat. The last words she'd spoken to him had been in the heat of the moment at the craps table, with a healthy dose of liquid courage lighting the fire. "Oooh-kay."

His mouth twisted into a smirk. "I'm just messing with you. But that look on your face was worth your insult."

Relief calmed her spastic nerves. Only a bit. Guilt gnawed at her gut with the ferocity of a hungry termite. She shouldn't be there. Darla should've stayed at her momma's side, not tattling on Jimmy like a five-year-old.

There'd been no other movement. No other sign that Nell was still in there. Nothing to indicate that the stroking of Darla's hair at the moment when she needed her mother most was more than a nervous system stretching its legs.

The doctors could talk all they wanted, but her heart spoke the truth. Her momma was still there. She knew her daughter was hurting. Was starting to break.

Steele women don't cry.

Darla got the message.

Loud and clear.

"So, what's with the secrecy?" She resumed stroking the car seat. It was likely to be the only time she sat in a Maserati, and she wanted to imprint the feel of the leather on her palms.

Enzo put the car in reverse and backed out without even looking behind him. It was like the car drove itself.

Darla really needed to get a car made in this century.

"We're going to meet someone."

"Who?"

The man navigated out of the parking garage and onto the busy street.

A storm churned overhead, thrusting them into dusk, even though it was early afternoon. The slate-blue clouds shot lightning out and thunder boomed like a mean drunk being cut-off at the bar. Even though she'd grown up in a trailer, thunderstorms never scared Darla. Her mother, on the other hand, panicked at the faintest rumble of thunder.

After several minutes, Enzo finally spoke. "You can't make successful investments being everyone's friend." The car glided to a stop at a red light. He glanced in her direction. "You of all people should understand the need to protect who you are in order to do what you must." He reached into the backseat and handed her a thick folder.

She flipped it open. A younger version of herself stared up. It was her driver's license photo from Texas. Twenty-something, fresh-faced. Happily working her way through community college to earn her associate's degree in business management.

That Darla was going to own her own business, or maybe become a paralegal. She had dreams. Maybe nothing as grand as becoming an actress, or a rock star, or even an internationally best-selling author.

That was the beauty of dreams. They came in all shapes and sizes, and all were equally precious.

The next photo was a few years later. This one was taken in Florida, after Darla had moved to take care of her momma. She stood on stage, her back arched against the silver pole, her black eye-shadowed eyes closed, obviously unwilling to look at the crowd of men more than happy to stuff their filthy money in her bikini bottoms.

The photos that followed were taken at a distance, candid shots. Darla getting out of her old-enough-to-vote car. Walking into the nursing home juggling boxes of donuts. Darla and Jimmy at a café, paperwork spread between them.

"You had me followed." She'd had a lot of shitty things happen in her life, but this took the shit-cake.

Enzo swung the car into a squat office building.

The nondescript stucco gave no clue as to what hid inside. It could've been a doctor's office or a front for sex trafficking.

"I protected my investment." He swung the car into two parking spots, straddling both so no one could fit on either side. "Like I said, Darla, we all have to do things we despise."

"Oh, so I see what this is. I grew up as white trash and you think I'm stealing money." Anger kicked up inside her like a thrashing bronc.

She might've been poor, but she wasn't a criminal. Just because Darla had danced didn't mean she was a money-grabbing gold digger. On the other hand, he was right.

She'd had to do things and become someone she despised, but she'd done it for her mother. If Nell had never gotten sick, if she'd never met that two-timing man who'd dragged her halfway across the country, Darla would've likely gotten her degree, a decent-enough job, married a good-enough man, and popped out two-point-five kids.

She'd danced because she had to, not because she got any pleasure out of being groped.

"For someone who doesn't want to be judged, you're doing a good bit judging yourself." Enzo killed the car engine. "Come on."

He heaved himself out of the car, but she sat still.

Enzo leaned back in. "You can be mad at me later, but for now, I need you on my team. Remember, you called me."

He was right, again.

She *had* called him, but in a jealous fit of anger. What had Darla unleashed? Whatever it was, it wouldn't go back into the chute.

Her only choice was to climb aboard and hold on for dear life.

She followed him into an unmarked office on the first floor.

Murmurings quieted when they entered.

It was a modest office with old, mismatched furniture. Stale cigarette smoke hung in the air like a toxic mist, once again reminding Darla of her time as a dancer.

"Where are we?" she whispered.

A man appeared in the doorway. He was tall, painfully thin; someone who could easily hide behind a light pole.

Was this the man who tailed her? Was that why she'd never spotted anyone?

"We thought you weren't coming," he said, his voice as gravelly as an old dirt road.

"Just needed some extra time," Enzo said. "Come on, Darla, have a seat."

Three other men sat in the tight room. One dressed all in black; black jeans, black leather jacket covering a black T-shirt. If he was a private investigator, he'd be better suited in New York. Someone dressed like him in Miami would stick out like a burr in the saddle.

The other one was an Enzo clone. Expensive suit, expensive haircut, expensive bug stuck up his butt.

The final man looked like he was hitting a Jimmy Buffet concert after their meeting. A loose-fitting Hawaiian shirt covered an abundant belly. His cargo shorts revealed tan legs, and he rested a flip-flopped foot over a knee.

Darla kept her eyes on the folders stacked neatly in the middle of the table. "Someone better start talking, or I'm going to think this is some weird fetish thing."

The Jimmy Buffet fan laughed. "You still crack me up."

She cocked an eyebrow.

Still?

"Jack Collins." He thrust his hand in her direction. "Glad to make your official acquaintance. I'm an investigator, and before you get all pissy on me, I only followed you for a few days. It took no time to see you're a good person."

"Thanks?" She folded her arms across her chest.

Enzo 2.0 spoke next. "What has taken a little bit more time was determining the same about Jimmy." He slid the stack of folders toward her. "My brother has a soft spot for Dire Enterprises." He pursed his lips, like he'd sucked on a sour gumball. "And, you."

I hope that bug in your ass stings.

Darla flipped open the folder. Much like the one Enzo had shown of her own investigation, there were photos of Jimmy at work, on the weekend, coming out of his house. Nothing that set off any alarms.

She reached for the next one. Same set up, just a slightly younger version of her boss. His hairline hadn't receded as much, the few wrinkles that creasing his forehead hadn't formed yet.

The final folder was mostly paperwork. Jimmy's license, the mortgage for his house, credit report, social security.

"I don't understand. It seems you have everything you need to know."

Enzo reached over and flipped to the last section of stapled papers. "At first glance, yes, but what do you notice?" He paused, giving her a chance to answer. "Everything starts in 1992. Nothing further back than that."

"So what? Maybe things weren't digital back then."

"We were able to go back to your school days," Jack said. "Selling your horse had to damn-near kill ya, huh?"

Darla swallowed against the lump in her throat. She'd loved that horse. "What're you saying?"

The man in black leaned forward. "His name isn't Jimmy Dire or James Dire. His first name isn't even Jimmy."

Those words buzzed in her ear like a mosquito. How could he not be Jimmy? The name fit him like a custom suit.

Enzo squeezed her shoulder. "We didn't really pursue it too much, as long as the company turned a profit, but the numbers went south, so we did more digging."

Darla whipped her head up. "He's not stealing. I manage the books, handle the checks coming in and going out…" her voice broke.

Did she know for a fact that he wasn't stealing? She knew him, didn't she? Thought she loved him. And, all this time…

His name isn't even Jimmy.

"We have a forensic accountant checking everything," Enzo's brother said. "Darla, if there's anything you need to tell us, now is the time."

"Wait…Do you think—I'd never do—" The room closed in on her.

What Enzo brought her into?

False accusations,

Hot tears flooded her eyes, but she shooed them away. *Steele women don't cry.*

"Okay, fine, here's what you need to know. Levi Livingston died of a drug overdose with a hooker in his room. Jimmy was too busy bumping uglies with Lourdes Peña to notice anything was wrong. Oh, and one of our Diers, Charlotte Claybrooke, isn't really dying, she's just thinking of offing herself."

The silence around the room told her they hadn't prepared for *that* truth.

Maybe something along the lines of what she kept tucked away, deep down where she loved Jimmy and would do anything to protect him. That spot was cracked open. Not quite broken.

He isn't even Jimmy.

"What's his name?" Her voice was deflated.

"Mark Mercer, Jr.," Jack said. "Grew up in Cleveland."

Darla laughed and covered her face, hiding the silent tears that broke the weak levee of her resolve. The tears that broke her. Broke *them*. "He told me he grew up in a small parish in southeastern Louisiana." She wiped her face. "There's two budgets. Dire's Enterprises has been losing money for the last couple of years, but he lied. Last year he sent you a budget that showed the company was growing slightly. It's even worse this year."

The men blinked, nodding to each other.

Enzo stood, offering her a hand. "You did good, Darla. Thank you."

The lump in her throat plunged into her stomach. "What happens next?" She let him lead her to standing.

He gestured to the tall man in a suit. "The lawyers get it now. You'll be fine, your mom will be fine. I'll see to that."

Darla nodded. For some reason, she didn't feel fine. She felt sick, as if she'd just stepped into the biggest pile of manure, and she'd be carrying the stink around with her for the rest of her life.

41

The gathering for Levi's funeral was much larger than Charlotte had expected. Which shouldn't have come as a surprise. Her charismatic friend's quick wit and quicker smile would've endeared him to even the grumpiest person.

It was also a relief to see so many people eager to pay homage to the late rocker. It would be easier to hide in a crowd, especially if Lourdes, Celeste, or Dylan showed up.

The security guard waved her through, and a parking attendant guided her to a spot along an adjacent road.

The white tent housing his memorial service gleamed on a hilltop, a beacon drawing the mourners toward it.

Charlotte hung back, waiting in the rental car. On the clear Los Angeles spring day, she could make out Celeste's black kaftan, with her white hair pulled back into a bun.

A tall figure in a dark suit walked beside her, their arms linked. His gangly stride gave Dylan away.

The way they walked toward their friend's graveside, like a condemned prisoner walking toward execution. The realization that, given time, they'd be joining him in death.

A shiny black SUV pulled up to the tent.

A man hopped out of the back driver's side and jogged around to open the back passenger door, offering a hand to the person inside.

Despite being dressed in a black suit, with a black hat and dark sunglasses covering her face, there was no doubt it was Lourdes emerging from the car.

Tears pricked at Charlotte's eyes. Seeing her friend, all of her friends, was like seeing the sun after a long period of rain, warming, yet the brightness burned. The bond they'd made in just a few short days was like a spider's web. Woven overnight, but no doubt strong and able to snag the wiliest of emotions.

Well, maybe not betrayal.

That seemed to undo her part of the web. Could she repair it? Was it worth trying to rebuild what she'd broken?

People filed by her, parting like water flowing around a boulder. Charlotte's mind flashed to Levi. He'd been the sickest of them all, but his will to live was the strongest. As if his spirit could drive his body forward, until his spirit got overzealous.

His ego had a losing hand, but bluffed anyway, folding when it was called.

What would he have said during her admission? She could almost hear his gravelly voice. *Char, love, there is so much life to live. Please don't give up.*

The thing was, she'd felt so alive with the other Diers. It had nothing to do with their deaths, but everything to do with the way they were living. With forgetting. With feeling like Charlotte belonged. She'd never felt more alive than when she was dying.

She took a deep breath and finished the journey to the funeral tent.

Only a smattering of seats remained, but she didn't mind. She'd already planned on finding a spot near the back.

Lourdes sat on an aisle seat in the back row. She kept her glasses and hat on, her back straight, staring ahead, but she could feel the woman's awareness of her.

Dylan led Celeste down the center aisle and into two open seats in the middle. His head turned in her direction as he helped the older woman into a seat.

Charlotte raised her hand and smiled, but the boy quickly diverted his eyes.

Levi's daughter, ex-wife, and the surviving members of Fistful of Devils entered. They each held a long-stem red rose, and as they entered, they bowed at the shiny black casket holding court at the front of the tent.

The service started with a cloaked minister taking his place next to Levi's casket.

Easels held over-sized pictures of the man. Younger, darker hair. Prime of his youth. Each photo held a different aspect of her friend's life. In a white suit standing next to his bride. A beaming Levi holding his baby daughter so carefully in his arms. His bandmates. Album covers. Photographic proof of a life lived large.

What would Charlotte's service be like?

People would claim to know her best, but did they? The only people who could truly eulogize her were already dead or dying. If they were in the dying category, they would most likely say, 'good riddance.'

People didn't live their lives with the end in mind. People lived their lives with as many good intentions as they could muster, and the assurances, if they messed up, tomorrow would be there so they could make amends.

Tomorrow was never a sure bet, and Charlotte needed to start making amends.

Where to start?

Her parents? Two people who'd done the best they could, but fighting their demons had robbed them of the energy to raise their daughter. She could start with forgiving them. Welcoming them back into her world.

And then who?

Her friends? Bless them, they'd tried. After Jason died, her girlfriends had hovered around her with the ferocity of hummingbirds, but they found no syrupy-sweet southern charm in return. Instead, they'd found a bitter, heartbroken woman who'd thrown their casseroles, cobblers, and sweet tea in their faces.

Charlotte hadn't grieved like a debutante. She'd grieved like the world had fucked her over.

The minister's words flew into her ears. The exact phrases were lost on her, but the intention was familiar. Were there only so many ways to eulogize a man's life? To sum up his entire being?

A soul was too complex to put into words.

Even though the tent had no walls, it suddenly closed in on her. The collective grief of Levi's mourners wrapped its fingers around her neck and squeezed.

Charlotte's chest heaved, but air betrayed her. Like she'd betrayed her friends.

"Let's bow our heads," the minister said.

She closed her eyes, but the assault of her friend's memory only intensified. Singing onstage. Hiking in Peru. The bloody spittle he'd tried to hide. His mischievous smile at the suggestion of running off to Monaco.

Everybody was different. Therefore, every life was different. Did some people leave a bigger hole when they left?

Would Charlotte leave a hole or a pinprick?

She took a step backward. She needed out.

To get as far away from the death and the dying and the lies she'd told. Out from under the shadow of Levi's death.

Into the blinding California sun.

Charlotte opened her eyes and whirled straight into the chest of the young man who'd escorted Lourdes in.

"Ms. Peña asks that you leave," he whispered. "Your presence is not welcomed here." He spoke with the emotional detachment of someone who routinely asked people to inconvenience their lives for his employer.

She swallowed the sob that crawled up her throat. "I-I'm, of course, yes, I-I."

How did one respond to that? To not being wanted?

A shoulder nudged its way between them, cloaked in a light gray suit.

As if shirking the darkness for something with a little bit of radiance. The sliver of a silver lining.

"Tell Ms. Peña, that funerals are a time for quiet reflection and reverence for the dead. Not for concerning herself with who else is in attendance."

Charlotte glanced up.

Jimmy's jaw as rigid as El Capitan. He narrowed his eyes at Lourdes' man. "Why are you still standing here?"

A few fellow mourners side-eyed them during the prayer.

The star's lackey slinked away, sliding back to his mistress' side.

"Want to get out of here?" Jimmy whispered. "Funerals are only for the living, anyway."

They walked out of the tent when the wobbly notes of a hymnal rose.

Charlotte could almost hear Levi's scoff. *Blech. So horrid. They couldn't carry a tune if they threw it over their shoulder. For the love of all things holy, please stop singing.*

They walked through the headstones of famous, the almost-famous, and the buried-by-the-famous.

The sound of Levi's funeral faded away.

"How're you doing?" Jimmy asked.

She shrugged and held up her arms. "Unbroken skin."

He shook his head and looked down.

"That was a piss-poor attempt at a joke." Charlotte knocked her bangs out of her eyes. "In all seriousness Jimmy, I want to live. Plain and simple. I thought I didn't, and maybe when the time came, I wouldn't have done it, but…I'm getting help."

They reached the top of the next hill and she stopped, glancing back at the tent housing the final memorial of Levi.

Death was the easy way out.

Living would be harder, especially now, but she owed it to Levi.

To herself.

"There's nothing worse than an early goodbye."

"Or, a French goodbye."

Charlotte tilted her head.

"Slang, basically means leaving the party without telling anyone goodbye. That's what Levi did."

"Technically, he left the party to snort cocaine with a hooker."

Jimmy winced.

"Sorry, that was too far. I guess when you admit the ugliest secret inside you, everything else doesn't seem so bad." She studied Jimmy's face.

His light, the one that flowed out of his body and energized those whose own lights were waning, dimmed. His skin was ashen and dark circles cushioned his eyes.

"Why aren't you sitting with Lourdes?" she asked.

He looked down the hill, back at the funeral.

It was coming to a close.

A line of mourners filed by Levi's casket, touching it, as if the lacquered wood could feel the goodbye for its passenger.

"We haven't talked since we got back." Jimmy shrugged. "Maybe it was a vacation fling. Dying people sometimes act out of character."

More mourners filed past Levi's casket.

Lourdes walked slowly.

The man with her held her arm. Was it for moral support or physical? Had her friend's health taken a serious turn for the worse?

Was it because of Charlotte's betrayal, or Levi's?

She pulled her eyes off the woman and focused on the casket. It was so easy to be mad at herself, but she hadn't given any of her anger to Levi.

What good did it do to be mad at him? He hadn't overdosed because he wanted to die. He'd overdosed because he'd wanted to live bigger. Higher.

He flew too close to the sun and crashed into the earth, bringing them all with him.

Death was the villain, not her friend.

Charlotte's attention was drawn away by two cars crawling up the road.

One was a police car, with its lights flashing, the other was a black sedan, the kind that could either be used for a funeral or official government business.

The cars stopped at the guard. The man leaned in, nodding as he listened before standing aside and pointing toward the breaking service.

The cars parked. Two uniformed officers and two men in dark windbreakers got out.

Charlotte had seen this scene play out several times during her legal career. She didn't need to see the back of their jackets to know they were federal agents.

Jimmy tensed beside her. "Shit."

42

Every person had a place deep inside them where truth lived. It was a secret compartment Jimmy protected like it was filled with precious jewels.

But, it was more valuable than jewels; it was his past, his truth.

Watching the agents and officers walking toward Levi's funeral, the truth escaped its vault and leeched into his stomach.

It'd started prying its way out when he'd talked to Darla after the group returned. It'd been in her voice. He'd lost her. The magic that'd held them together was broken.

In its place was the simmering pile of suspicion.

The officers looked around the mourners, their gazes bouncing from face to face.

One of them looked up the hill in their direction. His mouth moved and three other heads whipped their way.

Jimmy could run, but where would he hide? In Marilyn's tomb? Behind some famous director's headstone? The dead owed him nothing.

The foursome made their way up the hill.

The police officers held their hands over their guns, the federal agents walked with the ease of men who didn't have to face street criminals daily.

"Jimmy?" Charlotte's voice was a whisper.

He'd forgotten she was there. Jimmy glanced down the hill.

Lourdes and her boy toy watched.

Dylan and Celeste turned in their direction, her long dress rippled in the wind.

There was no sense in fighting. It was all over. Everything ended. Life. Love.

Lies.

"There's going to be a lot of things said." Jimmy assumed it'd be hard to speak, but the truth slid from his lips easier than a thousand lies. "Just know that it was never done for me; it was always for everyone else."

"You know why they're here?"

He took a deep breath and made eye contact with Charlotte. "Not exactly, but I have a pretty good guess."

"That guy in New York... He really did know you." She gnawed on her lower lip and narrowed her eyes. "Don't say anything. You got it?"

The men were now just a few feet away. "Jimmy Dire?"

He pulled his shoulders back. "Yes, that's me."

A federal agent held up folded papers. "A.K.A. Mark Mercer, Jr.?"

The name slapped him.

It was as much hearing his given name, as also his father's name.

Jimmy tried to speak, but that truth hadn't broken the surface yet.

"I'm Agent Hunt," the older agent spoke. "This is Agent Stone, we're both F.B.I. You're under arrest. We'll treat you with the utmost respect here at your friend's funeral, if you don't cause a scene."

"What charges?" Charlotte moved in front of him with the prowess of a guard dog.

"Fraud, theft of services, identity theft, extortion," Agent Hunt paused. "I could go on if you'd like."

Jimmy stepped around her. "That's not necessary. Okay, let's go." He took two steps toward the waiting cars, but the other cop stepped in front of him.

"Hands behind your back."

"Are you kidding me? I'm going willingly. I'm not going to do anything."

The man pulled the handcuffs from his belt.

"Come on, I'm a fraud, not a thug."

"Same in my book. Thought you weren't going to cause a scene." The officer gripped his shoulder and whipped him around, wedging one arm against his back and slapping the cuffs around his wrist.

The cold metal bit into Jimmy's skin. Although it'd been nearly a lifetime since handcuffs had last cut into his wrists, some scars never healed. The same ones that weren't visible to the naked eye.

The officer led him to his waiting car.

Jimmy glanced over his shoulder.

Charlotte was huddled with the agents, her head bent over the arrest warrant, her face pinched with concern.

He'd forgotten she was an attorney before launching her self-help business.

This wasn't going to be like last time, where he'd been dragged screaming and cursing and bleeding, to the cruiser.

No, this time he was going to walk with his head held high. Jimmy didn't have to worry about his father's abuse being covered up by his friends.

They passed the three Diers.

Lourdes pulled her sunglasses down. Her dark stare burned into him, full of confusion.

Celeste stepped in front of him, blocking their path. "Where do you think you're going with him?" She spoke in the tone that could've been used with a naughty grandson instead of an arresting officer.

"Ma'am, please step aside," the cop's words were full of I-don't-get-paid-enough-for-this-shit.

"Celeste, it's okay." Jimmy searched for the strength to tell her what she wanted to hear. "It's a misunderstanding, but I'm going to go with them to the station to figure it out."

She tilted her chin, her blue eyes calling his bullshit. "Why are you handcuffed if it's a misunderstanding?"

"Just a formality, please, tell the others that it's fine. I'll be back in touch soon." He glanced at the officer. "Let's go."

It was funny how some experiences imprinted themselves. Being led to the car, the officer helping him into the backseat, snapping the seatbelt in place.

The divider between him and the police.

A literal reminder they were on two sides of the law.

Even if he was never arrested again, Jimmy would carry this with him for the rest of his life.

The car lurched forward.

Charlotte stayed with the agents, still deep in conversation.

Lourdes, Celeste, and Dylan stood shoulder-to-shoulder, but as the car rolled by them, his Lulu pulled herself away from the group, walking toward the passing car.

Her glasses were back in place, hiding whatever she thought of him.

It was all part of the fantasy he'd built around himself. That someone like *her* could fall in love with someone like him.

It was a perverse Cinderella story.

Mark Mercer, Jr., son of a Cleveland cop, who'd grown up just on the other side of poor, his mother wasting away from cancer, first arrested at fifteen, a runaway before his seventeenth birthday, could make something of himself, and fall in love with a beautiful woman. Even better, she could love him back.

There was no fairy godmother to whisk Jimmy away from his father's abuse. He'd had to summon the strength to start over himself. The first step to doing that was to disavow everything to do with his father. Starting with his name.

They processed him at the station with the emotional detachment of people who routinely reduced others down to ink and a number.

Jimmy was led to a room where the federal agents waited. "Okay, I've played along." He lifted his cuffed hands. "But do I look like I pose any risk?"

The older agent, Hunt, who could probably see retirement on the horizon, nodded toward the younger one. "We're fine."

Jimmy sat across the table from them. He mindlessly rubbed his wrists, trying to wipe away the feeling of being restrained.

"Your attorney is meeting us in Miami, so this isn't to talk about your case, but simply the process for returning you to Florida," Agent Hunt's words were heavy with exhaustion.

He shifted in his seat. Where was Darla in all this?

Was she being escorted out of her mother's nursing home?

Hands behind her back, her tiny face pointed at the ground, blonde hair blocking her embarrassment from the people tasked with caring for her mother.

"I need to know about Darla Steele," Jimmy said. "Look, she did nothing, she works for me."

Agent Hunt lifted his gaze from the paperwork. "I don't know anything about a Darla Steele."

"Well, can you find out?" His words came out in a screech. "Come on, guys, she's my assistant. If this is happening to her in Miami, she's got to be freaking out."

The men exchanged glances, but neither moved.

"I'm not asking you to do anything to tip her off, I just need to know she's okay."

Hunt pulled out his phone and punched at the screen. He kept his ice blue gaze on Jimmy, as he held the phone against his ear.

The phone rang twice. "Yeah?" another male voice answered.

"Hunt here, with Mercer. You got anyone else we're bringing in on this case? Maybe a woman, Darla Steele?"

A tinny voice answered. No matter how hard Jimmy, strained he couldn't make out any words.

"Okay, thanks, that's all I needed. We'll be back in Miami before midnight." Hunt said before ending the call. "You're the only one listed in the indictment."

Jimmy blew out the air he'd been holding onto for dear life.

Thank God.

The rest of their prepared spiel flowed past his ears.

He wasn't paying attention to his rights or the explanation of what was going to happen when they took him back to Miami.

Instead, Jimmy played through the conversation he needed to have with Darla. Before any trials, talks with attorneys, testimony preparation, and legal strategy, he needed to come clean to his assistant.

There was so much he owed her.

Most of all, the truth.

43

The beat of Levi's band blasted through Charlotte's earbuds as she hurried into the courthouse for Jimmy's arraignment. The bright Miami sun shone down like a spotlight. Palm trees swayed in the meager breeze.

The song she'd sung onstage with the rocker had become an anthem.

Time to get out of bed. *She's the Girl.*

Have to eat breakfast. *She's the Girl.*

Get in the shower. *She's the Girl.*

Attend her first arraignment in nearly a decade. *She's the Girl.*

Offering to dust off her law career to represent Jimmy was the second most impulsive thing she'd done, next to signing up for Dire's Club. But she couldn't not do it. To stand beside her friend during his darkest days, like he'd stood by her when she'd admitted her secret. It helped that her business dried up like a flower in the hot sun after her video confession, affording her to take time away.

Charlotte hurried down the busy hallway to the courtroom, her heels clicking along with the backbeat of the song. If the docket was on time, Jimmy's arraignment had started ten minutes ago.

She pushed open the heavy wooden doors, pulling the earbuds from her ears mid-song.

The judge was speaking, his voice deep, lyrical, soporific. It was a wonder he hadn't put the entire courtroom to sleep.

"Miss Claybrooke, I presume," he said, cutting off his remarks.

"Yes, Your Honor." She joined Jimmy at the defendant's table. "My apologies to the Court for my tardiness. It won't happen again."

Judge Wilkinson pulled his reading glasses down to the very end of his nose, he either needed stronger glasses or a longer nose. "It says here, Counselor, that you are licensed to practice in Florida, but you live in South Carolina. It also says you haven't tried a case in ten years. Are you sure you're up for representing Mr. Mercer?"

Charlotte had spent half the night staring at the ceiling asking herself that same question. It'd taken a few extra affirmations in the mirror that morning to convince herself she wasn't a fraud; practicing law was a lot like riding a bike.

Riding a bike that was careening downhill on fire.

This was an arraignment hearing, not a trial.

When had she developed pre-arraignment jitters?

She cleared her throat. "Yes, sir. Even though I haven't actively practiced, I've kept my license up to date."

He dropped the papers and looked up. "Why?"

"Because it's a whole lot easier than sitting for the Bar exam again, don't you think, Your Honor?"

Judge Wilkinson nodded. "You got a point," he mumbled. "Very well, let's get on with this. We are here for the arraignment of Mark Mercer, Jr., in the case of U.S. Government versus Mark Mercer, Jr., also known as Jimmy Dire, for two counts of fraud, three counts of theft, and," the man pulled his glasses off his face, bringing the paper to the tip of his nose. "And *fifty counts of extortion?*" The judge looked at the prosecution. "Is this a typo?"

The prosecutor stood. He was on the short side, yet trim with hair that was more gray than black. "No, sir. Mr. Mercer ran a company that preyed on people at the end of their lives. Fifty counts is a conservative figure; we believe he swindled many more out of their money."

"That's a lie," Jimmy spoke from his seat.

Charlotte flicked her hand against his shoulder, shushing him.

"Miss Claybrooke does your client have something for the court?"

"No, sir." She cut a look at Jimmy.

Red crept up his neck, coloring his cheeks.

She's the girl.

The only one who could defend him. The only one who could truly tell his story.

The only one who's exactly like him.

The judge's gaze lingered on her, as if waiting for her to wilt. "How does the defendant plead?"

"Not guilty, Your Honor." Her words echoed in the courtroom, strong, clear, sure.

"Mr. Mendez, it says here you recommend Mr. Mercer to remain in jail until trial. That seems a bit excessive for this crime, don't you think?"

"Your Honor, Mr. Mercer has traveled extensively overseas, and we believe he may be a risk for fleeing the country," the prosecutor said.

Charlotte jumped in at the man's pause. "Your Honor is correct, that is excessive, especially given Mr. Dire's indictment is filled with false statements and slander." She'd studied the indictment on the flight home, and the best she could tell was it stretched the truth to the point it would break. There was no way the full charges would go to trial. "Additionally, the defense respectfully requests he be referred to as Mr. Dire during the trial. There is a reason he changed his name, which will be brought to light at trial."

Judge Wilkinson nodded. He pulled his glasses off once again, and brought the papers to his face. If he wasn't careful, he was going to get a paper cut on his chin. "I'm inclined to agree. Bail is set at one million dollars, but Mr. Mercer, or Dire or whoever the hell he is, will also surrender his passport, or passports if there's more than one. You're also not to leave Miami-Dade County."

"Thank you, Your Honor." Charlotte bent down to gather her papers. "Don't say a word," she whispered to Jimmy.

As soon as the judge gaveled the proceedings, the prosecutor made a beeline for her table.

"We haven't officially met." The man shoved his hand out. "Julian Mendez. My wife loves your books. It'll break her heart when I beat you."

She quirked up one side of her mouth. She had to admit, she missed this part of practicing law. It wasn't that different from running a race.

Psyching out the competition to think her insides were as soft as her face. Convince them the woman with the gentle eyes and pretty smile didn't have the heart of a warrior and a keen mind.

Charlotte met his hand with hers. "Oh, then I guess it'll be good that this farce of an indictment won't even see the light of day. I'd hate to cause any tension at home when you get your butt handed to you." She coated her words in her syrupiest Southern accent. "What's her name, I'll sign a copy of my latest book and send it to your office."

Julian cleared his throat. "You think you can charm your way out of this? I was trying to help you save face. What's the world going to think when Charlotte Claybrooke bombs the first case she's tried in a decade?"

"That's sweet, my face will be just fine, but you should worry about your case." She pushed past the attorney. "Come on, Jimmy, let's get to work on some motions to dismiss this thing."

Her client matched her quick pace as she fled the courtroom. The heels of his shoes echoed her snappy footfalls.

Fear and excitement battled inside her ribcage for control.

Charlotte tried to breathe normally, but her lungs refused air. Perspiration glued her bangs to her forehead.

She needed to get away from the courtroom, the near-sighted judge and short, cocky prosecutor. She even needed to hide from the man following her, who trusted her to represent him, but his desperation adhered him to her side.

Jimmy pulled his phone from his pocket as soon as they were on the sidewalk. "I can't reach Darla," he mumbled, his words as aimless as a drunk. "I've tried calling and texting her. I thought she'd be here today."

Charlotte pulled his phone from his hand. "Don't, Jimmy, she's not with us anymore."

His face fell like a skydiver tumbling out of a plane. "What? What d'you mean? What happened? Why haven't you told me? Who's going to take care of her mom?"

"No, sorry, not like that."

Hell of a way to choose your words, Charlotte.

"I mean, she's a witness for the prosecution."

This time it wasn't Jimmy's face that fell, it was his entire body. He hit the steps of the courthouse hard.

Charlotte knelt beside him.

"That's worse." He covered his face with his hands.

She pulled her pencil skirt over her knees. This conversation was what she'd wanted to run from, but they were at the point in the race where there was no turning back; only moving forward, one step at a time. "Jimmy, we need to have a serious conversation, but not here." She glanced over her shoulder.

People climbed up and down the steps of the busy courthouse. Their case would fall flat if Mendez walked out and saw her client crying.

"What does it matter?" Jimmy spoke into his palms. "If Mendez has Darla, there's nothing worth fighting for."

Charlotte gnawed on her bottom lip. Was this a huge mistake? She'd never shied away from a tough trial, but that was back when she'd been a fully practicing attorney. Back before her world had tumbled around her. Back before she'd had to become someone else to hide from the pain. "Are you and Darla...romantic?"

He dropped his hands. "No, I mean, I told her I loved her all the time, but it was in a purely platonic way. And, then...oh shit." Jimmy hung his head. "I kissed her."

"How long ago?"

"Two weeks."

She shifted on the step to face her client. "Two weeks ago, we were in Monaco."

His head sunk even further. Another admission and his forehead would be touching the ground. "It was at the casino. We just won big and I grabbed her, we kissed. I was drunk, she was drunk, I didn't think she'd remember it."

"I hate to tell you this, but if a woman's boss kisses her, she's going to remember it. Whether she welcomes it or not."

"What do we do?"

"We tell your story, no matter how ugly it is, or how uncomfortable it makes you." Charlotte looked out over the busy street. It was barely mid-morning but waves of heat already rose off the sidewalk. "I need to know; did you steal from us? From anyone?"

Jimmy lifted his head, staring at her through squinted eyes. "No. If anything I undervalued what I did. We're all dying, Charlotte. From the moment we're born, we march toward death. Not everyone can die feeling like they *lived*, but for those who I've crossed paths with, that's my goal. To give them something to hold on to while they release their final breath. To die with their soul happy."

Charlotte pulled her gaze off her friend. It was easier to stare into the sun than to look at the truth written all over Jimmy's face.

That she was once again an imposter, even if the trip had been completed, if Levi were still walking the earth and she was in the ocean surrounded by gentle giants of the sea, her soul was still wounded.

44

The driver stopped outside the gates of the upscale neighborhood. It took Charlotte listening to Levi's song twenty times that morning for the courage to get in the car to see Lourdes.

Her stomach curdled from the thick aroma in the florist van. It was deceptive and shitty, and quite frankly, beneath her. However, desperate times called for gaining access to her former friend under the guise of a flower delivery.

The driver punched a code into the speaker box. After a quick exchange, the gate opened and he jogged back to the van. "Are you sure about this, Miss?"

The short answer was no, but how could Charlotte say so, after flying to Mexico City for the sole purpose of convincing a woman who hated her to testify on behalf of a man who lied about his identity and his business dealings. She owed it to Jimmy to try.

The van parked outside a gorgeous stucco home built into the foothills. Desert fauna mingled with tropical flora in the front garden, creating a beautiful cacophony of colors and textures.

Charlotte grabbed the arrangement from the back. A heavy stone base filled with lilies and birds of paradise, brightly colored flowers that reminded her of their climb up Machu Pichu.

The driver waited.

She promised him a nice tip if he'd wait for her.

A bigger one if she made it inside.

She pressed the doorbell and a melodic chime filled the house. The arrangement hid her face, but she watched through the leaves as a man's shadow hurried toward the door.

"*Sí?*"

Charlotte moved the flowers to the side. "Hi, remember me?"

The man who'd been at the funeral frowned. "Why are you here? If Ms. Peña didn't want to see you then, she won't see you now."

"Well, you're going to need to tell Lulu to get over herself." She handed the man the heavy arrangement and pushed past him.

The house was beautiful in a stark, unfussy way. A white sofa sat in the middle of the living room. A single white orchid on a glass coffee table was positioned perfectly in front of two cobalt blue paintings.

The back windows looked out to a small dipping pool. Not large enough for swimming laps in, but the perfect size to sit in to escape the summer heat.

Charlotte crossed her arms over her chest. "You're still standing there."

He rolled his eyes and ran upstairs, mumbling in Spanish under his breath.

She took a deep breath to steady herself. The words of Levi's song flowed through her mind like a mantra. This could all be a colossal waste of time, or it could save Jimmy. Considering that Charlotte had bitten off way more than she could chew, she'd need every good luck charm, potion, spell, and self-affirmation ever written.

Several minutes later, footsteps overhead drew her attention from the exotic garden.

Lourdes appeared on the catwalk, a kimono covering her thin frame and her head wrapped in a scarf. "You're ballsy," the movie star said.

The woman made no motion to come down the stairs.

Fine, you want to reign over me, go ahead.

"Jimmy needs your help," Charlotte called.

Lourdes turned her head. "Why doesn't he ask me himself."

"Because he had to forfeit his passport."

The muscle in her jaw clenched. She looked away, surveying something on the hillside beyond the windows. "So, it wasn't just a misunderstanding." Lourdes' color was muted, no glow touched her cheeks. Without eyebrows drawn on or fake eyelashes, she looked like a coloring book outline of herself, nothing filled in on the inside.

"We need you for his trial. If you will testify, Celeste and Dylan will as well."

The *telenovela* star whipped her head toward her. "Oh, you're not done using me, I see."

Charlotte shook her head and took three steps up the stairs.

Lourdes' gaze drifted down to her feet, but she didn't retreat.

"It's not for me. It's for Jimmy, and as far as I can tell, he never used you." She took another two steps. "I'm not asking you to forgive me, or even talk to me outside of the questions I'll ask you at trial. You don't have to trust me, beyond the fact that I won't let opposing counsel embarrass you." Another two steps. "'I'm sorry' doesn't even come close to healing what I did to you and the others. But please know I wasn't mocking you. Or, Celeste, or Dylan or even Levi." Charlotte made it to the midpoint landing.

Her shoulders drooped a bit, and Lourdes angled her body more toward Charlotte. Not necessarily forgiveness.

Thankfully, also not full-on gonna-kick-your-ass.

"Would it have helped if I had told you in the beginning? Would y'all have accepted me?" She paused, waiting for a response. "I'm sorry, but I don't think you would have. I think you would've told me to leave before the orientation even started." Charlotte started her way up the final flight of stairs. "I didn't lie to you; I just didn't tell you the truth. Splitting hairs, I know. But…I found the person I was before with y'all. I thought she'd died that day with Jason. She's still there, just…scared…and lonely." She stood on the landing with Lourdes.

This close, her friend looked even more wan.

"Be mad at me for however long you want, just say you'll come with me to help Jimmy."

Lourdes locked eyes with her. Thick tears streamed down her face. "He never called me. After we got back, we texted some, but—" She wiped her face and laughed. "This is dumb. I'm Lourdes Peña, I don't cry over men. Men cry over me."

Heartbreak doesn't discriminate. It knew no boundaries. Rich or poor. Educated or unlearned. Beautiful and ugly. Despite the color of one's skin, the hearts were all the same. They beat the same. They loved the same.

Broke the same.

Charlotte wanted to wrap her friend in her arms, but she was afraid it was too much.

Lourdes peeked out of her shell. Any sudden movement might make her retreat beyond reach.

The starlet hugged her body. "At the funeral, he just stared at me. He didn't talk to me. Even try to approach me. But he came to you. He followed *you*." Her dark gaze pinned Charlotte to her spot.

Lourdes' jealousy washed over her like a tidal wave. "Because your boyfriend asked me to leave." She straightened her back and brushed her bangs out of her eyes. "And, why would Jimmy talk to you when you brought another man? Are you that accustomed to men fawning over you; you'd assume he'd face the embarrassment of you there with another man?"

She dropped her arms to her side. Her hairless brow knitted in confusion before her face relaxed into a slight smile. "Ha! Matteo is my nephew. I'm flattered that you think I can still entice someone as young and beautiful as him." Lourdes closed her eyes and shook her head. "He's staying here to help me around the house while he finishes university."

They stared at each other.

"How were you going to do it?" Lourdes' voice was a whisper.

It was Charlotte's turn to cry. The tears stabbed her eyes like cactus needles. "Drowning."

She blew out a breath. "Oh, you're sick. Wouldn't that hurt, or take too long?" The woman fell into a settee, leaving a spot next to her.

Charlotte perched on the edge. "It takes less time than you think. I've already done it once." Instead of saving her body, she'd hoped Jason would be there to save her soul.

"I have pills," Lourdes spoke to her hands. "For when the pain becomes too much. I've held them in one hand and a glass of water in the other, but that's the funny thing about pain. When you think you can't take anymore, you find the strength to push against it." She looked up from her hands. "That's the body. I can't speak to the heart, maybe the pain is greater there. The more you push against it, the greater it stabs back." She took a deep breath and closed her eyes. "I won't take the pills if you promise me to keep your head above water."

The sob burst from Charlotte's throat like a crashing wave. She'd been trying to keep her head above water for ten years. She was tired of treading. Wanted to swim forward but the undertow of her grief was too hard to escape.

Lourdes scooted over and wrapped her in a tight embrace.

She put her head on her friend's shoulder, finding a perfect notch in the protruding bones. "It's just so hard," Charlotte said between the tears. "I feel like I'm living this fake life. I'm a fraud. Telling people how to be strong and resilient, and I'm the weakest person I know. I'm telling them losing a loved one shouldn't mean their lives stop, but *mine* did. I'm not the person I'd hoped to be by now."

"You're not weak. Charlotte, you could've just killed yourself, but you didn't. You joined Dire's Club. That took strength, resiliency. Don't you dare call my friend a fraud." Lourdes squeezed Charlotte's hand. "As for not being who you'd hope to be, maybe you're a better person."

She shook her head and leaned up. "It's not that, I just…" Charlotte bunched her skirt in her hands. "I always thought I'd be a mom by now, and I wasted so many years mourning Jason, I forgot to live. I never let myself love again, or even think about having someone else's baby."

The star tilted her head; a sly smile crossed her beautiful face.

"Love is never guaranteed, even when you have a partner. But, a child? You don't need a man for that. Do you know how many children need saving?"

Saving.

Just like how Jason had saved her from a riptide. Maybe the life preserver he'd given her when he proposed, the one that sat in her bedroom, wasn't an albatross reminding her of a life she couldn't have.

It was a tool for her to use.

Maybe it was time for Charlotte to be someone else's life preserver.

45

Jimmy's office was a shell of its former self. When the Feds came in, they took all the computers, the files, his server. They even took his bourbon.

Bastards.

He needed a drink more than anything.

Charlotte had promised she had an ironclad strategy, but seeing the woman's panic after the arraignment; he considered calling the prosecutor to tell him to throw more than the book at him, but the whole damn library, too.

Jimmy couldn't do that to her. She was just so sure this would work, and after her admission in Monaco, he couldn't rob her of hope.

She needed that more than he needed his freedom.

He shook his head and stared at his reflection in the plate glass window. Dire's Club was officially out of business, yet he was still giving his Diers their final adventures. Even if this wasn't the one Charlotte had signed up for, her need to help him rolled off her like the fog off the ocean.

The chime of the office door clattered like Cinderella's clock striking midnight, the tone reverberating in his chest, in his heart.

Was he that close to everything turning back into a pumpkin?

"How are you doing?" Charlotte stood at his doorway. She was dressed casually, more casual than he'd assumed she'd been comfortable donning. Linen shorts fell mid-thigh, reminding him she'd kicked his ass on a run around Central Park just a couple of months ago. A beige shirt tucked into the waistband of her shorts was covered by a matching linen jacket. Miami was rubbing off on her.

Jimmy shrugged and shoved his hands in his jeans pockets. "This is like waiting to be devoured by a snail. I'm just waiting and waiting." He looked out at the flat ocean. "And, waiting." He glanced over his shoulder. "You're looking pretty casual there, Counselor."

Charlotte looked down, pink tinging her cheeks. "Well, I was trying to blend in." She crossed the room and plopped into his guest chair. "Do you have anything to drink? Preferably with alcohol?"

He took his chair across from her. "I used to have a nice bourbon. It disappeared when they raided my office."

"Those assholes," she muttered. She rested one arm on the back of the chair and twirled a strand of her hair through her fingers. "I'm more nervous about seeing them than I am about the case."

"You survived Lourdes." Jimmy's voice cracked a little at the woman's name. He'd stared at her name on his phone screen so many times, begging his fingers to touch it, to set forth the alchemy of modern technology that would bring her raspy, lyrical voice to his ears. "That's more than I can say."

His attorney's face softened. "You have to talk to her, Jimmy. You don't know how much more time she—" Charlotte looked away, studying the world outside his ravaged office. "She might appear to be strong, but she's an actress, and this is the role of her lifetime."

At some point, the director will yell, "That's a wrap."

He grimaced and studied his bare desk. Back in the heyday of Dire's Club, his desk was always covered with travel books and magazines, paperwork, doctors' forms, travel itineraries, and receipts that whispered that money flowed out faster than it came in.

The doorbell chimed again and voices haunted the empty lobby.

Charlotte craned her neck, glancing behind her. "Well, guess we're going to have to do this sober."

Sober, drunk, it didn't matter. The jury gathering in his lobby would be more difficult to face than twelve strangers. The Diers would judge him for who he was. For who he wasn't. For who he should've been.

Jimmy stood, slowly, his body, his heart, and his spirit stiff, as if he'd aged fifty years in just a few days.

"I'll be right here," Charlotte spoke softly. "I'll give you a few minutes to talk with them, then I'll come out."

He nodded and walked to the door.

"Just tell the truth," she added.

He tried to swallow, but a lump with the biceps of a nightclub bouncer refused entry.

Jimmy walked into the conference room. Only a few months ago, the people standing there had mingled over wine and a veggie tray. Excitement had hummed like the white noise of fluorescent lights.

They'd been at the beginning of their journey, about to make new friends, to live out their dying wish. Levi had been there with his gleaming white hair and a persona that could only be overshadowed by Mount Everest.

Today, the remaining Diers sat in a dark conference room. No wine flowed, no veggies for nibbling.

Darla wasn't there to welcome them with her Texas charm.

It was amazing how empty the room felt without her.

How empty Jimmy felt without her.

Darla wasn't dead.

Worse.

She'd walled him off. Blocked his number. Shut him out.

He cleared his throat and the light small talk dissipated like smoke.

Three faces turned toward him. Waited for him to speak magic words that would erase the hurt.

"Um, hi," Jimmy spoke to the conference room table.

Only a shuffling of chairs answered him.

He'd never had trouble speaking. Especially in a tense situation.

Quite the opposite. The tighter the vise he'd find himself in, the more eloquently his words flowed.

Standing there in front of his latest group of Diers, the *last* group of Diers, and the words were more stubborn than a jammed door.

"So." Jimmy let his gaze drift from the table. Instead of scorn, compassion stared back at him. Instead of judgment, understanding. When he looked at Lourdes, instead of hate, he saw love.

He pulled the chair out and slowly lowered himself like someone who'd lived two lifetimes.

In a sense, Jimmy *had* lived two lifetimes.

"Thank you for being here. Before I say anything else, I first want to say, I'm sorry."

Celeste held up her hand. "What're you apologizing for?"

"Well, I got arrested, Celeste. Remember?"

The older woman *tsked*. "Jimmy, this isn't an Alzheimer's thing. I mean, you have no reason to apologize. Unless you *did* swindle people out of money."

"I'd never do that, but I did lie to you guys. About my past, my real name. I was dealing with a lot of stuff with my business." He swallowed hard. "I embarrassed you when I got arrested at Levi's funeral. Hell, in Monaco, I shouldn't have let you guys gamble for me. I crossed a line and brought you guys with me."

"No, we were the ones who wanted to do it," Dylan said. The young man sat up straight, his chin held high.

Somehow, he'd grown from a self-conscious adolescent to a confident man in just the space of a few days.

"It was my idea. My adventure."

Jimmy shook his head. "I shouldn't have let you do it."

"We're the clients, you did exactly what we asked you to," Lourdes finally spoke. "And, we'd do it again."

Her words stung his heart with the ferocity of a horde of angry hornets.

Their compassion, *her compassion*, was exactly the flame to light the fuse of his truth.

He cleared his throat, readying himself to strike the match.

46

The persona of Jimmy Dire had been created before his tenth birthday. It was a natural progression of a game he and his mom had played. They'd started small.

"If you can be anywhere in the world, where would you be?"

The easy answer for his mom; not lying in bed.

The easy answer for Jimmy; anywhere but there.

It had nothing to do with his mother; everything to do with her illness.

"If you could be anyone in the world, who would you be?"

Jimmy had posed that question to her once, expecting the answer to be, "I'd want to be me, only healthy." She hadn't said that. She'd created a persona. Josephine Dire. Every day when Jimmy, or Marky, as his mother had called him, raced home from school, she told him more and more about this strange, foreign woman his mother wanted to be.

Her tale raced through unlikely scenarios: meeting a president, dinner with the queen, flirting with an exotic prince. When Josephine reached a certain age, she wove in the birth of her perfect son, James.

Mother and son traveled the world together on grand adventures spun in a dark room told in a raspy, breathless voice.

"I don't remember my mom ever being healthy." Jimmy cleared his throat again, his gaze stranded on a smudge on the conference room table.

A fingerprint left by a long-ago Dier, missed by the cleaning crew time and time again. Were there any fingerprints of his mother left in this world? After decades of being gone, has her last smudge been wiped clean?

The group in front of him were all dying. Each person in this room, on this planet, was headed for the same inevitable destination.

It was because of his mother that he refused to sit back and let people die without living out that final adventure. To die with a joyful smile knowing that yes, they did reach the final point in their journey, but they'd had a hell of a good time along the way.

It was only a matter of time before each person gathered around him would be nothing but a forgotten smudge on a conference room table.

Jimmy took a deep breath. "In some way, I didn't change my identity to hide who I was. I changed my identity to become who she wanted me to be." His cheek burned with the ghost of his father's strike. His breath rushed from his lungs, remembering the multiple punches to his gut. "In other ways, I changed my identity because I wanted nothing to do with my father."

Dylan shifted in his chair. The young man's brow furrowed and he opened and closed his mouth. Life a fish gasping for oxygen. Like a boy gasping for words. "I almost wished he'd hit me." His voice was quiet. Like a whisper against the wind. "I could've dealt with the physical pain, but the pushing, the manipulation—"

Celeste squeezed his hand. "Pain is pain, it doesn't matter if it's the heart or body. You're a brilliant young man, don't let your father make you think otherwise."

Dylan folded in on himself, as if to bend into non-existence.

Jimmy had done that, too. After his mom died, he'd tried to disappear. It was only when the beatings got so bad, he finally disappeared for good.

"My real name is Mark Mercer, Jr. I am the son of Yvette and

Mark Mercer, Sr. I left home at seventeen, changed my name, changed my past, because I couldn't stand to be his son anymore." Jimmy crossed the room and stared out the windows.

The bright blue sky was met with a mirror image of the ocean. Calm. Only the rhythmic rise and fall of the ocean, like an old man resting.

"I worked my way here, picking up odd jobs, mostly working in retirement homes. It was there, with the help of some wise residents, I got the courage to start this business."

"The courage or the money?" Lourdes' voice was as sharp as a spear.

He spun on his heel, eager to take her to task for the accusation, but instead, fell into a chair at the end of the table. "I've never stolen anything. Not even this identity. It was my creation."

The *telenovela* star leaned back in her chair, a smile spread slowly across her face, like the rays of the sun piercing thick rainclouds. "Good, I can love an actor easier than I can love a thief."

Jimmy rubbed his chest.

Love.

A word people tossed about like confetti. Throwing it around was like playing tennis with a nuclear weapon. Sure, he used it with Darla. He *did* love her.

Not the way she wanted him to. That much was obvious.

That was what happened when someone wasn't careful with the *L-word*. He'd lightly tossed it to Darla, hoping it showed his true affection for her, how much he loved her. *Kaboom!* His whole life had melted down.

The aftermath was uglier than Chernobyl.

He couldn't blame Darla. It was his fault. Jimmy had given her all the elements she'd needed. A first-row seat to his failing business. A casually-tossed declaration of fondness. A drunken kiss. The catalyst that ignited it sat right there in the conference room brandishing her own weapon.

"I'm guilty of changing my name and my past. I'm guilty of being a terrible business owner but I've never taken advantage of any of my Diers. The accusations Enzo lobbed at me are completely false."

"So, where's that little blonde?" Celeste asked. "She could set everything straight, right?"

"Unfortunately, she's joined the other team," Charlotte spoke from the door. "That's why we called you all here."

The energy in the conference room shifted, electrified. Like a quickly forming thunderstorm cell on a hot summer day.

"Why is she here?" Dylan gritted out. "She's not dying."

"We can't trust her," Celeste added, her face turned away from the woman hovering just outside the conference room. "She's a liar."

"She's my attorney," Jimmy said. He'd expected some resistance, but Celeste and Dylan's raised heckles made him worry he'd misread the chemistry of the group.

The older woman whipped her head in his direction. "Why would you do that? Jimmy, do you want to go to jail?"

"Yeah, I'm with Celeste, I can't help you if she's involved," the younger man sprung back in his chair.

"You all were so quick to forgive Jimmy," Lourdes said. She twirled in her chair to face Charlotte. "Why don't we give her a chance to explain."

His attorney gave his lover a soft smile and nodded. "Depression is a disease, and left unchecked, it can kill." She took a tentative step into the room. "You're right, Celeste, I am a liar. I lied to myself for years, thinking I was healing from losing Jason. What I didn't realize was the guilt from the day he died had turned rancid." Charlotte pulled out a chair, hesitating before sitting. "We always trained together. Except for one day." Tears flowed over her hazel eyes like the ocean filling a tidal pool. "I had a big case, the kind that made partners. It was a rainy Sunday; not my favorite weather for a bike ride and we didn't have any big races coming up, so I bailed on riding with Jason. I got so lost in my work, I didn't realize he wasn't home when he said he'd be. I didn't think anything was wrong until the cops came to my door."

She took an audible deep breath, breaking the levy of her tears. "The love of my life died alone, no one was with him. I was so busy preparing for a case I didn't notice anything was wrong." She wiped her eyes with the back of her hands. "I never told anyone that. I'm not naive enough to think he'd be here if I was with him, but he wouldn't have been alone. The hardest person to forgive is yourself. I don't think I have, might never. But the grief took up so much space in my life. So much, I thought the only way out was to kill myself." Her words hovered in the quiet conference room.

Jimmy imagined them hanging over each person, morphing and twisting, as each Dier considered them.

Dylan was the first to move. He pushed his chair back and stood, staring at Charlotte before crossing the room in two long strides.

She stood, her chin tilted up and back straight as if expecting to receive a blow.

Instead, the gangly young man wrapped her in a tight embrace. His back shook in silent sobs.

Jimmy watched Charlotte's stunned expression.

Her arms hung limply by her side before they reach around the boy and clung to his shirt.

After several minutes, Dylan released her. His face was red, wet, but his shoulders relaxed. The anger was leeched from his body, softening his face back to the young man who was dying well before his time.

Everyone turned toward Celeste.

"We're all in this together," Lourdes said. "It's all of us or none of us, but you have to be comfortable with Charlotte."

The older woman braced her hands on the table and pushed herself up. She didn't move toward Charlotte, only eyed her from down the table. "You have to make us a promise," her voice was a tight whisper. "No more of this wanting to die bullshit. You have to live. And I don't mean exist, Charlotte Claybrooke, I mean *live*. Live like your life depends on it."

Charlotte smiled and laughed. "I promise, Celeste. I'll be honest, we might not win Jimmy's case, but I'll give it everything I got, now and after the case."

"Good, now come here and give me a hug."

After the hugs were exhausted and the tears dried, Charlotte talked through her plans for the trial. Calling them as witnesses, having them share how Jimmy had made a difference in the sunset of their lives.

She didn't want to dispute the false identity, but rather embrace it. Explain how it was a coping mechanism for an abused boy.

Tears battered Jimmy's eyes as everyone readily agreed to help him.

To help Charlotte.

After years of helping the dying, the dying had come together to help him.

They made appointments for trial prep, discussed logistics, and as the sun drifted toward the western horizon, the gang broke up to head back to their hotels.

Except Lourdes.

She studied her siren-red nails, but he could feel her awareness probing him. Once the elevator bell rang somewhere deep in the heart of the office floor to ferry away the rest of the Diers, she finally spoke. "I don't do one-night stands, Jimmy."

His mouth opened, hoping his brain would have some words to fill it with, but his mind was as empty as a virgin canvas.

"I can understand if you want to pretend it never happened," he said, avoiding her dark eyes.

A heavy sigh escaped her full lips, and she pushed out of her chair, leaning against the table next to him. "You're not listening. I said I don't do them, in the sense that, when I sleep with someone, it's because I want to do it again." Lourdes leaned in, her spicy floral scent warming him. "Again." Her lips teased his, close enough for him to feel her electricity, but far enough away, the distance was a vast chasm. "And, again."

She tasted sweet and salty. Her body was both warm and cool under his touch.

Jimmy rubbed his thumb along the vein along the side of her neck, feeling the life strumming just beneath the surface, vowing to love her with every ounce of his being until her heart stilled.

47

There was something very ironic about Jimmy's trial starting on the hottest day of the year. Growing up in Charleston, Charlotte was accustomed to a heat that clung with the tackiness of honey, but this heat was different.

It slapped her the minute she stepped outside, teased with a brief ocean breeze, or a fleeting cloud over the sun. Miami's heat was made for people who lived in a bikini and coverup, not suits. She tried not to take it personally.

The air conditioner spewed cold air from its gills. The white noise, coupled with the enveloping heat had the same effect as a lullaby, putting the jurors, bailiffs, and witnesses to sleep.

Would a sleepy jury be a kind jury? Would they quickly find Jimmy not guilty in order to move on with their lives? Or, would the heat fire up their judgment and they'd find him guilty on all counts?

"Good morning, Counselor," the prosecutor, Julian Mendez, said. "I see you decided your reputation isn't that important after all."

Charlotte glanced at him from the corner of her eye while digging through her bag. "Oh Julian, I brought this for your wife." She handed the autographed book, watching as his eyes skirted over the inscription.

To strong women who prop up the men in their lives.

Color crept up his neck, like a red tide invading a normally placid ocean. "Yeah, I'll be sure to give this to her." He shoved it into his briefcase.

It didn't matter if the book never made it home. It'd done its job.

Jimmy and Lourdes walked in, their hands breaking apart when he took his spot next to Charlotte.

"You ready for this?" she whispered to her client. "Remember, the burden of proof hinges on the prosecution."

He smiled. The lines around his eyes looked smoother, as if he'd had plenty of restful nights. His skin held a healthy flush. Jimmy had to be the most serene defendant she'd ever seen.

"Whatever happens, happens. If I go to jail, so be it, but the truth is out there." His gaze shifted over his shoulder. "When you love and are loved, anything is possible."

She remembered that feeling. Being loved, and loving back. She hadn't known that feeling as a child. Instead of being buoyed by her parents' love, their indifference had been a lead weight. Maybe that was why she'd latched on to Jason, to his love.

Losing him was a tragedy, but losing that high of his love was like a junky suddenly being cut off from a drug cold turkey.

Deadly.

She made a mental note of bringing up the revelation the next time she met with her new therapist. Like being back in school, Charlotte was determined to be the model patient.

"All rise," the bailiff spoke in his deep baritone.

Judge Wilkinson took his seat behind his behemoth desk.

"The trial of U.S. against Mark Mercer, Jr. a.k.a Jimmy Dire, is set to begin."

"You may be seated," the judge commanded. "Good morning, all." The man fidgeted with a small fan. "I hope you don't mind; I'm wearing an extra layer of clothes." The little machine sprung to life, adding to the symphony of white noise, his robe dancing in the breeze. "Well, I won't draw this out any more than we need to. Mr. Mendez, would you like to start with your opening argument?"

The prosecutor stood, loosening his tie, and shucking his jacket.

Charlotte narrowed her eyes at his blatant tactic.

Julian spared a glance at the people in the jury, normal men and women who fanned themselves with their notepads. He was one of them. Coming down off his ivory tower of law to talk to the people.

She was already one step ahead of him in that game. Her sleeveless dress flared at the waist. Simple, beige, the muted color that said everything Charlotte needed to say about herself. Her hair was pulled back into a low, messy bun, a perfect mix of professional and casual.

"Ladies and gentlemen of the jury," the man began. "Imagine your grandmother found out she's dying, only has a few months to live. Wouldn't you want her to spend every bit of the time she has on this Earth with her family? You wouldn't want her to have her money and time swindled away by a smooth-talking man promising her bold adventures, would you?"

A few jurors' heads nodded, but many stayed still, their eyes locked on the man now rolling up his sleeves.

"Mark Mercer, Jr. is just that. A swindler. He swindled Fiore Venture Funding for money, promising a return on this bold idea. Granting wishes to dying adults. It sounds admirable." Mendez shrugged. "But I aim to prove he did more than take them on a trip. I'm going to prove, not only did he steal from the Fiore family, but he manipulated his clients and stole something that could never be regained—time with the people who love them most. Their families." He looked at the judge. "Thank you, Your Honor." The prosecutor gave Charlotte a side-eyed sneer, as he made his way back to his table.

"Ms. Claybrooke," the judge prompted.

"Thank you, Your Honor." She pushed herself up and approached the jury box, studying the five men and seven women.

This was a good jury, a few on the upper-income bracket, most were good, strong middle-class folks who would appreciate Celeste's story. There was even one young woman in her late twenties. Dylan would tug at her heartstrings.

"Everybody dies. You," she nodded to a fifty-something woman.

"You," Charlotte smiled at an older gentleman, a corporate executive. "Even you," she settled her gaze on the oldest man on the jury, "But that's still a ways off," she added with a wink. "Mr. Dire was focused solely on his clients, and while yes, it did take some time away from their families, in a way he was giving them freedom. Freedom to enjoy one last trip, one last adventure before they were unable to travel. Freedom from dier's guilt."

She paced the galley, her arms crossed over her chest. "Dier's guilt? I know what you're thinking. What the heck is that? It's the guilt we feel when we get a terminal diagnosis." She broke contact to look at her fellow Diers. "It's guilt over the anger of being told our time has come to an end. The guilt of leaving our family behind. The guilt of becoming a nuisance. The need to wrap up our lives in neat, perfectly wrapped boxes."

Charlotte turned back to the jury. "And yes, I'm using 'we' because I am, was, a Dier, and, the service Mr. Mercer—Jimmy Dire as we know him—offers is invaluable. It's a place we can come together to laugh, to cry, to scream, and ultimately, to find peace. I'm going to show the only crime Jimmy is guilty of is undervaluing his service, of operating at a loss so money was never an obstacle when it comes to having that last adventure of your lifetime. Thank you, Your Honor." She glanced at the courtroom.

Celeste dabbed her eyes with a tissue.

Dylan rubbed his nose, sniffing audibly.

Lulu smiled, a single tear cut down her cheek.

Jimmy squeezed her hand after she took her seat. "Thank you. I couldn't have said it better myself." He chewed on the inside of his cheek. "I've been afraid to look, but is Darla here?"

Charlotte had scanned the courtroom during her remarks for the petite blonde but didn't see her. Jimmy's former assistant was after the Fiores on the witness list, and they likely wouldn't get to her today, so she could've opted to stay home. "No, Jimmy, she's not here yet."

"That's good, right?" His eyes lit up like a Fourth of July sky. "Maybe she's decided to not testify."

She pursed her lips. The words were there, ready to leap, ready to kill his hope, but despite the brave, calm face Jimmy wore, his fear flowed just beneath the surface, like a shark waiting to strike at the first whiff of blood.

48

The prosecutor wasted no time calling his first witness. Enzo Fiore had filed the complaint, so it only made sense for Mendez to come out swinging.

Charlotte sat poised, ready to jot down any inconsistent comment, a slip of the silver spoon in his mouth, anything she could twist like a wet cloth and wring out the truth.

The venture capitalist seemed immune to the suffocating heat. His expensive suit was fully intact, tie perfectly knotted, long sleeves down and sporting diamond cufflinks, the dark gray jacket hanging perfectly on his athletic frame.

The man was handsome. Unfortunately, he knew it.

Fiore leaned back in the chair in the witness stand, arm draped over the back so the courtroom could have a full view of his lavish watch.

"Mr. Fiore, tell us about how you came to meet Mr. Mercer and fund his business," Mendez said, perched on the edge of his desk.

Like two college buddies catching up after a board meeting.

"Objection, Your Honor." It was a risky move, but Charlotte needed to strike early and set the tone.

Judge Wilkinson lifted his heavy lids. "For what, Ms. Claybrooke?"

"We'd like to use 'Jimmy Dire'. It's the name he's used throughout his association with Mr. Fiore."

"Your Honor, Mr. Mercer's false identity is part of the charges against him," Mendez countered.

"Yes, and by continuously using a name he wants no association with, and for very good reasons, you are essentially making up the jury's mind, before the trial even really gets started."

The judge heaved a heavy sigh on the courtroom. "I see your point, sustained."

Mendez's mouth puckered, like he'd taken a swig of vinegar. "Okay, Mr. Fiore, when did you first meet Mr. Dire?"

"I first met Jimmy about ten years ago. He had this business model, a really unique idea, and was looking for investors." His mouth pulled down in a quick grimace. "Sounded like a good idea, and we thought it would be a great service to those in the final stages of their lives." Fiore shifted in his chair and leaned forward. "We not only wanted this business to succeed because of our investment, but we believed in what Jimmy is doing."

Only white robes and a halo could've added to his attempted altar boy persona.

"Were there any complaints of questionable business practices over the years?" Mendez asked.

"No, which we initially thought was great, because who doesn't want a perfect business?" The man knitted his brow together, slipping on his next mask. "But then it made us wonder, because no one is perfect. So, we started to do some digging, and that's when we uncovered the families who felt they were robbed of precious time with their loved ones."

"Objection," Charlotte sprang into action. "Hearsay. Sadly, many of Mr. Dire's former clients are no longer with us, therefore they aren't here to speak for themselves."

"Sustained." The judge didn't look up, instead, he fiddled with the desk-top fan.

Mendez tossed more softball questions for Fiore to knock out the park.

Charlotte scribbled notes, hoping to scratch away enough of his I-truly-care-about-the-little-people veneer to find his black pulpy heart.

"What were some of the first warning signs that the business was running off course?" Mendez asked.

"Earlier this year. I asked Jimmy for his budget and, if I got a quarter for all the excuses, I'd made another million." Fiore chuckled alone at his joke. "I finally reached out to his assistant, Darla Steele, and she told me the truth."

At Darla's name, Jimmy froze beside Charlotte. The pen quivered as he scratched his former assistant's name on his notepad.

She glanced to her right, to see if the woman sat behind the prosecutor's desk, but she was nowhere to be found. "Hey, it's going to be okay."

His face was pale and his lips pressed together in a thin line. "I'm worried about her. Darla's the most loyal person I know. This has to be eating her alive."

Charlotte nodded. Loyalty was a commodity, like gold bricks. It hulked in the corner, glowing brightly, the weight of it filling the room, but once it was gone it left a gaping maw that stole everything around it. Joy. Confidence. Love.

Loyalty could also overstay its welcome.

Her loyalty to Jason was admirable, but it was time for it to go. To move on, let another guest in.

"You'll go easy on her, right?" Jimmy whispered.

She had no intention of tearing into the woman. Combative cross-examining was never her style, but also, their case hung on the woman's testimony. "I'll see what I can do."

"No further questions, Your Honor," Mendez said, pulling Charlotte back to the trial.

"Ms. Claybrooke," Judge Wilkinson prompted. "Your witness."

"Thank you, Your Honor." Charlotte pushed back from the table, but didn't approach the witness stand. Her questions for Fiore wouldn't take long.

The man was basking in the attention of the jury and courtroom and she intended to dim the glow as fast as she could.

"Mr. Fiore, you went into this intending to make back your investment, correct?"

The man shifted in his chair and straightened. "Well, of course, that's part of being in business."

"And, have you ever had a business that failed?"

He cleared his throat. "Well, of course, nothing everything is a total success—"

"You mean like your first three businesses?" She cut him off. She plucked a piece of paper from her desk. "Let's see, you had an internet start-up that failed its first year, I can understand that, tech is tough. And, a coffee shop. It's hard to sell coffee when it's this hot in Miami. A dry cleaner." Charlotte dropped the page and looked up at the man.

A strand of his perfectly gelled hair had come loose and quivered across his forehead.

"I know people are more casual here, but surely they still wore clothes," she said.

"Objection, Your Honor," Mendez shot up like a spring weed. "Is there a question in there?"

"Never mind, but I do have just one final question. If you invested in Dire Enterprises and Dire's Club to make money, aren't you in a sense trying to make money off dying people?"

Fiore's jaw dropped and his eyes narrowed. By the red creeping up from his designer shirt collar, he'd never had anyone speak to him like that before.

"Defense rests with this witness, Your Honor." Charlotte sat, not waiting to hear the man's answer.

Jimmy flopped an open palm in her direction under the table, which she met with a silent high five.

She'd forgotten how much fun it was to kick legal ass.

49

Nell's gaze flickered to the left. A quick move that would've been unnoticeable was a major milestone for Darla's mom.

"That's good, Momma. I'm proud of you."

Despite a slow start, her mother seemed to be finally making progress. Darla liked to think her mom was thrusting a middle finger in the faces of the doctors who said it was nothing but a fluke.

Some signs were small, a twitch of her eye, a flinch of her cheek muscles when Darla made a joke.

Others big, eye contact held while Darla put lotion on her mother's dry hands. Her hope was like a basketful of kittens, eager to pop out and explore the new world, but she did her best to rein them.

"I have to testify this afternoon. In Jimmy's case." She squirted more lotion into her palm for her mother's other hand. "I haven't talked to him or seen him in a couple of months. I'm nervous." She was more than nervous, but she was afraid to verbalize what she truly felt.

To breathe life into the emotion.

Regret.

Once she said it, the word would crystalize in her heart; growing and branching and spreading until it would shatter while she was on the stand.

"All right, Momma." Darla stood and brushed her black pencil skirt. "Wish me luck and say a prayer for me." Her reflection in the dirty mirror above the sink showed her more than she wanted to see; a woman who spent her entire life playing dress-up.

Rodeo queen. Junior college drop-out. Caregiver. Stripper. Office manager.

Backstabber.

Who would she be once the trial was over?

Nothing more than a one-dimensional paper-doll cut-out waiting for her suit to be draped over her.

The Towncar waited for her outside the nursing home's front door.

Enzo had insisted on sending a car for Darla, probably more to ensure she came to testify instead of a gentlemanly gesture.

Triple-digit temperatures and high double-digit humidity was hell on an unreliable air conditioner. Some days Darla's pride was shoved aside for good hair and makeup that hadn't slid off her face.

She should've read through her notes to prepare for her testimony, but instead, she found herself flipping through photos on her phone. It was a long overdue trip down memory lane. A trip that would surely result in a pickpocket reaching deep inside and stealing her resolve.

The most recent photo popped up first. The latest—last—group of Diers with Jimmy standing in the middle. His face glowed like a ringmaster, ushering frightened people through the hallways of death, giving them a much-needed sideshow of thrilling trips, bucket list check-offs, and life-well-lived smiles.

Her breath hitched with each photo she flipped past. The silly selfies she and Jimmy took. Jimmy hugging a woman, Claire, who'd passed away just weeks after her trip. The joy on her face shone through the photo, as if the picture itself was lit with her spirit.

Jimmy wasn't a criminal. He was a saint.

The only crime he was guilty of was not loving her back. Last time she'd checked, that was a non-prosecutorial offense.

Darla swallowed the bile rising up her throat.

Nothing tastes quite as bitter as eating your own words.

The car pulled up along the side of the courthouse. "Time to cowgirl up," she murmured, pushing open the door.

The heat inside the building was only slightly less suffocating than the heat outside.

She opted to climb the stairs to the third-floor courtroom, instead of the hot box of an elevator.

A bead of sweat dislodged from her temple and slid down her face, making a beeline for the corner of her eye. The last thing Darla needed was to look like a hot mess while on the stand.

It was fine if she was a hot mess on the inside. No one could see there unless she let them.

The images of the photos flipped through her mind even though her phone was tucked into her purse. How could Darla have done that to her friend?

He was standing at the guillotine and she was the masked man moments away from unleashing the blade.

Tears leaped to her eyes like flames engulfing a house. "Shit." She needed to get the tears, and their aftermath, under control or Enzo would lose it.

A restroom sign came into view in her watery vision. Without paying attention to the gender sign on the wall, Darla pushed open the door.

Jimmy stood inside, washing his hands. He glanced up, eyes going wide when they met hers. "Darla?"

She pursed her lips, a question trying to push its way through her crowded throat. "Why are you in the ladies' room?" The words came out in a rasp.

"This is the men's room."

She looked around at the urinals lining the opposite wall. "Oh."

He pulled paper towels out of the dispenser, way more than he could use to dry his hands. "How're you doing?"

Darla studied her former boss. Her former friend.

Jimmy looked thinner. His hair even looked like it'd receded a bit more. A few new wrinkles covered his face, his color pallid, despite the Miami summer sun bearing down on them. Was he eating? Drinking enough water? When was the last time he'd gotten a good night's sleep?

She nodded. "I'm good." Her mouth quirked up on one side. "Momma's making some improvements. She's moved her hands, making eye contact. The doctors say it's still too early to tell, but it's good to know that she's still in there."

His face broke into a grin, like the sun breaking the eastern horizon. His arm jerked as if to pull her into a hug before sticking tight to his side. "That's great, Darla! I know you're probably relieved."

"Yeah." For the briefest of moments, she felt like the old Darla.

They stood, staring at each other for several long seconds.

There were so many words that she wanted to say. The weight of her apology settled deep into her gut, making her feel more lethargic than the heat.

The door behind her pulled open, causing Darla to jump.

"Oh, excuse me, uh…you know this is the men's room, right?" A man said as he pushed past her.

She pulled out of her trance. "Yeah, sorry, wrong door. I'll be going."

"Darla," Jimmy called out. "Good luck."

She paused at the doorway. If she walked through it, she was going to swing the hammer on Jimmy's coffin.

If she stayed there, in the threshold of the men's room, she could even start to pull out the nail.

"Ma'am, do you mind?" The man's words snapped her out of her regret reverie.

"I'm going." She didn't feel her feet drag her down the hallway to the courtroom. Didn't feel her hand tug open the heavy wooden door. Didn't feel the worn wooden seat cushion her butt.

"Hey, Darla," the prosecutor greeted her. "You ready? You're going to do great."

She snapped her head up, unaware so many people filed back into the courtroom.

Jimmy walked in; his eyes cast down to the ground. He shuffled past the row with the surviving Diers.

Lourdes, Dylan, and Celeste smiled at their fallen leader, but cast side-eye glares at the Jezebel who betrayed him.

I stink worse than a three-day-old bull turd.

"All rise," the bailiff commanded.

It took Darla's knees a few seconds before they responded. Her name floated past her, inviting her to take the stand.

"Do you swear to tell the truth, the whole truth and nothing but the truth, so help you God?" The oath fled the bailiff's mouth in one breath.

The truth.

Which truth?

There were so many of them. There was the truth that Jimmy was offering people something special. There was the truth he didn't charge enough. There was the truth he also didn't want to ask Enzo for more money than he already had.

"Ms. Steele?" The judge asked, his glasses dangling off the end of his nose. "Is there a problem?"

Darla found her voice, hidden away from scary monsters and betrayal. "Yes. I mean, no. No, Your Honor, yes I do swear all that."

Mr. Mendez took his position in front of the witness stand. "Ms. Steele, how long have you worked for Mr. Dire?"

She shook back her hair and tilted her chin up. It wasn't just fake it until she made it, it was fake it until she no longer felt like throwing up. "Eight years."

"And over those eight years how often did you have to lie to cover Jimmy's losses?"

So much for making out before going all the way.

"Objection, leading the witness," Charlotte shot up from her chair.

God bless her.

"Withdrawn," the prosecutor said. "When did you start to notice the business wasn't making as much money?"

"Well, we made some money for the first few years I worked for him, but then prices started to go up, and with the economy being a bit rocky, Jimmy never wanted to price people out of the opportunity."

"Did he ask you to lie?"

Darla gnawed on her lips, surely staining her teeth with her bright red lipstick. "No, I did it all myself."

Jimmy's head snapped up.

Charlotte had been making notes, and her hand froze. Enzo's neck reddened. He was probably going to beat the hell out of a racquetball later.

"Excuse me?" Mr. Mendez said. "Maybe you didn't understand my question."

"I may be poor, and might've grown up in a trailer park, but my momma didn't raise no dummy." Flames licked in her belly, the same ones that smoldered whenever a friend punched above her weight in a bar fight, and Darla had to jump in and save her. "Jimmy never asked me to do anything out of the ordinary."

The prosecutor paced; the muscle in his jaw twitching, as he tried to regain control of Darla. He obviously wanted her off that stand as fast as possible. It rolled off him like his over-powering, expensive cologne.

"But, Enzo, now he didn't seem too worried about asking me to do something I didn't want to do. Dangling my poor Momma's health as a carrot in his scheme."

"Darla, you could go to jail for perjury."

She pulled her mouth into a calling-his-bullshit smile. "Did you know you can go to Hell for lying?"

The lawyer wrinkled his nose, like he got a whiff of a cow's fart.

Yep, he was officially done with her.

"Final question, Ms. Steele, what was the nature of your relationship with Mr. Dire?"

More tears filled her eyes, but these were calming tears, tears of release, tears of a broken heart that would do anything to repair the damage it caused. "He was my best friend," Darla turned to catch Jimmy's gaze. "*Is* my best friend, if he can ever forgive me."

50

Charlotte jogged along the beach, reveling in the quiet moments before the sun rose on the first day of presenting the defense case for Jimmy.

Defending against the prosecution's case had been relatively easy. It was just blocking the predictable shots Mendez lobbed in her direction. Like they were playing legal junior varsity volleyball.

Now it was time for her to step up to the big league. Time for her to tell the world that Jimmy Dire wasn't the swindler Mendez made him out to be. He was simply a man doing an impossible job.

It was her turn to be a woman taking on an impossible job.

She dressed quickly, choosing a white skirt suit. Powerful, yet pure. That was how she hoped the jury would see her. *Angelic*, would be a stretch, especially if the jury did much digging into her background.

Charlotte reviewed the questions planned for Dylan while she dried her hair. It made sense to start with the young man. His testimony would be simple, uncomplicated, yet moving. Who could fault a twenty-three-year-old for wanting to live his final healthy days to the fullest?

If Mendez attempted any snarky tricks, it would only endear the boy that much more to the jury, and, hopefully, the effect would trickle down to Jimmy.

She hurried into what was quickly becoming her second home; the courthouse. Her laptop bag hung from one hand, a tray of coffees in the other. "Good morning, Phillip, Joe." She handed each of the security officers a coffee.

It'd taken only one sip of the awful courthouse cafe coffee for her to vow to bring the security guys decent java from the outside world for the remainder of the trial.

"Ready for the day?" Charlotte asked.

One of the officers took the tray with two remaining coffees and walked it through the metal detectors for her. "About as ready as a rainstorm. How about you, Charlotte?"

"My defense argument starts today," she said, dropping her bag on the conveyor belt.

"You ready?"

She smiled. The short answer was no, she wasn't ready, like standing at the start of a race she forgot to train for. That gunshot was going to go off. The runners around her would start running. She'd be forced to move forward, whether she was ready or not. "I will be when he gavels in the day."

The courtroom was empty, except for a hunched figure sitting near the front.

Charlotte had gotten used to her and Jimmy being the first to arrive, but seeing Dylan sitting there, alone, stabbed her heart.

No matter how much she'd gotten used to seeing him on the trip and in the days preparing for his testimony, his youth always amazed her. She'd been twenty-three once, but that was her second year of law school, a time she'd spent reading, writing, studying, and working.

A year spent preparing for the rest of her life. What if she'd been like him?

Knowing that twenty-three *was* the rest of his life.

"Hey." She handed him what would've been her coffee. The butterflies with chainsaw wings fluttering in her gut would keep her awake throughout the day.

"Thanks." He barely looked up as he accepted the cup.

The boy's usually pale color was even more drained. Dark purple stained the skin under his eyes, augmented by his thick glasses. His pupils were thin pinpricks, as if they were trying to squeeze light out.

"You okay, Dylan?"

He shook his head. "Another migraine. Bad one. I didn't take my medicine because it makes me out of it." Dylan took a deep breath. "I'm going to try my best. For Jimmy, for you. But I don't know how long I'm gonna last up there."

Charlotte nodded and squeezed his hand. "I'll be quick, and hopefully Mendez won't draw it out if he sees you're not feeling well." She dug through her purse and pulled out her oversized sunglasses. "They should be big enough to fit over your glasses."

The boy mumbled his thanks and slumped lower on the bench.

She reviewed her questions again, trying to find places where she could economize her words. Keeping an ill brain tumor patient on the stand for pointless questions wouldn't help her case at all.

The courtroom filled and Jimmy slid into the seat next to her. "Dylan looks like he's seen better days," he whispered.

"Yeah, he's not feeling his best and didn't take his meds."

Her client's gaze floated from hers, drifting to the empty jury box. "Is it bad that I think this is good? I'm going to hell for that, right?"

The door for the jury opened, and the seven women and five men filed in quietly.

"I'll be down there with you."

The bailiff called for everyone to rise.

Judge Wilkinson took his spot and settled in, flipping on the small fan at his desk, like the day before. The tiny white-noise of blowing air filled the courtroom. "Today we hear from the defense. Ms. Claybrooke, would you like to call your first witness?"

She stood at her name and cleared her throat, pushing away concern for her young friend. "Yes, your Honor. The defense calls Dylan O'Keefe."

Their young friend pushed up from his seat and shuffled toward the witness stand, his gaze focused on his feet. After being sworn in, Dylan settled into the chair but didn't lift his head.

"Young man, are you okay?" Judge Wilkinson leaned over. His gruff demeanor lifted, and Charlotte saw him as a kind grandfather.

Dylan straightened his shoulders and lifted his head. "Yes, sir. Just a headache."

Mendez shot to his feet. "Your Honor, obviously this witness isn't up for questioning. I move that we postpone his testimony for another day."

Charlotte sucked in her lower lip. "Your Honor, may I approach?"

He waved her up.

Mendez was right on her heels.

"Sir, I promise my questions won't take more than twenty minutes. Dylan assured me he could do it."

The prosecutor pounced on her like a wounded animal. "She's exploiting these ill people."

"Mr. Dire has every right to witnesses, healthy or not." She flashed a tight-lipped grin. "Plus, standing here arguing, is prolonging how long Mr. O'Keefe has to be here. Don't you agree?"

Mendez's cheeks flushed. His mouth opened, as if ready to slap her with a word, but reason must've won out, because he turned and strode back to his desk.

Charlotte took a deep breath.

She's the girl. Just a quick run of Levi's chorus was all she needed to get back to the trial.

"Dylan, how're you doing?"

He shrugged. "I've been better."

"Can you share with the court about how you came to know Mr. Dire?"

Dylan shifted in his seat and sat up straighter, his eyes meeting hers. "I'm dying. An inoperable brain tumor, roughly the size of a golf ball. That's after it shrunk during radiation. I met Jimmy this spring when I signed up for a Dire's Club trip."

"Tell me, what drew you to spend time away from your family and with strangers?"

"I don't really have any family. My dad, but we don't get along." The man's shoulders hunched forward and he spoke to his hands, as if admitting his lack of a relationship was his fault.

Charlotte understood the weight that rested on children of broken parents.

"I'm really smart. Brilliant. Everything I did was for someone else. For my dad, for my teachers, colleagues, customers. I figured it was time to do something for myself before I couldn't," Dylan said.

She walked over to the defense table and leaned against the side.

Dylan looked much more at ease, and his color had returned.

She was still on borrowed time with him. "I'm glad you did. What did the trip mean for you?"

He laughed and looked away. "It meant…" He shook his head and took a deep breath. "It meant I was with people who expected nothing from me. On this trip, I found friends who didn't ask me about my net worth, or what I was working on. No one asked how I was feeling. No one told me I *shouldn't* do something. No one treated me like I was a child or a freak. I was accepted for what I am. Dying, just like everyone else." He paused, glancing down at his hands. "This trip was everything life wasn't." Dylan's words were soft, but they reverberated around the half-full courtroom.

Judge Wilkinson sniffed and wiped his nose with a handkerchief.

"Thank you, Dylan." Charlotte's voice came out in a thick whisper. "I have no further questions, your Honor."

"Mr. Mendez, your witness."

The prosecutor stood but didn't move from behind his table. "I'm so sorry about what life handed you, Mr. O'Keefe. Tell me, what *is* your current net worth?"

Charlotte popped up from her seat. "Objection, relevance."

"I'm inclined to agree with her, Mr. Mendez," Judge Wilkinson said.

"Considering this case is about a man known for swindling money, it is relevant."

The judge heaved a heavy sigh. "I don't like it, but okay."

"Two point three billion," Dylan mumbled.

"And where is that money going when you pass?"

"A good chunk of it will stay with my company, various pediatric cancer charities, and some other non-profits."

Mendez lifted his legal pad and jotted something down. "And how much is going to your father?"

Dylan looked away. "Four hundred and thirty-eight thousand dollars."

"Why such an odd amount?"

The boy looked at Mendez, his eyes hard. "It's what I owe him, by my calculations, for raising me."

"Final question. Your adventure changed, from a visit to a world-renowned scientific lab to a Monaco casino." The prosecutor tossed his pad on the table and hitched his hands on his hips. "Now Mr. O'Keefe, we know you're a brilliant mathematician. And, the group won a considerable amount of money that evening. Did Mr. Dire ask you to cheat for him?"

"Objection." Charlotte once again stood, her nails digging into her palms. "For so many reasons, but mostly because that's complete conjecture."

Mendez flashed a predatory smile. "I withdraw. Thank you, Mr. O'Keefe. I'm done with this witness, Your Honor."

She studied the jury, trying to determine if any were swayed by Dylan, either in Jimmy's favor or Enzo's.

Several of the women and two of the men looked at him with a softness that was usually reserved for babies and puppies. Two women glared at Charlotte, likely upset she'd put someone like him on the witness stand as fair game for Mendez. The other two men stared straight ahead, their expressions unreadable.

"We'll take a quick fifteen break before Ms. Claybrooke calls up her next witness." The judge gaveled and everyone stood.

If Mendez had no problem biting into Dylan, what would he do to Celeste?

51

Charlotte found Celeste at the far end of the hallway outside the courtroom.

The older woman hadn't been inside for Dylan's testimony. Strange, considering how close they'd become.

She was seated on a wooden bench, looking out a window into the clear Miami sky. Her notebook was clutched against her chest.

It was as if Charlotte was looking at a younger version of Celeste. A teenager with a diary full of secrets. Or, maybe a young girl holding tight to her favorite story of princes who saved the girls they loved.

"Hey Celeste, how you doing?" She sat next to her.

"Carly, dear. It's been so long. How are you?" There was a softness about her friend's face. Unburdened by a lifetime of memories.

"I'm Charlotte. Remember?" She lightly gripped Celeste's hand, hoping it would ground her in the present.

The woman's eyes widened before she squeezed them shut. When she opened them again, her expression tightened. The burden of living, and dying, was back. "Yes, I, uh, you just look like my niece."

Celeste's lie was as obvious as the Florida sun, but Charlotte ignored it like a teenager who didn't have to worry about wrinkled skin, sun damage, or trials.

"You're up next. Are you going to be okay?"

"Yes, honey." She patted her knee and stood. "How did Dylan do? Is he feeling better?" Just like that, the confusion and wrong name were gone, and Celeste slid back into her rightful place inside her memories.

"Good, he perked up during his testimony, but I think he was heading back to the hotel to rest." They walked toward the open courtroom doors.

People filed back inside.

Charlotte put a hand on the older woman's forearm, holding her back from entering. "Listen, Celeste, if aren't feeling up—"

Her friend rested a soft hand on hers. The skin vellum-thin, but still sturdy. Still sure. "If I'm not ready for it today, I won't be tomorrow. My memories are like leaves on a tree. It's early autumn. Right now, I'm just dropping one or two, but winter will burst in and blow the rest of them away. I need to do this now, because I don't know when the seasons will change."

She could only nod at Celeste's resolve. A few tears filled her vision, but she held them back. Later, when Charlotte was back at her hotel room, alone except for a glass of wine and mindless TV, she'd let them fall.

Her fellow Dier settled into the witness stand after being sworn in. She was as fresh as a spring day, dressed in her uniform kaftan and matching headband, this time bright green. The color of newly grown leaves, not yet scorched by the sun or thirsty from drought. Maybe it was why she'd chosen that color, as a way to dress herself to remembering everything.

"Tell us a little about yourself," Charlotte said.

The jury would fall in love with Celeste. They could bond with her in just a few moments. Someone who could be anyone's grandmother.

"Well, I live in Houston, I have three children and four beautiful grandchildren. I've been widowed for quite some time, but I keep myself busy."

She kept her smile firmly in place, hoping Celeste's slip up on the number of her grandkids would go unnoticed. "And why did you sign up for Dire's Club?"

Her face went soft. The sharpness in her eyes dulled just a bit, like a knife blade that'd been used too many times. "Clubs are good for us old folks, they keep us active, socialized." Her answer only a glint of the truth. Perspiration dotted her upper lip. Celeste sucked in her heavily coated lips, smearing bright red lipstick across her teeth.

"You're doing great, Celeste." Charlotte laid her hand over the woman's clammy forearm. "Are you feeling okay?"

She snapped back into place again. "Oh yes, it's just warm in here. You know how it is for women of a certain age." She fanned herself.

Judge Wilkinson aimed his fan toward the witness. "Here you go, ma'am."

The mechanical wind blew the top of Celeste's kaftan. Ripples of fabric undulated like leaves in a summer breeze.

"Anyway, as I said, clubs are good for people. Being around others, especially those who have something in common. Like death." The cool air revived her, bringing spirited confident Celeste back to the forefront.

"Tell us about the trip. About what it meant to you."

She glanced down at her hands, a deep inhale lifting her shoulders and she raised her head. "It meant freedom. It meant I didn't have to worry about the fact I'm dying, because for those precious days, I was living. We were living." Her gaze left Charlotte's. "Jimmy gave me permission to do something I never would've done in my life. To be selfish. Something happens when you have a child. Your needs and wishes and goals get put into a drawer, which at the time wasn't a problem. But when my kids didn't need me anymore, I never took my wishes out. Jimmy opened the drawer for me."

Charlotte stared at her friend. Wanted to say something, anything, but the expanse of Celeste's words filled the room. "That's…" The words refused to move past the lump in her throat. "No more questions, Your Honor." She kept her gaze down as she hurried back to her table. She didn't want Mendez to catch sight of the tears clouding her eyes.

"Ms. Bennett, you look beautiful in green." Mendez's voice had the respectful flirtation tone guys tended to use on older women. "And, I'm truly sorry that you're facing... I'm sorry, remind the court of your affliction."

The older woman's cheeks rose on the compliment, and fell on the reminder that she was dying a slow and terrifying death. "Alzheimer's," Celeste said softly.

"That's terrible. How long ago was your diagnosis?"

"Nearly a year ago." Her voice caught on the words. Even though plenty of time had passed for it to have sunk in, the diagnosis obviously still stung.

Mendez clasped his hands behind his back and paced the floor. "That must be especially tough on your kids. My *abuelita* suffered from dementia, and the constant worry was nearly unbearable."

Charlotte waited another second, giving the prosecutor time to ask a question, but nothing came. She stood; an objection perched on her lips.

The prosecutor side-eyed her and quickly spoke. "Were your kids okay with this little adventure?"

"Objection. What's the relevance to my client's case?"

He didn't even turn to look at her. "The relevance is whether Mrs. Bennett was coerced into joining Dire's Club."

"She's well equipped to make her own decisions. Her doctor gave his blessing. Anyway, Alzheimer's is a progressive disease that sometimes takes years."

The judge barely opened his eyes. "I'll allow it just this once, but this is toeing the line, Mr. Mendez. You may answer the question, Ms. Bennett."

Celeste's face whitened against her bright outfit. "I didn't tell them. Not that I'm hiding anything, but my kids are all very busy people. It's going to be hard enough when I become a burden on them."

Mendez nodded and shoved his hands in his pockets. "It's not that you didn't tell them about the trip. You didn't tell them about your diagnosis. Correct?"

"Your Honor," Charlotte sprang up again. She'd forgotten how a good trial could be harder than any workout.

"Counselor," his voice sharp with warning.

The prosecutor waved off his question. "So yes, your kids are busy. Your daughter with her three kids. Your oldest son and his two children, but he's living overseas. And then your youngest son, where is he again?"

Celeste's face softened at the mention of her family. "He's in Hawaii."

"And I have the number of your grandchildren, correct? Five?" Mendez cupped his chin with his palm, drumming his fingers in the worst portrayal of thinking that she'd ever seen. "Because earlier you said four."

Horror crossed her face, like a storm cloud at the start of a picnic. "Did I? I'm sure I misspoke."

"Can you name them for us?"

That does it.

Charlotte allowed Mendez to ask too many questions about Celeste's disease. It was obvious what he was doing. Hell, she'd do it herself if she was in his place.

But, she wasn't in his place. After her time with the Diers, she'd never do this to someone suffering like Celeste. "Your Honor, I'd like to remind Mr. Mendez, Ms. Bennett is not on trial here. He's badgering her."

The man shifted, angling his body to look over his shoulder to address her. "I'm simply trying to establish how much Ms. Bennett remembers. It's very much relevant."

Judge Wilkinson waved his hand in a hurry-up motion but said nothing.

"Ms. Bennett, let's talk about the trip. Tell me what went through your mind when Levi Livingston was found dead."

Celeste stared at the prosecutor.

Charlotte counted off several seconds, waiting for her friend, her witness, to answer.

Instead, the older woman's face softened, slowly like forgotten butter left out on the counter.

Charlotte popped up. They needed a recess.

Celeste needed a moment to remember where she was. Who they were, but her friend spoke before Charlotte could push the words out of her throat.

"Who?"

52

Charlotte wasn't surprised to find Lourdes at her hotel room door.

After Celeste's disastrous testimony on the witness stand, she'd checked her phone obsessively, waiting for a text from Lulu saying she wasn't going to subject herself to that kind of abuse.

"We've got to kick that *pendejo's* butt tomorrow," she said, pushing her way into Charlotte's room.

Jimmy followed behind, looking less fired up and more like he wanted to get off the rollercoaster of his trial.

The *telenovela* star paced in the living room of Charlotte's extended stay suite, muttering under her breath a mix of Spanish and English. "I can't believe he treated Celeste that way."

Charlotte fell into the criminally uncomfortable armchair. "That was all my fault. I shouldn't have put her up there. It was late in the day. I should've put you up this afternoon." Instead of preparing for Lourdes' testimony, she'd spent the evening beating herself up by reading everything she could find online about Alzheimer's. They called it sundowning, that as the day wore on the patient tended to be more confused, forgetful. If only she'd read this before...

Lourdes shook her head with so much fury, her wig slid sideways.

"No, don't you dare second-guess yourself. All that did was show how much she needed this trip." She pointed at her lover. "And, how much Jimmy helped her."

"Lulu, honey," he shook his head. Even though the trial was still going on, Jimmy wore his guilty verdict like an ill-fitting coat. "Let Charlotte do her job."

Imposter syndrome crept up on her, like a thief in a dark alley. It'd been years since she'd tried a case. What was she doing trying this one?

What made Charlotte suited to go up against a man who'd been practicing in the years she'd worn the disguise of someone who'd survived heartbreak and preached to others to move on?

She wasn't moving on with her life, she was treading backward. This trial was as futile as Dylan's attempt to go back in time.

After a quick run of Lourdes' testimony, Jimmy convinced her it was time to go. She needed to rest, save her energy. The last thing Charlotte needed, Jimmy needed, was two witnesses back-to-back who validated Mendez's claim they were too sick to make sound decisions.

Charlotte tried to sleep, but it was as forthcoming as the lies she'd told herself. The dark shadows on the ceiling lightened to a gray-blue, and before she knew it, a pale orange glow stretched into her room.

Back at the courthouse, Charlotte held her on to her coffee like it was oxygen. If only triple espresso shots could help cover the dark circles under her eyes.

She was accustomed to being one of the first to arrive. Sometimes the bailiff would be there, reading his paper or scrolling through his phone. Today, the bailiff was rolling in a large TV, positioning it next to the witness stand, the glass screen facing the juror box.

"Did someone order a TV?"

The man was crouched behind the cart, unraveling the plug. "Prosecution did."

Charlotte flipped through every possibility in her mind. News coverage was light. Due to the nature of Jimmy's business, most of his past clients were already deceased. Family members had moved on, barely giving a second thought to a trip their departed loved ones had taken. What had Mendez dug up? What did it have to do with Lourdes?

The courtroom door sighed open.

She glanced behind her, hoping the opposing counsel would be in early and could shed some light on his tactics, but it was Lourdes and Jimmy.

Like Charlotte, her friend's eyes zeroed in on the addition to the courtroom.

"What's that here for?" Lourdes' voice was even huskier than usual. "What's he going to show?" Her skin tone seemed two shades lighter than usual, and sweat shimmered on her forehead like rhinestones on a couture gown.

Lourdes was dressed conservatively. A black suit, with a silky cream top peeking out of the top of her buttoned-up blazer. Instead of looking like an internationally famous *telenovela* star, she looked like a CEO running a board meeting.

"Is he going to show clips of me?" Her voice went from husky to thick. "Is he going to show the *old* me?" Red flooded her cheeks.

The door opened again, and this time Mendez entered, his phone stuck against his ear and a coffee cup in his free hand.

Charlotte stood in the middle of the aisle, blocking him from making it to his table, but that didn't stop his conversation.

"Uh-huh, yep. Yeah, I doubt the jury would take too long so sure, I can make that tee time." He glanced up, just enough to acknowledge her presence. "Sure, then maybe after that, we can pick up some steaks, get the families together. I've got a nice Bordeaux I've—"

She plucked the phone from his hand and ended the call.

"Hey, that was a very important call," Mendez whined, snatching the device from her hands.

"Why yes, golf and steaks and a nice Bordeaux are important." Charlotte let all of her annoyance fuel her words. "But so are trials, especially *this* one. Care to explain that?" She hitched her thumb over her shoulder. "Planning to show videos of your swing? Or, maybe you want to watch Mexican soap operas?"

The man's mouth quirked up to a self-satisfied smile. Like a cat who just knocked a full coffee mug off a counter to spite his owner. "All due time, Counselor." He pushed past her and dropped his briefcase on his table.

She followed, waiting to speak until she was right next to him. "I'm serious, Julian. My witness is panicking that you're going to pull some stunt." She lowered her voice. "Listen, you have to understand what the treatments have done to her self-confidence. If you're planning to show clips of her before cancer, I beg you, as a human being, to reconsider. There's nothing worse than being confronted with who you *used* to be."

On the surface, these words were spoken about her friend, her witness, but deep down they were for her. This trial, reliving the trips with her fellow Diers, was nothing but one big slap in the face of her mistakes, her failures. Her lies.

The prosecutor's eyes narrowed before they softened just slightly. "Look, we might be on opposite teams here, but I'm not an asshole." He rolled his eyes. "How about this, it's for her but not about her."

She nodded. "Thank you." Charlotte turned, heading to her table to prepare for her questions.

"But Charlotte," he called out. "I still want to win."

With Lourdes sworn in and settled into the witness stand, Charlotte automatically went through her questions. Like someone walking through a haunted house, she kept waiting for Mendez to jump out and shout *'Boo!'*.

She cleared her throat, preparing herself for her final question. It was one they'd decided Charlotte would ask to diffuse any venom Mendez might try to inject into the testimony. "Ms. Peña, tell the court about your adventure."

A warm smile crossed her face, the kind that was usually brought forth with fond memories. "A night under the African stars. It was such a fun night, being able to share it with new lifelong friends." Lourdes held her gaze.

They'd been building to that trip, from singing with Levi to shouting obscenities off the end of the world, to just watching a perfect sunset in near seclusion. Those three trips were everything about life. Highs, lows, and peace.

Charlotte swallowed the tangled emotions in her throat. As much as she wanted to leave it there, she couldn't. It would be like leaving Mendez a wounded animal to prey upon. "But it didn't end perfectly. Tell us about that."

The star's smile fell. "Bandits attacked. Thankfully, no one was seriously hurt, but still, it scared us. But you know, a slow death is like being cornered by a lava flow. It's coming, and we can't run away from it. That, I think, is more terrifying than a quick end. When a volcano explodes, it happens before you can process fear."

She let her friend's philosophical musings hang in the air for an extra second. "That's profound. You say no one was seriously hurt, but there was an injury."

This time Lourdes shifted her gaze to Jimmy. "Yes, Jimmy and I were awake when the bandits showed up. He was trying to protect me, us, and they butted him with a gun."

"Wouldn't that make him irresponsible?"

"The opposite. I live in Mexico City, and I can honestly say not many men would stand up to thieves like he did."

"Thank you, Lourdes. No further questions, Your Honor." Charlotte sat back at her table. Her stomach clenched as if she were climbing up the big first hill of a roller coaster. She was going over it, but she just didn't know how bad the drop would be, or where it would level off.

Jimmy must've felt the same way. His legs jostled under the table, shaking the floor under their feet.

Mendez pushed himself away from his table. "Ms. Peña." He chuckled. "I have to admit to being a bit starstruck. My wife couldn't believe it when I told her you'd be on the stand today."

"We'll have to take a selfie later to prove it." Lourdes' voice was pure venom.

Charlotte had to suck in her lower lip to keep from laughing.

Mendez asked some relatively mundane questions while he fiddled with the TV.

What is he up to?

Finally, he got it where he wanted it, pausing at a black screen. "Ms. Peña, everyone on this trip was dying. Including Ms. Claybrooke, correct?"

"Yes."

"And what were the ailments?"

"Excuse me?"

Mendez shrugged. "What was killing everyone? For example, you have cancer."

Lourdes narrowed her eyes, her pretty mouth set in a hard line. "I think we've established what everyone is dealing with already."

The prosecutor turned; a slow, predatory smile spread across his face. "Ahh...almost." He aimed the remote at the TV.

Charlotte's face filled the screen. *"You all look to me to guide you..."* Her stomach dropped, threatening to splash the coffee back up her throat. The temperature in the hot courtroom dropped to Arctic levels, and her lungs refused to take in a new breath.

"I joined this trip with the intention of taking my own life," the Charlotte-from-the-TV said while walking around the cemetery holding the remains of her dead fiancé.

"Charlotte, do something," Jimmy's urging shook her out of her shock.

"Your Honor, this is absolutely nuts," she shouted, hoping to drown out her voice. If she could run over and rip that remote out of Mendez's hand, or yank the plug out of the wall she would. Instead, she could only grip the edge of the table to keep herself standing. "There are so many things to object."

"Mr. Mendez, pause that, please. Both of you, approach."

Charlotte walked forward, her legs on autopilot. They had to be; all her brain was doing was telling her to run. "I'm not on trial here, this is ridiculous." She ran her hands up and down her arms.

"Mr. Mendez, what exactly are you doing?" Judge Wilkinson's jowls shook as he spoke. "What is the relevancy to this witness?"

"Your Honor, I have it on very good authority Ms. Claybrooke's state of mind and her admission to the witnesses was not well received. My questions following this will dig into that."

"I've not hidden from the fact I struggled. You pulled this down from my social media feed. It's not exactly a secret."

The judge studied them both. "I'll allow that line of questioning, but no more video. I think we've got the gist of it." The judge paused. "Ms. Claybrooke, how are you doing?"

The tenderness of his question warmed her, smothering the rush of emotion.

"I'm getting help and doing much better, Your Honor. Thank you for asking."

Mendez clicked off the TV. "Ms. Peña, when you learned Ms. Claybrooke intended to take her life, how did you feel?"

Lourdes tilted her chin up, her gaze finding Charlotte's. "I felt angry. Here was someone whose body was strong, no delinquent cells." One side of her mouth pulled up to a smirk. "A full head of beautiful hair. But then, I felt sad, because a sick mind must be so much harder to deal with than a sick body." She pulled her wig off, her bald head shone under the glare of fluorescent lights. "Most people wear their illnesses; it would come as no surprise to learn that I'm dying. People see me as I am and I get sympathy, I get help, people wanting to do whatever I needed. But you see a gorgeous, healthy woman, you don't know the sickness she fights when she's alone." Lourdes looked back at Mendez, her eyes heavy with tears. "That's what's so unfair. Charlotte had to carry her disease all alone. Until she met us."

53

Jimmy beat Charlotte to the courtroom early the next morning. Sitting alone, his head hung low; shoulders slumped. His posture told her he agreed with what her traitorous mind had hissed at her over and over. She'd botched his case. Because of her, Jimmy would be going to jail.

"Hey," she said, sliding into the bench next to him. "Where's Lourdes?"

"She'll be here in a bit," he spoke to his clasped hands. His face was more lined, hair a bit thinner. The suit hung on him like his body was no more than a clothes hanger.

Did she look as bad as he did?

Her coffee to food ratio was sorely out of proportion. If it weren't for a couple of glasses of wine before bed, she'd never drift off to a restless slumber.

Charlotte glanced down at her bright yellow dress. She'd intentionally chosen this dress to project confidence that she wasn't worried about the outcome of the trial. Wearing a sunny color would signal to the jurors she was certain she'd win. Instead, she just felt like a giant lemon drop melting on the sidewalk. "Is she mad at me?"

"Lulu? Not at all." Jimmy glanced over his shoulder. "I can't promise she doesn't want to slash Mendez's tires, but you, no. She meant everything she said."

The jury had barely looked at Charlotte after Mendez's ambush.

It'd been so unexpected, so out of line, and just, so *so*, that the judge called an early end to the day.

Jimmy stared straight ahead. His Adam's apple bobbed with hard swallows. "I want you to call me up this morning."

"Jimmy, if I do that, you're fair game to Mendez, and I can't do anything to protect you." She tried to read his tired face. "Why're you doing this? What do you want to say?"

He didn't answer. Instead, he looked away and sniffed.

"We have closing arguments this morning and then it's up to the jury," she said.

"I want to tell them why I did it." He whipped his head around. "I need to tell my story. And, if that sends me to jail, so be it." Jimmy gripped her hand. "You told your truth. Let me tell mine."

When Charlotte announced to the courtroom that she had one more witness to call up, Mendez looked like a yuppie who'd just been told he had to push back his tee time. However, when she announced it was Jimmy, the man turned hungry. Ready to dig into her witness like a starved man at a buffet.

"Jimmy, you run a very unusual business," Charlotte said. "Why do you do this?"

His chest puffed up, clearly proud he could do something no one else dared to attempt. "Western culture is equally afraid of and obsessed with death. Everyone dies. It transcends class, ethnic group, politics; any line that's drawn, death is immune to that. I do this because I know how hard dying is, not just on those left behind but on the diers as well. My mother was ill, and the guilt and grief she held on to, knowing she'd be leaving me was unbearable. She died when I was ten." His voice broke, and he cleared his throat. "Yes, I lied about my identity, but it was only to have a fresh start. My father was abusive, and when I left home, I left behind the boy I was, so I could become the man my mother wanted me to be. I couldn't do that if I carried my father's name."

"Why didn't you tell Mr. Fiore the truth about the business? That it was losing money."

He took a deep breath and looked past Charlotte into the gallery.

She glanced over her shoulder and found Darla at the end of his gaze.

"Because I knew he'd make me charge more, which I couldn't do to the people who needed these trips most. Or, he'd make me close up the business. I'd be fine if that happened, but Darla needed the job to take care of her mother." He glanced at the jury. "She'd been in a vegetative state after a stroke for several years now, and her care is quite expensive."

Charlotte nodded and paced in front of the jury box.

They were held captive with Jimmy's story. Even a couple dabbed their eyes with the backs of their hands.

She hadn't prepared for this. Didn't have the energy to think on her feet for something witty.

Truthfully, she'd been ready to accept defeat and crawl back to her secluded house on the barrier island off the coast of South Carolina.

Charlotte wandered back to her table, leaning against it and crossing her arms. "Knowing everything you know now; would you do it all over again?"

"Absolutely. Even if I have to spend the rest of my life in jail, I wouldn't feel like my life was wasted. I've fulfilled my purpose."

"Thank you, Jimmy. For everything. Your Honor, no more questions." She took her place behind her table. Her heart was a little scared bird fluttering in her chest.

"Mr. Mendez?" Even Judge Wilkinson seemed affected by Jimmy's honesty.

The prosecutor rose and straightened his tie. His mouth opened, then closed. Mendez cleared his throat and shook his head. "No questions for this witness, Your Honor."

Charlotte cocked her head in the prosecutor's direction. That was the last thing she'd expected. Had he read the jury enough to realize any hard-hitting questions would cause him to lose precious legal capital?

After a brief recess, it was time for the closing arguments. This was even more important than her opening statement. More important than any questions posed to witnesses. Or cross examination. Even more important than Mendez's stunt of playing her video.

Her summation was the bow on the wrapping of Jimmy's trial.

Mendez was up first. "Ladies and gentlemen, there's no doubt Mr. Dire offers something unique to his clients. And, I can't say if I were dealing with a terminal illness, I wouldn't seek out his services. That's not what's on trial." He paced in front of the jury; his hands clasped behind his back. "What's on trial is that he repeatedly lied to his investors, he committed fraud by operating under a false identity. While the witnesses we heard from sing his praises, we're also here to stand up for those who lost precious time and money on one of his trips. Ladies and gentlemen, Jimmy Dire, Mark Mercer, Jr., as he was born, is no saint. He can't play with other people's money, Mr. Fiore's included, like he's God. I implore you to find Mr. Mercer guilty of fraud. Thank you."

Charlotte took a deep inhale, begging the abundance of oxygen to calm her nerves and fuel her argument. She pushed her bangs out of her eyes and smoothed any flyaways from her ponytail. "Mr. Mendez is right; Jimmy Dire is no saint. None of us are. But he's wrong about one thing, Jimmy is no fraud. He might be the most real person on the planet." She took a few steps and stopped. "We live every day, denying our existence will come to an end. That the world will continue even without us in it. But not my client. He fully understands our mortality, and instead of seeing the morbid side of death, he sees the beauty in it." She walked back toward the defense table but looked past her client to the row behind him. "Jimmy doesn't save lives. He untangles the knot of emotions of the dying. So they, we, can die unburdened."

Her fellow Diers sat, shoulder to shoulder. There was even a spot at the end of the bench where she could almost imagine Levi would be seated; his white hair glowing under the fluorescent lights.

"He gave us permission to be selfish, offered fatherly words of encouragement, or even just one last raucous good time. He reminded us that we are much more than a diagnosis." She focused back on the jurors. "But in my case, he did save my life. If Jimmy didn't have his business, I would likely be dead by now. As you go back to deliberate, I ask you to keep one thing in mind. If you knew you were dying, really dying, wouldn't you want to have someone like Jimmy there beside you? Thank you." Charlotte fell into her chair, her legs no longer able to keep her upright. Her ears hummed with her rushing blood, drowning out the judge's instructions to the jurors for their deliberation.

The courtroom emptied, except for Jimmy, Charlotte, and the Diers.

"What now?" Dylan asked.

"We wait," Charlotte answered.

Lourdes glanced down at the rosary tangled in her hands. "And, we pray."

54

With the jury deliberating, there was nowhere to go but Jimmy's office.

Charlotte found him there, sitting among the remaining file folders spread across his floor; only the bright Miami sun streaming through the windows lighting the room.

"Hey," she said. "Figured I'd find you here."

This was the worst part of the trial. In past cases, she would've even settled for a loss if it meant the waiting would end. Maybe that was what it was really like with a terminal disease. Living to just wait for it to end. Which wasn't that different from how she'd spent the last decade. But now, she wanted to win.

Now, she wanted to live.

Jimmy tossed some papers into a pile and dropped the folder into a bank box. "Yeah, thought I'd get some packing done while we wait. I have to be out at the end of the month, and in case—" he dropped his gaze and cleared his throat.

She knelt on the floor next to him. "Defeatist thoughts will only make it worse. There's still a chance—"

"Charlotte, it's okay; you did your job. Now it's up to the jury. There's nothing more you can do."

She sat there amidst the packing of a closed-up business, waiting while her friend's future was being discussed by twelve total strangers across town.

It was all one giant distraction from her own future. What'd started as a drive to help a friend in legal trouble had become a full-fledged distraction of her own wilting business. Her video admission was like a late-season frost, and in the aftermath, the speaking engagements and book deals faded away. Everything died. Even businesses.

"I'm shutting my own business down." The words slipped from her lips like a secret.

Once they were out; she was free. Like she'd fought her way out of a rip current.

Liberated.

Charlotte laughed and lifted her chin. "I'm shutting down my business!" She shouted to the ceiling.

To the universe.

Jimmy's cheeks pulled up, but he kept his gaze on the floor. "Going back to law?"

"Nope." She was drunk with opportunity. "I might tackle a bigger job. I'm going to be a parent." Like a dandelion seed, the idea had floated from Lulu's lips, planting itself into Charlotte's heart, where it'd slowly grown until sitting there in a dark office, it finally broke the surface, flowering into undeniable destiny.

He looked up, his jaw dropping and eyes wide. Then it was his turn to laugh. "That's your adventure. Except for you, it's not a final one."

"Just a lifetime one." Her phone buzzed in her pocket. She read the words on the text, a flare of cold flashing from her heart. "They're done."

"Who?"

"The jury." She fired off a group text to the Diers. "Judge wants us there in a couple of hours." Charlotte pushed herself off the floor, smoothing her pants. There was more she wanted to tell him. That he might want to spend the time making sure his affairs are in order.

Tighten up any loose ends. Prepare as if this were his last day in the free world.

"Charlotte, this is good, right?" Jimmy's face pleaded for her to lie to him.

To tell him when juries finished this quickly it was a good thing. He'd be okay.

They'd all be okay.

She pulled her mouth up into a tight smile. "We'll find out soon enough. I'll meet you there."

The downside to not being the first in the courthouse was dealing with the lack of parking. After circling and gunning it to try to beat other cars, Charlotte finally found a spot and sprinted to the courtroom.

Jimmy was already there, seated behind the defense table.

The Diers were all together, lined up in support of their leader. Once again united in their shared destinies. It was as silent as a funeral, as they waited for the judge and jury to enter.

The door to the hallway opened again. Darla entered, her normally big hair was pulled back into a simple ponytail, her face clean of makeup. The woman walked down the aisle, hesitating, as if deciding which side to sit on. "Jimmy," her voice was quiet, breathless. "I just want to say…" Her eyes filled with tears, and a vein popped on her forehead.

Jimmy stood and pulled his former assistant into a tight hug. "It doesn't matter. I love you, Darla, and nothing you do or say will change that."

Her petite shoulders shook with a flood of tears.

Jimmy held tight until her sobs subsided. When he finally let her go, a damp spot stained his jacket.

"Here, honey, you sit with us," Celeste said, reaching for Darla's hand.

The door for the jurors opened and they filed in.

Charlotte studied their faces, trying to get a read on their mood.

Were they distressed by sending a man to jail? Or, did they walk with their heads high, elated to be done with this trial?

The judge entered next.

Everyone stood, as they'd been trained to do over the week-long trial.

"Members of the jury, have you reached a verdict?" Judge Wilkinson asked.

The forewoman stood. "We have, Your Honor."

"In the trial of the United States versus Mark Mercer Jr., how do you find?"

The woman pulled a sheet of paper from her pocket. "In the charge of extortion, we find him not guilty."

Charlotte's heart thumped hard.

"In the charge of theft of services, we find him not guilty."

Waves crowded her vision.

Did we do it?

"In the charge of fraud, we find him guilty."

Her legs went numb.

Two out of three wasn't bad. It was much better than she could have asked for.

Jimmy sucked in deep breaths beside her.

"However, we don't recommend jail time, sir," the forewoman continued. "We suggest that the business be liquidated and absorbed by Fiore Investments."

"Thank you for your service," the judge said to the jurors. He turned toward the courtroom. "Mr. Dire, I think forty-eight hours is enough time for you to turn everything over to Mr. Fiore, do you agree?"

"Yes, sir."

"One more thing, Mr. Dire, maybe next time be a little more forthcoming. The truth is always the better choice, even when it's hard to speak it." Judge Wilkinson gaveled out and fled the heat of the courtroom.

Mendez and Fiore had their heads close, their whispered words lost in the cheers of the Diers.

The prosecutor picked up his briefcase and stopped in front of Charlotte. "Like riding a bike, huh?" He thrust a hand out.

She gripped it. "A little wobbly at first, but I managed to get into the race."

Mendez nodded once. "Nice work, Counselor."

Fiore stepped up to the table, his mouth pinched tight. "I can still sue you for the money I lost."

Jimmy shrugged. "Go ahead, but you'll spend more on lawyer fees than you'd get out of me."

The man spun on his expensive heels, and strode out of the courtroom.

With the prosecution gone, the celebration kicked up a notch.

Celeste grabbed Jimmy's face and planted a bright red kiss on his cheek.

Darla laughed and dabbed tears from her eyes.

"We should celebrate," Dylan said. "Maybe hit a bar or something, go out afterward."

Lourdes shook her head. "Are you any better at holding your liquor? If not, it'll be a short party."

Charlotte couldn't hold back the bark of laughter; for the gentle ribbing of her friend and the lifting of the weight of someone's future bearing down on her.

They found a restaurant with a view of the ocean. Their timing was perfect, after the lunch rush and before happy hour.

They settled in at a patio table in the shade, a cool ocean breeze lifted Charlotte's hair off her neck.

Conversation flowed as freely as the champagne. Jimmy sat at the head of the table, Lourdes to his right and Darla on his left.

Celeste and Dylan laughed over her attempts to take pictures of the group with her phone, but she kept inadvertently turning it to selfie mode.

Charlotte joined in when a question was lobbed in her direction, but she mostly sat and watched.

The empty chair next to her caused an ache for Levi she hadn't felt in some time.

While they laughed and drank and celebrated, the clarity of closure washed over her.

Not just the finale of the trial, and her decision to close her business, but the end of a journey with the most unlikely traveling companions.

Nothing could last forever.

Vacations were only exciting because they ended.

Life had thrown this unlikely group of people together, but they were bound by Jimmy.

Tomorrow they would go back to their lives. Whatever time was left, at least.

Charlotte stood, bid her goodbyes, made excuses about being tired, needing to pack. The truth was, she didn't want to be there for the end.

Because seeing them all together, flush with life, happily buzzed, was how she wanted to remember the Diers for the rest of her life.

55

The unexpected ring of a phone cut across her strange dream. Charlotte sat in a coffee shop sipping hot tea with Levi. Just two old friends chatting.

Despite knowing him for only a couple of weeks, the man had made an imprint on her soul that time couldn't wash away. She'd had more dream conversations with Levi in the six months since his death than she had while he was alive.

The phone rang again, a glow illuminating the darkness.

Who would be calling at two in the morning?

Unless...

Charlotte's cold hands fumbled in the dark, sliding the answer bar before voicemail intercepted. The call could be either life or death. Literally. "Hello?"

"Charlotte." The now-familiar voice was only slightly more awake. "It's time. How fast do you think you can make it to the hospital?"

She was already out of bed, flipping on lights. "Forty-five minutes, an hour at the most. Is that fast enough?" Her heart pounded against her ribcage like frothing waves.

"You'll be fine. Just don't get into an accident. We're counting on you making it here in one piece." The smile in the woman's voice was stronger than any calming cup of tea.

Charlotte didn't wait for her shower to warm up, eager for the blast of cold water to finish the job of waking her up. Soapy water ran down her arms.

This was a fulcrum moment. The last shower before. The last night before.

These moments happened all the time, but people didn't realize they existed until it was over.

She dried her hair quickly, just enough to keep it from freezing in the early morning autumn hours. She dressed in jeans and the softest sweater she could find, tugging her quietest sneakers over her feet.

Charlotte spared just a moment to fire off a group text, grabbed the pre-packed bag waiting on the chair in her room—the same chair that for a decade had held Jason's life preserver.

The next time she came into this room the chair would have a new job.

The night sky on the far end of the island glistened with stars. With no moon, the stars tumbled into a calm sea.

Charlotte took a mental snapshot. She wanted to remember every detail for when she told this story over and over for years to come.

She pulled into a parking spot at the hospital and jogged to the waiting room. Her adoption caseworker greeted her with a warm hug.

"Am I late?" she asked, breathless, not from the run, but her racing heart.

Marcy smiled. "Not at all. Let's go meet your daughter."

Her breath hitched.

Her daughter.

Ever since she'd started the adoption process, she'd practiced those words in her head, but to hear them spoken aloud caused a tidal wave of emotion.

Fear. Excitement. Hope.

Love.

She followed Marcy down the hall to the nursery. A few babies slept, two fussed, but one studied her surroundings with a fearless intensity.

My daughter.

She knew her before the caseworker pointed her out. Maybe maternal bonds were less dependent on shared genes than a shared destiny pulling two lost souls together to ride out the waves of life.

"It never fails," the caseworker spoke, reminding Charlotte that she and her daughter weren't the only two people in the world. "The parents always know exactly which is theirs."

The baby was swaddled tight, but her little fists move under the blanket. Her head was covered in thick dark hair that matched the fringe of eyelashes. A healthy flush of pink kissed her plump cheeks.

"Want to hold her?" Marcy asked.

Charlotte barely let her gaze drift from her daughter for the first time since she'd spotted her. There would be many times in the future when she'd have to let her out of her sight. Today was not going to be one of them. "Can I?"

The woman laughed. "Of course. You hold her while I get the paperwork ready."

The baby in her arms felt like home. Not a physical space, but an emotional home. A place where the two of them would always be safe. The walls of her love for this little person would stand through any storm until the day Charlotte died.

The thought stole her breath.

Before, she welcomed death. Welcomed the possibility of seeing Jason again. Of not having to carry on in this lonely world without him.

Not now...

Now she wanted to live forever. Or at least until her daughter grew up to become an old woman herself. Now she wanted to fight for every day, as if it were the fight of her life.

For her life.

Charlotte leaned down and inhaled the newborn scent. Her daughter smelled like warmth and happiness. She smelled like a new beginning.

The phone buzzed in her pocket with a text message.

Lulu's name flashed on the screen. *You better send pics.*

She opened her video call app and pressed her friend's picture.

The star's face filled the screen, her bald head uncovered, shrouded in darkness.

"I can do you one better," Charlotte whispered to the screen. She turned the phone down, giving her friend a view of her sleeping daughter. "Meet your namesake, Lulu. This is Lourdes Olivia Claybrooke." The name for her daughter came naturally, an honor to both the woman on the phone and the man who left them all way too soon.

Her friend smiled. A lone tear trickled down her face, reminding Charlotte that one day she'd be the lone survivor of the last group of Diers.

"I wish I could see her grow up." The star's face was thinner, her cheekbones no longer prominent but protruding. Dark circles discolored the hollows of her face.

That was the middle of the night call Charlotte had expected. The one where she'd learn that Lourdes was gone.

"If she's one-tenth as brave and bold as you, I'll be so incredibly proud. And, so incredibly screwed."

Her friend's laugh was weak. Not that the sentiment wasn't there to power it, just that her life force was weakening, like a waning car battery.

They remained on the phone for several more minutes, both watching the sleeping child.

The caseworker poked her head in the room. "Are you ready to make it official?"

"I can't wait to hold her," Lulu said, her voice cracking. "I'll be there as soon as I can." She kissed her middle and index fingers and pressed them to the screen before ending the call.

Charlotte knew better. She'd never see her friend again. Lourdes' body wouldn't be strong enough to make the journey to meet the child bearing her name.

Everybody died. But everybody was also born.

Everybody lived. Through bumps and bruises, through first loves and scalding heartbreaks. Through wins and losses. Through joy and grief.

Everybody lived. Some longer than others.

Because of that, because of the child sleeping in her arms, Charlotte vowed to honor her loved ones whose time was cut short.

Everybody lives.

Especially Charlotte.

The End

THERE'S HELP IF YOU NEED IT

Like many, Charlotte suffered through her grief and depression alone. It doesn't have to be that way. If you or someone you know is suffering from this silent killer, please get help. The National Suicide Prevention Hotline has someone available 24/7. Help is only a phone call away. 800-273-8255

A NOTE TO MY READERS

This might have been the hardest book I'd ever written. A large cast of characters to get to know, including one who was so consumed by grief. There were many times I'd be writing Charlotte and have to take a walk to clear my head. That's the beauty of fiction - the empathy we feel to the characters we write and read makes us better fellow humans.

Thank you so much for going on this journey in Dire's Club. It might have been a hard one, especially now, but hopefully, it was a meaningful journey.

If you enjoyed Dire's Club, please help spread the word by leaving a review on the site where you purchased it or on BookBub and Goodreads. And, if you'd like to hear what I'm working on next (it's totally different!) then follow me on social media or sign up for my newsletter.

Until next time!

xoxo,

Kim

ACKNOWLEDGMENTS

It takes a village to bring a book into the world. I'll forever be indebted to my parents for supporting their budding young author. To the WTWA Bangers (Jolene, Carol, Linda F. & Linda T., Christine, Lana, Jenna, Vaun), thank you ladies for helping me with the bones of Dire's Club. So much gratitude for my critique group - Christine Broderson, Vanessa Foster, Chris Crawford, Sarah Hamilton, Susie Sheehey, and Chrissy Szarek. You let me show my dirty laundry and don't judge me too hard. To Marcy Sherman, not only did you help me realize just how strong of a character Charlotte was, but you gave me the confidence to say it was ready for the world. To my wonderful sister and brother-in-law, Angie and Mike Madrid, I am always humbled by your faith in me. And, to Colby, the days are brighter with you in my life.

ABOUT THE AUTHOR

Kimberly Packard is an award-winning author of edgy women's fiction.

When she isn't writing, she can be found running, asking her dog what's in his mouth or curled up with a book. She resides in Texas with her husband Colby, a clever cat named Oliver and a precocious puppy named Tully.

Her debut novel, *Phoenix*, was awarded as Best General Fiction of 2013 by the Texas Association of Authors. She is also the author of a Christmas novella, *The Crazy Yates*, and the sequels to *Phoenix*, *Pardon Falls* and *Prospera Pass*, and her stand-alone titles *Vortex* and *Dire's Club*. She was honored as one of the Top 10 Haute Young Authors by Southern Methodist University in 2019.

ALSO BY KIMBERLY PACKARD

The Phoenix Series

Phoenix

Pardon Falls (Phoenix Book 2)

Prospera Pass (Phoenix Book 3)

Standalone Titles

Vortex

The Crazy Yates